The Fate

Copyright © 2016 by

Sarvar Kodirov

Translator: Hafiza Allanazarova (From Uzbek into English)

Editor: Mirabbos Iriskulov

ISBN: Jasmaya Productions and Publications 978-0-9983940-0-8
10000 E. Paseo San Ardo Tucson, Arizona, 85747

JASMAYA
Productions & Publications
The Eyes of Independent Publishing

The Fate

Author: Sarvar Kodirov

Translator: Hafiza Allanazarova (From Uzbek into English)

Editor: Mirabbos Iriskulov

This book reveals the life story and at the same time a huge collection of the lessons to be learned for pursuit of success and happiness. By reading this book, you will see that miracles do exist when a human being strives to achieve and works hard. A boy of four, orphaned after his father died in the world war, who didn't even have boots to wear in the winter snow and chilly days, fought each challenge, hunger, oppositions and through hard work got promoted to a very high position in higher education. He has become a man who has earned the confidence and trust of thousands of people who have needed his help. Every human's soul is like a bottomless ocean which can't be seen, and a scientist can love, and dream, and also withstand the challenges of love. There is an answer hidden to the question "Why are we living in this world?" in this book, and the answer will allow you to learn about journeys, useful lessons and love...

While you are reading the novel "Fate", it's recommended that one approach it considering the stages of history in which that the author has lived. By taking into account the social and economical state of those periods, one can grow to understand that these periods have resulted in some harsh realities of life which the author have encountered.

This novel portrays the seventy years of life lived by the author and it's possible to infer he was born in 1940 with most of his life occurring during the former Soviet Union period. Like many other people in this era, he was also forced to live under totalitarian and communistic pressure. Despite many encumbrances, he fought against them with dignity and made   all of his dreams come true. In return, and for the tortures he underwent, he has become a prominent and well-known scientist worldwide and has contributed to the scientific and technological development of his motherland. He has also become famous as a professional teacher, preparing graduates of distinction for his independent motherland.

Sarvar Kodirov, a prominent scientist, and an honored statesman of science, looked forward to Uzbekistan's Declaration of Independence and on that day his heart filled with joy, when at long last his motherland became independent. The President of independent Uzbekistan, the founder of Independence, and leader of scientific development, Islom Abduganiyevich Karimov had great trust in this scientist.

He headed the Tashkent State Automobile and Road University as president for ten years, putting this university on the map., and had the trust of the President of independent Uzbekistan.

Sarvar Kodirov has celebrated his seventieth birthday anniversary and is still working strenuously in order to teach the younger generations with his utmost discretion. The novel "The Fate" portrays his past life routine, and the obstacles he encountered prior to reaching the peak of scientific pursuits, and career, as well as his scientific, practical and pedagogical activities.

In the third part of the novel there are more opportunities to read the writer's inner thoughts and in "The Recent Days Gone by" some events are repeated. Despite all these vital and loyal repetitions, the author's soul vehemently combines these events into a unique unit.

You'd better read this novel and you will make sure that a human can achieve all of his goals, can make every dream come true if he doesn't bear any malice aforethought, if he has good ambitions and if he does his best. Reading this novel your soul will get replete with energy and unbelievable strength leading you towards your great future!

Kutlibeka Rahimboyeva

FOREWORD

A person can learn a person, can describe him. But no one is able to know the human as well as he does himself. Therefore, in all periods of life there has been exclusive interest in autobiographical novels.

"Boburnoma" is a valuable book of all stages of life. Soul and image of Bobur reflects in all of his poems. But his dignity, deep agonies, grief is well witnessed in "Boburnoma".

These autobiographical novels such as "Childhood" by Oybek, "Memorials" by Sadriddin Ayniy not only provides information about the author's life, but also about the history of the period he lived in.

"The Fate" is also a novel devoted to life of Sarvar Kodirov, a doctor of technical sciences and a prominent specialist.

The first part of the novel "Divine ties" portrays strong feeling of love between the hero's parents. How strong was this love? Why did this feeling experience much more misfortune than happiness? To all of these questions you can find an answer on any page in this novel.

` The Part "Dreams Came True" is about the hardships and difficulties of science, the pursuit of success and the feeling of happiness that comes to your soul after sleepless hours at night. Events in this novel are divided into small reports. Occasionally it may seem to you as if the author is describing everything in detail. This may remind you about "Memorials" by Sadriddin Ayni. As the novel covers a wide range of information, this style is really worth utilizing. The author mingles in the events in this book, with all the conversations about engines highly widening and enriching the outlooks of a person.

By reading this novel it's highly possible to understand how a patient and hardworking man, with clear conscience and dignity, has made his own life replete with reputation and happiness. He shares his travels abroad: the cities and educational systems are described in a way that one could see it as if a painter has drawn every stage as a masterpiece. This novel will lead the reader through the route of love, loyalty, traveling and science. We are confident that it will become quite a favorite book for you in your private library, dear reader!

Every experience of the author will urge the reader to realize that life and its realities are very complicated. You will learn how the author overcame many difficulties and see how you, as a reader, can also reach the peaks he has.

If you travel through the pages of this book, following the steps and the beckons of the author, you will find a fathomless response to your questions "Why do we come into being?" "Why do we live in this world?", with the response being; there's a dream, love, divine and advice...

THE FIRST PART DIVINE TIES

A HUMAN

The older you get, the more questions you ask which aren't that easy to answer. I've been reading lots of books seeking answers to my questions following the route of life, living with its heroes, thinking about them, but I still endlessly suffer looking for an answer to one question. Reading Torah, Koran and Bible more than once, I've made sure that all the creatures are created by Allah.

When was the first man created? A very complicated question which is impossible to answer! Why did Allah create a human? Of course, he did in order to lead and head the creatures and the world he has created on his own.

But who has headed these people for millions of years? They were increasing in number or reducing by eating each other, weak ones fighting in the same team against the strong. Allah has created them for this purpose and in the way they really are. If God hadn't created them on the basis of certain rules, the entire world would've been replete with wild animals. But it didn't happen, I wonder why? But in those stages of life, human being hadn't come into existence yet, had he? These are questions for which there can be no exact answer. I remember reading in manual that even before Adam was born, some people had been sent onto the earth, they could each live for at least eighty thousand years. Let's just imagine that it's true, but what could these people do in so a huge planet?

In all the holy and religious books gifted by Allah the whole nature surrounding us (the earth, the sky, clouds, the moon, stars, animals and plants) is predicted to have been created within six days. Perhaps this estimation's true, but as far as I am concerned there should be millions of years between each of those six days. I even have a definite proof for this. According to what's written in books of Allah historically it hasn't been so a long time since the first human Adam came into existence. (Look at the book "Generations of Adam and Eve". 2009. Tashkent State Islam University)

During the period when the former Soviet Union controlled Central Asia, teachers used to explain the hypothesis that a human is originated from monkeys. Even today millions of people trust in this theory. More precisely, this hypothesis infers that monkeys had their mind developed, having got rid of their hair on the skin, learned to walk upright with two fee and then evolved into a human. It means that these monkeys gradually started sewing and wearing clothes, at first heading one tribe and then a group of people, a team and even they coped with governing very big countries and cities. If this hypothesis were true, it could also be possible to find any monkey which has turned into a human. Therefore, atheistic theories are false logically. No animal is able to think or communicate as well as a human does. A human was created by Allah and he was gifted with the sense of intelligence by this Almighty. And the rest of this approximately accepted hypothesis can be proved invalid when these facts are compared with them.

We always try to understand and learn scientifically the statements cited in the Koran and as a scientist I admit that all the predictions stated in holy religious books have yet to be established by any scientists. Even some of those statements to which the key has been established leads to the understanding that the Koran is really a sacred and holy book. In the Torah, there is sufficient information about human beings. More vividly the woman Eve was created from the of a rib of a man Adam and they were expelled from paradise as a punishment for their notorious sins. At that time, Allah says of them: "You will further be having children and they will increase in number on the earth. Therefore, you will be called Adam and Eve." It means no matter what nationality, or race people relate to, they are all Adam and Eve's descendants. This is the truth which no one can deny.

Unfortunately, blood's thicker than water, and this can be confirmed by some of greedy people (this negative quality has been passed on from Kobul who murdered his own brother out of envy). Obviously, every human in the world generates from this man, Kobul, which means every human carries envy in his genes, with this sort of genetic negativity prevailing in some Heads of State and leaders as well. Therefore, one could still witness the unfair attitudes of successful people everywhere. Every ignorance of nationality or invasion of a country is due to genetic factors. Can we get rid of these negative factors?

A prominent writer Chingiz Aytmatov wrote that Cassandra felt the sign of God sending negative genes to one woman on earth, who would give birth to Cassandra's brother. Cassandra predicted that the disaster could be prevented if a baby is murdered with just a drug when on the seventh day of its birth. If a human being doesn't want to fight for a happy and peaceful life, and if we as humans don't even try, no one can help us to achieve this. If we all start fighting for our own happiness and for a peaceful life, a miracle will enhance the development of all societies. Consequently, all nationalities, and citizens of different countries will be living as friendly as if they were in the same family. All the blocks and barriers would come to end. However, it's incredible that most people seem not to want to live in peace, and it's impossible to see their attempts to live in this manner. Currently, citizens in twenty-seven European countries are living in happiness and in peace, and it's possible to render peace and prosperity to two hundred and forty more countries.

Allah is witness to this and I really want these days to come…

The Fate

Both Adam and Eve lived together as if they were halves of a unique creature making one together and this feeling was certainly gifted to them by the Almighty. As everybody in the world has their own life-partner, they usually find each other only through the Glory of Allah. Therefore, according to Islamic theories, unless Nikah, which is a holy a Islamic marriage is administered, couples can never get married.

There aren't any couples who do not believe that love is given from god as a gift. If it were not true, people couldn't find their love in another part of world or from other nationalities. One more proof for it is that living just round the corner as neighbors a boy and a girl can never fall in love with each other even though they are both good-looking or equally clever. But a fellow, never married may fall in love with a woman divorced from her husband no matter how much his parents object to their marriage. Love is a precious feeling which God will only gift to good people.

I made sure that every creature in the world is governed by the will of Allah. Even though a human being doesn't understand Allah's will or feels astonished by it, he will grow to realize it when he sets off to wherever he is going (one day, perhaps to the sky).

Let's just analyze some love stories of the past centuries from which we can still learn. Even though they are just called "couples" with one word they all have their own history.

Yusuf and Zulaiho. Yusuf was a slave to Pharaoh whose wife was Zulaiho and he adored him most in the world. If love hadn't appeared from Allah's will, Zulaiho wouldn't have fallen in love with a strange man. Sacred love made them meet each other and the Princess pride, as well as luxurious life, forced her to admit weakness in front of love.

Layli and Majnun. Maybe Layli appeared to be a dark looking girl to some people, but she was a unique and the most beautiful girl for Majnun. She was a Princess and he was a poor young man. He could never have thought to cut his cloth according to his coat, and he didn't even think about her wealth. Despite Majnun being insane, Layli valued him as if he was the cleverest ever. This is the actually the will of Allah.

Mohammad and Hadicha. A twenty-five-year-old young man of honest disposition fell in love with a forty-year-old woman of means. At that time, there were fifteen years more before Muhammad was to be anointed as a Prophet. But neither age, nor other troubles, put a barrier between their love.

Romeo and Juliet. They were children of two tribes who were continuously fighting against each other. Regardless of these contradictions, two innocent children fell in love with each other and the struggles between this true love and their parents led Romeo and Juliet to ultimately die. That they fell in love is no coincidence; it's the will of fate set by the Almighty.

Farhod and Shirin. Is the story of a princess and an ordinary boy who worked in a cave etching decorations on stones? However, their love was not ordinary; it came from God.

Tohir and Zuhra. Tohir, whose job dealt with stones, and Zuhra, a princess, loved each other. They had come into existence on the same day, so they departed this world on the same day. If it hadn't been the decision of God, Tohir wouldn't have fallen in love with the daughter of a man who murdered his own father. This is incredible. Due to the power of this love Tohir didn't want to marry the King in Khorezm's daughter. On hearing that Zuhra was murdered by his father, Khan BabakhanTohir killed himself responding to murder with murder.

Otabek and Kumush. Is another example and proof of the existence of true love. No matter how many good- looking girls there were in Tashkent city, Otabek fell in love with a beautiful girl, Kumushbibi as soon as he saw her for the first time. This can be defined with just the willing of Allah, with fate. Otabek married Kumush as God wanted it, but as he was forced by his mother to marry another girl, Zaynab this marriage has ended with death of Otabek and Kumush.

If two people do not love each other, they can never get married. Love is an ancient feeling, but every time it's renewed and therefore each love bears its own history. In the story, which is going to be read now is different from the others somehow.

First glow of love

In one small part of a huge Tashkent city there lives one boy, Sarvar who remained as an orphan after the bloodshed war, and despite the poverty, he lives there in happiness with his widow mother, brothers and sisters. All the other people living in the same mahalla treat him as a very clever and honest boy. He is studying in his third year at the university and he is one of the most brilliant partners for a conversation as he had already read hundreds of literary books at that time. Like all the heroes in romance books he always lives dreaming about everlasting love.

In the house, opposite to theirs, there is one rich woman recently married, her sister Rahima has started visiting her house much more often than before, perhaps it's because she has fallen in love with her sister's neighbor, a clever and handsome boy studying at the university. That girl has just finished school and it is the time when a season of romance started for her. The boy felt his heart creeping when he saw her for the first time, seemingly the girl wasn't also indifferent as she goes into their home trying to find some foolish reasons for that. Besides she could become friends with his little sister. In this way, gradually they started feeling closer to each other, whenever they glance at each other, their eyes seem to be talking in a way that only their souls can hear those voices. Thus minutes, hours, days and months are passing one after another.

One day the boy bared his soul to his mother at long last after so many inner tortures:

"Rahima is going to get married soon, mummy. If her parents tried to be patient a bit more, I would marry her right after I graduate from the university."

Every mother thinks that her son is the best. Therefore, with good intentions she went into her neighbor's home to ask the girl to marry her son, but unfortunately a bit later she came back, giving way to despair. The rich man, Rahima's uncle, living just round the corner said that Sarvar was just a student and could feed neither his wife nor his children as he had not a penny to his name. By that he meant that he couldn't afford to marry yet. This ignorance hurt the soul of the mother whose expectations about her son were high up to heaven. She was also a woman of means, and when her husband was alive, he made golden jewelry but, he died in the bloody war. She was bereft, and alone, raising five children, and even though somebody hurt her heart, she didn't even let the King hurt her children. At the time, when this rich brother brushed her off, she responded bravely:

"It's ok if you do want your sister to marry my son, but you mustn't talk about my son like that. He will soon graduate from the university and I know he will reach the peaks of success one day because all of his grandfathers were great men of means. "She tried to explain all that had happened to her son, and Sarvar, found insulting that his proposal was rejected due to their poverty. Glancing at his mother's glittering eyes he said:

"Will you please be patient Mummy? One day I will become a greater person than they have can ever imagine. There are plenty of fish in the sea mum, so if she wants to marry a rich man, let her do whatever she wants!"

Maybe it was her destiny, but Rahima's parents forced her to marry a rich man and she became pregnant several times by him. The torture and tiredness of being a mother at an early age affected her health badly and she died while giving a birth to her third child. She certainly wanted to live in happiness, but her husband seemingly didn't want it and he treated her as if she didn't deserve to be treated well. If he had understood her and had let her rest at least one day, maybe she would be alive today. Her husband had lots of money, but he was devoid of a sense of intelligence. On hearing about her death, Sarvar's heart leapt out of his mouth. At that time, he was doing his postgraduate studies in Moscow. No matter how much he felt sorry for the girl who was cut down in her prime, there was no use grieving because he could never find her again. But as time is a great healer, that girl turned into a sweet memory for Sarvar. He longed for his interest in love, but was absorbed in his own world of science.

Sarvar was one of the most leading students of the Mechanics faculty in the Asian Technical university. He did well in each subject and all of his teachers and friends respected and valued him all the time. He also did his best to help his friends who couldn't do well and shared his own views with other students. At that time, agricultural activities, especially cotton planting, were the main part of being a student. Sarvar was one of the best students, even in the cotton fields, and he received high grades during all five years of his education. He did his best to not bother his mother by asking for money, and on though being a student, he frequently helped her, and his brothers with money. Those years, many beautiful girls were eager for his love, but he paid no attention to them because he first wanted to excel and become professional enough to earn money. Since he was really good-looking, there were many girls in the Mahalla wanting to marry him. One of those girls was Lobar, a daughter of a rich man. Had Sarvar shown a bit of interest, both the girl and her wealth could have belonged to him from that day forth. One more example was Guzal, who lived with her rich uncles and grandpa even though she was an orphan. She lived in a family of scientists. Sarvar also wanted to look like them all. But he treated all those girls as if they were his own sisters, and didn't even think about marrying them at all.

Actually, everyday they did their homework together, with the boys and girls gathering in the same house and discussing several topics. They didn't stop, even though they stayed there until the late evening. When dusk fell, the boys accompanied the girls to their homes. None of girl's parents were concerned about their daughter's as they trusted Sarvar a lot and they knew he would never do something bad. Sarvar was aware of the feelings those girls were hiding inside their souls, but he sensitively controlled his emotions. Sometimes Sarvar's sister got on his nerves saying lots of things with irony:

"Why won't you take Lobar or Guzal to the cinema? You wouldn't refuse to love these beautiful girls, would you? They'd marry you with pleasure as soon as you hint at it?"

Sarvar said in response:

"But I do love them as much as I love you, I look upon them as if they are my sisters. If I take them somewhere today or tomorrow, other people around may think that they aren't good girls. They might think that we are going on a date. Imagine, a girl is like a white paper, as soon as it has a dot, no matter how small it is, it's easily seen on the surface. Anything perceived as bad behavior could destroy their reputation."

When Sarvar was studying at the university, he would often visit his friend Tohir and they would study together. In that house, Tohir's sister seemingly liked Sarvar a lot, and when she glanced at him, her eyes always flashed with happiness.

After Sarvar graduated from the university, she entered Tashkent Foreign languages university. Sarvar appreciated the feelings of clever and good girls, and he invited Zulfiya to the cinema once or twice, and he even brought a present to her after he returned from Moscow. Zulfiya's parents really wanted him to be her husband. One day when her parents said that many people were asking for Zulfiya as a bride, and that they were waiting for Sarvar's proposal, Sarvar answered his mother's unspoken question.

"Zulfiya is a very good and clever girl, but she'd better marry another man. I don't want her to wait for me, mummy!".

In his opinion love was not something to feel after seeing each other once or twice. Maybe you think that Sarvar has loved someone else. Perhaps not. He has seen the people in love, suffering and …

Coincidence or …

Sarvar's parents loved each other so much that there's not another love story which may be compared with theirs. Sarvar's father was one of the most famous and the richest men in Tashkent city, and Alimjonboy's grandson. His grandfather had a big guest-room, concert hall, land measuring no less than five hundred hectares bordering with Tashkent and no less than ten shops. Being one of the richest men, he even ran trade relationships with Russia. They were living in a two- story house and he forced his son, Sarvar's father, Mukaddir to marry a girl who was as rich as they were. He didn't have a feeling of warmth towards her, and besides that, the girl had a physical flaw. Even though she gave birth to a son, there was no love in his heart since he was forced to marry her.

At the same time, there was a wedding in Chigatay mahalla, and one man who was well-known as a Toshpulat jeweler gave a wedding party for his daughter Hojiya. They made their beautiful daughter marry their own relative. The girl gave a birth to a daughter, but sadly her husband became seriously ill and breathed his last breath leaving his wife a widow at 25.

Perhaps it was fate that the widow and Sarvar's father who was forced to get married suddenly met each other at another wedding in Chigatay mahalla. As soon as they glanced at each other, they fell in love. However, Sarvar's father, Mukaddir, had a son and a wife, and the widowed woman Hojiya had a daughter at home. Moreover, their parents were really famous all over Tashkent. What could they do so that they wouldn't cause their parents to feel shy because of their children? They wondered if there was any solution to that problem.

After that first meeting in Chigatay, Mukaddir started sleeping in another room and this lasted for several days. During the daytimes Mukaddir was lounging near the house where Hojiya lived, and he was ready to die to see her just once more time.

 Mukaddir's wife noticed a strange change in her husband's behavior and explained it to her mother-in-law. Then his mother tried to talk frankly to her son: "What's up my dear son? Is anything wrong with your own bed? Why are you sleeping in another room these days?"

Muukaddir didn't try to hide anything:

"Don't pretend not to know what's wrong. You know that I haven't had any feelings for my wife since the first day of our wedding. Allah gives us every torture and happiness if we are patient. Do you think my heart can stand this? I've only been living with her at your bidding. But a man is born just once. Everybody has the right to live with love. Let me take her to her own home, I will not leave my son without care, I'll be helping them all the time."

His mother was quite disappointed:

"Aren't you a bit crazy? Her father is a man of means. What are we going to do with people? They'll start gossiping about it all over Tashkent, won't they? Don't dare to do it! Never! You have a duty to fulfill for your marriage. Marriage makes everyone love their partners one day. Try being a bit more patient. Ok my son?"

"Mummy I've been patient for two long years, but nothing has made me love her still. I will a divorce. Don't try to convince me. Please, mummy. I will explain to my father, and even talk to father-in-law. I can't see any other way but this one…"

His mother tried to change his mind somehow: "As you've become too arrogant, you seem to have fallen in love with someone, haven't you?"

"Mummy, I'm in the dark about what it is, but I saw her at least once or twice and I still can't realize what to do. I don't even know if I am on the earth or the sky. I am wandering here where she lives to see her once again. But still I can't."

His mother felt that all what he said came from the bottom of his heart: "I understand, but how can we explain it to people, and what are we going to say to your father?"

"I'm not going to live depending on what the neighbors might think, or the willing of my parents. I want to get married relying on love that Allah gifted me with. I've already made up my mind, I'll talk to my father about it," Sarvar said.

Indeed, love had made him quite brave at that time.

As his father was busy with trade in Moscow, several days later he came back with lots of presents. Of course, when his father came home, they would first sit silently for some time, His father had noticed on his own that his daughter-in-law was very different, and his son looked upset. Calling him to the living room, he said:

"Well, my son, what's up? Is there anything wrong with you? Why do you look so upset and why does your wife look the same?"

"Daddy, you know that I've been living with her for two years, but still I feel as if I am dead. I didn't dare say a word for the sake of your reputation. Why is a man born then? I think he needs to be born so as to live in happiness. I came clean about everything to my mother. Therefore, I really ask you to talk to my mother and come to one decision about my future dad!" said Mukaddir and went outside slowly.

His father was deep in thought. But his son wasn't also guilty, and he had been hiding his anguish in his heart for the sake of reputation for a long time. He had to explain it to Mukaddir's wife's father. After he called his own wife, Mukaddir's mother, everything became clear. His wife was quiet. She dared not look at the woman's parents, to explain everything to her. Even though she was in despair about her daughter-in-law, it was obvious that she took more pity on her own son. The woman came from a rich family, maybe she would quarrel with them if she was told the truth. At long last Mukaddir bared his soul to his wife:

"Malika, I don't want to hurt your heart, but mine is really hurt a lot. For two years, we've been living like two strangers in the same bedroom. You also have enough pain in your heart. This anguish has brought me to the end at last. Please, talk to your parents unless I kill myself somewhere today or tomorrow. Let's solve it without any problems, shan't we? I hope your parents will understand my situation."

"Oh, my dear, what on earth are you talking about? You are the first I've ever been together with! We were gifted with a son. Whatever trouble God gives, he will give the healing as well. I do not mind even though you'll be living in another room, dear!"

"But, Malika, I fell in love with another woman," he didn't want to lie to her. Silence fell. She heaved a deep sigh:

"Now I understand. A Broken heart is impossible to be healed entirely. I don't mind. If you really want it, I will explain everything to my mummy and dad."

Seeing another woman grieving for her husband is a death-like torture, and just imagining the situation the woman is in at that time makes a person tremble out of pity.

Getting permission, the woman left. Several days later her brother came in a horse-cart to take all of her things back to home.

Both Qodirboy, Mukaddir's father and his mother Oynisa were in a very awkward situation, but the only thing they could do was to soothe each other reminding themselves that everything happens due to fate. Now their son was single.

The divine ties

Mukaddir told his parents about how he fell in love with that girl, and afterwards his mother started visiting the beaut home where the beautiful with the good behavior lived. Seeing all of this Mukaddir said to his mother:

"Mummy, I don't want you to worry so much, anyway I will marry the girl who I like. It's true that I have seen her only once. I didn't even talk to her. She just gave me a delicate smile, I need to somehow see her somewhere and talk frankly about everything. If I feel that she is ready to marry me, then I will ask you to go to her home mummy."

"It's a shame on us, my dear son, love isn't something that suits Muslims. If your father gets to know…"

"Mummy, when will you stop making a decision to save my life? I am already an adult at 28. I can feed and build my own family on my own, can't I? Why do you think I should live the way you want me to? Why has Allah gifted us with intelligence? Would you please, mummy convince my daddy to agree. As you see both my elder sister and brother think that I am doing the right thing" he begged his mother sincerely.

"What kind of a girl is she? I wonder if she comes from a good family? Once we forced him to get married even though he didn't love the woman, so we can't make any more mistakes." She brushed off.

"Mummy, if you are patient I will find a good reason to meet her somewhere. If I can convince her to marry me, then you may have to visit her home dear mummy! Only then I can answer all of your questions no matter how many they are!"

A few days later some theatre artists were going to come to Tashkent to perform. Hojiya would certainly come with her sister to watch the performance since her uncle worked there as the head and his wife, whose name was Marusya turned out to be a Russian woman.

Reading information about this, Mukaddir went to watch that performance.

A bit later when Mukaddir looked at the front seats, there sat the girl who stole his heart at first sight in the wedding. She looked very beautiful, especially with her long hair plaited forty times. His heart started beating fast. Should he go to the front row?

There's no seat vacant. There's a crowd of people. He didn't even realize how good the first part of the performance

was. His thoughts were busy with that girl and looking for a way to have a talk. He remembered the wedding where they met for the first time, his friends whispered into his ears saying that she was single, and that it had been more than a year since her husband died. But that day she didn't even look like a married woman. She was as beautiful as the Moon shining for eighteen days.

Fortunately, when the first part of the performance came to an end, Hojiya went out to the foyer and Mukaddir   slowly stepped towards her.

"Good evening, Miss! Thanks to God that I saw you at last week. I've been looking for you since that wedding party. I was about to go insane wandering around where you live. I hoped you'd to come to this performance. My heart didn't lie to me."

"Aha, it's you who made me shy at the wedding party, isn't it? Everybody around felt how much you looked at me that day.

"Yes, that's me. I always...er... love at first sight..." "I don't know. But I read about it in books."

"I also didn't believe before, but now I do."

"Would you please excuse me? The next part of the performance has started. Do you like it or...?

"I'm not even watching that performance. I'm just sitting there relishing your beauty."

"I am just an ordinary girl. It's usually possible to relish the beauty of the Moon, not ordinary girls like me."

"No, you're different, and you don't seem to be ordinary. I've never seen a girl more beautiful than you.

"Oh, gosh, you seem so strange. You may put me to shame if my uncle suddenly sees us."

"Is your uncle also here?"

"Yes, he is. He works here as the assistant Director."

"I see. It means I can find you here whenever I start missing

you then. It'll be on the days the performances are scheduled, won't it?"

-       ...

"I know many things about you, Hojiya."

"For example…"

"Your husband died and you have a little daughter."

"Why are you interested in a widow with a daughter,

there are plenty of fish in…"

"I am single, and I got divorced. It seems to be my destiny   that Allah has gifted me with insight and I now understand what love means… I realized this as soon as I saw you for the first time."

"This must be hard for your wife then. Poor woman, is she …"

"It's been hard for me too. Until now. We were only together once. Now I am free of my tortures. She'll be living in peace with her child, and I will do my best to help her all the time. There's no life where there's no love and I really want to live being loved and loving somebody. I've already made up my mind Hojiya. The only decision is for you to make. I want to know you more and more."

"Next week my sister and I will come to a performance, and every time we watch it we'll have a conversation about our impressions. That's it…"

"I see that you aren't like the other girls."

"Maybe… Good-bye. Will you watch the next part of the performance or are you leaving?"

"I will certainly watch it!"

They were both excited after their conversation and happily returned to their own seats. This excitement remained alive in Mukaddir's heart even after the performance ended. After the artists were given some flowers, everybody started leaving. Mukaddir waited for the girl pass him, but she walked out with her sister and a very handsome man. Mukaddir stared at her and he didn't know what to do. Glancing at her at least once, the girl went on walking with her partners. Soon they got on the phaeton and left. Mukaddir looked at the girl a bit longer, sat in one of the service carts and left. It took him about an hour to get home as Kodirboy's home was far outside the town. At home Mukaddir's mother was waiting for him.

"Oh, my son has come! Where on earth have you been for so a long time?"

"Mummy, my mummy, today I am the happiest in the world! When I went to the Hamza theatre to see

the new performance, you won't believe it. I saw the girl who I fell in love with at the wedding party! I recognized her after seeing her long and plaited hair. My heart missed a beat, I don't know how the first part of the performance ended. Fortunately for me, she came out to the foyer and we talked for a bit. I made sure that she is a well-educated and very docile girl. It was easy to see it in the way that she answered my questions."

"She seems to have stolen your heart really! Didn't she do anything wrong my son? Are you sure? I think she has asked someone to help her gain your heart with magic."

"Mummy, what on earth are you thinking about? I just saw her for less than five seconds. Today we talked for at least three minutes. She didn't even take a look at me, mum. If she had been someone with a bad past experience she would've shown it in how she talked."

"What are you going to do now?"

"I don't know yet... I am ready to get married right now, but I don't know about her. If you ask her parents to give her to me as a wife, and if you get they refuse... No, never, no! I think I couldn't stand that at all."

At this time his mother was busy with her own troubles, and she wanted her son to get married as soon as possible. Therefore, she was visiting many homes in order to look for a suitable woman worthy of her son.

"Today we visited Abdullaboy's home with your sister. There we were reminded that you could marry his daughter if you see and like her, and we admitted that you weren't the type that would obey somebody. Even though they were taken aback, they agreed to show their daughter to you. So tomorrow at five you can see that girl. She is going to come to the park in Charsu, with her sister. You will also go there with your sister. I hope you'll like her…"

"Ok, I don't want to make you upset, mummy, if I see that girl, I will have a chance to compare her with the one I like. Then after that I will tell you what I think."

Mukaddir went to a park with his sister the next morning and met the girl. She was good-looking but not only beauty was important for him; also, he found inner beauty to be equally important.

"My mother asked you to marry me, but I don't need a wife, I'm not even going to get married. I've come here just to see and talk to you. Have you ever studied at any school?"

"Unfortunately, I haven't" said the girl suddenly without hiding her astonishment.

"Have you ever read books "Layli and Majnun" and "Farhod and Shirin" by Alisher Navai? Asked Mukaddir again. "Who is that Alisher Navai? The girl answered that question

with a question.

"Do you visit Hamza theatre then, if yes how often?" asked Mukaddir as he didn't want to treat someone unfairly. He tried to compare her with Hojiya.

"I know that this theatre is somewhere around Charsu, but I've never been to theatre. I'm not so interested in it" she answered carelessly, but she didn't know that these questions and answers could even decide her future.

"What are you busy with all the time?"

"Well, mainly, cleaning inside and outside the house, laundry, dishwashing, cooking and looking after the cows."

"Sorry, but I'm afraid that I'm not suitable for you at all" he said

They said goodbye to each other. Mukaddir compared this girl with Hojiya, but he grew to understand that Hojiya was quite different, no one could be compared to her. He got even more convinced about everything.

From now on he will take advices from his own heart obeying any of its orders.

But it's interesting who is that girl Hojiya who could attract Mukaddir so much to herself, such a man with a strange behavior! It's incredible! Hojiya's relatives keep calling her as "Bonu" and her ancestors were generations of a famous saint Eshonbobohon. At the beginning of the last century girls in Uzbek families were forced to get married at a very early age, at 12 or 13 and it became popular as a tradition. Hojiya's father, Toshpulat jeweler also married according to the same tradition to a thirteen-year-old woman. In consequence, the immature girl wasn't ready to become a mother, hence she died immediately giving a birth to a daughter, who was later given the name Hojiya. Again, according to traditions after the mother died, her sister was forced to marry her husband and she further looked after the orphan daughter. The girl was brought up in a rich family and luxurious conditions, and when she pushed eighteen she was also made to marry her own cousin. In the past people usually made their children marry their own relatives so that the family ties would keep stronger despite many years have passed. In 1933 Hojiya gave birth to her daughter, but this happiness didn't last long as her husband died because of a serious illness. After all the mournings came to end and when the widow with her daughter started forgetting her anguish, there seemed to be no end to people visiting their home asking Hojiya as a wife. But for some reasons unknown Hojiya didn't want to get married and she carelessly convinced her parents to be patient as she was still in the very despair. They were hesitating about what to do and trying to convince her that they could look after her daughter. But she didn't even say word… Right at that time the meeting in the wedding and in the theatre has changed everything. The girl seems to have some kind of a warm feeling in her heart, but she didn't dare to tell anyone about it. But no matter what part of the day or what time, where she was, the image and the voice of Mukaddir kept invading in her thoughts.

She kept telling to herself: "What's happening to me these days? Why isn't he failing to escape my mind? Isn't he more than a stranger for me? No, never, I must control my emotions somehow."

In this family of well-educated people there were two sons who were very clever. All the news and events were always discussed in this family, therefore they used to go for a walk, concerts very frequently. This was a simple tradition for this family.

One day Hojiya's brother Gafurjon said: "What if you take your daughter to a concert? If you'd like I will get a ticket for you for the concert held by the Azerbaijani singers."

"I don't mind at all. Have I ever refused when you invited somewhere? Not really."

Next morning her brother Gafurjon indeed bought a ticket and Hojiya went to a concert with her daughter. After they came out of this concert in which they enjoyed listening to Azerbaijani songs and musics, suddenly that man Mukaddir came into sight again. Mukaddir immediately lifted up her daughter and she also hugged her with pleasure as if she had known him for a long time. As Hojiyabonu felt awkward she asked her daughter to get down saying that she might seem heavy for him.

"No," she insisted, "I am not heavy, am I?" she talked in amazing tone and her eyes were glittering like a brilliant in the dark.

"Let me hold her for a minute more please, she looks as beautiful and clever as you are! Let me carry her until we get out of the gate, then you may further go by yourselves" he said. "What's your name, little honey?" he asked the little girl in his hands.

"Please, excuse my daughter confused you with someone I think. I am afraid we may bother you er… you don't seem to have much free time, do you?" Hojiya said to him feeling a bit shy.

"To be honest I came to this concert so as to see you at least once, but I came a bit late. Therefore, I just waited outside. Fortunately, you have come I see! My heart felt that you would as I know that you're a fan of culture" Mukaddir said joking, but all that he said was actually true.

"Oh, really! You turned out to be a telepathic then. You seem to know all the things in advance then, don't you?" she started talking sincerely this time.

"Errr… What does telepathic mean?" asked Mukaddir wanting to make her talk more and more.

"I read about it in one of the fiction books, that a man who is telepathic could predict about future as easily as he saw it in the movies. It's a rare ability."

"Now I see! If I am telepathic let me predict what might happen in future."

"Oh, well, let's see…?"

"Well, I see the wedding party in this autumn, oh and this party is going to be ours!"

"How did you predict this?"

"It's my heart speaking to you, not me. Me is just giving sound effects to my own heart that so much wants to talk to you, share feelings …"

"What if my heart refuses agreeing to proposal…"

"Then I will beg your heart to… as you, as you deserve being happy. I promise to make both of you happy. If you agree I will ask my mother to visit your home for proposal…"

"My honey, get down, come on, we'll go by ourselves further. Say thanks to your uncle and give a kiss on his cheek!" Hojiya turned her face towards her daughter as if she didn't hear what Mukaddir said.

"Thank you a lot, Sir! What's your name" asked the little girl.

"Mukaddir, what about yours?"

"Bakhtia" (it represents happiness in Uzbek).

That sounds really beautiful. Good-bye then. My mum will go to your home then!

"Bye-Bye" said Hojiya.

Both Hojiya and her daughter got home with a smile on their faces. The girl hugged her grandma running up to her immediately and she started talking non-stop:

"We saw a wonderful concert today, granny! And while we were going out, one man came up and carried me until we got to the gate and I thanked to him."

"That's a good idea to say thanks when somebody does a favor to you, my baby!"

"I wish I also had a father like him."

"Oh, my little kid, if your mother finds her happiness with someone, you will certainly have a father, my honey! You see, it's your mother who doesn't like anyone."

Hojiya denied carefully: "Don't pay attention, let her say whatever she wants. She is a kid still, and doesn't know what she wants."

"Ok, time can heal everything. We'll see it one day…"

Mukaddir was glad and came into home reciting poems by Navai.

"What's wrong, my dear son, you're up on the clouds, aren't you?" his mother seemingly felt everything in her bones. "Sure, mummy. I am very happy today as I have met that person of my soul. I even hugged her little daughter. She is a wonderful girl. It's very nice to talk to her."

"Oh, it's ok if she is suitable for you, my son. But I don't like the sounding of her daughter and that you will marry her despite that. You aren't going to marry a woman with a daughter, are you?

"Mummy, don't be so weird. If people love each other, they should love the way they are."

"I shudder to think of anything. I don't know what your father may say about this? He always changes his mood."

"Mummy, daddy isn't even interested in what happens at home as he is out days and evenings. You understand me all the time. I really want you to convince him, mum!"

Indeed his father, Kodirboy leaves early and ca, me home late whenever he has business. His days were hectic especially these days. Several businessmen arrived from Russia, and he needed to control the farmers working in the field of 500 hectares. It's not easy to gain wealth and maintain it, and a man needs intelligence and special skills for this. This is also enhanced by Allah.

1930s... Unfortunately, the wealthy USSR started to chase Uzbek rich people. Everyday one could hear bad news. For example, when one man of means tried to not to allow them to take away their lands, they were arrested and sued, then were exiled to North. Another news was that one rich man escaped to Afghanistan with all of his gold as the authorities kept chasing all the rich families.... Therefore, Kodirboy looked sad and in despair when he came home from work. For this reason, his wife couldn't find a chance to talk to him frankly about Mukaddir's problems with love, and she thought that it wasn't time for love. But love is such a strong   feeling that it can make any huge problem seem small. Mukaddir was impatient for his father's decision about his marriage.

"Mummy, couldn't you talk to my father? Have you convinced him yet? I might appear to a liar to Hojiya, mum!" Mukaddir begged.

"Hope to Allah, I will certainly talk to him tonight. I hope that he'll would feel good when he comes home!"

At last that night Kodirboy came in home with lots of gifts. Mother immediately brought pilaf and they all sat around the table. After they had eaten, mother started talking carefully.

: "Dear, it's been a year since our son is living alone. He is as stubborn as you are, my darling! He fell in love with a daughter of a well-known jeweler, Toshpulat. If you allow me, I would go and visit their home to ask their daughter to marry our son. If we go together, we could even have a chance to see that girl."

"I don't mind at all, dear. I don't want my son to live alone all of his life. You'd better go and see what happens… We'll come back to it later on."

Feeling happy, the mother told this good news to her son after what Mukaddir immediately started imagining Hojiyabonu nearby. He was about to fly towards her taking the air if he were able to. His mother and sister went to the home where Hojiya lived and the girl's family welcomed them and invited them inside. According to tradition the girl who brought a pot of tea in seemed very good-looking and pleasing with her slim figure and beauty. Maybe this is what the will of Allah for marriage is as two hearts yearning for each other at long last could be together without any objections. Everyone, even her father, agreed to the marriage and finally Mukaddir would have reach the opportunity to be with Hojiyabonu, the Angel of his heart.

The night of the wedding party, when the Moon shone brightly through the window of the bedroom where Mukaddir and were, Hojiya spent sleepless hours of night talking until the dawn of the day! Each of them melted in the embrace of true love that night and this gave them a chance to get to know each other much better than before. Happy days began for each of these young people…

Days were passing, but the grief in Hojiya's eyes didn't seem to fade away. Mukaddir grew to understand that she wasn't entirely happy and he asked the reason for it. She said:

"I miss my daughter a lot..."

"Ok, we'll go your home then tomorrow."

Asking permission from her mother-in-law Hojiya and her husband left for their home. They were taken there on a horse cart.

Having come home Hojiya greeted everyone there and she hugged her daughter tightly clinching her to her breast. The whole day they'd been together and kissing on her cheeks Hojiya asked her:

"How are you feeling my honey? Aren't you bored here my baby?"

"I keep dreaming about you every night mummy. What if you take me together mum? I won't make any noise and I'm going to be a good girl there, I promise mum!" Her mother felt terrible after she heard what her innocent kid was saying.

She didn't say anything to her husband about it. She was wondering about how his parents would react if she brought her daughter to their home, and if they would welcome a step-granddaughter or...Suddenly she remembered what Mukaddir said in the park and she felt calm. When dusk fell, Mukaddir came bringing some presents for all of them. He even brought a beautiful toy to Bahtiya. After they had supper, the young couple were allowed to leave when, at that right moment quite unexpectedly little girl Bahtiya cried out: "Mummy, I want to go with you, it's going to be very hard for me without you mum!"

Awkward silence fell around the room, and suddenly, hugging her tightly Mukaddir said to her:

"My little honey, don't cry, will you? I will take you to our home, we'll be all living there together.

Mukaddir, his wife and her daughter, returned to their own home that night.

It was quite strange for Hojiya and she said:

"We should've warned our parents before we took her home, dear". She said this as if she was guilty of something and impatiently waited for her husband to respond.

"Leave it. I will solve this problem with them. A little child isn't guilty here, is she? Even the time when I saw her for the first time I treated her as my own daughter, and I will continue to do so!" He wasn't aware how glad he made Hojiya by saying that.

Mukaddir's relatives had heard that his new wife had a daughter, but they didn't expect her to live in this house. Therefore, they were thinking that the girl would leave soon after she stayed there for two or three days. But a week later, even ten days later the little girl was still staying and playing there. All the neighbors and relatives started gossiping about this at that time because it's wrong in the Uzbek tradition for a woman, or especially for a man, to marry someone who has already been married or has a child. These rumors were unpleasant for both Kodirboy and his wife, Oynisabonu as they were a well-known family in Tashkent with their own reputation.

Kodirboy beckoned his son:

"What are you going to do with her daughter, my son?" "Daddy, this girl is my wife's daughter, and your daughter-

in-law. She must somehow live with her mother as she is too young, dad! I think it's unfair to make them live apart from each other."

"Well, you need to be fair and just, so I'll have to think about my own reputation. Do you get me or not?

"Daddy, I didn't understand what you mean. How can I take her back to her grandma's home? I wish you had seen how she begged her mother and me to take her with us!"

"My dear son, I may understand it with my heart, but thinking as an intelligent man, I can't even imagine that a daughter of her first husband is living with us. If you don't want it, you'd better buy another house and move there and live apart from us. Maybe then all the rumors will somehow stop."

"If I don't have any other way out, I will do what you want me to do!"

Blowing the lid of the Soviet system

In the autumn of 1935, not only leaves fell from the trees and other plants, but the houses were also falling with troubles caused by the USSR who were taking lands away from rich people and using them as unique property for the whole community. Those who objected could be exiled to Siberia and the Ukraine with all of their families and even people in Kodirboy's house were also fearful at that time. Kodirboy was also hesitating because he didn't know what to do; allow his own home to be taken away or save his own life rather than a home? Those who wanted to stay alive voluntarily submitted their own lands and houses to the government and as a result, they could be accepted a unique collective-farm to be founded by the government. 500 hectares of lands of apple- trees, grapes, apples and apricots remained at the disposal of the USSR within just one day... Kodirboy spent many sleepless hours at night, in order to gain this wealth.

Besides submitting their lands to the government, they were forced to give their shops in Tashkent city. Now Kodirboy had nothing left. The NKVD1 group and investigation teams came from Russia to Uzbekistan and they were involved in organizing massacres. They were inquiring about the richest people of the country, and those who tried to object to them were going to see themselves in the great beyond. Kodirboy also had the same trouble[1].

"You've become rich gaining wealth by stealing money from rich people, and now you're objecting to gathering all the wealth in the same collective farm, aren't you? It's high time to return everything you took from the people. Or, if you don't, you will be exiled to Siberia with all of your family"

The prosecutor brushed him off, treating him as if he'd murdered someone.

"I gave you everything I earned during my whole life. Isn't it enough? Do you want my children to remain jobless?

They should eke out their living somehow in our shops. I wish you hadn't required us to give our own shops. Can you give me three days more so that I could talk to my family members and then I will come here again"?

 Kodirboy begged them feeling that if he hadn't obeyed he could die with all of his family.

---

[1] The ministry of the internal affairs, during the former Soviet system. It was very cruel towards citizens.

After Kodirboy came home everybody sat around the table to have supper and at that time he explained everything to his children. It was useless to make them suffer just because of the wealth the USSR was waiting for.

Then his clever son Mukaddir sighed.

"Daddy, we'd better not joke with the USSR as they are greedy for wealth and they aren't going to stop until they carry away all the wealth that our people have. I heard some rich people took some parts of their wealth to Russian NKVD in Moscow and in this way they could get official information about exemptions from punishment. They are getting rid of them by showing that sheet of certificate to Russian investigators here. In that case, maybe they will stop disturbing us. Maybe you should do the same".

"I think that's a good idea. You'd better prepare my warm clothes as it's very cold in Moscow. I will try to bring the necessary documents by asking for help from my friends there."

Mukaddir hid many things in the basement. Hiding all the golden jewelry and other golden coins in his leather suitcase Kodirboy set off for Moscow buying a ticket and saying good-bye to everyone. Now dear friends, I ask you to think a bit more! Is it correct from either legal or religious point to force somebody to give all the wealth and money they have, and they earned their entire life? Isn't it something that a real thief can do? Isn't it a crime or cruelty?

Kodirboy sent a telegram to his friend living in Moscow before he left. Seeing him in at the Kazan railway station, his friend helped him to book a room in a hotel. While the two friends were having supper in a restaurant, Kodirboy explained the reason for his arrival. He described how the awful situation the Republic was and he came clean saying that he wanted to get rid of all his troubles.

His friend promised to help him solve the problem after talking to his friend in the administration building. They said good-bye to each other, and in order not to waste his time, Kodirboy went to a performance so that he could slightly avoid his troubles.

The next morning his friend came and asked him to meet colonel Novikov in Moscow NKVD as everything was seemingly settled a day before. Kodirboy said what his friend said, and the colonel Novikov welcomed him with a sincere smile. The conversation between them sounded as follows:

"What are you interested in Comrade Alimdjanov, how can I help you?" asked Novikov.

"Controlling measures reached a peak in Uzbekistan nowadays and I am in a big trouble. Therefore, I came here hoping that there's justice in Moscow. Gathering all of my wealth I came here to submit them to you."

Novikov was on cloud number nine. And he asked in a rush where the money was.

"It's in the street. I left it with my Russian friend, errrr, it's in the suitcase" said Kodirboy.

It wasn't hard to feel that Novikov was in the seventh heaven.

"You can go and bring it and I will tell the guards to let you in."

Coming in he brought the suitcase with the money inside and opened it to show the money. On seeing all the money, and gold, Novikov's eyes were bulging out with astonishment and he encouraged Kodirboy with a handshake saying that he had done the right thing.

"Thanks Kodirboy, you turned out to be a brave rich man. I ordered the accounting department to accept the money you brought. After you submit them one by one they are going to write a certificate and give a you copy. I will write an official license to you on behalf of the NKVD. From now on no one will dare bother you, I promise."

"Thank you a lot. Would you please come to Tashkent to visit us? We are going to be very glad to serve you as a guest."

"Hope to God"

Submitting all of his property Kodirboy went outside, quite calm as if he got rid of all this troubles. At night getting the Moscow-Tashkent train, he returned his home.

Coming home he talked to his children very frankly:

"My dear children, now we will also have to eke out our living like all the citizens of the Soviet Union, working in the field because there's no another way out you see."

During the Soviet Union period, everybody accepted these tortures as destiny, with millions of people trying to be patient.

If you remember, there's an interesting story popular among people. In ancient times, there lived citizens of one country and they all were patient with everything and were also invaded by another country. One day the despotic country complained about the fast population growth rate and announced that they wanted them to reduce the number since it was hard to provide all of them with food. Do you know what, the despot country asked the citizens to hang the other citizens with a rope? When one of the enslaved citizens begged for permission to ask a question the chief despotic member said:

"You can ask, but as quick as possible."

"Where do we need to get ropes from, will you give it or shall we look for them by ourselves?"

This is a funny story for someone, but if you pay attention, it can make you both laugh and cry. Maybe there's more than a grain of truth in this story as Kodirboy also encountered the same situation. More vividly he thanked the man who forced him to give him all his wealth, and money he had. His children also accepted this as destiny. What on earth could they do except   this?

Nothing actually...

"I will try to find another job" said Mukaddir.

"I am going to enter the university" Mukaddir's ambitious brother Mirgiyos said.

"I will go to the field to work" Mirtoir, Mukaddir's elder brother made up his mind.

When Mukaddir and his wife were having a rest in their bedroom, he told her everything that happened to his   father.

Now it was high time for every couple to eke out their own living.

Attempting to appease her husband Bonu said: "I have an idea, what if I will try to talk to my uncle. He has many friends who can help us somehow. Maybe, I hope to God, he can somehow help us."

"Ok..."

The next morning after Bonu did what she said, and indeed talked to her uncle, asking for help and she coped with it. Three or four days later her uncle called Mukaddir. It was really awkward for him to go to her uncle's house, and it was a bit strange to ask for help from his wife's relative. He could also barely go there because he was shy. Bonu's uncle greeted him   with a smile. He gave him the news that he'd found him a job, but it was very far from his hometown. The job turned out to be in Boysun, one of the districts of Surkhandarya.

The uncle gave him a recommendation letter so that he could work there with his wife. Mukaddir agreed because he wanted to somehow get out of his money troubles. Later he told his decision to his father Kodirboy, who didn't object because he knew that his son wasn't good at fieldwork. So, fate brought Bonu and Mukaddir to Boysun city.

They came to this city, because Bonu's uncle asked help from his son-in-law who worked in NKVD Secretary. At first working there as just a secretary, Mukaddir could be eliminated to the position of a responsible specialist. He worked a long time there. In 1936 Mukaddir and Bonu were gifted with a daughter, but the infant's life turned out to be quite short and she died when she was just three-months old. Not long after Bonu again became pregnant and a son was born in Tashkent. A year later Mukaddir also came back to Tashkent where he was appointed as the chief of the shop. At that time, there used to be various dairy products such as foods and clothes in the shop and he started building a house by buying a yard measuring over 0,8 hectares in the street called Allon. This land was surrounded with a clay wall and the rest of 0.6 hectares of land were to be occupied by a garden with fruit-trees. But   this wasn't that easy for either of them, Bonu was in charge of cooking food, and preparing tea for the builders even though she had a daughter and a little son to look after. Moreover she became heavy with one more child at the same time. In 1939 in late autumn when the house was completed Mukaddir and Bonu moved there with their children. But Mukaddir's mother, Oynisa didn't like the way that her son was leaving the house with his wife and children, as the proverb says: "All the birds will leave the nests one day". Thanks to god his parents gave up complaining about it to neighbors. But sometimes she made it known to them that she didn't want them to leave:

"I don't care what you're going to live on. You can move into your new home only having the things which Bonu brought. The rest of them is ours, I ain't going to give you anything."

Both Mukaddir and Bonu moved to their new house getting all of their bits and pieces. However, it was only enough to fill in the terrace and the house. All the cushions they had placed into the chests and the dishes they put into the cupboard. A big wall clock made in Paris decorated the middle of the house. The new house looked as nice as a home for honeymooners. Of course, it's good when the father and mother-in-law live together with couples, but it's much better when the happy people are alone. Looking forward to the next morning they saw each evening with lots of joy. Sometimes their parents visited them, or sometimes they went to see them. Going out in the early morning to go to work, Mukaddir was in a hurry to see his children and beautiful wife at home every evening. Most often Mukaddir's youngest brother Mirgiyos and his sister Sohiba came to see them and their mother Oynisa was in the dark about it. Moreover, Bonu's father was also helping them with money.

The happy hours seemed to be like minutes as they passed quite fast and easily; happy moments can infuse endless joy, and sweet memories into the heart. Planting some fruit trees in the garden they also grew many flowers on the both sides of the ditch in their yard. In the middle of the yard they built a wide-bed which in the centre there was a table and some cushions around where they could sit to have meals, and rest at night. The nights seemed to be very fascinating with twinkling stars in the sky and the moon glowing afar. On such beautiful nights, they used to talk for hours until the dawn of the day. It was in 1939 in autumn, when there was more news about this couple. Bonu was about to give birth.

Bakhtiya was running from left to right as usual, Anvar also started taking his first steps. Four months later, Bonu gave a birth to a son! At that time, there weren't any maternity hospitals, so it was a midwife who gave a hand to women giving birth. Mukaddir was in seventh heaven, and all the neighbors, and the aunts served as a midwife to the baby. The tiny innocent creature came into existence jumping out s on the cushion around the sandalwood.

At this time Mukaddir was very lucky as his shop was always crowded with clients. Everyday he comes home singing his favorite songs and as usual Bonu saw him in with an innocent smile as if they were a newly married couple. They decided to buy a cow for the house because they wanted to save money on milk, and sour cream for the children every day. Mukaddir's aunt taught Bonu how to milk the cow and after that they started growing clover in their garden so that there could be enough fodder for the cow to eat.

Bonu's father named the new baby "Sarvari olam" (which means another holy name for the Islamic prophet Muhammad) and he wanted him to become a great person in the future. Bakhtia started going to school and helping her mother around the home, and it is she who looked after the little baby. And the mother cleaned, swept the house everyday, preparing meals and looking forward to the evening when her husband would come back from work. Their life was replete with happiness, like that of heroes in the fairy tales, peaceful and there seemed to be no trouble worth thinking over. At long last the youngest baby started making his first steps and speaking initial words.

Bloodshed

In 1941 when Mirgiyos, Mukaddir's youngest brother had just graduated from the Tashkent State Railway roads institute, the fascists started a war against the former Soviet Union. Mirgiyos left for the war like many other young men in the city. His eldest brother Mirtoir stayed to look after the collective farm[2] as a chief. The eldest daughter of Kodirboy was living with her father and there was one more home being built for the youngest child to live in when he got married. In Uzbek families parents start building homes for their sons starting from the time they are born, as they all want to live together, having a meal around the same table.

Kodirboy was also a businessman and he owned a good oriental tea-room where most passers-by stopped to have a drink. This place was a traditional pastime for almost all the elderly people of the mahalla2.

Life seemed to be interesting and strange at the same time. No matter how much a person loves his life-partner, there may be some obstacles through their lifetime. When life of Mukaddir and Bonu was going well, one girl from the countryside started visiting his shop quite often which caused the other people around to disperse some rumors. She was a daughter of a man popular with a religious background, and at least twice a day she had to come into this shop to say a few words to Mukaddir on her way home. She started following and chasing him all the time. Her home was quite close to the shop, and she treated him very differently, inviting him to their home. Mukaddir couldn't reject the invitation as the girl's father, an old person of high reputation invited

---

[2] A common street-like place to live where Uzbek people live counting each other as members of the same family.

him personally, and Mukaddir thought that he might just have some business suggestions. Then he noticed that something was wrong with their attitude as they treated him as the future groom at home, and indeed the girl's father wanted that his daughter was old enough and not needed anywhere. There aren't many people living in the countryside and therefore they all know each other well and can even keep posted what right or wrong each is doing. Soon people started gossiping about the relationship in the village. Despite Bonu trusting in Mukaddir's loyalty, these rumors were very bitter pills to swallow. Bonu wasn't such a brawler to say much about such nonsense. Therefore, she spoke to her husband.

"If those rumors turn out to be true, I warn you that you're never going to see me and the children. That girl is going to cry for the moon, barking up the wrong tree, I assure you!".

Although Mukaddir was not guilty he stood quiet, his head down.

"Bonu, my dear, I fought death to be with you. Trust me, won't you! The shop is always crowded and anyone can get in and out of it. Will you believe the rumors of women who don't want our happiness to last longer? You're very clever, but don't give up and loose yourself in that nonsense. Soon we're going to have one more child which is why we are even happier. Everyday I am living with fear that I may be sent to war and I shudder to think that I am going to live without you, my dearest. You're thinking about the things people are telling you, Bonu!" he said feeling a bit sad.

"The person who loves doesn't want his partner to look at someone else, and this jealousy as they say may even kill the person, dear. Next time I beg you to not allow the people around us to hinder us, will you!"

From that point forward the rumor at long last disappeared.

In January of 1942 this family was gifted with one more daughter whom they called Gulnara, but Mukaddir and Bonu call her Muhabbat (which means love) as she was born thanks to their strong love.

Half a year later, Mukaddir came back home in a depressed state as if something serious had happened. He didn't dare say anything to his wife at first, but he was forced to. It was because the head of the farm bought many things promising to pay for them later on and this lasted for one year. At last when Mukaddir tried to calculate all the money he owed, it turned out to be thirty thousand soum, which was a really huge amount at that

Time, leading the shop to a crisis. No matter how much he tried to ask, the head of the farm wouldn't attempt to cover the costs and therefore Mukaddir was forced to pay fifty percent, about fifteen thousand soum. The head promised to pay the money back and asked him to write everything down. If the tax control system came to check the shop, it might even get closed because of debt. He somehow paid a part of the debt with his own, but he was still worried about it.

Once when the head came into the shop Mukaddir reminded him about the money he owed saying that he had paid half of it, that's fifteen thousand on his own. He asked him to pay all if he had a chance. However, the head looked indifferently at him.

"How much did I owe for the goods I bought more exactly?"

"Thirty thousand soums...

"It's impossible that I owed you so much money, friend! I don't even remember it!"

"I paid extra 15 thousand on my own, now it's high time you..."

"Ok then, you will have to wait for some days."

For many days Mukaddir had been hoping he'd bring the money back, but he didn't. It was awkward to ask him again now, seven days passed, then ten... Controllers came into the shop to examine and they ordered it to be closed.

They had checked it for a week and found an illegal outcome. This meant products were sold, but there was no payment for them. The Controllers warned him to call him the main office. Mukaddir was in bad mood those days, returning home a bit drunken. Bonu looked at his angry face eager to know what was wrong with him.

"I am fed-up with all the things happening. I seem to be punished for what I haven't done. There's a 15 thousand illegal deficit and this is because of the headman who hasn't paid a penny for what he bought during the year. When I showed the controllers my notebook of debts, they rejected it insisting that there was no sign confirming that. He couldn't show any documents proving that. It seems that they are going to call him tomorrow as well as the head. What if he won't admit anything?"

If he didn't Mukaddir would be found guilty. He was so sorry that he had wanted to do something good to people, and this what he got in return. Mukaddir was really irritated.

Despite the fact that Bonu tried to calm her husband down, she was fearful and shuddering to think that he could be arrested. Who would listen up to her? Who would give her a hand? They could hardly see the morning in. No sooner had two or three days passed, than a man from the main office of controllers came to leave an order about calling Mukaddir for inquiry. The next morning when Mukaddir went there, the investigator told him:

"Comrade Kodirov, yesterday we inquired the head of the farm, but he gave us a written assignment confirming that he didn't owe any soums. Here it is, you can read this".

Seeing what was written there, Mukaddir was stunned, and stood stock-still. The investigator averted his eyes.

"I am going to give you some time. If you don't pay the sums back in two weeks, you're going to be sued unfortunately."

"Thanks, I will think it over a bit..." He got a terrible pain in his head and he was thinking about how unfair it was. The situation was hard enough to hide from Bonu.

Both of them didn't know where to go and what to do. At that time when the war was going on, it was impossible to find such a huge sum of money, and no one would even trust them. They couldn't go to talk to the head who was a real thief and he had already denied it. More vividly he had actually invited the controllers so that he would get rid of the debt and they had showed him how to do it. An innocent man like Mukaddir had trusted them in vain and he hadn't expect them to do cheat him. How could he get rid of this trouble? He had no one to give him a hand!

He had a four-year old child, besides his wife was pregnant again.

In vain, he asked quite a few people for help.... No one could ever understand him as well as he did himself.

Moreover, his little brother came back from the war, wounded, and had started his studies at the university again. He thought over it for a long time, and didn't know how to overcome this. At long last he made up his mind to leave for the war rather than being arrested due to the crime someone else had done. Being arrested with the sale unpaid was nothing but shame for him. He preferred to die in the war for it. However, he didn't dare to tell this to his wife. Millions of people were fighting in the war for their motherland, now Mukaddir was thirty-six, strong enough to fight.

The next morning Mukaddir went to the Department of the Military service where he came clean about all of his troubles to the chief. At that time, when people had injured themselves, to avoid being called to the war, they volunteered. The chief was stunned to see the man who was going to combat death to defend his own pride and reputation. The chief said:

"I wish all the men could be as brave as you are! The army needs people like you! Within a week, I wish you could tackle all the problems you have at home, and convince your parents and wife that you must gather all the things needed and come up to their where the soldiers usually gather. It's going to be at the beginning of December. After you're all registered, we'll go to the station where soldiers from the other regions will join you. Getting on the train, all of you will set off for the warfield."

"Thank you a lot. Now I feel myself much more confident" said Mukaddir to the chief giving an innocent smile. Maybe this sort of being brave seems to be a crazy idea for some people today, but at that time, it was a holy duty for all of the people. There were millions of them who wanted to voluntarily join the army.

Going to see his parents he tried to explain everything. His parents didn't even try to object, and instead they encouraged his decision as they were of clever disposition. They were praying for him so that he could come back safe and sound preferring a man's braveness to money. After Mukaddir made sure that he was doing the right thing, he confidently came up to his wife. "You can congratulate your husband. Like many other brave men, I am also going to fight for your peaceful life. You see, my brother returned from the war safe and sound within just two months. I also made up my mind to serve. If I stay here, I may be arrested which will no doubt put me to shame."

Women are women anyway, and no matter how confidently he said this to her, it was immediately obvious how she turned to despair:

"What are we going to do without you then?"

"Leave it, Bonu, that's what many people have to be patient with. You will lead your lives the way the other people are living. My parents and my brothers are alive, and they will give you a hand I hope."

Bonu couldn't do anything, no matter how much she tried. She cried the whole night and the pillow she lay on became wet through from her tears. She was suffering from the bitter anguish of an unfair life. How long will money be ruling over people, not justice? An innocent man could be easily arrested because of money and there's no one to give you a hand. Her husband decided to fight in the war so that he wouldn't be arrested. He preferred to die as a brave man than to being arrested because of an unfair decision by the administration. Bonu added as an afterthought: "The more I do for my husband, the more outstanding duties I'll still have. Therefore, I mustn't let him feel sad, instead I must show my happiness and that I will see him off to defend our motherland, my children, and our peaceful life. I wish he will return quickly as right as rain for the sake of happiness of my children!"

When a man is happy he it is said that time to passes quickly. So, the last happy days of this couple were going to come to end, maybe for a while. This day was the first day of them being apart from each other. The train was said to be arriving at 10.00 am.

In 1943 on December 5 they woke up earlier to have breakfast together. It had been many days since Mukaddir became weak because of troubles, but he was still trying to look strong in front of his wife. Before his departure to   the bloodshed field, he stood still for a long time with his children and his wife.

 "Wait for me, ok, and I will be back!"

He added his sweetest words and feelings as an afterthought. After Mukaddir left the house, Bonu's brother came to take her to the station which was already crowded with people. There were soldiers dressed in military uniforms, all of which looked the same. It was hard to find and recognize her own husband among those soldiers in the crowd. She handed something wrapped up inside some paper to his son, and gave it to her son. Sarvar shouted loudly at Mukaddir.

 "My dearest, will you get the thing in your son's hand". At this time the soldiers were given permission to stand free– (order "Vol'no") three-year old Sarvar ran up to his father and embraced him tightly like he was going to lose his father forever. Mukaddir shouted loudly: "Bonuuu, I got it! I got it!". All the soldiers were ordered to get into their own wagons.

All of them got inside the wagons. As soon as they took their own seats, they were allowed to say good-bye to their close people. Children and Bonu could barely find the wagon in which Mukaddir sat. Leaning her face against the window looking down in fear with her eyes glittering with tears, Bonu made her son Sarvar get into the wagon. Running up to his father, he sat on his knees. Hugging him tightly Mukaddir was too weak to hold his tears from trickling down his face. Mukaddir said to him:

"My sweet son, you're already a big boy now. Don't make your mummy angry, will you? Immediately do whatever she says." After he said all of this, he could hardly set his son loose and out of his hands. The first signal was already given so that the train would move. Sarvar was about to cry. He could feel these last moments with all of his heart. However, he kept patient like the adults:

"I want you to murder each of the fascists, with no trace, dad!"

He then went down the platform. The station was as noisy as the ocean filling with waves. Someone was crying, some shouting, and others were screaming with anguish. Two innocent children and a mother went out of the station to get into the tram. After they arrived in Juva, their uncle took them in the cart to their home. The days were seeming to be longer and longer, and the nights even longer as they were passing without Mukaddir for Bonu!

Bonu was in agony like a bird bereaved of its wings. Different thoughts about her husband were invading her, torturing her, and making her toss and turn in her bed. A day seemed as long as a year. When winter came to end, she got a letter from her husband: "Bonu, my dearest, how is it being hard for you alone with children? Do not worry about me. We are in the military sector in the Ukraine, and quarantine has also come to end. We took the holy oath and learned to use guns, and soon we will take part in the fighting. I just want you to pray for me and not to worry my darling so that I can kill all the fascists torturing us so much. Kisses and hugs to our children. Wanting to hug you! Mukaddir".

Crying and sobbing, Bonu sent a response: "My Darling, my days are like years without you here. May you be safe and sound for the sake of my children. My endless love, may

God save you from any trouble or disaster. You shouldn't worry about us, as our relatives are always giving us a hand. Both your and my parents are taking care of our children. The only thing I want from you is to take care of yourself, for me and for our children!".

Bonu was heavy with a child and on the first day of April in 1944 she gave a birth. A son was born. A baby which wasn't yet born when his father left just five months ago, came into being. Aunt Sohiba and grandma of Hojiya were the midwives there for her. In March Mukaddir wrote another letter: "Bonu, one day when I went to sleep I had a dream. There, I saw you and my children. I dreamt that you gave birth to a son!". That's what he felt, what a father feels, and indeed she gave birth to a son! Two days later Bonu asked her daughter to write a letter to her father saying that they had one more little brother, a new guest, and that his dreams had come true. They wrote a letter delivering the news about a baby son, and left it in the post-office.

"Game" of the head

In the beginning of April, they got another letter from daddy. "Bonu, right now we are leaving for Moldavia. The bastard fascists are losing one by one but they aren't giving up that easily. They started escaping from the territory of our motherland. I know that you're about to give birth. Are you feeling good these days, dear? If you have problems with money, show this letter to the head."

Even though Bonu knew what Mukaddir could write to the head, with curiosity she opened the letter hidden inside the one for her. She started reading the letter for the head:

"I don't even know how to address you now, sir, but because of you I've been walking through bloodshed, and I've abandoned my five children at home, with my wife alone. You know the reason very well. You owe me thirty thousand soums. Sir, I swear for it in the name of Allah, if you deny this, you're going to burn to ashes in hell when you die one day. I really beg you to help my children. I hope you won't make my wife sad after you read this letter...".

For a while Bonu didn't show this letter to the head hiding it in somewhere safe.

Half a month or two later someone came knocking at the door. All the women and elderly people were looking forward to the postman to come as he delivered letters of joy from their close people, and bread-winners of their families. Bonu looked at the postman with a strange feeling, he said:

"Mrs. I've been avoiding giving you this letter for a long time."

He handed the letter to her and Bonu flinched out of fear. Bakhtia saw how her mother fell to the ground and she called out for Sarvar and Anvar. They could hardly bring their mother inside the house, and once they had her inside, they squirted water on her face. When she opened her eyes she immediately remembered the letter. Running outside quickly Bakhtia brought the letter inside and didn't show it to the children, even though they insisted. To their curiosity, she answered:

"All the things written in here are false. Your daddy isn't dead, he will never die, he will never leave us alone, he will never abandon me alone. I don't believe it. No. Never. One day or the other he will come through this door, and you, we'll be waiting. He will come back some way." The children also didn't believe that their father had died and they believed whatever their mother said. .

Isn't that brave of an Uzbek woman? That woman focused on making her children believe that their father was alive, even though she was in absolute distress. She didn't want her children to feel the same agony.

Quite often, when the children were sleeping, Bonu went outside and sobbed for a long time, staring at the photo of her husband, with unique love. As children were young, they didn't understand many things. She didn't want them to see that she was crying and suffering. Time was passing somehow.

Day by day all the jewelry Bonu had was sold just to buy some food to eat. There was none of them left now. Even all the cushions on the chest were sold. But Bonu didn't sell the cow, she thought that children would better eat milk foods everyday.

Whatever she did, she worked hard to somehow eke out living. Getting the letter which her husband had sent, she decided to show it to the head, a thief, she read it once more carefully. Going to the Secretary of the Party Committee in the village, Risolat, she carefully explained the reason for her visit. After, the woman, Risolat read that letter.

"I don't believe that he could be so greedy, that man, Mukaddir used to be a very clever man, I don't believe it. I will go with you to talk to the head. We'll solve this problem together".

Both of them went in the office where the head sat. Welcoming them with open hands he expressed his condolence to Bonu. He said many things about Mukaddir and that he was a very good man. Risolat handed the letter to him. There was no change in his facial expression when he was reading the letter. He then put the letter in the drawer saying that he would help.

Thanking him once, both women left the room together.

Weeks, and months passed but there was nothing sent by the head to give them a hand. The secretary came to their this house more house, more than once, promising somehow get them the money, but sometime later that woman also died in the hospital.

There was no one to help Bonu now and only that woman was aware of that letter, which was given to the Head, a very dishonest man.

Harsh realities of life

Now it was time to forget about that money and Bonu needed to find another way to somehow feed her children. Every week, her father and brother sent food to feed her children, but it wasn't enough. At this time, all the women in the mahalla were being called to help the soldiers by sewing cushions for them to sleep on. It was a good chance for Bonu to earn money and she started sewing for them at home. Bakhtia also helped her very much by sewing the cushions together, and it became much easier to earn money for bread.

At those times widows having five children used to be given financial assistance by the government, but to receive assistance, the last child should've been born in 1945. Her youngest child was born in 1944, and she didn't know what to do. Five innocent children were hungry at home, and as soon as she was told about the assistance her brother-in-law Mirgiyos helped to write a certificate confirming that her youngest child was born in 1945, despite he was born in 1944. This cost them a pair of brilliant ear-rings, and the financial assistance started being rendered soon to that poor widow, Bonu.

In 1945 there was news informing people that the fascists were losing the war, but now the soldiers didn't need any cushions. Therefore, there were no orders for them anymore. Now Bonu was obligated again to find another way of earning money to feed her children. A woman, Hakimakhon in the neighborhood was sewing sweatshirts, and trousers selling them around.

Now Bonu was seeking all possible ways to somehow feed her children. Asking her father for help, she bought a Zinger sewing machine for a very cheap price and she learnt how to sew clothes in her neighbor's home. Bakhtia was capable of doing all the housework at home, and Sarvar helped his mother by pulling the thread on the machine tight so that   it would work smoothly because the machine didn't work very well as it was old. With her neighbor, Bonu went to the shop to buy some calamine cloth, thread, needles and all the other necessary tools. Selling the clothes ready made in the shops, she bought food to eat for children. Although Bonu seemed to get engrossed in family and housework troubles, she didn't forget her husband even for a moment. In every instant of being apart from each other, she looked forward to news about him.

One day a gypsy woman came along the village to foretell people about their lives. Bonu also tried to ask her about her husband. She foretold that Mukaddir was alive, not dead, just kept captive somewhere and that he would come back many years later...

She didn't know whether it was true, or not, but anyway she believed it remaining forever loyal to her husband, remembering him, every time she took breath. Several months later the war ended and life started going at a better pace, Bakhtia started working on a farm. Anvar was late to attend school as he was weak in health. Witnessing the harsh realities of life being, and so little and innocent, the children were growing up day by day. In 1947 Sarvar and his brother Anvar were accepted to study at school 111 where a teacher whose name was Musayev Giyoskori taught them to read and write. Their living conditions improved a lot, now people didn't need to buy cheap sweatshirts or trousers and earning money became much easier than before.

Bonu decided to learn one more skill, it was sewing suits with trousers from the cloth named "thin Chinese silk cloth". But, when it fell out of fashion, she once again had trouble of eking out a living. Then she learned to sew beautiful fashionable clothes for women after what her life started going at a better pace. Now she had more clients and more money to feed her children with.

Bonu had a lot of trouble, but being a mother was a priority to her, and she didn't let anyone hurt her children. It was the time when Sarvar was a very curious and a temperamental boy, and one day when he was playing with a ball outside in the yard, he kicked it once and it bounced over to the place where a cow was eating fodder. The cow was seemingly greedy for the fodder, and it started attacking him. As soon as Sarvar started screaming Bonu rushed to him. She always kept being alert to her children. Though she didn't dare sell the cow when she needed money during the war time, she sold it immediately after it attempted to harm her child.

During wartime, the government members visited homes with many children asking parents to leave their child in the orphanage as it was a hard time to cope with so many children. These people visited Bonu many times as well.

They said:

"War has left you alone and bereft. Therefore, what if you leave three or two of your children in the orphanage and after that it will be much easier for you to feed and bring up the rest. They are going to be under the state control where they will always be happy, and have enough to wear and to eat."

"Excuse me please. But I think that my children are orphans in your opinion! Actually, they aren't. My husband, their father is alive. Therefore, I will never allow my children to be taken to the orphanage. Despite my loneliness, I will bring them up with no needs, and they are going to be great people one day that all people will admire."

All those who came with this suggestion went back being astonished at this brave woman, because she was not afraid of anything, and had strong dignity.

Bonu never spent her time in vain, and all the neighbors liked chatting with her in their leisure time. Although they came into her home missing her a lot, she welcomed them with a smile, and though she was never free, she kept sewing something for the clients. The neighbors said to her one day:

"Bonu, dear, you've strained yourself working non-stop for your children, and they never give up reading a book whenever we see them. Why don't you teach them to do something to earn money?"

"What can they do to earn?"

"One of the children of your neighbor Ibrohim is selling kerosene, another one sells some milk foods. It might be easier for you then if you try it, Bonu."

"I know it's ok to learn to earn, but I want my children to become educated people. No matter how much I suffer, I will do my best for this, hope to God. Before their father left for the war I promised him to do everything so that they could study. I will never break my promise."

"Sorry we've said this. It's because we feel sorry for you, dear!?"

No matter how much she had to work, and suffer, Bonu didn't go to her parents or brothers asking for help. Sometimes she sent her children to visit her relatives, uncles, aunts and grandparents, as they had many children to play with there. They often came home saying many things which hurt their mother. They were innocent and didn't understand anything:

"Mummy, yesterday we saw that they threw the beets with pieces of bread to their cows. But we never throw them, do we? I told them that it was the only thing we had at home to eat. But they, I think don't eat it."

"My baby, my honey kids, whatever you're eating today, will be forgotten tomorrow if you study well and work hard."

"Mummy, why doesn't our uncle give that bread to us, instead of giving it to the cows. We are eating bread with ants mummy. Isn't it wrong? If we had a father we wouldn't be suffering so much, would we?"

"My son, you should be very strong and patient with everything. The only thing you must do is to study hard and be a man who will show them that it was wrong. You shouldn't wait for help from anyone."

Bonu knew very well why her husband's relatives didn't want to treat her children well. But she didn't want to tell her children as she didn't want them to hate their uncles. Working hard non-stop she gave two of her children to school, controlling all the tasks they accomplished. Seeing their love and interest in study, she felt very glad.

Again, winter came freezing everywhere, covering the lands with white snow. All the snow gathering on the roofs   brought the snow to the ground and made a dome in the same corner. These domes created a skating ground where they could play going up and down. All the children of the mahalla played there no matter how close or far they lived.

They had to set off earlier to go to school. The streets were narrow, there was no trace of the carts, and therefore the snow hindered them from walking. Just try to imagine, seven or eight-year-old children walking through the snow wearing only galoshes on their feet, not boots. They were forced to walk one and half kilometers on foot in cold weather. Somehow, they moved onto a wider street, but their feet were aching as if needles had penetrated their skin, which was due to cold snow. While walking there the bigger children tried to appease them as they were crying on the way. Their faces were sore because of the cold, and their skin got blue. As soon as they came into the classroom, blood rushed to their faces, because the teachers didn't immediately start the lesson since they waited for children to get warm inside. Especially, the teacher Musayev, who was very kind to the children and wrapped up their feet with blanket as soon as they came in. He made them sit in front of the central heating where they could get warm their feet.

He was a kind teacher, loving the children and treating them as if they were his own kids.

Her sons studied very well despite the difficulties, and that year her little daughter went to school. She had a strange habit of keeping every note-book her children filled and was assessed by teachers inside the chest as if they were precious gifts. She accepted many thank you letters from the teachers, and after the children started reading without difficulties she made them get registered in the library and required them to bring different fairy tales home every day. They did it, and every day they brought home a new book and made them retell everything they read. Bonu was really satisfied that her children were getting a wider and wider outlook day by day.

If you could imagine how this family lived after the war, you would even cry feeling sorry for them. As the house they lived got older because of rain, and snow, every time it rained the roof got soaked with water which trickling through, and the floors, and ceilings, were soaked all the time. Their neighbors helped them to cover the roof with clay and straw, but it was useless.   It rained a lot in the winter of 1945, therefore the open wooden roof broke after one of the cow's horns' broke. They couldn't afford to rebuild the cow-shed any more, and therefore they had to sell the cow. After that they destroyed the cowshed.

Bonu was quite busy with earning and feeding the children, and in 1947 all the lands were cultivated for cotton and the people were called to pick the white delicate, soft, cotton. Bakhtia was one of leading workers in the cotton field and her brothers helped her all the time. Her photos were published in the newspapers for her contribution to cotton picking activities. In 1949the winter weather started earlier. At that time people had to squeeze spatter-dock to get the cotton out of it, because the cotton wasn't ready enough to pick. When dusk fell, each worker was given one ray of bread, and therefore Sarvar also went to squeeze spatter-docks to help his sister and to get a ray bread, despite his hands aching and bleeding. His hands were bleeding due to the scratching injuries caused by the sharp tips of the spatter-docks. Bonu used to wash his hands and smear cologne with cream on them as soon as he came home.

Bonu never forgot about her female beauty, and even though she didn't have a husband, she kept taking care of herself by doing her hair, and wearing makeup. She looked so beautiful that those looking at her, couldn't stop staring. Yes, though her children were wearing old clothes, she always they kept them clean and ironed. Her yard and home were also full of aroma of different flowers. War made the neighbors kind to each other as they all shared the same troubles with needs, and poverty. No strange man ever came in Bonu's house, except for the tax controller or the head man.

Since Mukaddir left for the war when his sons were young, he couldn't cope with celebrating the sunnat[3] party for them. Now it was high time for all of them to undergo this tradition. His eight, six, and two-year old sons were gathered for the party   which, according to this tradition, the head man, and the

special Master would visit to accomplish the main tasks. Actually, they should've treated the whole mahalla people to pilaf, but they couldn't afford it, hence they just treated the head man, and that special master with a wide plate of pilaf. If they had had a father they could have afforded the celebration.

---

[3] A religious tradition according to which boys under seven will undergo certain customs at a certain age.

Bonu made up her mind to sell their land for a garden measuring ten meters wide, the same length long, and in this way, she could cover the costs for the school needs. Before all the income from selling fruit in this garden would be enough to feed children because the price for those fruits were very cheap, Bonu invited some young men in the mahalla to help her to pick the fruits with the following terms:

"You can eat, or take as much fruit home as you want, but you need to pick a big pan of fruit for me."

The young men were pleased to help her, but the income of their assistance wasn't enough to cover her daily expenses.

THE SECOND PART
DREAMS CAME TRUE

Freedom can be reached through torture and only a stone can turn into a pearl being kept in a shellfish.

Omar Hayam

Introduction

A hospital, not so big and not so small. As soon as I opened the window of the hospital ward, I could smell a very pleasant odor which emerged from the flowers growing outside. She turned into the palata 13 after putting on her smock, then got a tonometer and a stethoscope. There were two patients in this room, one of which was reading a book, and the other washing his face. After we greeted each other, one patient spoke "Mrs. Doctor, what diagnosis do I have for my sickness?" "Dear professor, you don't need to discuss or ask about your

disease. It's enough for you to take the pills, the treatment, because in time you'll soon lose your former self. I think, you know what's written in our holy books: "Before feeling sick, you need to take care of your health and all the things nature has gifted you with!" the doctor said.

"Thanks doctor, I will try."

A woman about thirty, good-looking, Zulhumor walked alongside the hospital and went inside the Cardiology department. It had been three days since I felt something wrong was upcoming. I could feel that in my bones. The days which used to pass quickly for me before, started passing very slowly, and the raindrops falling on the ground seemed to be reminding me of the harsh realities of life I'd witnessed, and the challenges I'd experienced. They at the same time hurt, and gave me a chance to concentrate on my memories of the past days.

Life is like a book. Memory is a book itself.

The dawn was breaking after the night which was giving up to the morning. Loneliness is a thought to cure any pain and in this case, a man can sort out everything bad or good, happiness or sadness while he is alone. A doctor isn't needed in order to cure the inner pain we have, but time, it seems, can heal everything, and be even more effective when we have the privilege to come clean about our troubles to someone we find reliable.

In spring of 1989, I was ill, in a second state-owned hospital, and to be honest, it was the first time I became ill. According to how philosophers interpret it, every occasion has its own categories of consequences and motives. And in this respect, there was a good reason for me being sick at that time. Unexpectedly a very good-looking woman doctor came into my room to see me.

When I wondered what diagnosis they had for my sickness, she told me not to think about that.

I was suffering a lot due to all the non-stop medications I was taking; six sorts of drugs, five injections, and two drops in a glass every day. Both of my hands were in pain due to needles which penetrated them. My body seemed to be full of drugs, and I had pain everywhere. The main my illness was tiredness, and nervousness.

One day the same doctor wondered aloud.

"Mr. Professor, you actually look very young, but your hair has already turned grey, why's that?"

"Do you know what doctor? Someone's hair turns grey early due to fear, or because of genetic factors. However, it's actually science and getting knowledge that caused my hair to turn and look so grey. Therefore, I need to tell you about what I encountered before I reached the peak of science and research."

Every human being would like to come clean about their personal troubles to someone reliable and honest, so not long after that the same doctor came to me asked to have a talk as she was on duty and had plenty of time to chat.

"Don't you think you may get bored if I tell you everything I faced during my lifetime Mrs. Doctor?"

"No, no, never. Getting to know whatever pain you feel inside will come in handy in order for me to treat you more deeply and effectively psychologically. Besides, I am also involved in research. You can no doubt trust me with everything you say."

The depth of science.

The world of science is like a deep ocean having no bottom, and the deeper you search, the more you realize that you need to learn more.

To prove it one can cite a very good statement told by a great Uzbek ancestor Avicenna who said:

I thought no one left I had unsearched and unknown, quite a few mysteries which I haven't plumbed, to look at my knowledge just deeply now, today

I understood in fact there's nothing I have solved.

"If you become a scientist learning the world, the whole world will seem to be yours!", This proverb is very famous, and is not in vain. Scientists are said to follow the footsteps of the prophet. But the peak of science, and the happiness of being a scientist, is reached through climbing up mountains with sharp rocks and stones, and a man should be prepared to fall at any moment, but get up immediately, and get ready for the rocks that will make his hands and feet bleed. But the worst part of striving to be a scientist, are the many obstacles which can cause a heart to bleed from pain.

"Do you think all the scientists who have achieved this degree of success have faced all these difficulties?"

"It's possible to be a scientist by working hard, but it's much harder to be a real human with proper sense of honesty. Unfortunately, in the 1980s, the number of artificial scientists (carrying out their research by bribing the responsible members) increased due to the level of science, research and intelligence in the country had decreased considerably. Scientific degrees and research were easily accessible to some people with malicious forethought. There appeared to be different ways, other than knowledge, in order to get state awards and scientific degrees. Besides, in the Supreme Certification Committee real scientists started being ignored as they didn't prefer those different ways to obtain their degrees. To prove this I can assure you that some people without any knowledge got scientific degrees and awards. Isn't that surprising? It was all due to those dishonest people preferring money to their commitment and duties.

We know very well that more than a third of the world scientists work in the former Soviet Union. However, the dishonest people certainly impacted the scientific and technological development in Uzbekistan and consequently we couldn't go on at the same pace as other countries such as Japan, FRG. and the USA because many artificially intelligent people destroyed everything by occupying the highest positions in our country. These people only thought about their own interest and personal profits. Nothing good can be expected from them and Alisher Navoiy confirmed it:

Whoever uses knowledge and authority for his own profits will bring people nothing but misery.

It isn't a secret that if a dishonest man who doesn't want to share his knowledge with students is appointed as the head of any educational institute, that organization can never have talented students or other intellectual people. (Moreover, talented people may become useless toys at their disposal). Additionally, the expenditure on education and science in the Soviet Union was twenty or thirty times less than that in the USA. It's now high time to compare the actual results of research in both countries. We are talking about new products and products, but aren't we buying all those new products from abroad even though the government spends a lot on the development of science, inventions and technology? Moreover, all the talented inventors are having many problems with showing their talent, and this is what makes it hard for our country to develop. These inventors cannot apply their inventions in the practical spheres. All of our initial inventions are prepared to first be produced abroad. This can be confirmed by many facts, and this is the main trouble inhibiting their development. Can you use disposable injections? Don't you think we have experimenting examples, and samples, so that we could produce them in our own country. We have, and we do have everything to develop, but somebody inhibits their utilization. We don't have scientists like Elizarov, and there aren't enough conditions for improving the system due to some reasons....

To look back at the history of scientific development in Central Asia, there are thousands of years of history to explore. A simple ancient water pump has been serving our people since ancient times. The evolution of the astronomical science is closely related to Omar Hayam and Mirzo Ulugbek in the world. The medical science without Avicenna, Algebra and geometry without Beruniy and Al Khorazmiy are just impossible to imagine as they made great contribution to their foundation, and development all over the world. The Development of the Uzbek language, and literature, is always associated with Navoiy and Bobur. All the historical monuments, buildings, establishments, their style, and ornaments can easily prove how wise our Uzbek ancestors were. Therefore, the sunshine is associated with the east, and even in ancient times the reputation of the eastern kings were the highest among the rest. Those who know Uzbek history will not require proof of this, and to confirm this it's enough to remember Emir Temur in whose period bloodsheds, wars and fighting slightly inhibited science from developing. Thousands of manuscripts were burnt to ashes or stolen away. The fact that the invader Kutayba ibn Muslim burnt a huge library in Bukhara shows how many attacks the Turan had encountered before. Consequently, most of our ancestors' manuscripts are unfortunately kept in other foreign countries.

We can surely be proud of Uzbek great ancestors, and I don't mean that there used to live a few poets, writers or prominent people in other countries. Every nation should know its own history and origin, and it's necessary not to forget that this means the memories of the nation from the past must certainly be respected. The nation who isn't aware of own history, will not possibly have an upcoming future.

There used to live so many prominent people in the East that it's really important to discover the heritage they left as most of them are still unknown. I really hope in near future we will get back to our previous wealthy, historical cultural heritage, and gain all our unknown discoveries. For instance, just ten or fifteen years ago, we didn't know anything about Forobiy, but today the former Chigatay street is named in his honor.

Since eastern nations were mainly involved in agriculture, trade, and the architectural sector, technology has yet to be well developed in our country. However, it is well developed today and among the western countries such as the French, English and German scientists are taking the leading role in inventions and technology. Today's generation can't imagine life without computers, planes, cars or TV, can they?

Could these inventions be created in the XVIII or XV century? No, it's impossible as the necessary foundation hadn't been laid at that time. Our Uzbek ancestors made up stories and legends about a flying carpet, the fairy mirror etc. Today all these dreams came true as there are inventions substituting those legendary items. The main technology of the eastern nations were the catapult, water pump, cart, handmill and the spinning wheel.

The XX century has been interpreted differently by different scientists, a century of electronics, century, of cybernetics, century of the space. If this chance for interpretation were given to me I would call this century as the "century of automobiles" because in Uzbekistan 80 % of agricultural products, and 90 % of the passengers are transported by an automobile. No doubt it leads to infer that this century belongs to automobiles.

To look at history, engines are deemed to be the heart of the automobiles. The first internal combustion engines were invented by a French scientist Lenuar in 1860 and a German engineer N. Otto in 1877. Russian scientists V. Grinevetskiy, E. Masing, N. Brilling, B. Stechkin made a great contribution to development of "The theory of engines". Academician of the automobile science was E. Chudakov, development of automobile and engines developments are closely related to their names.

The authors from Uzbekistan were first introduced to this sort of development for the first time in 1977 with the manual "Automobile engines" in their own language, and as always, they had materials in Russian. For further development, Uzbekistan needs scientists who can make a contribution to research in the Uzbek language.

After telling all this Sarvar addressed the doctor with a question: "Now I want to tell you about myself, Mrs. doctor, if it doesn't interest you, I won't even try."

Doctor: "Oh, leave that, whatever you say, is interesting to me".

Sarvar: "If you allow me I'll start by telling you about my grandparents and my mother."

Doctor: "Oh, that's fine, in that case I will be able to know more about your genetics."

My ancestors

There are some proverbs confirming that being great depends on genetics. Therefore, Emir Temur wanted his sons to marry after getting information about a prospective bride's genetics, and seven previous forefathers, before the wedding. Every person should know his seven previous ancestors according to the tradition, therefore I prefer to tell you a bit about them if you don't mind.

My elder grandfather (father's father) Alimjon is said to have been one of the richest people in Tashkent. According to historical information, in the XIX centuries most the crop grown on Tashkent's lands were cotton or wheat. I heard that my grandfather had so much gold that he used to give his golden coins to his sons Tuhtaboy, Rahimboy, Kodirboy, Abdullaboy without counting, but by measuring them using cups. He wasn't only a wealthy man, he also was a very wise man favored among his friends and all his neighbors. One of my old aunts told me that he had a two-story house on Chakichmon street.

All sorts of eastern fruit used to be planted here, and once you ate apricots, it tempted you to eat more and more. I still remember how my grandparent's gardens were, and how they used to smell with flowers, fruit, fresh apples, apricots, cherries and many others. Once I ate the apricots, I wanted more and more, and I loved the garden's pools which gave a relaxing look to the garden. The fruits were useful for many people during wartime when everyone was suffering from hunger.

My grandfather Kodir's brother was one of the most intelligent people of his period, and to prove it, one only need to know that he built the Mosque, Sharq hotel and hospital near the Eski Juva shops. Besides being rich Tokhta used to be quite a generous person. He was carried in a cart led by two horses which turned into a tradition in the XIX century. According to some specific information, the rich men in Tashkent at that time provided consumers with the raw materials made of cotton.

My grandmother (my mother's mother), used to sell golden jewelry and they used to live a very good life, with all of my uncles being intelligent and very well-educated men. When my mother's father got married, his first wife died and afterwards the late woman's sister was forced to marry him according to the tradition. Even though my mother, her sister and brothers were step-siblings I've never noticed it in their attitudes, and they were always very friendly.

I can assure you that I've been proud of my grandparents, parents all my life. I've always been proud of my both culturally and financially wealthy ancestors. Therefore, I have never had any malice, or aforethought towards my friends for instance who have reached the peak of wealth, which I haven't. One more thing, I hate compliments, as compliments may eventually lead to committing crime according to what one of the philosophers wrote. I was especially never greedy for wealth.

Thanks to God, I don't think that my life is worse than someone else's. My salary is no doubt enough to feed my children, and the money I get for the books I write is more than enough for my personal outcomes. I have two daughters and many students. Until now, whatever award, degrees, or achievement I've gained are all due to my own hard work and pursuit. Maybe that's why I have a special reputation among the people, and this is I think the greatest happiness I have. My mother actually married her own relative, not long after my sister Bakhtia was born. But unfortunately, after her husband died, she remained a widow and when my father Mukaddir met her for the first time, they fell in love and got married. As my father's parents didn't like her much, they had to move to another house. My father got married only because he fell in love, despite his father's objections, and my grandparents didn't even help him to buy a carpet or another thing for their new house. However, I still remember how my distant grandparents used to help us by bringing chests of pearls, gold and jewelry. I still remember how we eked out a living by exchanging those jewelries for food. My mother used to be a very beautiful woman, and only the happiest man could love her. After she married my father, she had five more children, two daughters, and three sons.

She really was very clever and good-looking, and I still remember how clean she kept the whole house, how she liked beautiful flowers, which she planted all around the house. She really liked nice and pleasant smells, and even in her last moments, asked for perfume for her tomb, not flowers. She had a very strange habit, before she used to lie on her bed, where she would be fast asleep in no time, of asking us: "If my father comes back alive from the great beyond, don't wake me up, ok?"

I always try to concentrate on my childhood memories and attempt to imagine how I lay in the cradle inside the hut listening to a lullaby sung by my mummy to me. I can still feel the smell of the wood our hut was made of, and both my daddy and mummy used to sing very well, and my daddy was also very handsome. I can still remember how I saw my father off to the war with my mummy and my brother. It still pains me to think how he dabbed the tears on his face with a handkerchief. I still feel like crying whenever the memories of how he hugged me, dandling me on his knees and this memory still always haunts me. As soon as he forced me to leave his embrace and gave me to mummy, the train started moving. I was going to run after him, but I had no strength, and there seemed to be something stuck in my throat. I stayed there longing for my father. We lived waiting for him for a lifetime, and it was awful to lose someone when you don't witness his death or the dead body. We couldn't believe that he died when we got the letter about his death.

Childhood and teenage (1940-1957)
Nothing in the world can render a human generous and gentle except his days spent in childhood or teenage. Strong social support will help to preserve these human qualities.

A.I. Gercen

I came into being in 1940 on February 11, in Tashkent city, the Shayhontohur district, Allon mahalla, in a family of peasants.

Regardless, I was small in figure, and I grew up being quite strong and healthy. My brother (Anvar), little brother (Marvar) and sister (Muhabbat) were taller, but I was not too short, but not very tall. Since my eldest brother was often ill, we attended school together. 1947 it was the first time that my eldest brother and I attended school together. The school was number 111 in the Shayhantahur district. It was about 1. 5 kilometers to get to the school, and you can't imagine how hard it was to walk such a long distance because those narrow streets were crammed with lots of sand, and the wind used to raise be so strong that we weren't well able to open our eyes because of the dust (of course this was during the summer days). As for spring and autumn, we had to walk through clay, water, as there weren't any asphalt roads at that time. Boys from the same mahalla, Sobir, Soat, Boriy started studying in the same or separate groups. I am forevermore in debt to my first teacher, Musayev Giyoskori who taught me how to read the alphabet, write and the basic knowledge of life. May God bless him, I hope. At that time my surname was Mukaddirov, then it was changed into my grandfather's name, Kodirov, because it was compulsory to use the grandfather's name as a surname. I still have a pain in my heart as soon as I remember the times of the war, when there was no electricity, no bulbs, and we kept doing our home tasks under the dim light of the wick lamp. At that time, I used to have another surname, Mukaddirov, which was my father's name.

A big channel used to flow through the middle of the street where we lived. After swimming for a long time in the water, we   used to sunbathe lying with our face down, and our skin would become as rough as those of frogs. When dusk fell, it was our favorite thing to play Hide and seek, or listen to fairy tales. In the third form, we were taught by Mr. Kuchkor, in the forth by Mr. Yusuf, and one by one we had more and more lessons and different teachers for every subject. Later on, Russian and English we had in addition to our time-tables, and we were especially engrossed in learning foreign languages. Our teachers of Russian, Vera, and of English Bella Semenovna treated us very politely. I am very grateful to my teachers as the knowledge they gave me came in handy at the university a lot. Every educated man should know one or two foreign languages as the more ability of speech a man has, the more influential and useful he is going to be for the people around him. Otherwise he will remain in his own circle for a lifetime without any progress. Although most young people do not want to admit it, foreign languages were the main weapons of our period.

It's really beneficial to know foreign languages since most of the manuals, books, and useful information are in English or in Russian. If you know a foreign language, you can easily read and understand them. It is not a secret that in highly developed countries such as Japan, Southern Korea, Thailand, France and Germany, many lessons at university are taught in English. The point is that they all know that all of the information on the internet is given in English or in Russian. A man knowing foreign languages will never fail in his pursuit of career, for instance the fact that I learned them very well at school helped me a lot in order to make progress at the university. Certainly, all of my teachers helped me to cope with this a lot, Lyubov' Tepatovna, Farida Ahatovna and one more teacher from Moscow contributed a lot to my further achievements. It's necessary to tell that we didn't have any friends to speak with in English, and therefore I couldn't develop my oral communication though all my classmates used to feel astonished seeing the way I used grammar correctly and how fluently I wrote in this language.

When I was a schoolboy, gradually I got interested in subjects like Algebra, geometry, geography, history, zoology and biology as well as physics and chemistry. All of our teachers were very satisfied with the progress we had while learning. I still remember how we made a performance about the war at school, and conducted an amateur conference from physics. Since the graduate students of Tashkent State University (Current National University of Uzbekistan) taught our group, our class students were the strongest in mathematics. Our teachers Mr Fathulla, Majid Kodiriy (mathematics), Mr Zokir (physics), Hamidulla (history), Ziyovutdin (chemistry), Ahat (zoology), Mr Rafikov (geology) contributed a lot to further our careers and our achievements at the university.

Childhood, for me, was the sweetest, the most innocent, and happiest stage of my life. I still remember how we played different games at the age of 10 or 14, like game of nuts, stick- throwing, football, wrestling and hide-and-seek. At that time there wasn't any TV, radio or cassette players.

Of course these games we used to play only at the time when we got free of our home tasks and housework, or working in the field. Every game was different in its own way, for instance in a game of nuts we used to throw nuts into a hole, and if there were an even number of nuts in the hole, the last person to throw the nut would win. However, if there were an odd number, the last person to throw was the looser. I still remember how many nuts I gave to the winners in case I lost the game. For instance in a game of chillak4, those who threw the chillak[4] the furthest, will be the winner, if not then, he is the loser. The second game was giving some nuts to take part in the game, and we had to win our own nuts and nuts given by other participants while playing this game. This required honesty and quickness. All the nuts were located in an accurate range, a meter far from each other. A participant needs to get one nut and standing afar, he needs to aim at the nuts on the ground. If he can beat any of those nuts, he can continue the game, if not the next participant will try. I still remember I joined the game putting just one nut on the ground, but won the game, as a result I brought 50 or 60 nuts home, which means I won 50 or 60 times a day. In this way I could even gather up a sack of nuts for the winter season. All the children were afraid to play nuts with me as I would win and get all the nuts they had.

As for playing football, all the children living in our mahalla5 played much better than those living in the village. All the people in the mahalla[5] would see how we played football with children.

In the evening we used to go out and play kurash[6] on the grass-field. I was seven or eight years old at that time. In summer months sometimes I used to go to the village Telkman and I would play with my own relatives who were the same age as I was. I used to go there because my uncle lived there and worked as a brigadier, so those I played with were actually his sons. My uncle made us play kurash. The most interesting thing was that my uncle used to scold his sons as they often lost and we won, though they were living, and eating whatever they wanted, and weren't as hungry and poor as we were.

---

[4] Chillak is a type of a national game which is played by minimum two children, the main tools in this game are one long and one short stick which is thrown during the game.

[5] Mahalla is a national unit where many families live like one family.

[6] Is a type of sport like wrestling, played without any weapons by maximum

All the people living in the same mahalla with one child had rights to advise him, and to tell him what's right or what's wrong to do or to say. But young people today are more independent and confident than those in the past. Unfortunately there are some too confident young people who are spending their golden time on disco bars and video chatting. Who is guilty for that? Of course, we are guilty for their disruptive behavior. If we show them all the right way in life though they may not like it, one day it will be of use for them all. But as for my childhood, when I was a child, our neighbors kept supporting us all the time no matter what happened. It's the basis of our national culture to live in friendship and have mutual understanding with neighbors.

The years of war … Although many people were living in poverty among our neighbors, they were still kind and generous to each other. No matter what we had at home to eat, pottage or boiled beetroots, we shared it with each other like we were living in the same family.

I think life's challenges and poverty make people closer to each other, but getting too arrogant because of wealth, is dangerous for any society, and it can also destroy the peaceful harmony between members of different nationalities.

There were some Tatar or Russian neighbors living in our mahalla, and I can never remember having any disagreements with them, never. We played games together, no matter what, football, nuts, and they all could fluently speak Uzbek fluently. I can slightly remember children like Misha, Valentin, and Kolia. Unfortunately, in 1971 we were forced to allow the government to ruin our old houses and had to move to another place, which actually caused us to lose each other, and because of this, we lost our closest people, friends and neighbors at that time.

Remembering my childhood

I think I will not be mistaken if I say that during the years of war and starvation, we survived because of fruit like water melons and melons. I still remember it like it happened just yesterday. My eldest uncle used to plant water melon, melon, and corn in his field, and most of the water melon were the type with red seeds. We, as children, used to gather them and crack them to eat, and we ate it without a knife, or a spoon, enjoying eating them with our hands. As they were very sweet, our hands used to stick to each other… I can never forget taste of those water melons.

In the 1940s, the Arabic alphabet was replaced with Latin. Those days I saw one book "Days Gone By" by Abdulla Kodiriy in my uncle's house, it was written in the Latin alphabet. At that time I was about 10 or 11 years old and read that novel barely. Because in the 1947s we started writing in Russian alphabet. We didn't know the Latin alphabet that well.

As my mother said I was born at the time when my father was lucky in business, so they built a house on the land they bought (until that house was built we lived in a hut). There used to be a yellow snake in our house, it would sometimes hang down to my cradle…. it was said to bring happiness for our family. Until our old house was destroyed, I saw this snake more than once. One day when I had a vacation (in Ph.D.), something suddenly came down quickly to where I was lying. It was on the terrace, and was a snake hissing and showing us the tip of its tongue. Mummy shouted:

"Don't be afraid! This is your own snake! It won't harm you."

After we moved to another house, when the old one was destroyed I didn't see that snake any more.

Aha, by the way, we've started talking about snakes, let's listen to one more story about them. One day when I went into the kitchen, guess what I saw there? I heard something actually hissing there. As I turned round, oh, my god, I was scared to death because I saw a snake right beside the stow fire. I immediately called our neighbor's children and told them to go out to the street. That happened when I was at eight or nine. All of my friends saw the snake. However, they didn't dare to kill it. On hearing about the snake, a little daughter of the neighbor living next door to us came running into our kitchen. On seeing that snake, she grabbed a thick wood off the land and murdered it by hitting it over and over again. The rest of the boys were very shy and they couldn't do what the girl had done.

We used to have a beautiful dog nicknamed 'Kashka", and it didn't let anyone pass the street as it barked out loudly and everyone was scared of it. It would chase away all the strangers out to the border of the street. If it was chained, its loud voice could just pierce the ears. Although it had never bitten anyone, it used to frighten people by just barking loudly. One day when the boys caught and brought a snake in front of that dog, surprisingly it didn't feel frightened at all, and instead it grabbed the snake, shook it up and down and killed by whirling it around and biting off the snake's head. When we looked at it, the snake was dead.

One day our neighbor's son boasted:

"Our cat is really strong, let's make my cat and your dog fight together, shan't we?"

I agreed immediately. Could you imagine how a cat and a dog fought. It was incredible! The cat snatched, and scratched the dog with its sharp claws. The dog bit it back on the neck and legs, and at long last the cat was forced to escape.

I still remember, there was only one thing our dog used to be afraid of; it was thunder, and whenever thunder boomed, it used to sleek into the kennel and tremble. We would calm our dog by patting and hugging it repeatedly. The dog is said to be very loyal to its owner, I made sure about this lots of times.

Now I really want to say a few words about the loyalty of our favourite dog. This dog Kashka suddenly disappeared somewhere for three days, and mummy started looking for it. There was no place left where we didn't look for it. A week later, when I was playing around the farm field, I could hear Kashka's barking. It seemed to be far from me. Running up to it, I saw it wagging its tail in front of another dog. As soon as I called, Kashka made a few steps towards me, but then stepped back towards its own female partner. Walking alongside that garden (it measured about two hectares) I knocked on the door of the house there. After we greeted each other, I told the person why I came, and that I wanted to take my dog back. He said to me smiling:

"You can get it back, of course, if you can!"

No matter how much I tried I couldn't convince Kashka to go home. I finally chained it and dragged him home. Can you imagine how much he whined while looking back at his female partner? For three days he rejected eating whatever food I gave him, then I grew to understand that even dogs can have feelings.

During the war years, with hunger, and starvation, we were even happy when we found a piece of bread to eat. It was hard for everyone, notably for those whose husbands had died in the war. At that time all the poor people had a special certificate, a so called Zabor, confirming that they were indeed poor. We used to show it to the shop-assistant and after that we were given a loaf of bread weighing just a kilo, and two hundred grams. It was just for one family. There was neither sugar nor butter to eat for breakfast, and there was no way out, other than living thanking   God. We were weak enough to change something. The Tajik people in our mahalla used to eke out their living by begging for food in the other mahallas. They would bring some bread and other things to eat, and we would exchange these spoiled foods with our old and dirty patched clothes. We witnessed how insects crept through that bread, but we were obligated to eat it anyway, so as not to die of hunger.

To earn a penny, mummy and sister would go to the farm where they could cut some trees and sell them in the Eski Juva bazaar as firewood. For this, and for just a few pennies, we had to walk three kilometers with the logs on our back and   shoulders, which used to pain our body because of the sharp tips of wood. I still remember how we sold those logs and with the money, mummy bought us two pasties with potatoes inside. No sooner had I drawn one of the pasties close to my mouth, I remember a little boy snatching it out of my hand and running away. I just stood stock-still, because I could do nothing else. You see what hunger can do to a human being!

As the roof on our house was covered with clay, when it rained, especially in the spring months, we felt like it rained inside our house because the floor, and carpets got soaked. Sometimes there was no place dry enough to lie on. Everywhere we put pans, deep plates, and bowls down so that the water would drop into those dishes. Only after I graduated from the university in 1962, could we somehow afford roofing slates. We also didn't have electric energy until 1957 either. We didn't have any money to pay the bills and taxes for the electric energy we used. Therefore, for three or four years we were forced to illegally use electricity without money. We would tap the electric wires from the electricity column for our electricity at home. Ok, we got the wires at night, and connected a bulb to one, after that we somehow lit our homes, then we disconnected the wires the next morning again. Nobody knew that we were using electricity this way.

We were forced to stand in a queue for just a loaf of bread from the early morning, at around eight o'clock, when the bread would be brought. One day something interesting happened. We were waiting in a queue with mummy, and there was no trace of the flour to be brought. I was late and suddenly seeing my teacher passing by me, I started getting furious, I was studying in the second or the third form. Maybe I made mummy get fed-up from waiting from the early morning, and she just slapped my face.

"If you need to study and go to school on time, I need to earn something so as to feed you! To feed you!"

At that time a kilo of flour for every person used to be given to a family and therefore she wanted me to stay up. It was wrong of course to feel sad about mummy for that, because she was doing everything she could, only for us, for her children.

We were living in a town and it was hard enough for the administration to make profits as they used to make a report on every expenditure to the Higher organizations. Maybe that's why we would go to the farm and bring whatever was worth selling, logs, melons, watermelons, fruit and so on. All the people in the town were living at subsistence levels.

To be honest, I was very naughty and mischievous in my childhood. We would go to steal fruit, apricots, apples in the garden when there was no one there. When one part of our group was busy stealing apples, the others were stealing apricots. One day, when we went to steal some pears, we were almost caught by the brigadier at that time.

One more thing happened when all the apples were ripe in the same garden. After going up to a tree branch, I remember how I picked and hid ten or eleven apples inside my shirt, but as soon as I wanted to climb down, I saw the water carrier man below. I stood stock-still, and my heart leapt out of my mouth.

"Who is your father?" he asked me sounding a bit more calm.

"Mmmm... Mukaddir's...

"What on earth are you doing   in this   apple-tree?

What?"

"My daddy came back from the war, that's why I've been picking apples here for him..."

On hearing this news, he was stunned, and as it turned out, he knew my daddy very well as they were very close friends. Moreover, he knew my daddy had died in the war. Making use of the time he was stunned, and not scolding me, I climbed down and ran away. Arriving home, I told mummy about it, but she brushed me off.

"You did wrong, my son. That man is your daddy's very close friend. If he understood you well, that's ok, if not, what would happen then? He must've felt very astonished."

We used to tell many lies when we were frightened. I made myself believe that my daddy would come back, staring at the gate through which I yearned to see him once more, and hug him even tighter, much tighter than I did when he left for the war. It becomes clear that a human being can remain patient in order to endure any torture in life.

Days were passing following one another. I was one of the leading school children among my friends, and we had a little library in the corner of our school where I finished reading one book completely in one day.

Sometimes various thoughts haunted me: Why didn't we die at the time of war, when hunger was torturing us so much? I think God has gifted human beings with magic power, and when it's necessary humans can use all their inner deposits of energy, when called for. Starting from April after classes, in June during the whole day, we worked to earn some money. We worked in the field with my brother Anvar from 1954- 1956, and even though our brigadier Mr. Solih was very strict, he was a very honest man.

There used to be two horses in the village, Turik and Opoy, which we used with carts. One of them, Opoy, was very energetic, a type of Vladimir horses, and was so wide that he was wide enough to lie on. Being blind in one eye, it was being used for the fieldwork during the wartime. What's was funny though, was I couldn't jump onto it becuase I wasn't tall enough, besides   it kept baulking all the time. After it baulked three or four times, it used to calm down. That's why brother used to bring it under the cherry tree shadow. And in this way, I used to jump onto this horse from the tree, as I was short enough to get on by myself. So, we helped do the fieldwork in this way.

Giving water to horses seemed to be amazing, and even sometimes we played racing. One day, brigadier Solih asked me to give water to his young horse. There was 1-5 kilometers until I got to the river. Riding on a cub horse I felt excited, it walked smoothly, and didn't even bulge. I remember how I made him run after giving him some water to drink. I've never relished riding on a horse so much.

It was both amazing and hard to work in the field, as you feel exhausted by the hard work, but after that it's possible to have a rest, stretching your legs on clay pellets.

It was very exciting and relaxing to sleep on the clover reaped and gathered up, and I still yearn for the smell of clover flowers, and the plants that mummy planted in our house.

Something very interesting happened to me and my brother one day. After we did our bits, brother whipped the horse. As we were riding, there were many nut trees, and suddenly my brother's collar got hooked up on a tree branch. However, the horse was still walking with me, leaving my brother hanging from the branch. Fortunately, his shirt was old enough to hold him there a bit longer, then it tore and my brother jumped down into the sand. He was very dusty, and crammed with dust. Can you imagine a teenage hanging up on the branch? Getting scared to death we came back home and stunned mother and sister all with our dusty clothes, hair and face. Not long after that everyone in our house started cackling loudly and blood rushed to their faces. I am not going to boast but we, two school children, used to accomplish tasks quickly which other people on the farm could barely do in a day. I remember how we won the fridge "Saratov" in the lottery we played at the time (it was given by the administration). It was great news for everyone, and at that time my sister Bakhtia had already gotten married.

The children whose fathers died during the education era used to be given some clothes once a year. It was a great occasion for all of us.

Both my brother and I did very well at school, I finished school with the golden medal, brother with the silver. At this time, we got knowledge not only from school subjects, but also from the harsh realities of life at the same time. Because of our happiness, dreams and ambitions, we not only were related to life…. only to life. It's hardly possible to be eager to succeed for a person without learning life realities.

When I studied at the university, we baked some bricks to sell with our brother, neighbors and other friends, and it was possibly at that time, that I got a permanent pain in my back and legs. Besides our friendship being very strong at that time, we used to treat each other like real siblings. We would sit together for many hours so as to do our home tasks, and I was never eager to teach someone something I knew very well. I didn't take pity on my time doing that. We mostly did our hometasks together, at home, belonging to the healer, especially Holik, eight boys doing homework there all the time.

When we started studying in the eighth form, a new maths teacher, Majid Kodiriy started teaching all of us. He was the mathematician who returned with health troubles as a result of a massacre, and imprisonment by Stallin. However, though he was ill, he was a priority to everyone with his knowledge, and only within just a year, he made us excel in mathematical appliances much better than children in other groups. Some graduates of the Tashkent State university were also practicing with our schoolchildren. As all the cousins in our family were almost the same age, we would often gather around in the same house to discuss the homework given. Here my elder brothers Mirgiyos uncle would organize a little competition between us, by asking us four or five equations, and questions in math, which we participated in to see who will be the first to work them out all. In the rating note-book all of our marks used to look the same, but when all the less and more clever students lost the game being held, I would always be the winner, turning out to be the cleverest. I don't know why, but I always dreamt of being   first all the time in my childhood and It's true, that the soldier who doesn't aim to be a General, isn't a real soldier.

In the autumn of 1956, when we were studying in our eleventh form, we, the school children from town, were taken to the cotton field in the Okkurghan district. Even though it was   hard work, our happiness didn't seem to end, and we returned after working hard for over a month. Many ants and worms attacked us there at that time, especially where we slept which had thousands of ants creeping under our cushions. Suddenly, we heard on the radio that the first artificial satellite had flown into the sky and we decided to watch the sky the same evening. We saw how that satellite was moving in the sky among the other glittering stars, and it was the greatest victory of human beings, and especially for scientists.

When we were staying in the far cities to pick cotton, our parents visited us several times even though the transport was a big problem for all of them.

One day we had one more interesting event in the cotton field when our classmate Mirsoat was serving the cook as an assistant. As soon as we came in hungry for dinner, he beckoned us aside and told us in a whisper us not to eat anything cooked that day. When we asked the reason for this he just insisted, but didn't say why. Of course, we did what he said, and when we became hungry to death, we started making our friend Mirsoat more furious, minute by minute. Then it became clear that a little dog had jumped into the cauldron all of a sudden, and even the cook wasn't aware of it. Not long after that, as the cook tried to stir the food with a ladle, something heavy got on the ladle. The cook was stunned about this heavy ingredient as he hadn't added any big pieces of meat. He suddenly realized that the dog had been cooked, and indeed yuckily boiled inside the food! Both the cook and the assistance decided not to tell this to anyone and consequencely, there were one hundred and twenty people who refused to eat that meal they cooked. Since our friend didn't dare hide this from us, he told everything honestly. Anyway, in this way we finished and contributed to cotton picking activities and afterwards we returned to our school days again.

I still remember how I had an argument with my supervisor in my tenth form. The reason was the vignette onto the pages of which the supervisor wanted to list the students in order of the initial alphabetic letters of our surnames. I didn't agree as the list was organized in order of the highest scores obtained in all the controlled work and success of graduation. My supervisor Mr. Mahmud felt very upset about it and promised to mark me with a point "Good" in the exam instead of "Excellent" for what I had actually studied. Turning my head towards him I convinced him to pass the exam to the committee, not to him and said that assessment was going to be fair enough anyway. He didn't talk to me until we had a good-bye party in summer because he didn't keep his promise to me. The point is that the committee assessed my knowledge with "Excellent" marks and therefore I finished school with a gold medal and we finally mended the fences at the good-bye party, as you know.

The sin I had when I was a schoolboy still pains me whenever these thoughts invade in my mind. That's right I did very well at school and all the teachers were confident in submitting to me the control papers in order to check and assist them as they didn't always have time on their own. Of course, I didn't let them down and always accesessed those papers fairly enough. Therefore, I was in a friendly relationship with all of my teachers. In higher forms of school I was appointed as a member for wall-paper administration in our school providing that the wall-papers was of a good quality. As I wrote very accurately and attentively, almost all the things I accomplished by myself and I had a very good reputation in our school.

I still remember… The school head asked us to fill in the school and Secondary education certificates, Anvar and I were responsible for this. I sincerely did what I was asked, but only one thing was the exception. That was when Abduboriy, my friend, had good and excellent marks from all subjects except only one "satisfactory" from native language. We thought the teacher was unfair with his assessment, and all our friends begged us to help him by changing that "satisfactory" mark on his certificate as we were responsible to write them all.

I at long last agreed and when it was high time to write assessment of Abduboriy for the native language I left it without any note and brought them all into the Head's office to be signed and sealed. All the certificates were issued to their bearers. Only after that I corrected what I did in Abduboriy's certificate by writing there "Good" instead of "satisfying". This was the only wrong thing I did when I was at school. Later on, I had one more chance to correct the mistake I made. Abduboriy, my friend passed the state entrance exam to the Andijan State Medical institute and was assessed with "excellent" in the native language studies. Then I grew to understand how strictly our teacher approached assessing us all.

Eight classmate boys remained very close friends forevermore. For over fifty years we've been gathering in our special meetings, later on our wives joined this occasion. Unfortunately, some of those boys died before their prime, but their sons sometimes joined our occasions.

These sorts of special meetings and occasions were founded by the healer Holik as his son Abduboriy didn't do so well at school and his father wanted him to prepare for school homework together with our friends. It started in 1955. It was because that healer asked us all schoolchildren doing well at school to visit and stay in his home and do their homework there. In return he'd make all the necessary conditions available. After asking our parents for permission, we all agreed and got involved in studying with eight other students together. It was vivid that starting from April I had to give up that tradition as I was forced to earn money working in the field. The healer and his wife looked upon us as if we were his own children to tell the truth.

I remember how my mother came to see us in the early morning in their house when we were sleeping just to make sure we were safe. It was sometimes when we stayed there for a night. As I was always alert, I felt it in my bones, then I understood that mothers will always think about their children... every moment, and every passing instant.

As we all did our homework and studied together in partnership, four children finished school with gold and silver   medals, while the other four did well with good and excellent assessments. All of us entered the university without any encumbrance, and successfully due to our hard work and strong ambition.

There are many prominent people in Uzbekistan and most of them are known to have studied in our school. The President of the Uzbekistan Republic Science Academy Obid Sodikov (died in), The head of the ToshcityNur S. Tolipov (died in), general Utkir Komilov, the former Tashkent region ruler Kozim Tulaganov and etc. studied in the school where I studied in my teenage years. Most of our classmates are well- educated: Nigmat Goipov, graduated from the Central Asian Polytechnical institute in 1962, worked as a mechanician in Tashkent State university (current National University of Uzbekistan) and Tashkent Automobile and Road university, died in 2000. Akrom Ziyakhodjayev, graduated from the Samarkand Trade institute after he worked as an inspector in the Tashkent State Professional union later on being employed in Universam shop as the chief. He used to be a very polite and gentle man, who unfortunately died in 1992. Mirsobir Miragzamov

–   graduated from the Tashkent Polytechnical university in 1962 and was involved in scientific research all of his life, doctor of technical sciences, professor, worked as the chief in the scientific institute of the Uz Standard, we still recall him as a very good person close to religion, unfortunately he also died in 2007. Abduboriy Yusupov – graduated from the Andijan State Medical institute, was a very experienced doctor. He could even treat ulcers in the stomach. He also died in 2008. Anvar Haydarov – graduated from the Tashkent State Communication technology institute in 1962. For many years, he effectively worked at the Tashkent television station and Tashkent railway station. Nowadays he has been given the award "Honor". Tulagan Odilov – graduated from the Samarkand State Trade institute in 1962, working in the commercial sphere for many years. Despite he is old and was awarded with "Honor" he is a businessman in addition. Ubaydulla Abdullayev – graduated from the Tashkent State railway institute, a builder-engineer, worked in very high positions in Uzbekistan Republic Agricultural Construction Ministry as well as being the department head in the Tashkent Automobile and Road university for many years, awarded with "Honor". Olim Orifjonov – graduated from the Tashkent &&&&Polytechnical university in 1963, chemist, unfortunately died in 2003. Mahmuda Ziyahodjayeva –joined in our class in the eighth form, later married to Akrom Ziyahodjayev. All these people have been meeting on special occasions almost every month since we studied in the tenth form, you see fifty-two years have passed since then.

Since 1970 we've been meeting with our families usually once a month. In this meeting, we always remember our jokes, and happy events by recalling them together and having fun for a long time. In this meeting, all the people were close to each other since our childhood feel as if we were flown back to those days of innocence again. Everybody treats each other   informally, just like the closest friends forever. We don't even obey each other, as we are all equal, and I think true friends should keep this sort of relationship. Both critics and jokes are made in the same degree to everyone, we always keep visiting each other, together in both rainy and happy moments of life, as loyal friends. I wish they will always be safe and sound.

As a man witnessing the encumbrances of war, and the harsh realities of life, I would really like to mention to the young generation of Independent Uzbekistan: "There are many chances to get knowledge in this country, and the only thing left is to study hard, and to work hard, thanking all the happiness we have today. If you suffer today, tomorrow you will witness your happiness forever, and if it's cloudy or rainy, tomorrow is going to be shining with the bright sunny rays." An educated man will never suffer in the future, and unfortunately some of the young people are involved in fun activities in cafes, restaurants and disco clubs (of course due to money of their rich parents). If their parents sometimes don't give them enough money they may reluctantly get involved in easy ways of earning money such as theft, robbery, drug dealing and so on. Once you get trapped in it, everything is over! You can get rid of this burden only by being incarcerated or by dying before your prime. I   alwaystak e pity on them, and somehow I want to claim: "Oh, you, why are you so careless and light-headed? Don't you want to come to your senses, you'd better study hard and achieve some goals like many intelligent people. If you're intelligent, you can enter any university you want!"

My youth (1957-1962)

Youth is a dream, belief. It's yearning for braveness, it's lyrics and romance. It's great expectations and plans for future. It's the beginning of happiness.

N. Hikmat

"Now, Mrs Doctor, if you aren't bored I would be pleased to tell you about the times I studied at the university."

"Yes, of course, how come can I be bored or tired of such an interesting conversation with you, dear professor? Can you please go on, I've already started being curious!"

In 1957 I finished school with a gold medal, and, at that time, it could provide the privilege to enter any university without passing any exams.

I made baby steps towards science since the time I started going to school by studying hard and simultaneously working hard to earn money. When I studied at school we had a neighbor Mr Abdulla, docent, the head of the department in SUCA (State Univeristy of Central Asia) who was much respected in our mahalla. He used to wear beautiful and clean clothes with a tie, and looking at this man I also wanted to look like him, living in happiness like he did. My mummy also worshipped god so that I could also become a scientist like that man. Later on, one driver was driving and dropped our relative, Saidmurod in car named "Volga". Later I asked why and, I was told that this man graduated from the Central Asian Polytechnical university and was working as an engineer at the Gasapparatus factory. I also wanted to drive a car, or to have a personal car with a driver. I won my dreams and made them come true at long last, because I made up my mind to eventually be a specialist of automobiles.

The knowledge passed down from the Hojaparkhon

Virgin lands named after Hojaparkhon turned into a narrow street during the period of the former Soviet Union. Belonging to the Allon mahalla in Tashkent city, one corner of it crossed Chigatay street, and another one the Uzbekistan farm. Nearly twenty families lived on this street during the years of the Second World War, and most of the houses occupied much bigger land around 0,18 hectares. Some neighbors lived here only in summer, but we lived there permanently in all seasons. All the houses were destroyed in 1971, and instead, sky-scrapers and schools were erected one by one.

Every place is beautiful and wonderful not only with decorations, plants and scenery, but also with regular people who are somehow equally important. In the Allon mahalla there used to live not only famous people, but also those who put our country on the map with their attempts to excel. Nuritdin Akramovich Muhitdinov, a famous philosopher Abdulla Ayupov, and Saidmurod Sultonov who worked as the director in the "UzgasApparatus" factory for many years also grew up here.

Assistant to the minister of Higher and Secondary Education Ministry, Shavkat Ayupov, the administrator of the Republican Science and technology center Marvar Toshpulatov, Scientific department head of the State scientific examination institute of the State Standard Mirsobir Miragzamov, the former department head of the Tashkent State Pedagogical university Mirortik Muminov, prorector of the Tashkent State Information Technologies university Nigmatilla Muminov, candidate of medical science, docent of the Tashkent State medical specialists experience development center Jaloliddin Tojiyev, Assistant of the Director in the silk industrial institute for many years Odil Gapporov, a member of the State Press Committee and Erkin Komilov all grew up all in our mahalla, Allon.

The specialist of the Uzbekistan Republic History institute, candidate of science, Ahmad Yusupov and brothers Mirfayoz and Mirsoat Musayev are also the stars of this Allon mahalla. Bahodir Abdullayev is the master of Radio and Television activities, I was also brought up here, and in this respect, I decided to mention about the other people who lived in the same mahalla with me.

One of those people was Abdullayev Bahodir who was a prominent specialist of radio and television science.

Nuriddin Akramovich Muhitdinov – secretary of the former Communistic Party of Soviet Union Central committee, the man who had the greatest professional position among Uzbek people during the Soviet people. At that time, Soviet government didn't allow Uzbek people to get positions as an authority representative.

Abdulla Ayupov – combated in the Second World war, was a famous philosopher, professor, an honoured scientist of Uzbekistan, and the department head in the National University of Uzbekistan for more than 30 years. He is still teaching young people at the university.

Saidmurod Sultonov was – the first engineer in our mahalla. He was later promoted to the positions of the chief engineer of the plant and then the director. Wanting to emulate him as a specialist, many young people in our mahalla decided to be engineers in the future.

Ahmad Ayupov – historian, junior and senior scientist at the institute of History at the university, also worked as the head of the department, and at this moment he is retired.

Jaloloddin Tojiyev – candidate of medical sciences, docent, worked in the institute of developing Experince and skills of medical specialists. He is an experienced doctor.

Gafforov Odil – a great scientist in the silk industry, had three brothers in the family, Orif, Obid and Odil.

Mirsobir Miragzamov - is also an engineer, and a prominent professor and scientist of cybernetics.

Here I'd like to tell you a bit about the Muminovs. Mr Mirortik has for many years taught youg students in geography, and has written many books and manuals. Mr Nematulla was also a prominent scientist of machinery science, a professor, and an author of several books.

Shavkat ayupov – a famous scientist of mathematics, was one of the youngest academicians. He worked in many high positions and as a chief member of the Supreme attestation Committee. He has also nurtured many prominent scientists for the Republic.

In our family, the Kodirovs, all the boys finished school with gold and silver medals, and graduated from the technical universities. The eldest son Anvar worked in the chief positions in the Communication Ministry, Central Telegraph and died in 1995. The youngest son Marvar is a professor, an author of several monographs, works as the chief representative in the Science and Technics Centre of Uzbekistan and also works in the Tashkent State Technical University. His son, Davron is a candidate of medical sciences. The elder son in the Kodirovs family, me, Sarvar, has worked for ten years as a president of the Tashkent Automobile and Roads university, served a lot for educating young people with patriotic feelings, and taught them to learn national culture and about the motherland. I was admitted as an honoured professor in Moscow Technical University, am a real member of the New York sciences Academy, and I was awarded with "The man of the year" several times. An Honoured Scientist of Uzbekistan. I am also proud of saying that my daughter is working to pursue her doctoral degree these days.

In the Musayevs family Mr Mirfayoz is a scientist of pedagogics, and he also grew up where I was born, in our mahalla. He worked as the chief editor of the newspaper

"Toshkent haqiqati" (Truth about Tashkent city), and after he retired, he started working as the head of the department in the State Scientific Publishing House "National Encyclopedia of Uzbekistan". He is an Honoured Journalist of Uzbekistan.

Erkin Komilov – after graduating from the Tashkent Law institute, worked in different positions in the Adminstration of Publishing literature. From 1991-2002, he worked in the former Uzbekistan State Press Committee, an honoured specialist of culture. He is retired these days.

Bahodir Abdullayev – after he graduated from the Tashkent State University, dedicated his life to the radio, and worked as a radio journalist for 25 years. He was awarded with "An honoured specialist of culture in Uzbekistan", and since the 90s, he has been loyally working in television, and he has contributed a lot to many films which were successfully dubbed.

Look how, in just a small mahalla, street, so-called Allon, there were many prominent people who dedicated their life to development of the motherland, shared all of their opportunities with other people, and helped them throughout their lives. I think that I was also able achieve my goals just because the environment of patriotic feelings has certainly influenced me.

University

Each passing day had something special to memorialize and cherish. To be honest, at first I didn't even know how to go to the university. As I spent my childhood working in the field, I had no time to visit the city. Therefore, my neighbor Abdulla Ayupov helped me to find the university and submit my documents to apply. Today he is a very famous scientist in the Republic.

I applied to the Central Asian Polytechnical university, Mechanics faculty, Automobile transport sector, and I was accepted as a student without any exams on the basis of an interview. My golden days had begun.

When I was a student I didn't entirely understand the basic meaning of being a student, and this golden privilege. It's true that this time is a great chance to find the closest friends. I started appreciating this chance only after I had grown up and became an experienced specialist. Doing something good for someone you never expect something in return, and those days are a symbol of innocence, hard work and dignity. When it was time to pick cotton, we still remembered how about twenty of our friends slept on straw bedding together.

Our practical experience in Moscow, Minsk, and the Kiev automobile manufacturing plants and factory never escapes my mind, along with dating girls. The privilege of youth is that it will give and has its own future. Youth is the stage of life when the first feelings start invading the heart. Unfortunately, these days of youth will never come back.

To be honest, before I finished school, I didn't even have a suit to wear when I became a student. I had shoes made of tarpaulin, and my youngest uncle Mirgiyos gave me a suit as a present and so I started studying at the university. I found many friends among the students who came from different regions of the Republic.Of the eight friends who did homework together at home, we all successfully entered the university. At that time, it was impossible to enter the university illegally by means of assistance of some big shots with money. The only criteria of the entering university used to be knowledge.

In our group at the university, almost all the students had golden or silver medals, so each of them started struggling to become a leader. Some students gave up their education because of their fear of testing for exams. I still take pity on them. I didn't feel any challenge when I studied there, and in October we were all sent to the Chinoz. District to pick cotton, I was the third to pick the biggest amount of cotton. However, those from the far regions were the real leaders in this activity. The net weight of cotton picked used to be around 115 kilos. That year we were supervised by the young scientist Mr Okil Salimov (dean- assistant) and later other assistants such as A.M. Muhamedov, K.A. Horoshev etc.

Despite it being hot, the cottons looked as white as snow in the cotton field, and when it started getting cold, there were fewer and fewer fields where cotton wasn't picked. However, we found out that there was an area flooded by water and there was lots of cottons there. Despite the cold water and the weather, we picked all that cotton which eventually weighed about 250 kilos in total. This brave work still pains us and we all have back troubles. So, to become a hero, we didn't even care about our health at that time.

I could afford to buy a coat and boots ffrom the money I earned by picking cotton. Me and my brother once promised our mother "you will never work again after we enter university, now it's high time we started feeding you and our brothers!". Me and brother received a scholarship of about 800 or 900 soums at that time, and it was a huge sum for poor people like our family. We lived for five years being patient with just this money and we had nothing more. At this time, Bakhtia's husband, Hamidulla helped us a lot by frequently visiting us.

It sounds very funny today if we tell our students that we wore tarpaulin shoes or galoshes even in the winter months. However, it is exactly these difficulties which enabled us to adjust to everything. Life is the best teacher for any human being.

If a man can't learn the lessons of real life at all None of the strongest teachers can teach him overall This has been written by Abu Abdulloh Rudakiy.

In real life, nothing good can be gained without any difficulties.

The years were passing at a high speed and in our third year, me my friends Marat, Tulkin, Zayniddin and Sharofiddin started participating in a scientific group about the discipline "Materials resistance". The name of the union was "Students". Our teacher docent Nigmatilla Tursunov helped us a lot, as there aren't many books relating to the discipline we were frequently forced to visit his home. One day when he had to stay at the university, he asked us to go to his home and read all the books there saying that his wife would see us in. As he said we all went to his home and his wife welcomed us with open arms. When I was going to take my shoes off at the corridor, my friend Tulkin urged me not to, reminding me that the carpet covered just the middle of the whole floor. Following whatever they did I also stepped on the floor without taking off my boots, there was a table in the corner. Some time later our teacher came and suddenly threw a glance at my boots, I was so shy that I was ready to disappear out of his sight at that time. I didn't even know what to do, it seemed to be weird for me at that time, but the teacher seemingly forgave me for this all.

I think all my interest in science was born at that time, my first lecture was on the topic: "Identifying flexibility of electric lines and wires in hot and cold conditions". We made a discourse with my friend Marat in the hall with which could sit no less than one hundred people. I was rigid   with excitement, and disappointment, and I did my best to explain everything clearly concentrating on the topic and looking at the same point somewhere on the wall. Our dean Okil Salimov gave us a book "Automobiles" as a present which I still keep in the centre of my bookshelf.

Due to my vehement interest in studying, I didn't feel any difficulty at all, and besides being active in social activities I preferred to help the other students having problems with understanding the lectures.

At that time, we didn't have enough books, and therefore we paid all of our attention to the notes we took during the lectures. We used to listen to every lesson with the utmost discretion and with all of our concentration. There, one more interesting adventure I had occurred. The exam from "Geometry of schemes had to be held at 3.00 pm in the Construction faculty, and no sooner had we arrived, that we saw that the teacher K. Aytikin and the assistant L. Hakimov were just about to finish up everything and leave. Later we got to know that on the day of the consultation when we weren't obligated to be present, all the students made up their mind to take the exams not in the afternoons, but in the morning. This meant we failed to take part in the exam because we were completely unaware of this decision. Even though the teachers were upset, they somehow allowed us to write our responses to the questions. Answering all the questions with positive results, we were assessed with "Good", and of course we were considered guilty at that time, so the rest of the exams we passed with only excellent marks. This was the first term which taught me to be attentive to everything. Inferring from all that happened I started studying for only Excellent marks in the next second term.

All the second-year students were sent to the Mirzachul (desert) located in the Syrdarya region for the cotton-picking season where the director of the collective farm introduced us all with Ganisher Yunusov, Social Labour hero and the other brigadiers there. Everyone was speaking one by one, and now it was time for Shutak, secretary of the Party Bureau, who greeted everyone with a handshake and introduced himself as a docent and candidate of science. All the students laughed silently greeted everyone and the brigadiers threw a strange glance at us then, because they didn't know what the award was this candidate of technical sciences meant to actually give. They didn't know anything except growing and picking cotton.

In 1958, our second year, we were busy with picking cotton in the land of Ganisher Yunusov, Labour hero, and someone would be on duty boiling tea among us. Doing that, it was necessary to get up at six and fill the big pan with water to boil. It was my turn to boil tea one day, but I suddenly fell asleep. Waking up and on the brink of sleepiness I got some water from the canal, poured it into the dish, and set in the fire to boil. When the water started boiling, I opened the lid so as to put in some tea leaves. Do you wonder what I saw there? A big dark green frog was boiling with the water. I quickly got it out with a dish and threw it away. I didn't know what to do, because soon all the students would start asking for tea. I put some tea leaves in the pot and closed the lid. It was once said that a frog can be a remedy for different diseases, so I kept silent begging God to forgive my sins. I didn't have another way out.

That year it started snowing earlier, and obviously, it was hardly possible to pick cotton in this cold weather. All the snow on the cotton plants used to be knocked off by men riding on horses and we were in charge of picking cottons with our feet freezing to death. Soon, the students of Russian- speaking groups started complaining about that unfair policy, and all the deans, and teachers, came back immediately and tried to calm them down. They could barely do it. However, the Uzbek students didn't utter a word of dissatisfaction, as cotton was the pride of Uzbek nationality. If we studied for five years at the institute, after calculating carefully, it became clear that one year of these five years we spent in the cotton fields. This meant we studied at the university not for five years, but for three years and ten months. The knowledge was also worth th e hard work, and despite all the encumbrances, being a student was a golden privilege. It's enough for you to study, and if you do, victory is yours.

Mrs Doctor, I am eager to tell you about our mahalla.

People in our mahalla were living quite friendly and we used to respect each other a lot. Our neighbor Saidmurod bought a car GAS-21 Volga, his brother Utkir studied with me together at the same faculty. As we studied in the special course teaching how to drive a car, we had no problem with that. Usually me and Utkir travelled along the street driving Mr Saidmurod's car, sometimes on the smooth roads I was also allowed to drive, until that time I hadn't tried to drive a car "GAS-51" under the control of the teacher. One day handing the gear to me Utkir said that I needed to drive the car until we got home. After that I was of course on the seventh heaven. Our street wasn't very narrow, and after driving for some five minutes I had to change the gear to turn into the narrow street where Utkir lived. However only one car could barely be driven in that small space. Besides that, our friend who also lived there installed and buried tram rails so that the cars passing wouldn't destroy the wall he was building. As soon as we approached the narrow street Utkir asked me to stop, but instead of braking, I stepped on the gas pedal, so at full throttle the car skidded suddenly and crashed the rails. It was quite late when I stepped on the brake pedal. When we went down we saw that the bumper was ruined. The front apron looked awful, but the rest of the parts were all ok. The brand-new car had to now be repaired. There was no use of feeling worried, concerned or sad, becuase it was time to think fast and very clearly. Utkir didn't say a thing, and in order to hide what wrong we did, we decided to take the car to the Tinchlik street where we hoped to find a good master. The day before I got a scholarship of 450 soums (in the currency activated throughout the time from 1947 to 1961). Fortunately, we found a master and he somehow mended the front apron. Unfortunately, it was hardly possible to mend the bumper which had an awful crack. After paying for the service, I was really worried about everything and took the car to the garage. I felt like time was going to stop passing, and everything seemed to be over for I lost interest in life and fell into despair. Everytime I saw Utkir I wondered if his brother had seen the car. He kept saying "Not yet" for a while. Three or four days later Mr Said finally saw and found out about everything after Utkir came clean about what we did... more exactly what I did. Maybe because he was upset or irritated, he didn't say a word and took the car in order to have the bumper repaired. After that I kept avoiding seeing that man as much as I could. One day, at long last, no matter how much I tried not to see him, I came across him and I had to greet him. When I expected him to scold me for what I did, he asked me politely instead: "Why did you stop visiting us, or our home? Is everything ok with you?" At that time, I realized the basic meaning of one philosophy of real life." A thing like a car, or a TV, we can find anytime, with no problem, if we have enough money. But a human being can never be found again once you loose them. All those things which can be damaged, can easily be created by a human. Most of all people need to pay attention of the people close to them, not their money or expensive gifts."

In 1960, in our third year, we had our practical lessons in Minsk. We had to first spend five days in order to get to Moscow by train. This was the first time I saw Moscow. We visited the Mausoleum where "the very Geniuses" Stalin and Lenin were lying, then we set off again. We were very glad to see how friendly and hospitable Byelorussian people were, and even at that time we knew all the capitals cities of all the fifteen countries of the USSR, and the surnames of the secretaries in the central committee because when we had to be included into the group of pioneers or the young communist league, we were asked everything about them. For those Byelorussian people, we were all Chinese. After working hard for two months in the same factory which we were astonished to see, we all developed our knowledge on how to apply our theoretical knowledge in practice when there's a need for it.   We finally returned to Moscow where we got a room in a hotel. Leaving all the new jumpers we bought on the beds in the rooms, we started traveling along the streets of Moscow. As soon as we came back we found the jumpers had been stolen. We couldn't believe it, but no one working in that hotel admitted to stealing them. Everyone was pretending not to know anything, and we could do nothing, because we weren't careful and were all thinking like Uzbeks believing the others were as honest as we were. In fact, in our cities, we really didn't touch another man's things without permission. We even left our houses unlocked when we went out.

After we finished our fourth year at the university, we were all sent to the Vostriakovo village in Moscow where we relished a lot. Afterwards we were again sent to another city and the Kiev Auto repair factory where we had to apply theoretical issues as part of our graduation work. I can assure you that the friendly relationships between Russian and Uzbek people became even closer after picking cotton and other practical work.

We always cherished the memories of our dearest teachers in the Automobile department, N.S. Abramov, N.S. Munster, K.I. Afanas'ev, A.A. Mutalibov, O.U. Salimov, K.A. Horoshev and others.

 I would like to recall two events. My and Marat's surnames sound the same, mine is Kodirov, his is Kodirkhonov. It was time for exams and the teacher N.S. Münstr was going to give exams in the discipline "Theory of Automobiles". Marat Kodirkhonov was the first to pass and to be assessed with an excellent mark. However, this assessment was registered in my note-book, and he knew much more than I did about this subject. The teacher didn't even realize it at that time until I sat in the chair in front of him to answer. My knowledge was worth the mark which was close to Excellent, but the teacher decided to ask me a bit more, all plus was excellent at last, of course after asking me hundreds of questions to which I could barely answer. Today Marat teaches this subject "Theory of automobiles" at university, he is a docent.

One more event is that K.I. Afanas'ev was giving exams on the subject "Internal combustion engines", and this time the same thing happened, Marat was the first to answer and he was assessed with a Good mark. this was again written into my notebook due to our similar surname, but this time I couldn't manage to warn the teacher about this. It was high time for me to answer, but I had already been mistakenly assessed in the note-book. Since I answered all of his questions, the teacher had to change my good mark to excellent in the notebook. Today I am a doctor in the same discipline, which means even at that time I could establish the foundation for my future.

In the 1962 summer season, after successfully defending our graduation papers, 63 ambitious and successful people left for 63 different parts of the Republic in pursuit of their careers. After graduating, I was given a month of a rest so that I could gather all of my energy and concentration. At first working as a chief of the exploitation in the Yangier Automobile company, I started to be paid one hundred and eighty soums a month despite having graduated with a diploma of distinction and with honors. There was no job for me in Tashkent, so I couldn't stay there.

One day my scientific advisor K.A. Horoshev invited me to the department on behalf of all the members of the Automobile department, and they suggested I work as an assistant, and the salary was going to be 105 soums a month. I promised them to think over this suggestion on talking about this with my mother. She said to me: "You'd better talk about this with your brother Okil. He will advise you. I will encourage him. That's ok if we have this burden with money for five or six more years. We'll try to be patient, so don't think about earning money. You should take care of your career". At this time our dean was promoted to a proctor, and I visited him, somehow finding a little time. He welcomed me and promised to accept me as a Ph. D student. His advice gifted me with wings and I was seemingly flying out of joy and happiness. So, I signed with confirmation and I applied for a job at the university, as did the head of the department N.S. Abramov. When this happened, we were both standing in the university corridor. I could see the statement on my application: "On the basis of probation period". Starting from July I started working as an assistant.

From 1957 to 1962, my course mates shared their grief and happiness together, passing all the easy or challenging exams together, carrying out research and graduation work. We always supported each other until the last day of our studies. After the exams, all of us started our carriers in different regions in the Karakalpakstan Republic of Uzbekistan. As for me, I left for Moscow to study for my Ph. D and finally came back to my unique motherland. Different thoughts started invading my mind, 63 course mates graduated, but we have never tried to meet each other. It was ten years after graduation at that time. I made up my mind to invite all of my course mates to gather. The poet Rudakiy mentioned:

Even all the happiness of the world people

Can not be equal to meeting of friends, that's simple!

Indeed, friendship is appreciated everywhere.

It's a must for all of us to meet, and within ten years, ten years, whatever might happen during this long period, everybody wonders about their dearest friend, don't they? After consulting with five or six classmates in Tashkent, I got all the employment recommendations that were given to all of them. They showed our course mates addresses, so we decided June 6, 1972 as the meeting date for all of us. At long last we met, and all those who got the message about meeting came, with only those whose address we couldn't get unfortunately not attending.

We also invited our teachers, who were absolutely overjoyed visiting us all, and even the president of the university, A.A. Mutalibov came to see us.

Here it's worth showing the statement mentioned by Alisher Navoiy:

Through honest, those who taught you a thing with efforts,

Nothing's enough to pay for it, no money or no complimentary words!

This confirms how much teachers should be appreciated as they devote all of their energy, thoughts, labour and mind to the upcoming future of their students, even though they aren't relatives or there aren't any other extra interests between them.

The meeting took place and our faces were replete with sincerity, and everybody seemingly missed each other, as they all greeted each other by hugging each other tightly.   Our conversations seemed to have no end. Only after that we made up our minds to meet each other like this on the first Saturday of June every year and every time in different cities. I was eventually appointed as a leader of both groups for preserving this tradition. This happened in 1972, so from that day forth it was me who took charge of organizing the next annual meeting of our former course mates. We met each other later in Namangan, Samarkand, Nukus and Karshi. Those days were indeed fabulous and unforgettable. Everytime we met, our sweet memories of youth could wake up, an alert in our hearts, renewing everything funny, mischieveous or the other. Most of the meetings took place in Tashkent and we went to rest at the most beautiful and scenic places in the Republic. Most of our friends were promoted to higher positions at that time and they were having more and more privileges day by day. Four of my friends would become doctors of sciences, seven of them were candidates of sciences, Lerik was appointed as a Minister, Timur the assistant to the Minister, Sadir – the director of the Science Institute, seven or eight of our friends were working as teachers at our university devoting their life to teaching and educating young generation.

The basic symbol of friendship is equality, as no high position, no reputation due to arrogance can inhibit this relationship if it's real. Where there's suspicion, friendship will end. However, thanks to God our friendship has been and will always be eternal. For over forty-seven years we've been giving a hand to each other, encouraging and supporting as much as we could. Unfortunately, up to today we were bereaved of most of our true friends. May they be blessed by God all the time!

Pursuit of science and knowledge (1962–1969)

If once a bit of knowledge is infused into your mind,

It brightens the world much more than the sun has ever

shined. A. Firdavsiy

I actually think that the time I was studying for my Ph. D lasted seven years and I defended my graduation work on June 19, 1962, and then I was given an opportunity, to defend the candidate's research on June 19 (as you see both on the same day). Everyone voted in my favor, as there was no one to object. This was one of my happiest day ever.

Of course, achieving this goal was absolutely challenging, as I was forced to learn spending sleepless hours at night being engrossed in different books, experiments, waiting for results, overcoming different invisible blocks and barriers. Not everyone can afford to do this, and there are many who failed and back off this pursuit. I think only those blessed and loved by God can become a scientist as science is something saving the world.

As the Ph. D studies were going on I went to Moscow Automobiles transport university to enter and target Ph. Studies, but I failed. On coming back and after working as an assistant, I worked hard experiencing being a constructor. I then returned to Moscow for a one-year experience and afterwards I was at long last accepted to the targeted Ph. Studies in November of 1964. Three years passed, but the scientific work still wasn't over as it was being written on an absolutely complicated issue.

The date for my defense had been prolonged for 8 months and at last my research and investigations came to end. I started working as an assistant in the Tashkent Polytechnical university in the department of "Exploitation of Automobiles". I was charged with collecting the huge amount of academic- methodological materials from the Moscow State Automobile and roads university and I was sent on business for six months. I am quite grateful to the head of the department, Okil Umrzakovich. I coped with all the tasks and I succeeded in initial defending my dissertation.

Initial victory!

I came back to Tashkent and started my own activity and I met my future wife Alokhon while studying for my Ph.D.

The date to defend the dissertation was appointed for me on June 19, and for my wife on June 26. It was of course unfamiliar when we both could defend our research. But both of us were eager to get knowledge. We were working hard all the time for the sake of the mother-land. All our talks when we were on a date were about science and learning. Our love was just like a part of the world dearest to us. On October 25, 1969, we had our wedding, and this day was the outset of our life in partnership, charged with love and loyalty.

- Mrs Doctor, if you don't mind, I'm going to tell you about the time when I was an assistant-Ph.D. student. We'll go back a bit more to the past. In 1962, my brother and I graduated from the university. According to a decision by the university administration, they sent my brother to Kazakhstan, Karaganda province and at the same time he was engaged to his future wife. Now we had a serious problem to be solved: where could they live after they got married? We didn't have any space except a terrace and a little home. I was working as an ordinary assistant, earning just 105 soums and 89 pennies a month. But anyway, we were forced to build a house for our brother and his wife in which they could live. So, me and a younger brother Marvar could hardly make 12 thousand bricks and bought a thousand more at the end. Later our neighbor Saidmurod gave us a hand to buy some wood and roofing slates. Our neighbor Mr Vossib showed us how to make bricks, and the rest of the things we learned by ourselves. At that time, I grew to understand that there was nothing a man can not do. Although we were just students, we learnt to construct a house. We coped with daubing as Mr Mahmoud and all the other neighbors helped us a lot with that. At long last we finished building our home, and our brother got married in September of 1963.

The days seemed to be passing in the same way, but there are also some changes in life, some bad memories embedded in your life for a lifetime, to tell the truth. I was talking to our head of the building, Dina Michailovna, and it was the time when we were cleaning outside the university. Suddenly one young fellow came up to us, he turned out to be working in Comsomol Committee, and I was stunned by the way he rudely asked me why I wasn't taking part in cleaning. Then Dina said that I was a teacher there, in a higher position than him. So it also infered that some young people start feeling arrogant and dismissing their own teachers as soon as they are promoted to a slightly higher position.

I went to the Moscow Automobile and Roads university, "Autotractor engines" department in the autumn of 1962, to be enrolled in my Ph.D studies. As soon as I came here, I felt like I came along in a completely different world. Although I graduated with distinction, I made sure that I didn't have enough knowledge. Actually I didn't even read a book relating to any of those subjects because the books were rather hard to find in our country. I just thought it was enough to read my notes written during the lectures.

The head of the department, Max Samoylovich talked to me for a long time, checked my knowledge and advised me to stay for a year to get some experience. Without experience I knew that I couldn't start my Ph.D. courses, but it was also impossible to stay without permission of my own host university. They said they wouldn't allow me to stay, but they could just let me stay a year later. In that country I found all the necessary books and started working even harder in that country and started having a different outlook about life and the world. I seemed to feel a bit upset with my teachers who assessed me with high scores although I didn't deserve it. They aren't guilty at all for that. They probably assessed me by comparing my knowledge with that of the other students. I started thinking for a long time after I left Max Samoylovich. because I needed some money in order to go back to Tashkent. For four days later I earned some money for transport back to Tashkent by working in Horoshevsk station, helping to load potatoes and cabbage. Although I failed the exams, I made up my mind to come back for my Ph.D. courses again. I was then working hard for my dear university in Tashkent for another year . and after another year I went to Moscow with the intention of working as an assistant-teacher in on October 5, 1963.

Docent S.E.Nikitin was appointed as a secondary advisor for me. Sergei Yevdokimovich contributed a lot to my interest in research.This kind of person isn't easy to find . He had of strict and kind disposition at the same time. Within a year I became an engineer-constructor. I recalled all the lectures delivered by my professors, and reworked all my course work and laboratory work. I both worked and studied because I knew if I didn't work hard I might fail my exams again. All the lectures I listened to all my life came in handy. I also delivered some lectures when docent Morozov supervised me there.

Within a year I prepared schemes of a future engine, and submitted it for production. In the autumn of 1964 I succeeded in all the exams and was enrolled in target aspirantura, though I hadn't even passed my exams for special subjects. This was a quite a rare success for Ph.D. candidates. The working schemes of the engine were submitted to the Factory of experimented constructions, and the engine was to be constructed there. I had to become friends with the planning department. Frankly saying , all the money I earned was spent on creating this tool. I at long last invented this engine with one cylinder.

At this time I had completed one year of my Ph.D. course, and we collected the engine in a special GDR.

Unfortunately the engine we invented couldn't meet economical requirements we aimed at. This was invented structurally imitating the engine produced in the USA, and using Soviet technology. It means the quality of the engine couldn't meet the requirements.

The engine we designed required a lot of fuel and energy, so we talked to professor Mr Hovach and made up our minds to replace the cylinder punger with that of SMD-7 engine. After we did what was needed, although with some challenges, we made real progress, and the expenditure on fuel decreased dramatically. Decreasing this expenditure was my job to cope with. We had to provide a coincidence of the combustion camera, and the injection pressure and air motion. For three years I did my best to provide this, and I was able make the engine modern enough to meet the requirements of the current science. We were forced to make and use measuring instruments, conductors and tools. As the engine we made, had a high speed, it was stubborn enough, to say figuratively. One night we were running an experiment with that engine, when suddenly it seemed something flashed in the head of the engine, because I heard cracking sounds at that moment. It was about 10 at night, and I immediately pressed the emergency button to stop the engine from working. We all left for home thinking that Vlas Prokofyevich, engineer Nicolai Petrovich wouldn't divide the engine into components, thinking to start work next day again. I couldn't fall asleep at all, and I was feeling it in my bones that the engine stopped working properly because several minutes passed until this engine started rotating 3800 times a minute,;yes it had stopped operating.

In the morning at our workplace, we opened the engine head, and saw that a flap had fallen down into the cylinder, which it made a hole in the piston. Both the cylinder and the head was in a terrible state. Nikitin helped us to rework and reinstall all the details, and after working again from three or four months, the engine started working again. After we examined the motives for failure in the first testing, we found out that the internal spring of the flap operating at a high speed turned out to be operating wrongly, and the details were falling out of place. When we tested the number of rotations, it was also incorrect, as the tool used for calculating the number of rotations wasn't operating at all. We found out that the engine was actually working with 4300 rotations, and obviously couldn't stand it because it was too much for this engine. Assembling the engine once more, with all the components properly installed, so we decided to let it work with fewer rotations In the next experiments we got all the results as properly as we'd planned.

The mechanical engineer couldn't stand this hard work and eventually quit. To be honest, he could stand this work, but the salary he earned was worth much less worth than what he did there. Those who value themselves will surely accept this as ignorance. Instead of him, we got a new colleague, a young officer, Bantush Vasiliy. Despite his quick temper, he was a good man, and we got along well together. We were forced to break the engine apart and recollect it the same day, which was almost impossible to do within 24 hours.

In this regard it's necessary to remember what Abu Raihon Beruniy said about that:

"If you want to take steps towards science and knowledge, you need to get rid of jealousy, nonsense, different strange habits and other negative feelings."

All of my life I've been trying to follow this statement non-stop.

The head of the Ph.D, courses department insisted on passing one of the entrance exams in Russia, but I had already passed this exam. I said I was ready, but in case it would be in Uzbek as I studied in Uzbek course. Seeing he didn't agree I addressed the president of the Moscow Automobile and Road university, L.Afanasev. I was right, but the rector said: "you need to pass it in Russian, if you can't get the mark, I will solve this problem". I agreed and started reading all books in Russian and those about the history of the parties. Next day at the exam professor Akimov attended it, and after listening to two of my responses to questions, he immediately left. But the next morning he gave me a friendly hug seeing me outside the university. I thought I could never get along with this man, but later we became the closest friends. I always used give him a hand since I had an accurate handwriting and good writing skills in Russian. A year later this man died and Nikitin explained to me why he caused me so many challenges before and after the exams. Working as a political leader for many years, he came to the conclusion that all the students arriving from Central Asia and studying for their Ph.D., were doing so just because they had lots of money. In short, illegally. He also thought students in Central Asia didn't have enough knowledge. However, I tried so hard that he changed his mind about Central Asia students. I am always proud of being such a student and deserving his attention and his good attitude.

The first victory

It isn't easy to carry out scientific research in technical science. You must first of all help the metal to be alive and then carry out necessary the experiments. You are always faced with possible failures, especially in the field of "heating engines", which combines physics, chemistry, heating techniques, electronics, mathematics and other essential subjects.

All the constructive parameters of the fast moving diesel engine were all similar to the best American engine Cammins, and we took an example from this operation. These engines were the result of hard work by a member of the USSR Science academy, N.R. Briling. Previously this engine wasn't valued enough, and caused many disputes before use, but it was approved anyway, and another engine passed approbation. For three years we kept exploring new ways of proving that we were right, and yes, we won, we got the results, again successfully, and we submitted it to the Scientific Auto motor university.

Within that time I widened my outlooks and grew up considerably. I started having scientific discussions with teachers. The engine was broken several times and repaired. These days this tool and the one cylinder-engine is being explored for soon creating a new ceramic engine .

Completing all the experiments in 1968, I reformed all my dissertation's content and finished with it entirely in August. One of the docents brushed me off one day with irony: "Now you can leave us for two years or a bit more, and within this time, I would be really satisfied if you could at least finish writing your dissertation ". This made me upset, hurt me deeply in the heart. But I bit back. Redrawing all the graphs, I immediately went to the house where Mr Nikitin lived and rented a house 120 kilometers from Moscow. They came there for summer vacations from Algeria. He looked through my work within three days, then I ran to the senior teacher. Professor Max Samoylovich who looked through the dissertation within a week and I gave the checked version to a secretary woman to have it typed. After some days for rest, the department teachers looked through and discussed my dissertation. M.Hovah declared that the dissertation was worth considering as complete. The docent who predicted that it would take me at least a year to write it didn't believe it. M.Hovah calmly handed the dissertation to him tobe introduced, and the second and third copies were passed to the famous professors I.Astahov and N.Voinov.

That year, in autumn, my research and results were positively assessed in all the seminars of the department. . The dissertation was very well assessed by two science doctors and one candidate of sciences.

For the initial defence of my dissertation, I hung 55 schemes and delivered a lecture for an hour. My brother Marvar and the girl, technician, prepared the graphs for me. All the professors supported my ideas in the dissertation, but they noticed some faults as well. This day was the happiest day of my life. The basic part of the research hasn't been altered and they suggested it for further formal defense. However, suddenly it suddenly became known that I hadn't passed any of the exams for the discipline " Internal combustion engines ". I really forgot it because of all the pressure. All the members of the scientific seminars and the department supported me claiming that I could've been assessed for that exam automatically as I had shown my own talent with the lecture discourse. So I got the mark without taking any exams. This displayed the utmost confidence in me, and ever since, I've been trying to warrant this confidence throughout my life.

From August of 1968 to January of 1969, thte staff of the "Autotransport maintenance department did their best to help me with the completion of my dissertation, I also brought many necessary materials from the Moscow Automobile and Road university and submitted it to the training and teaching process.

All the Ph.D students of Moscow automobile and Road university used to live the dormitory near the subway station "Sokol". In the neighbouring dormitory lived students from the Medical institute . There were a number of students from my home country in the dormitory I lived and in the neighboring one.

 All the friends I met in Moscow kept visiting me quite often, and so did I. Even when we were in Moscow, we used to spend lots of time together telling jokes, and anecdotes together.

 I was in Moscow those beautiful days, mummy and brother stayed at home, and I would send many expensive things there with the money I earned so that they wouldn't have financial problems.

Indeed as L.N.Tolstoi, the great Russian writer said: "Regular problems, hard work, and a lack of money are all necessary in the pursuit of a better life, as these challenges prompt the pursuit of a better life ahead".

Moreover, there's a proverb the the Uzbek language "You aren't deemed as a Moslem unless you try to live away from your home".

I at long last went back to my hometown, Tashkent, in 1969 where I proceeded with my career as a teacher.

In this world, we come across with different sorts of people, good or bad, good or bad ...

I still remember helping one teacher Mutalibov and two of his students, who started visiting me quite often as their scientific advisor, Mutalibov couldn't cope with helping them at all. They hoped that I would help them to complete their dissertation. I asked most of my friends in Moscow to look through those dissertations, and at last I succeeded in my pursuit as a rewiever.

After Mutalibov, the scientific advisor of those two students was appointed as president in Tashkent Automobile and Road university, and one by one all my friends started to blow their lids because they thought that I would tell all the gossip they made about Mutalibov. They were probably unaware that I am not that type of a man at all. One of the students of Mutalibov was M.Miryunusov, I helped him to reform the plan of his dissertation, and as a result, his research was successfully completed. This man was really honest without any malice, or aforethought.

"Moscwich" is good as a car, "Jiguli" – even much better.

I used to live in Hojaparhon mahalla,then in 1971, I moved in Korakamish 2/4. At that time buses were quite rare, and commuters used to wait in the street for hours. First I took two buses and then a train. So you can imagine how hard it was for me to go to work.

I taught "Internal combustion engines" to students and was one of their most favourite teachers as I did my best to help them all the time. They shared all of their personal problems with me. Ties of friendship were very strong, and at this time I was working as a docent and my daughter was already one year old. Most of the docents came to work driving their own cars. Although there were two docents in our family, my wife Alokhon and me, to get to work we had to get off one bus and after we got to a certain bus-stop we had to take another bus. All of our students knew how hard it was for us to get there.

One day one of my older students came to see me to say that he wanted to help me with the transport. He said: "There's one old car on sale, Sir". I told him that I didn't have enough money enough to buy a car, but he insisted and said that his own uncle who served in the world war wanted to sell his car for a very low price. The car was a Moscwich -403, but he said we were forced to go to Karakalpakstan just to take a look at it.

I agreed and we set off. To get to the Karakalpakstan Republic we passed Tashkent, Gulistan, Jizzakh, Samarkand, Navoiy, Bukhara, Khorazm and Tortkol provinces. His uncle turned lived in Tortkol province, which was one of the towns of the Karakalpakstan Republic. Getting there safe and sound we had to be guests in one of the weddings. They welcomed us and treated us very well. On the table one could see meat, meals with meat and alcoholic drinks. I begged the guests around not to make me drink those drinks as I couldn't stand that at all. We had a good time, and listened to songs. The next day we saw the car, and it was indeed old, and required general repair. However, it moved somehow. We had a good conversation and the host told us about his experiences, and the challenges he came across with during the world war. I also told him about my father who died in that war. I told them that he died in Moldavia in 1944 leaving my mother alone with five orphans to take care of. I think this was something that touched their heart and they sold the car to me for a very cheap price, of only 1000 soums. I was the owner of the Moscwich 403, and on cloud nine. We had the car sale confirmed right there and set off to Tashkent. This car was a gift on the first birthday of my daughter Nigora. After some time the Tortkol admistration permitted to have the car confirmed as legally owned by me. It was a bit uncomfortable to drive that car as the body required repair. All of students heard that I bought a car, and they all immediately came to take a look at it. One of my students who worked as an engineer in the auto saloon said: "Dear teacher, you have done many good things for us, so if you can buy some details for the car, I would mend your car for free with pleasure. He took the car to his own workplace, and I gave him enough money for all the details he needed. After two or three months the car looked brand new. Now it was possible to easily drive the almost new car. We started arriving to our to be workplace in our own car. One day I happened to be driving along after shopping and on my way home when people ran up to me asking me how much I wanted to sell my car for. I just joked and said seven thousand soums. At that right moment one of the clients looked through the car and said that he would pay me cash if I sold it for at least 6500 soums . I said that I couldn't sell it at the moment and I quickly left. But the price seemed ok for me, and at that moment I realized it was rare to find this sort of a car because it was only distributed to one or two families once or twice a month.

I went to Moscow on business where I first visited M.S.Samoylovich. He said to me:

"You don't need to bother yourself going to hotels. Here's the key of Masha for you. You'll be living there." Having thanked to him, I took the key and went there to stay. I thanked God a thousand times for it. I must admit that if my teachers Nikitin and

Hovach had been alive, they wouldn't have allowed me to stay at the hotel. They always treated me as if I were their son. May God bless them both. Look, in the apartment where I lived one could see the car shop. On the weekends I went for a bit of walk to that car shop. One by one I started observing all the cars on sale, price, quality etc... I didn't have an idea to buy a car at all, but I got interested in cars like the "Volga" "Moscwich" and "Jiguli". They weren't that expensive. Suddenly I saw one of my friends Sergei with whom I lived in the dormitory. We greeted each other and asked about each other's personal life news and health. I asked: "What are you doing?" He said: "I was called to render military service. Therefore actually I came here to sell my car." He pointed to his car Jiguli-01. Getting interested I tried to take a seat in that car and inserted the key. The engine started working without any noise, and as I was a scientist of engines, I fell in love with that engine. I asked him:

"How much will you sell it for?".

"For you it is just 6500 soums" he said. I started calculating, I could buy the Jiguli for the money I'd get selling my own Moscwich. But I wasn't able to drive it alone to Tashkent because I wasn't experienced enough.

I told him: "Ok, I will buy your car, but if you will drive it to Tashkent, this would be a chance for you to see that beautiful city. Then I will help you to go back by plane".

We shook hands as a sign of agreement, but I didn't have a penny in my pocket. I immediately went to the post-office to call my brother Anvar and asked him to loan me 6,5 thousand soums for one or two months. He agreed as he'd sold his house for 12 thousand soums, and his new house was going to be built soon, and was even sold just before that.

Sergei left for his own home in Smolensk promising to have the car excluded from the registration list in three days. The next day my brother Marvar came to my flat in Moscow bringing me 7000 soums. Two days later Sergei handed me the keys to the Jiguli registered in my name. Now it was time to set off for Tashkent. We bought some necessary items and other things for the car. It was the last days of October, and Sergei went home after I handed him the money and came back to see me again. However, he received note about his duty as a military servant, and according to that official note he was forced to report to the military department in two days and had to pack all the necessary things. Therefore, he promised to drive us to Orenburg, then we had to drive on our own. I agreed as there wasn't any other way to cope, and I thought we could somehow get to Tashkent. I said goodbye to my teacher in MADI, and we set off with Sergei in the driver's seat, me next to him, and my brother in the rear seat. We bought all the food we needed and drove to Stalingrad. Walking in this beautiful city for a bit, we trsveled to Orenburg, and after we said goodbye to Sergei, I bought a ticket for him back to Moscow. I had bought a guide book for the USSR auto roads, which came in handy for us.

We drove through all the passages, stopping our car to wherever they asked us to, and they showed us where to drive, which direction, which way to turn and so on. We got to the Ilgiz river where there wasn't a bridge, and where all the cars were crossing river without a bridge! How stunning! After crossing this river we reached a village where we bought some fuel, and since there were many tracks in the desert, we lost our way. Again we came close to some kind of a village. and fortunately we saw a truck and asked the driver to show us the way. He asked us to follow t him. We drove some 5 or 6 kilometers following that truck, but the car crashed against something and skidded. After we got out of the car, the truck was already out of sight and the car turned out to have crashed against a big tree , the branches had scratched the car,which was broke, and engine's fuel was leaking out. Oh, how lucky we were, you see! We then had to spend a night there somehow. I didn't sleep all night trying to calm my brother down as he was in complete and absolute anxiety. We got up early in the morning, both washed up, and after eating some snacks for breakfast, we waited for a truck to pass us. After about an hour, and as we expected, a truck came and stopped. The driver was stunned seeing the tree blocking the way and he agreed to drag our car with the truck he drove. He helped us free the car from tree trunk and I left my brother in the car and went to the village nearby, I decided to find a specialist to replace the car's tray. I came upon the head of the garage and explained what happened. The manager introduced me to a Kazakh boy and asked him to help me with the car. But unfortunately he said: "I can't do anything with that." What could we do for that car? Can we repair it? Tens of cars were passing us in that desert, and not one of us tried to help us. At last I decided to stop a truck VAZ, and five men and one Russian man got out of it. We met, I showed my certificate and explained what happened. In short asking for help. Fortunately, there turned out to be a locksmith master among them and they lifted up one side of the car by using a hoisting jack, the they removed the tray. There wasn't any fuel and the fuel pump was broken. They tightly tied the broken part of the pump to the car, and one man tied two pieces of the oil motor to the other using some wires. He leveled the tray by beating it with a hammer and repaired it using a blowlamp, making it tight with bolts. They took their own oil from their can and poured it into the engine of my car. Where else could we find oil suitable for the Jiguli in the desert?

One of those men took the key from me and started driving the car, which started moving as if it had always been new. The engine started working and the car started moving. It moved 300-400 meters and back. Everything was fine! The truck driver sat next to me and drove me to the village. In the village we bought some fuel and I gave them some money for their service. They even accompanied us to the city of Aralsk, said goodbye to us and then left to go fishing.

In this life it's possible to meet lots of good people, and once more I must admit admitted that Russian people are very friendly. Those who helped me with the car were all Russian, but there were Uzbek drivers who didn't even stop when we asked for help in the desert.

Now we, as brothers, set off for Uzbekistan in a very good mood. After driving some 10-15 kilometers we saw a Volga which was on the edge of the road. In front of that car there were three people: one young man, one woman and a child.

Stopping the car immediately, I went there and asked if they needed my help. They were really depressed. I suddenly remembered the situation I was in. As I knew the car working system very well, I looked through the car and got to see that the bolt of that Volga was apart and needed to be fixed. We could The driver and I barely fixed the car together, which was now was in a state to move. We both then agreed to go to Tashkent together. They all turned out to be from the Chirchik a province of Tashkent. While we were driving, three or four more cars joined us there, and we set off again together. There, on the road there were domes of sands in the desert blocking our ways. After we drove some 10 kilometers, the Moscwich stopped working at all. The engine wasn't working as the fuel was empty. The Russian driver was depressed, and he asked his partners for fuel, who refused. Even though I didn't know him I gave him my own fuel which I bought in the village. I thought I could get to Aralsk with the fuel I had left. After we drove for a bit, our car stopped somewhere we didn't even know. It was a dome of sand which blocked the way, so we decided to go on the next morning. In Aralsk we filled all the containers with fuel.

We quickly found the autobasa and I left the woman with the child there and went inside where I met my former student who the Director there. He saw me and gave me a spontaneous hug failing to hide his excitement. Then I realized that some of my former students were working there in different positions. They immediately arrived where we were, and one of my students took my car and started examining what wrong was with it. They concluded that everything was ok. They asked me what kind of fuel I was using, and I frankly admitted that I was using A-76. They poured some fuel from the container in my car and then took it somewhere to pour aviation fuel.

At that time I was also having the Volga car repaired. They looked through it quite well and made it ready for driving. During this time they ordered some pilaf and we sat together all eating some pilaf. Two people from Namangan arrived, we met, and got acquainted. Those two men were also in a trouble as their car was stuck in the desert. Then I asked and it became clear that they were working as a taxi driver for one of my friends Zayniddin. We made up our mind to go to Tashkent together.

In the afternoon my students promised to accompany us, and three automobiles left on the highway along the Aral Sea. After we drove some 10-15 kilometers, smoke started bulching out of the engine and it made it hard to see through the front window. We immediately got out of the car to see what was wrong. Oh my God, the ventilator blades were broken, there was a hole in the radiator, and a crack in the water pump. As a result, hot antifreeze was overflowing and it had already evaporated . We were feeling terrible, and didn't know what to do. A truck dragged the jiguli to help it move towards the highway, it was dark enough. Three drivers of an automobile were eager to see if any trucks on the highway would help us to get out of that desert. Some time later we stopped two trucks GAZ-53 both which were empty, didn't have any loads. Both the drivers were Russian, just one passenger seemed to be Kazakh. We explained to them what happened, and though the Russian driver was ready to have our cars lifted on the body of their truck, the Kazakh man didn't allow them to. Then it became clear that those automobiles had been bought from the Gorky automobile plant and were being driven to Kurgan city, they were brand new, and it was impossible for them to lift heavy loads. We agreed to drag it with a trailer. We tied the truck to the hook of the Jiguli with a rope (but it was thin) and I was to drive the car. A taxi driver from Namangan sat next to me , and after we started driving, my students left saying good-bye. It was dark around, the headlights were flashing, and I drove some ten kilometers. It was the first time in my life I was driving a car with a trailer. Some time later I felt that I was falling asleep, and suddenly my partner beeped the car and sat in my seat to drive it further. Just imagine driving a trailer for 100 kilometers. This was because of that Kazakh who didn't want to help us, though my friend who was a taxi-driver helped me a lot.

At mid-night, two cars, a Volga and a Jiguli, and two trucks stopped at a village and we decided to rest there until the morning. all of us fell asleep inside the car. My brother Marvar tried to convince the Kazakh man to agree to drag the Jiguli with the truck GAZ-53 all night long. At last, in the early morning he agreed. We were calm now, and it was possible to let the Volga drivers go home. We said good-bye and thanked them after that. They left and we sat in the cab and started moving. However, on the way we noticed that one of the trucks was missing. Then it came into sight, but with a Jiguli upon it. Then it became clear that some men had had the same accidental problem with the Jiguli which they'd recently bought. They were also driving it to home like we were and the radiator, ventilator and water pump had stopped operating. We started driving to Turkiston, and while we were driving into the city, the traffic wardens stopped the two cars and took away their driving license after that. The Russian drivers were feeling sad, but I said them: "Don't worry, everything's going to be ok!" The Kazakh policemen were really threatening us, saying that we were doing was wrong and illegal. I asked them to take me to their administrator. We sat on the motorcycle and went to the chief administrator in the police office. I was greeted by the administrator wearing a lieutenant's uniform. On his desk I put my certificates confirming that I was a docent and a business traveler to Moscow and I said : "Sobir Sodikov,the director of the bus station studied with me at the institute, and if you could please call him, he will tell you who we are.The truck drivers aren't guilty of anything. It's us who are guilty because we were forced to drive our cars this way. You can punish me as much as you want, please." The lieutenant was silent for some time and gave my documents back wishing us good luck. I thanked him, and asked him to send my regards to Sobir Sodikov. After we got to there where our Russian friends were waiting, the policemen returned their all documents immediately. We started driving to Chimkent and soon got to the border some time later. Suddenly we saw some Uzbek people coming out of their homes, we met and introduced each other. They helped us to release the cars from the trucks GAZ-53, and afterwards invited us in. This was hospitality, a symbol of Uzbek culture, and we exchanged our addresses with the Russian men. All of us were really glad to be there. When we were sitting there as guests, we enjoyed eating the meals the housewife cooked. I promised the man who helped us to find all the details of the "Moscwich-408".

In the afternoon, two trucks left for the Kurgan city, and we said good-bye to our Russian friends.

Now we stayed in the street with two cars and with the Jiguli not working. I brooded over it for a long time, then made up my mind. My brother Marvar was going to stay there, to have all the radiators repaired while I'd go to Tashkent with our friend from Namangan city and bring all the other necessary parts. After we stopped a taxi, we got to Tashkent within sixteen hours, but I was thinking about meeting my friend Kahramon, the head of the Station of Technical Service, but he was out. His subordinates recognized me and immediately found two ventilators, and two water pumps for us. Later we returned to Chimkent where my brother stayed with the Jiguli cars. After we drove some 15 or 20 kilometers I groped in my pocket, but I couldn't find the registration certificate of the cars. Oh, no, I probably left them in the Station of Technical Service. We came back with the same taxi to the Station of Technical Service, but it was later than 5 pm, and it was already closed. Then I asked the driver to go to the Karakamish district where I lived, because I thought my poor mother was very worried about us as we didn't even call her for five days at all. I came home, our friend from Namangan city went to Chimkent, and I promised to get him all the documents we had left from the Station of Technical Service and get to Chimkent at 11 in the morning.

We had so many challenges with driving to Tashkent that when I went into the house, my poor mummy felt high up in the seventh heaven seeing me, and asked where was Marvar . I told her that I left him with an Uzbek family as we had some problems.

In the early morning I woke up and quickly prepared to set off to go there where I had left my brother. I didn't even notice how I got to Chimkent after driving 130 kilometers away.I arrived in Chimkent at 11 o'clock and I saw that my Jigule was already repaired. We thanked the owners of the house and we said goodbye to those people who took care of my car and brother. The two men from Namangan and I got to Tashkent safe and sound.

Thanks to Allah! We arrived home in the "Jiguli".

Everyone in our family was glad.

The next weekend I sold my Moscwich for 6.500 thousand soums and paid my brother the money which he had lent me when I had been in Moscow.

This "Jiguli" served our family until 1975, it never broke, and I really enjoyed driving it all the time. At this time I was appointed as a secretary for the faculty Party Bureau. The administration promised to gift me with a jiguli 06. Then with my sister's husband we went to the car shop where we sold my old jiguli for 7.500 soums, a much higher price than what I bought it for in Moscow. The car was in really good shape, and the customers didn't even try to get a discount. They immediately decided to buy it after examining the engine.

Unfortunately I had already sold my own car,and the problem to get me a car took three years to be solved. I felt sorry that I sold my own car, and at last, in 1977, I coped with buying a new one jiguli 03.

If you do something good for people, there will be someone else to help you. I've tested this a lot of times throughout my life. I started getting deeper and deeper into the world of human soul.

It isn't so easy to be a doctor of sciences (1969-1984)

The whole meaning of life is to overcome all the things which are abstract and to long for learning, getting knowledge more and more.

E.Zolia

- Now Mrs Doctor, it's high time I tell you how I became a doctor of sciences...

There are millions of people who couldn't achieve this happiness. According to statistics, just 4-5 % of candidates of sciences successfully continued their research for a doctoral degree. To achieve this success, it's important not to be afraid of difficulties, to be resistant, and to have a peaceful family life. This means that the man gifted by God can achieve this happiness.

I can never forget my teacher, professor M.S.Hovach's prediction . When I went up to him for advice he said: "I taught you whatever I knew, now you know what is useful for your own motherland. I don't know what exactly you need,and you need to find whatever problem you need to solve." The main constructor of the Oltoi engine factory found me and asked me to solve a problem in the Central Asia. I agreed although it was hard to tackle it. It took a year to establish the causes of the problem and ways of solving it. This was a great innovation. The work duration of the tractors in the Central Asia was prolonged and made even more effective, and they started working without any technical pauses. After all the results were published in an article, most directors and researchers started ordering the research results. The research was wide enough and as a result I found the theme of my doctoral dissertation. In 1975 I was enrolled in Moscow auto mechanics Ph.D courses and professor R.P.Dobrogayev was appointed as a scientific advisor for me. This man contributed a lot to my success in achieving the doctoral degree of sciences.

After I defended my Ph.D dissertation, my opponent M.D.Apashev came to our university to deliver some lectures. He advised me to create a manual in Uzbek language and I was really proud if I could create it within just a year. I understood that it was really hard after two or three years.

At this time I prepared lecture texts on the basis of the dissertation theme. With my teacher S.E.Nikitin, I wrote a little book "The work process and exploitation of diesel in conditions of Central Asia" and students soon got the chance to read it. For four years I translated the book by Hovach called "Automobile engines" into Uzbek, and it took me four years. Unfortunately I tried to publish it two years ahead, but at that time it was prohibited to write a manual in Uzbek in technical field, and only a few some books were allowed to be translated into Uzbek for schoolchildren and students in the 1 and 2 year. Starting from their 3rd year, students learned all the subjects in Russian.

I was more and more busy with my main activities and research. At that time my younger daughter Oydin was born. It happened in the spring of 1974. This was great happiness for me. She prompted me to secure newer and newer victories. At last in 1977 the book "Automobile engines" was the first book to be published in technical field in Uzbek language. The book having 7000 more copies became quite common among the students. Now it's time to think about the second edition as it turned into a rare book in the library.

In 1979-1980 I went to Yugoslavia with my wife and to the Budapest technical university, in Budapest alone in order to learn a higher educational system.

1981-1982 were really effective years for me, and I published a monograph, a manual and a book. I finished the doctoral dissertation and showed it to the head of the

Moscow automobile and Road university and professor V.Lukanin agreed to serve as an opponent. My student M.Orifjonov defended the dissertation for the degree of candidate of sciences.

I submitted my doctoral dissertation on November 26 1984 in the Leningrad agricultural university. The challenges I faced up to that day is like a big novel to tell about. Unfortunately although there are wide opportunities for doctoral research nowadays, some scientists don't know how to take advantage of it. A bit later the first president of the TARU, Mutalibov was forced to resign after he served for thirteen years. Some people with malice tried to find reasons for it. One day the Minister of the higher education S.Pulatov invited me for a conversation. He said that he would support promoting me to the position of a new president for the university and they even planned to have several conversations with me.

But later everything changed. The higher education Minister S.Pulatov resigned and became the president of the university.

At this time different positions were offered to me a lot. I didn't accept any of them because I knew that it was required to spend sleepless hours at night in order to achieve goals.

I had been working in the Automobile roads university since the beginning of 1969. There were in total 4 departments in the faculty, and our dean was the man with who I shared the same room.

Not long after that I realized that there were two test benches in our department which had been bought from Germany. They hadn't been used for six years, you see and were gathering dust in the store. The Controlling agency criticized the university for that several times, as they are really rare for a university. But there weren't any good scientist to use them effectively and unfortunately, O.U.Salimov served a lot to bring those stands to our university.

When I was in Russia, I experimented with this type of machine for four years. We needed some space in order to use those instruments, so I decided to take the initiative to create the necessary conditions with my students and partners at the university. My friends Slavik and Abdugani helped us with this a lot. When one of them helped buy some concrete and cement, the another helped with slates, and some others for tubes.

The laboratory rooms were being prepared, and inside the rooms we installed two sorts of instruments, and two rooms for laboratory were at last made ready. To do this, we had to rebuild one side of the room as a window.

One day we got an announcement urging all the teachers to take part in a meeting where the dean Salimov would also take part. There were several people who contributed to building those laboratory rooms . I was wondering what we would discuss, and the dean then told everyone what I was doing for the faculty. When my opponents were allowed to speak, they started telling lies about me, with five of them saying that I was not giving permission to anyone to train in the laboratory. I was alone. I stood up and said: "Those who are saying that I didn't allow them to use the laboratory are all lying to you. I didn't object to anyone else, and I will really be glad if someone uses these conditions to learn something. You're all welcome to this laboratory!" All of them were silent.

Mr Salimov then suggested putting forth further forward issues to be solved and tasks to be accomplished. He said: "let's go downstairs and see what Sarvar has done!" Seeing all the tools and laboratory conditions, he was really glad as these results we achieved within six months without any assistance and done alone.

He said: "Sarvar, you can go on with all these tasks, and thank you a lot!". He then left without saying goodbye to the rest. Now we had a great opportunity in the new laboratory and I invited young specialists from the aviation production department. I also had electric tools repaired there. We started working with the test bench bringing some necessary equipment, helping to preserve temperature at the same degree, which we brought from MARU, and it enabled it to cool and heat at the same time. Some of the students defended their dissertations using all this equipment. I also carried out the main part of my doctoral research by using these instruments and tools. Those who told lies about me during the meeting, and about the laboratory, didn't even try to visit this room.

The worst feeling a human can have is envy, which harms not only the envious man, but also those around him. Envy is like a weapon hurting the souls of all the people.

My mistake

In the 70s I made a big mistake as I was immature, young, and at that time I thought that entering and studying at a university is all based on justice. Moreover, I had been in Moscow for 5 years, not knowing what was happening in my own hometown. In the beginning of the 1970 s the first assistant of the higher education Minister and O.U.Salimov invited all the teachers to a meeting and they criticized the teachers for their wrong attitude towards the students. It was because 35 students complained about them all. I was appointed as a responsible teacher for the course "Engines". It was a tradition for me to complete any and every task on time. I examined 11 students because according to a special decree, none of the teachers could assess the students for course work and projects. The assessments of just 11 students were accepted and recorded in the archives, but the rest didn't even try to pass exams. However, it became clear that 85 students were all assessed and submitted all the course and project work on time. This means they did this illegally in cooperation with teachers because I didn't see them passing exams. So they could have paid money for being assessed by some other teachers, because I've never got money from any of them , I wouldn't even do it. I was just 30 years old, and couldn't stand this unfair. I required in depth control over all these assessments as a result of which I made enough enemies for myself. I sent letters to home addresses of the students who didn't even take part in exams, but who had already got their marks. I required justice here, required the teachers working illegally to be punished. For being so naïve and fair I kept being punished for the rest of my life working under the eternal pressure because of having so many enemies among my own "less than honest" colleagues. I worked like this for 15 years…. for 15 years.

Teachers are my dearest

Well-educated men are always nice to talk to, and one relishes conversations with them, because they always infuse you eternally with their wealth of knowledge. They need to be honest, self-conscious and gentle at the same time.

I would first of all mention my own teachers as worthy of being called well-educated. Every man starts being educated by a mother since birth, as she feeds him with milk, and sings a lullabies to him all night long. Therefore I know my own mother Tashpulatova Hojia as my first teacher in my life. I couldn't get support from my father, as he died in the world war in one of the villages in Moldavia.

The main education I got at school for at least ten years, was the first teacher who taught me the alphabet, how to read, and write, was Giyoskori Musayev who I can never forget at all. The people who later taught me at school were Mr Kuchkor, Mr Yusuf, Mr Hamidulla, Mr Latif, Mrs Vera, Mrs Bella, Mrs Farida and many others. Almost all of them have unfortunately already died .

I continued my education at the university for five more years and I remember all the teachers who taught me and helped me a lot. O.U.Salimov (materials of auto exploitation), Nigmatilla Tursunov (Opposition of materials), Tukhtahonov (history), A.Musalov (theoretical mechanics) and many others.

When I was a Ph.D student my teacher Sergei Yevdokimovich led me to new routes of science, I could open the first of them and became a candidate of sciences. I became a teacher by myself, teaching the subject "Internal combustion engines and their construction, dynamics and theory"., and I had several researches on my doctoral theme.

R.Dobrogayev, who served effectively for science development in Russia was a very strict man, and at the same time, a hard working teacher for me, I was privileged to celebrate his seventieth birthday anniversary with him in Russia.

For example when we studied in Moscow, our dear teacher Okil Salimov often came to visit us. Seeing how hard we worked, it was often suggested that we stay there for huge salaries, but we'd decided to contribute to the development of our own motherland.

One of my teachers Voinov scolded me because I joined the political party, saying that I was not needed there so much, I was actually needed in technical science.

In 1971 I started translating the book "Automobile engines" written by Maslov into Uzbek.

I translated the book which consisted of 480 pages, from Russian into Uzbek. But the director of the publishing house rejected the book saying that he didn't need the book translated because they had their own translators. So I didn't even know what to do.

I was working with scientific research on the basis of a house holding contract. While traveling to Moscow, I told my teacher Hovach everything which had happened with the translation . He asked me to connect him to Okil Salimov as they were very close friends. He helped me to solve this problem, and the book was now to be published.

In the 1970s it was almost possible to publish books in technical science for Uzbek scientists. Uzbek scientists could only write books about silk, cotton, agriculture and etc. The Russian government didn't allow us to write books in the technical field, maybe because they were thinking that we weren't able to work in the technical science.

In 1977 the first book in technical science in Uzbek language was at last delivered to Uzbek students.

Okil Umurzakovich Salimov had always fought against the wrong assessment of students. He had many students years ago, and even now, although he is retired and old, he doesn't take pity for his time for sharing his views and giving his golden advice to us.

Scientific problem was at long last found

An important scientific problem in Central Asia was put forward when in 1971 the main constructor of the Oltoi engines factory approached me with a special request. The purpose was to scientifically prove why the pumps of a diesel engine were having disorder in so short a time. I thought about it for a short time and then I agreed. In our university for the first time we signed a house holding contract with a cost of 10 000 soums, which a year later I successfully completed the research. When we submitted all the reports to the Oltoi factory, they approved all the results. I had to rule on 2-3 contracts within two or three years.

When I was busy with my doctoral research at the university, I wasn't given any extra chances to work at it. I was forced to run 760 hours of lessons each year as well as being active in the cotton picking process. Some teachers didn't even run classes, and they had all the awards and all the ease. I thank them for at least not discouraging me with what I was doing, because they kept disturbing me all the time.

None of my colleagues had any idea about what I was busy with, and although they were aware I was doing something , they couldn't even interfere , as they didn't have the patience to work on research by themselves.

In 1981 I completed the first version of the dissertation "Heating engines", and after I submitted it to Lukanin, he approved all of the final results. However, it took me six months to have it examined by my own department teachers, who tried to find different reasons to not confirm my dissertation. At long last they organized a meeting between nine departments and they started discussing the results.

When my teacher Dobrogayev looked through my dissertation, he objected to submitting it for approval as he thought that the first part lacked theoretical information, and besides that, I had taken the wrong approach to differential equations. This research took me a long time and hard work in order to complete.

Loss and happiness

When I came back to Tashkent I showed the certificate confirming the fact that the dissertation had excellent organization and the results were positive. But in September in a letter posted by the president of the MARU7[7] it was written that the dissertation had been assessed negatively. This letter didn't contain any figures or dates. This was betrayal, or worse than betrayal, and ignorance of hard work, was obviously arranged by someone. I immediately consulted the proctor of our university and got my dissertation back after writing an application to Lukanin. After my teachers Hovach and Voinov died, I didn't even notice that the rest of the colleagues were really envious of my success in science. I didn't have important people or lots of money like those teachers, who could help me in when I was in such a difficult situation. Then I asked myself a question; , who needs the results of my dissertation? This was really vital for agricultural development, as it portrayed scientifically proven solutions to problems of prolonging effective activity of agricultural automobile engines. Just one or two paragraphs were devoted to MAZ automobiles. Then I decided to show this dissertation to other teachers and the prominent professors, Dobrogayev, Archangelskiy and Nikitin who certainly supported this idea. I went to Kiev to meet B.Draganov. He advised me to address the Leningrad Agriculture university, but there wasn't any council there relating to my direction. I did, and there I found out that there was a special council relating to

---

[7] 7 MARU. It is abbreviation of the Moscow Automobile and Roads university.

this direction. After I showed him the results, he said that it was absolutely what was needed and the secretary Shkrabak took it home to check.

They came to the conclusion that the dissertation really related to the council of the Leningrad Agriculture university, I left it for the council head, professor Nikolenko and his assistant Lofinov to check, and they promised to check it within a week. For a week all the scientists of engine science knew me quite well as I had twice headed the Soviet Council of those scientists in Tashkent. At the end of September, I got the conclusion from the council which showed exactly what to alter, and what changes to make in the dissertation. Then for the third time I did my best to rewrite the work. One-third part of the work had been altered, and in December I took my research to the rector of the Leningrad agriculture university. I didn't spend a penny of the university's money for all the expenses I had for traveling, living abroad etc. I spent the money I earned from the results of house holding contracts I made on my own.

In January of 1984, after the research was looked through by the Soviet council, it was positively assessed and recommended for defense. In June the list of opponents was confirmed. In 1984 on November 26 I had my main defense. It lasted for six hours, and was discussed inside out and the talks were really vital. Academician Kryajkov, professor Burkov, professor Lebedev took the main part in the talks as members of the council, and after a six hour-talk, I secured the victory. Everything was in my favour, at 13:00. This was one of the happiest days of my life.

When there were ten days left for the dissertation defense I flew from Tashkent to Moscow. I had a partner, a colleague from the university, Mirzamurod. When there was just one day left, my brother Marvar, Ph.student Shuhrat and my wife arrived. I didn't even see both of my opponents until the day of defense. Once I talked to them on the phone. They were professors Ivanchenko Nikolai and Boris Ulitovskiy. They said they had positive opinions, therefore we met on the day of my defense. On November 19 the council head gave me all the notes and main opinions of the opponents so that I could be prepared for the questions and answers. When I asked permission to talk to one of the members of the council ,he said that it was banned until the day appointed for the talk. I just wanted to know what Mishin thought about my dissertation as his opinion had a great role in everything. I was worried as I saw how he had negatively assessed a doctoral dissertation of one man in June.

In order to pass the exams, and get positive assessment, it was necessary to get well acquainted with the members of the council. I remember going up to Bagdasarov on November 19, He said that I was late. According to what he said I had to treat the members with gifts, presents and … In response to him I said "But the scientists in Leningrad don't want anything from us, they have enough salary in their own."

The defense started on time. The illustrations on the walls were worth millions. I discussed the main issues for thirty minutes, and the defense lasted for five hours. Professor Mishin asked me 21 questions, and he criticized me as well. He focused on the main formula and said that the calculations weren't matching the results and units of measures. I politely proved that he was mistaken. He said that I was too talkative. At the end everyone approved the results of dissertation. The most interesting point was that Mishin was the first to vote in my favour and he left the room first after congratulating me with good wishes. He was eighty two at that time, and he showed his courage to everyone sitting there.

After that meeting was over, we had a small party with all of my close people, my best friend, Normuhamedov, Dobrogayev, Bagirov, Marvar, Mirzamurod, Shuhrat and my wife. None of the opponents and council members were invited to that party.

Marvar took my dissertation and left it in Moscow, in the Soviet scientific and technical information university which was as the rule.

We prepared all the documents for commission, and there wasn't a charge for the exhibitional materials. We wanted to go back to Tashkent. I had to come with Shuhrat, Mirzamurod. tut there weren't any ticket left for either the trains nor the planes, so we had to stay in a hotel, then visited Ivanchenko to say goodbye.

Mirzamurod suggested we travel by train without a ticket, which meant illegally, paying some money to the conductor.

Besides buying the tickets for the plane, have you ever heard about a doctor of sciences who traveled by train without a ticket like thieves! We left the hotel for the railway station thinking that we could get a ticket. Mirzamurod talked to the conductor of the last coach and we got some seats there at last. Suddenly a controller went inside the coach where I slept, and I felt scared to death not because I didn't have the ticket, but because it could've put me to shame, so I pretended to be sleeping while he talked to the conductor instead of me. In the early morning we arrived in Moscow and stayed in my friend Bagirov's home, then after we flew to Tashkent.

I am grateful to all the scientists in Leningrad for the way they fairly assess in favour of society. There's a strange tradition among the scientists in Moscow, which is they tend to require money from everyone. This results in the failure of development, as real scientists will not succeed in this case, and this allows only the rich scholars to get positive assessments.

After the dissertation was submitted to the black opponent, there were two letters without a surname in the Dissertation commission. This was written by scientists of the "Autotractor engines" department, and was certainly arranged.

All the analysis cited in that letter absolutely contradicted that written in the third real version of my dissertation. I was happy to know that my "true friends" had never seen the final version of my dissertation.

Those sorts of letters were again sent to Leningrad to my astonishment. They required me to explain everything in detail. The dissertation was examined once more by those three professors and they at last concluded in 1985 in July that the dissertation was worth a positive assessment. In 1985, on September 19, I was invited to discuss of my dissertation. All the members of the council voted in favour of my dissertation in a meeting which lasted for 45 minutes.

In 1985, November 28-30 we were going to hold the Soviet council. I was the head there. In 1985 on November 29 presidium of Supreme Certification Commission (SCC) was going to be held. Usually one in a thousand dissertations could be rejected by this organization, and unluckily and unfortunately it was me . This wasn't a coincidence at all. This was all arranged in advance because my "true friends" weren't strong enough to delude the council in Leningrad. The reason they rejected my work was they proposed the dissertation be examined by the council of power engineering. In this council there was a friend of my "true friends" Pokrovskiy. My "true friend" tried to delude the professor Murashov many times and the assistant of the department head Sh.Soliyev, but he wasn't successful at all and because he couldn't cope with all of this he took advantage of Pokrovskiy, who unfortunately didn't understand my sphere at all. The dissertation in consequence was submitted to another doctor of sciences, and although he understood the research well, he failed to analyze the theoretical part of it.

In general, the dissertation had to be written up in the field of heating engines, but there wasn't enough theory for that theme. This conclusion was submitted to the council of agriculture.

Finally they invited m e to the meeting of experts in 1986 on April 24 for the second time at the SCC office. I hoped they would discuss the dissertation fairly, but I was wrong. Pokrovskiy was 15 minutes late for the council. The head of the power engineering dropped him in his own car. For the second time they attacked me with lots of questions. There had to be a specialist in this field, and they just murmured saying that only Kragelskiy and Mutalibov worked in this field. Here they all followed one saying by the Greek theorist of illegal acts Media: "If you want to attack someone with words, don't be afraid, in any case there will be some scars left on the skin no matter how much you bite him."

I completely answered all of their questions. It is right that the theory of detail erosion was created by Kragelskiy, but his theories aren't suitable for the regional conditions of Central Asia. Mutalibov investigated the possibility of using gas condensations as a fuel.However, he didn't indicate the methods of predicting rates of engine and fuel apparatus. I created a new theory. They let me out for fifteen minutes and invited me back. They said: "We made a negative conclusion about your dissertation". I was indeed taken aback.

"What's the reason?" I asked. "We came to this conclusion. "

"Can I talk to SCC administration face to face?" "You aren't allowed to"

"Excuse me, but I have citizenship rights, and besides, I am the member of the political party. If you like, I will defend the dissertation in presence of the strongest specialists in the Political party".

"You can do whatever you want."

I went to the department of agriculture, I told the specialist what happened and asked where I could talk to the head of the SCC. He advised me first of all to meet the assistant of SCC, Ermakov. I was asked to wait for a bit in the secretary's room. After that I explained what happened to Ermakov. He asked me to write an application and sent it to the head of the department Shapavalov. At this time the meeting of the council was over and the head was still in his own office. He also took part in the council with the decisive vote. I asked him: "what's wrong?The last time I was positively assessed, but now they rejected my dissertation".

He said: "It is Pokrovskiy who did all of this. He negatively assessed your dissertation on behalf of the whole council. As half of our council have recently been elected, they didn't even dare to mind it".

I asked him again bravely: "Could you please repeat what you've just said in front of Ermakov ?"

"Of course" he said.

He repeated everything frankly to Ermakov. Ermakov ordered him to reject the decree of objection to my dissertation and allowed me to leave. I calmed down for a bit and returned to Tashkent.

I wrote a seven page letter to the controlling agency of the SCC administration, and in the last days of September of 1986 I received a letter from SCC. According to the letter, the dissertation was forwarded to Cheliabinsk for an additional conclusion. Unfortunately there wasn't a council examining doctoral researches there, and I had to wait for it until December again. After the council was organized, the opponent for my dissertation was V.I.Vinogradov. I phoned that professor. He promised to look through my dissertation until January 10 and invited me to a meet with him, for a talk about the main issues. I met with him and he seemingly didn't have any positive ideas about the results and theoretical part. We started debating, and the more we debated, the more he changed. I practically confirmed every disagreement I had, and at last he said Bravo. This man was one of the most famous scientists in the history of the world. He finally said : "Sarvar, now I am ready to defend your dissertation not only in front of the SCC or the council, but also in front of God, I had the same oppositions previously when I was young."

The repeated defense of my research was appointed on February 12, in 1987.I turned 47 on the 11 th of February the same year. The defense was appointed in Cheliabinsk. Three doctors of sciences from the Technical university were included in the list of the council members with permission from the SCC. My defense lasted for 5 hours, I got 14 positive and 2 negative votes. Those negative belonged to friends of Pokrovskiy (my "true friend's" friend) According to the rule, 50 % votes in my favour were enough for me. My opponents and my teachers who were always supporting me there, and I was really happy to feel their support.

 March 27, 1987 (the day when my teacher Dobrogayev was born) I was awarded the scientific degree "doctor of sciences" by the SCC of the USSR. This award didn't bring the happiness I expected. My "true friend" forgot to congratulate me, and instead he offered to have a drink. The heads of the university didn't even want to inform the others about this news. If other young specialists who wanted to carry out doctoral research in our university started to believe in justice thought that I wasn't able to defend because of an unfair administration, they wouldn't even bother themselves with that. "Some colleagues wanted to kill me even, causing me stress and a stroke afterwards. But they couldn't. This struggle for a peak of science and pursuing justice requires lots of courage and hard work. It's compulsory that the work should be done out of the heart and it must certainly meet standards, and serve for the state's development".

Thoughts about the USSR SCC

The SCC scientific council had no importance at all. The dissertation could have possibly gone in vain if the council was unfair. Even though the opponent is honest, he may be deluded any time for money. In that case the whole work, and hard work, under pressure would go in vain and the author would accidentally die because of stroke or a heart attack. I know many scientists who died two or three days after their dissertation was confirmed. This is the real face of the former SCC.

The pursuit of a scientific degree is full of challenges, hardships and obstacles. Until I reached my current reputation, the many obstacles I had caused me to suffer a lot. I didn't change my mind at all, I'd made it up already, and I guessed that there wasn't any brave man in this world. As French scientist Jan Fabr said : "the man who has had many challenges in life is the happiest ever".

"Mrs doctor! I have grey hair, and the pains in my heart are the wealth I gained during my entire life. Anyway, I secured a victory in overcoming the difficulties in life. The difficult days I had when I was busy with doctoral my research are really precious to me, and it wasn't easy at all for me to be patient with all of them.

It isn't so simple to secure a victory, We will gain it after hundreds of battles

Having much bloodshed and hard work,

We will welcome this happiness after that into our hearts.

I am thinking:

After my dissertation was defended, it was forwarded to the council of experts. I often wondered why the man who carried out doctoral research with so much effort have to encounter across so many difficulties? I didn't know. If a dissertation is supported once and confirmed successfully, the candidate needs to be awarded with the diploma, or otherwise, there won't be any development in science. But the opponents had to be kept secret until the day of defense. They also have to take part in voting. If the amount of votes is enough, the candidate needs to be handed a diploma. For this a summary should be necessary and the research should to be submitted to the SCC. The rest of the research needs to be examined by the secretary. The secretary needs to be under strict control while the research is examined. He needs to be re-elected every year, I mean, annually. The doctoral candidate's opponents need to be scientists and they must be honest.

I mean only the research should bring benefits for the government and needs need to be confirmed. It isn't easy to be a doctor of sciences, and it requires fighting against obstacles and envious people. My enemies prompted me to find further innovational approaches in science. If I hadn't had those enemies, I wouldn't have had so many victories. The famous writer Togay Murod said : "I wish my enemies would live a longer life, because they are the only ones to urge me to succeed!" I carried out different research non-stop. I completed two manuals in Uzbek and in Russian, and one book and two monographs. My hard work didn't go in vain. They were immediately published and delivered to my readers. I wasn't angry at all during this time. I knew that after some time of challenges I would certainly achieve what I wished to have. At this time my teachers Dobrogayev, S.E.Nikitin, the administration of the science council Iofinov, Nikolenko, and my opponent Lebedev were always by me with support.

My working activity in the Uzbekistan SCC experts council.

I contributed considerably to awarding people with scientific degrees and awards as an expert from 1991 to 1995. I have always tried to support real scientists. I could also distinguish reality from lies. I was against the people who wanted to get scientific degrees illegally by means of money.

I remember how the president of the Tashkent textile and light industry, Alimova H.A. was defending her doctoral research. There were 13 doctors of sciences on the council of experts. She couldn't respond to some questions about the theoretical part, and seven or eight experts expressed their opinions, which were almost all negative. I kept silent, but I couldn't stand this unfairness.

The proctor of this university was also taking part in the council, but he couldn't do anything as it was the president of the same university to be examined. I was looking around, and there was no one else to comment. Then I asked a permission to express my opinion. I picked up the list of the requirements for the candidate of doctoral degree, and the requirements were officially set by the SCC. It was written: "If the candidate created at least one new technology, he deserves to be awarded with the doctoral degree". That woman candidate had created four sorts of new technology using residues of cocoon. I mentioned these as advantages and in addition said that she was a bit weak in theory. That meant she deserved being awarded with the doctoral degree of technical sciences. The voting results were 7:6 in favour of the candidate. It was fair, the candidate secured a victory, and she was the unique female president at the University in history of Uzbekistan.

One more event, we were listening to dissertation overview of the doctoral dissertation by the director of one famous company. It was obvious that someone else wrote that dissertation for him. He didn't take part in the experiments personally. In short it was the research carried out by someone else for money. Some members of the council were even supporting the research, again I stood up for a speech and said everything I thought about the results. The results of votes were negative, the director didn't deserve being awarded, the results were in favour of justice: 3:10.

Science and scientific achievements should have just pure background, illegal acts and money mustn't interfere it at all. I know hundreds of doctors of sciences who have never prepared candidates or doctors of sciences, the government doesn't benefit from them at all.

My teacher Dobrogayev

Rostislav Pavlovich Dobrogayev moved in Tashkent in the world war during 1943. He graduated from the Kiev Polytehnical university with a diploma with honours and left to fight in the war. After the war he was sent to Bronetank academy to teach young officers there. Until 1970 he worked in that academy as a colonel, doctor of technical sciences, professor, head of the department after that he was appointed as the head for the department "Engines of automobiles and tractors". He was born in 1917, between 1971 and 1985 he contributed a lot to raising reputation of the Tashkent State automobile roads university. He delivered lectures on the construction of internal combustion engines. He wrote thousands of articles and annotations to all the scientific researches which the students requested . His wife Galina Mihaylovna and his son Pavlik had lived for many years in a flat measuring just 6 and 8 м2. Now his son Pavlik is a candidate of sciences, married, and has a daughter. All of their attempts about buying a new flat were in vain all the time. It's unfair that a prominent scientist of technical sciences in Russia, a warrior in the world war, and professor, was living in a flat measuring 14 м2 But this man had never complained about his life, and the walls of his flat were decorated with the butterfly exhibitions collected from different parts of the world. He was a man in favour, and whoever talked to him just once, would certainly want to meet again.

Our families have always had close relationships, and he looks upon me as if I were his own son. I could hardly remember my own father, therefore I treated him like my own father. Thanks to God, he pushed 70 this year. I wish we could meet each other many more years . Everytime we meet, with every glass he raises, he makes a wish for Uzbek nationality. This man was the shoulder I could cry on, and he showed me the right way, whenever I was in a trouble. He had worked as an expert in the Soviet SCC for more than 10 years, being aware of all the people, and illegal acts relating to research and their assessment. He had always said that research I was carrying out could absolutely meet the SCC's requirements . We did our best to fight for justice to get the proper assessment of research, and we secured a victory. This is what we say "The dreams that came true".

A year after I was awarded with the doctoral degree, I was privileged to be admitted as a professor. Thanks to God. I was admitted as a prominent scientist throughout the whole   Soviet Union. This all happened in March of 1988 . This year I had the book "Internal combustion engines" published.

Longing for newer victories

In February of 1986 I was suggested to work for the department "Producing and repairing automobiles".This showed a lot of great trust for me by the new rector. The working environment was really awful in this department and was being criticized in every council of the university administration. I accepted this proposal.

My acceptance was first because this sphere was closer to my doctoral dissertation, and secondly I wanted to prove to my colleagues that I could succeed in management. The department staff made this suggestion , and the university president accepted this with pleasure. Until that day, for fifteen years, I had never been trusted by anyone else like that. I could only take an active part in the political party's activities.

Later on, during the period of reconstructions, the struggles against protectionism reached its peak everywhere. In order to fight against protectionism , it was required to get rid of the teachers with immoral behavior, or those who were bribed by students. It was important to identify the teacher's level of knowledge by organizing a special commission. Today, the students are asked to answer anonymous questionnaires where they freely express their opinions about teachers fairly, and they will be assessed fairly. Sometimes these measures are called "That's what the students think about the teachers". Their opinions will be assessed with scores from 3 to 9. The teacher who gained the least scores won't be punished or given the sack. Nothing will be changed, and all the teachers will be employed again by the university. Only in the USA will teachers who gain the less scores be invited for a meeting with university president, in which the rector will warn him about being fired the next year. And you? In our university it's impossible to be rude to even an ordinary secretary. Most people are afraid of them saying that they have a big shot to rely on if something goes wrong in the workplace. I wish at least one student could be assessed by taking into account his abilities and hard work! The only thing which is important in this regard is the family background, social status and so on.

For six years I've worked in the new department as the head, and was awarded with the best professor award. During this period our department got the first rank in terms of scientific achievements among the rest of the university departments. This happened three times. The lesson process was reorganized for our specialty. We established a new academic and scientific organization so-called "Auto repair specialist" in the first auto repair factory. We ran all the classes and training in the same tune with the activity in the factory. All the graduation projects started being carried out on the basis of the orders we got from the factories. The most important thing was that we did all of this on the basis of a house holding contract and the tools, and instruments we created were to be utilized during the working process of the factory. Our students involved in all of this have developed their skills as an engineer. While being busy with technological practice, they thoroughly learned the technology of repairing engines. In the fifth course, throughout the first term (11 or 12 weeks) they worked as a substitute engineer. This was an essential factor to nurture talented engineers in our department.

This wasn't all that easy for us. But anyway, despite all the encumbrances we had to fight against them, otherwise it was impossible to restore the time lost. No matter what position the scientist has, he needs to constantly train,and pursue higher peaks in his/her career. Therefore I never complained about the difficulties I faced, because the success gained through hardships seems to make you indeed relish your hard work.

Through the last years I prepared six Ph.D. students who are these days working as docents in different departments and have their own reputation. They are all preparing their further doctoral research.

The more contrasting views there are against me, the more success I will have throughout my life... this rule has become really efficient in my life. I have plenty of proof that the truth of this rule hides in itself. The encumbrances of people around me have prompted me to succeed even more in my life: The Doctoral dissertation, being found as a worthy candidate for the award "the Prodigy of science serving effectively in Uzbekistan" and many others have made me believe that God always helps those who keep working hard and do their best to pursue happiness.

In 1987 different candidates started offering themselves to be certified with different awards. Being one of the members of the exam commission in these events I felt quite shy as most of the candidate weren't deserving any of the awards at all. Our dean Mr Galob noticed that I didn't quite like all of this. Suddenly he asked me why I wasn't submitting my own documents for the award. I told him that it was within his remits to do this and he immediately ordered me to prepare all the documents needed. At that time he also added"The books for teaching our specialty in Uzbek are the first manuals in Uzbek in this field, and many young people have been effectively using them all. Besides, you've been working as a teacher for over 25 years, and you're a doctor of sciences. You deserve being recommended and to be awarded, Sarvar!"

All the documents were made ready, and the whole faculty staff consisting of forty people supported the idea of suggesting me as a candidate to be certified with the award: "the prominent scientist considerably contributed to Uzbekistan development". As many prominent scientists gathered, all in our faculty, they all confirmed this idea in the council held in September. One more professor O.Murashov was also suggested along with me. To continue the process, a special application was filled in and was signed by the faculty council, and it was forwarded to the Higher Education Ministry. The ministry also confirmed it , immediately signed in it, and after it was confirmed by the city Party council, was now forwarded to the Province special Council. I was feeling awkward and wondered if my published books deserved special attention or if they were all useless.

A year passed after that but there weren't any results, neither positive, nor negative. I had a friend, Mirahmad who worked as a secretary in the Tashkent provincial council. He knew that I was also among the candidates recommended,   but he was afraid to sign, and therefore he didn't. All the documents were sent back, delivered to the Tashkent city council, afterwards all the terms of awarding the candidate changed a little bit. Two professors were recommended to be awarded, one of them was me, and the second, my colleague. He always claimed: "It is hardly possible to get this award, and honestly, we'd better find another way of winning the game", He said this to me every single day, but I insisted that I could at least get a letter of rejection in case I was found not suitable for the award. It defied logic that I could be rejected, and If one compared what I did with those who had already been awarded, mine deserved even more significant awards at that time. That friend of mine had never written a book and I was forced to wait for a long time; I'm still waiting.

To tell the truth, all these awards should actually be given fairly, to honest people and their efforts without any greed, or thought of wealth, and without fear of those who are dishonest. These two sorts of people have always been fighting against each other. "It's probably possible to chase honest people, but it's impossible to ruin their real reputation. If one stops being honest, he will be accustomed to bad and illegal deeds, and furthermore, he will be entirely accustomed to leading an illegal way of life." (N.G.Chernishevskiy). May God save us from this happening.

"Now, dear doctor, you're asking why my hair turned grey so early. Is it possible to look young after so many unfair things have happened? Don't they cause a man to feel sick, and to be nervous all the time? God has many gifts and tests for us. It's a must for us all to be brave in the heart. I told you everything I faced during my life to now . First of all, I believe in God while waiting for a recovery. Then I can believe in doctors, as God is the unique one to decide who will survive, and who will not. Now I trust you, dear doctor, and I suffer from all the tortures I came across during my lifetime, non stop"

"Thanks, dear professor, thanks a lot, I got what needed. Besides, I enjoyed talking to you to tell the truth. Now I am really sure that you're going to recover soon."

Indeed, after that I got additional treatments for two more weeks and left the hospital safe and sound. I'll never forget the help I got from that doctor. Never! I will not forget it at all.

Famous in the Republic and then in the world (1989 – 1995)

Ask God whatever good you want, because you aren't going to ask him to give you something that belongs to another man, are you? Live in this world as if God is seeing all that you do, and pray for God as if all the people can hear what you ask him for.

Seneka I came across my doctor again one day in the hospital in 1996. She was now also a candidate of sciences. This is a great award (especially for women). I was being treated for preventive measures there. We kept talking quite frequently and we got quite close to each other like a brother and a sister, besides her surname was the same as mine, Mrs Kodirova. One of those days we again had some time for a friendly conversation . And I again I started telling her about myself, the stories showing all the hardships I faced during my life,

from 1989 to 1996.

"I'd better tell you what I faced during my life as you may also surely face them in your own life soon. This is going to be a good lesson to you. To be famous in the Republic you certainly need to pursue a doctoral degree in the future. If you want to be famous in the world, you should also become an academician not only in the universities of our Republic, but abroad as well. To become an honoured professor of universities, you also need to have your own academic manuals admitted as worthy in foreign countries, and have your articles published in many other countries. It's also good idea to have at least one international award.

However, to pursue a doctoral degree, figuratively speaking, you must be ready to walk barefoot on the hot sands of the deserts, and on the rocky tracks of the mountains . It means you need to withstand all the difficulties alone, with no support from others. Those who can, do cope with all this , and they will certainly reach the peak of success.

As you know I was appointed as the head for the "Automobile manufacture and repair department" with a special recommendation from the university president S.Pulatov. In the next three years, the department was the first to carry out successive scientific work in those years, and to take all this into account, I was privileged to get a free ticket and certificate to get experience in India. In the autumn of 1989, I bought another ticket for my wife and we traveled to the magically beautiful country, India. We enjoyed traveling there for fourteen days, and we got quite a lot of impressions from traveling. Perhaps I will tell about this later in detail.

Mrs Doctor, do you remember that I told you about being recommended for the award "The most Prominent scientist serving in Uzbekistan" in 1987, and I had to wait for more than two years to receive it.

It became clear that as the city council had no way of rejecting my documents, they confirmed the recommendation and forwarded it to the Supreme Council. My friend who was with me also found a way to solve this problem, I mean the "special ways" which honest people can not be aware of. Two years later on June 29, 1989, I was awarded with the " Most Prominent scientist serving in the USSR. Justice secured a victory at long last, and that day, I felt that I was the happiest in the world.

Within this time, one more nonsensical thing took place. There was a chance to get a car, a "Volga" in our university. The people who had that chance were first my teachers, A.A.Mutalibov, O.D.Murashov, then me. At that time, those who got the award I had recently had received, could be given the Volga without any waiting time. My partner didn't want to wait for his turn for the car, so he agreed to replace it with a "Jiguli 09".

As soon as he got it, he sold it for a much more expensive cost. This type of a car was really rare, and the "Volga" was almost the same. I gathered all the money I earned from the books I earned, and submitted it to the savings bank office waiting for my turn to get the "Volga".

That money, roughly 15 000 soums ,is still kept in the same bank office.

Usually each university was given one Volga each year, and even though I could get this without a turn, I waited for my teacher and friend to get it. At last, on October 16, my teacher got the car. I was really glad, and I was thinking that now I could try and get the car without any problems. We went to talk to the first secretary of the District Committee with my friend Muhsin Goziyev, (who was working as an Assistant of the Minister of the Automobile transport). The secretary welcomed us and treated us very friendly. As soon as I showed my document to him, he promised to give me the car immediately after he got a chance for it. I felt very satisfied and glad. However, it took a long time for the region to receive the cars, and moreover, the price of cars rose as high as four times in 1990. I didn't have 65 thousand soums , and I didn't want to owe money to someone because of my desire to have a car. Therefore I was unfortunately robbed of buying a car. Maybe I could have been much quicker to have my problems solved, as I had the chance to get a car, but I gave up first for my teacher, then for my friend, and at last I couldn't get what I wanted. In 1992, even my own Jiguli which was designed in 1997, and which I had driven for over fifteen years, was stolen by someone. Thanks to God that after that my students and old teachers helped to get an old car, hardly possible to use, which is in the repair store(car shop) every two days.

I got even more tasks to do the last days. These years (1987 and 1990) our department was the first to carry out scientific and academic research and activity. During this time we had two special manuals published, one of them was in Uzbek, and the other in Russian. Great scientific research started being carried out, and for this we had to establish four laboratories. Young scientists started working hard to get use of all the conditions created. All the scientific work and results gained in the department were implemented in the whole Republic.

At last, in1990, when I pushed fifty, I invited all of my relatives, friends from childhood, from the university, Ph.D studies, and all of my close friends, and we had a big party together.

I received the "Honoured automobile specialist" that day, and I didn't invite anyone I knew in the Ministry and university. What I needed was a team of real friends. That year was full of achievements for me. After many battles, 5000 copies of my book and manual on "Automobile and tractor engines", written in Russian, was at last handed to readers . What makes me happiest to know is that 15 countries in Asia bought this book at 20 copies each. It was even approved in Russia. I know that not everyone is privileged with this happiness, and it meant I had become a world wide famous scientist.   On December 19, 1991, I was appointed as a correspondent member for the Uzbekistan Agricultural sciences academy, and at the end of the year I had my own book "Harsh rules of becoming a scientist" published. Everyday in my department was very hectic. It gained a reputation in the whole world, and it was obvious who had enabled the department to establish an academic-scientific and manufacturing organization, and who initiated the ritual of the graduation projects on the basis of the order and requirements of the manufacturing enterprises.

Academy – academician...

I heard that there was a competition for the award of a correspondent member for the Uzbekistan Sciences Academy, "Mechanics" specialty. I submitted all the documents on behalf of the staff of the Automobile transport Ministry. I didn't want to be recommended by the scientific council of the university. The documents were accepted, and then I learned that all of them were examined in the Uzbekistan Science Academy Technics department, and that they'd decided that my doctoral research wasn't suitable for the direction "Technics". However the head of the department only had to inform me about the conclusion of the experts appointed for my research. It was easily seen how human rights were not enforced and defended in such a great university. One needed to have a lot of money or a close friend among the big shots in order to join the Academy as a member. When there's money, some academicians forget about human rights entirely. Let's analyze the members of the academy at that time. All the members were elderly people, and around seventy-aged

. When they started fighting for the award, the young specialists couldn't do anything. It's possible to see here how human rights were dismissed in this organization of higher education. It became clear that it was necessary to have a friend among the big shots or some money to join the Science Academy as an academician. When there's money, all the people in charge of the future of our country will fail to think about their own real commitments. If you try to analyze the age of the academicians in the Science Academy, everyone can notice that all of the members were old and they were all prominent people with good reputations. They didn't let young people become a member for the Academy at all, and it was because they all occupied all the vacancies there.

Wasn't it impossible to make them retire after they turned 70? If it was, there would appear more vacancies for young people . Why didn't they want to have a rest for the remainder of their lives? I thought that the only scientists who devoted their life to independence of our Republic should deserve being accepted as a member for the science academy. Unfortunately this was just a dream and unlikely to come true. If you look at this issue generally, it seemed to have fair exam system, which worthy candidates were actually winning ...

In 1991 after the USSR was fortunately terminated the , scientists started to open The Academy of the Uzbekistan Republic Agricultural sciences. They announced the opening of a competition for vacancies and appointments for this academy. So I thought that I could also take part in it. Taking this into account I decided to phone the head of the Tashkent university of Irrigation and Mechanisation of Agriculture (TUIMA) department, professor Sh.Yuldoshev. I asked him if the competition in terms of "Technology of constructions of agriculture machines" was declared for his specialty. I told him that if it was how I thought, I wouldn't submit my documents, and that I wouldn't apply because I didn't want to be an opponent to this man. However he said: "Oh, Sarvar, don't think about it at all, You can apply for this competition without a problem, and there's also a good chance for you to win."

I think you, my dear reader, wonder why I addressed this man ? It was because at that time, when there were many prominent scientists applying for a certain specialty, I, as an ordinary scientist, couldn't apply for the same competition. This would first seem strange to anyone around , and secondly I would waste my time bothering for documents. If these men applied, they would certainly win the competition anyway. Therefore, I again went up to my teacher Okil Salimov whose specialty was the same with that of mine and with that of Sh.Yuldoshev. Okil Salimov who was the rector of the TUIMA at that time. I asked him if he was applying for the same position, and he said no. However, I felt that he was in an awkward situation, so I changed my mind about applying for that position. Twenty days later after this happened, one of my friends informed me that one more professor had applied for the same position for which I wanted to apply. I made sure that I was right to change my mind as the third candidate for the two vacancies was something weird. Therefore I decided to apply for the Tashkent engine factory, and I submitted all of my published books and monographs . The administration welcomed me there quite friendly and I was recommended as a potential member of the academy in terms of my own specialty. Even though I worked in the Automobile Roads university, I didn't ask for a recommendation letter from my own institute's administration. I had my own reasons for doing that of course. Besides I was also recommended by the Uzagropromremont" scientific council, and I managed to submit all of the documents just at the time when the offices doors would close in three or four hours . Three candidates were competing for just one position. Some time later the surnames of the candidates were announced in the newspapers. There I saw that three candidates were competing for two positions. The forth candidate turned out to have changed his profile into another one as a correspondent member. All of my teachers and colleagues supported my efforts for that position claiming that I deserved it more than the others. They advised me to visit the Council to show and to discuss my own scientific research results, monographs and books there, and then it would be possible to be elected and to get most of the votes in the competition. I was pleased to hear this.

I first had to meet all of the members on the expert Council, and the head of that council, Academician Yuldosh Sadriddin Hujayevich was the first with whom I got introduced. But at that time I didn't know anyone who worked as the directors or scientists at the institutes. All of my scientific activity was devoted to automobiles of agricultural industry, and I had mainly worked with manufacturing and agricultural enterprises. I asked the professor Erkin Yuldoshevich (the Head Doctor in the first hospital) to go there with me. He studied with me in Moscow when I was busy with my Ph.D courses. He praised Sadriddin Yuldashev as a very honest and hardworking man. We visited their home together, but unfortunately he was out somewhere. We left all of my books and monographs and his wife promised to let him check all of them. Three or four days later I called him and went to see him once more. He met me with a smile he said: " I didn't know we have such a great scientist in Uzbekistan and I'm surprised! I approved of all your work and scientific achievements" I was high on clou nine, and I didn't expect my scientific work to be so highly assessed. Other scientists also recommended me to apply for the position after seeing all of my books and scientific achievements. I met the directors of all the scientific laboratory institutes and introduced them to my scientific research, and even though they seemed not to have welcomed me at the beginning, when I was going to leave they saw me off with a smile on their faces. Perhaps they were deeply impressed. I was glad.

My dear readers, I beg you not to think that I brought some presents to all of those people who I met and talked. I didn't have anything else to give them except my own books and monographs. All of those people who I met were each members in the Experts Council. If they voted in my favour during the council meeting, I would be privileged to become a member for that academy, and that's why I tried to have a talk with all of these expert members. Some of them frankly said that they would surely vote in my favour, some of them admitted my real efforts, but said that they didn't have any way to do this, as they themselves were dependent on someone else. At last the council of experts started. In A huge building,

on the second floor, all the candidates aiming for the position were waiting for their turn to be interviewed in the entrance. Okil Salimov was first, A.Hojiyev was second, Sh.Yuldoshev was third and I was the fourth candidate to go into the interview room. I went in with my folder in which I carried all of my books and monographs. After greeting all of the results of my scientific research, and seeing all what I had done, the head of the experts academician Sadriddin Hujayevich said: "You have ten minutes. What problems could you solve for Uzbekistan, what did you do for the higher education development, what other problems do you want to tackle in the future? Can you tell us about it in brief?" I responded to all the questions within the time given, we had a short debate consisting of questions and answers, and I answered all of their questions. I was then allowed to leave the room.

My advisor in all of these efforts and achievements was an academician Oleg Vlamirovich Lebedev. When I applied for that competition, some experts were going to force me to withdraw my application, but Lebedev urged me to fight until the end. I didn't withdraw my application, and I decided to wait too see what would happen. I was told that one day at a wedding Mr Erkin came with Usmonov Saidmahmud and that man said to him: "Please, could tell Sarvar to visit me tomorrow?" He seemingly knew about our friendship with Mr Erkin. Mr Erkin had his own reputation among the directors as he headed the first hospital in the city. He was absolutely a loyal scientist.

When I went to see him the next day, Usmonov Saidmahmud welcomed me really friendly and said:

"I wish you wouldn't make it hard to work for us. If you could please change your mind about applying for this competition, and if you do what we want, we'll announce an opening in one more competitions in six months , and then you can apply again. If you insist on keeping your choice, I suggest you to talk to Mr Okil Salimov." I left his room and rang Okil Salimov while going to the institute.

He said: "You'd better think it over for a bit, and we'll talk a bit later on the phone."

I was a member in the Central Asian university of Mechanisation and Electrification (CAUME) special Council and I could be present in some defenses there. After the names and surnames of candidates were announced in the newspapers, one scientist laughed at me and teased saying:

"You're barking up the wrong tree, Kodirov. The wrong tree. You will never get this position. You don't have enough power in your hands for that."

I can't remember exactly, but I think it was December 18, when me and O.Lebedev were driving to Yangiyul district in the Tashkent province. We were both thinking about what to do against all of these obstacles and what finally came to our minds was the following application:

To whom it may concern:

President of the Union Academy of Agriculture of Sciences Central Asian branch

A. Imomaliyev

From the candidate recommended for the position as an academician S.Kodirov

APPLICATION

As the number of vacancies for the position of an academician in this specialty is limited, I ask you to recommend me for the nomination for an academician to the nomination of a correspondent member. The Expert Council members have positively assessed the results of my activity.

December 18 . 1991 (signature).

After I typed this letter on the typewriter, I phoned Okil Salimov. It was when I read my application to him twice in a loud voice that he approved of what I was doing. I went to talk to the Vice-President to show the application. As soon as he read it, he became happy and asked me to follow him until we got to the room where the President A.Imomaliyev was sitting on the first floor. Blood rushed to their faces out of happiness to see that I was giving up. They promised to do their utmost the next day in the council of experts. It was the next day when the meeting was to be held, and the first academicians were to be elected, then correspondent members. On December 19, I had gone to work very early, and maybe that's why I nodded off as soon as I got home. When I was fast asleep I suddenly heard my telephone ringing. It was Omon Hamrokulov from my institute. He said:"You're wanted in the academy, you need to go there as soon as possible". I quickly got dressed up and immediately went to the academy. I was standing there not knowing what to do, when a man came out and asked :

"Are you Kodirov? You must immediately come in. We've just finished voting, and now you're all going to hear the results."

When I went inside I learned that all the academicians had already been elected. I immediately went up to Okil Salimov, Nosir, Sh.Yuldashev, A.Sadriddinov, R.Matchonov, and congratulated them sincerely for their success. Mr Nosir made me take a seat, saying that I was registered on an additional list.

At last academician Mahmud Mirzayev declared all those who were chosen. It was high time to announce the votes I had in my own favour. The result was : "supported by 23 experts, not supported by 3 experts". There was a tumultuous sound of applauses. So I was finally elected as a correspondent member for the Uzbekistan agricultural sciences Academy, the specialty

: Technology of agricultural automobile constructions. All of my true friends congratulated me there, but the other "strange friends" were silent. Even our university president forgot to congratulate me, as it was the first time that an academician was elected in the history of the TARU8[8].

I heard that there were a lot of disputes over electing me as a winner, but I was basically and firmly supported by the academicians Sh.Akmalkhanov and O.Salimov.

On that day the content of the Academy was elected again; all the members, President, Presidium members, vice-presidents were re-elected. The next day the list of the specialists elected for the academy were announced in the newspaper. There I saw my own surname. This was a great happiness for me. All the scientists in the Republic found me worthy of that and I wrote it down in my diary as an unforgettable moment.

Suddenly, a very famous scientist who'd laughed at me before that day rang me, and congratulated me. He said:

"Congratulations, I am absolutely stunned seeing that you overcame so many challenges!"

Let's try to remember what happened until I secured this victory. One day when one academician talked to one of my close friends, he said some things about me to him, and described me as a man who wasn't aware of how to get to the top illegally. Indeed I achieved everything with my own hard work and with lots of patience. However, that academician only helped those who could solve problems with money. Most of the scientists knew him like the back of their hands. Ok, it's his job to do what was necessary to survive, how to work and how to live. As our President said : "We need to assess scientist without taking into account how many big shots he has, but merely according to his knowledge."

Time and life were passing, and flying by. What had I done for the people living in my motherland, and what could I do for my motherland?

During the last years I had one more book published, "Engines of tractor and automobiles", and I wrote another dictionary of auto tractor terminology in Russian and in Uzbek with a co-author. It was allowed to be published as a book. I've been carrying out different scientific research funded by the government budget. I dedicated all of my scientific research to the most important problems of Uzbekistan science and

---

[8] TARU is an abbreviation of the Tashkent Automobile and Road university

technology as well as Uzbekistan agriculture. Even more work could be done, and it's a must to do all of them. For this there needs to be necessary conditions. I wish we could have them all soon. Life consists of fights and struggles, and without them life isn't interesting at all. Maybe if there hadn't been obstacles I couldn't have succeeded in my efforts. Probably yes. I could have lead my life running a profitable business or do something different from science. But if all the scientists start working in business or entrepreneurship, who will work to preserve the independence of the Republic?

After I was elected as a member of the Academy, I worked as the head of the department for three years and six months from 1991-1995. I translated my own book from Russian into Uzbek and had it published in 1992 at the publishing House Ukituvchi. 7000 copies were delivered. This was a unique book in Uzbek for higher education.

The department became famous all over the Republic succeeding in many scientific and academic achievements. All the work done and being done was regularly reported in the newspapers.

During the same years between 1991 and 1995 I served the high Attestation commission as an expert member of technical sciences. I contributed to provisions of justice in awarding the scientists of our Republic with doctoral and candidate degrees. I went on the same activity until I was appointed as the university president in the TARU.

Thieves of automobiles

Until I was appointed as the university president, I travelled and gained experience in many countries like India, Yugoslavia and Hungary. They have different customs and habits. There cars are usually stolen in the streets, but what about our country?

In 1977, the administration of the institute promised me to sell the car Jiguli 2103, while,at that time I was a secretary of the party. This car served us and came in handy until 1992, for over 15 years . I can assure you as an automobile specialist that our car was brand new, being driven just for 50 thousand kilometers of road.

In 1992 several doctors of sciences, me among them ,were invited to the Office of the President. We passed different testing and interview exams there which were conducted by the State Counsellor.

The aim of the exam was to choose the new prospective university president of the TARU. I think that the fair tests and interview were successful for me.

A week later, and after that exam my wife and I, docent Alo Kodirova came to work and I parked my car next to our rector's car. After the lessons were over, we again walked together and went where I parked our car.

My wife suddenly asked me: "Where on earth are you going?

" Where we parked the car, my dear! "But, where's the car?

I saw that the car wasn't there. I had a habit of handing my car keys to students and I thought I again might have given them to someone else. I groped in my pocket, and the key was in my pocket. That's very strange, isn't it? Again we went inside the institute where I phoned my student working in Tashkent city State Automobile Control administration (SACA), I explained to him what happened and asked him for help. I then phoned the big shots who I knew regulated these sorts of robberies. I was really sure that they could find my car soon.

We got in the tram and went home without any trouble in our hearts. That night one of the big shots phoned me to inform me that it wasn't their people who did this.

The head of the SACA also phoned me to say that all the signs and other properties of the car were forwarded to all the necessary places, and everything was under control.

On hearing this bad news one of my kind students ordered the director of the Taxi Parking area to give me a car to use. It was an old GAZ- 24, we had it repaired and somehow used it for some time.

I am always proud of having my own personality and character: I don't have any envious feelings, I am never envious of anything. I am never interested in wealth or the money earned for someone's hard work. I never try to talk to envious people, or to those who gossip. I am not optimistic to a high extent. I never feel depressed and try to be alert to everything. If by accident I lose something or have it broken, damaged or stolen, I just calm down saying : "That was what God just gave me for a while, now he took it away this time".

My intuition never lies to me, and it wasn't by accident that my car was stolen. The candidates to be appointed as rector were thought to have done this because nobody felt anything wrong about car robberies in the whole Tashkent city. It means everything was planned before it was accomplished. Even though I had a good reputation in the city, the car wasn't found anywhere.

I think all this happened more than three years ago. It was February 1995. At around 10 pm at night, somebody suddenly knocked on the door of our flat. After I opened it, I saw two men wearing police uniforms. They asked:

"Are you professor Kodirov? "

"Yes, is there something wrong?" "Has your car been stolen? "

"Yes, but that was three years ago"

They entered our home, and my wife treated them to some tea and sweets. We started talking about everything, and they made everything clear after several minutes of conversation. At that moment they asked me:

"Could you please now come with us to take a look at the car? We need to finish up with some documents."

My wife said:

" I am afraid it's a bit late. Can we please meet you tomorrow?"

"Ok, then we'll be waiting for you tomorrow at 9.00 am in the Tashkent city Internal Affairs Ministry office."

" All right"

The next day we went to the appointed place appointed, all the documents turned out to be prepared, they saw us in, but I went in to see the prosecutor alone. According to what he said, I wrote down all the signs of the car which I was aware of, and nobody except me. This is what I wrote :

"There was hardly a visible trace of the stone on the front window of the car, a hole measuring two millimeters on the upper part, and there was also a letter C on the edge of the engine block."

The Prosecutor took everything I'd written to the head and I was finally invited inside. I was welcomed by the colonel and he assured me that the car was mine. He permitted me to take the car, but the engine was at the office., and told me they'd examined our car according to what a very honest car repair specialist had said. The number of the car had all been removed, but when we examined it with a magnetic flaw detector, it became clear that the old number there belonged to your car. The engine also turned to be yours, and the rest of the things you'll learn from the prosecutor.

I thanked him and left the office. After that the prosecutor called me to his office, where he invited the young man who had bought the stolen car . The young man came, and he turned out to have graduated from the Tashkent State Technical institute. It became clear that he had bought that car for a very cheap price, and his friend who had sold it to him was studying at our institute, the automobile roads institute. He wanted to have the body painted. Taking the car to a car repair shop he left it for a very good Russian master to be fixed. There's a strict order: each master needs to check the car number and the engine number with the registration certificate. As a result of an examination, it can be clear if the car is stolen or not. This Russian master therefore informed the police.

The young man who brought that car to the repair shop was arrested, and the police officers took advantage of him to find the real thieves. Perhaps a group of students in TARU organized a special team to steal cars and set false numbers. Look, they even arranged a robbery of a car. They divided the car into different components and seemingly started selling all of them. They certainly did all of this stealing based on someone's special order.

I say this because six of those seven thieves who had stolen my car turned out to be former graduates of our TARU, and they came from the same province. I am purposely not telling you which province this is because one of the candidates was recommended to be appointed as a rector had also come from that province. So now I think it's become clear for you what's wrong. That day me, theowner of the car, my nephew, and the prosecutor, went to the home 54 Segeli, where I saw my precious car. I had the key with me, but when I attempted to insert it, the car door failed to open. Yes, I was naïve, completely naïve. Being an automobile science specialist, I forgot that the stolen car had all the locks changed. The prosecutor once more checked the coincidence of all the signs I told him about. He was seemingly satisfied and handed the car key to me saying :

"No doubt, the car is yours Sir! Here are your keys!"

My nephew talked to one driver of a truck asking him to take my car to the back yard of the institute, where I left it for the master Sanich. The next day the engine was to be brought, and two weeks later I was told that the car was ready to drive. I sat in the car and drove it once around the territory. This car seemed to me to be a completely new car. After I handed the key back to the master, I asked him to sell the car because some days before he had told about a client who was going to buy it.

The next day San Sanich handed me two thousand dollars.

So, the story about my car came to end at long last. The thieves of the car were sentenced to ten years or more in imprisonment. I didn't attend the court at all as it was something not proper for me, with the position I had achieved. Perhaps this is the proof to the saying that everyone is to be punished for what wrong they do in this world.

All the good and bad people will anyway be judged by God sooner or later. We mustn't forget that nobody can escape that punishment, never.

Becoming a university president at university is the trust and responsibility

(1995–2005)

 was asked :

"Dear teacher, now I see that you wrote   many workbooks and manuals, and the one in Russian was even published in Russia. Did you receive any benefits from that book?

"Oh, benefits ... I hope that any hard work will not go in vain. One day I will get to know that young people eager to learn will get the benefits from those books. I can assure you all the books I wrote came in handy to young people. I'll be talking about this all in detail later, so If you want to know, let's go!

International awards

It was in June 1994, June and I was invited to the second International Al-Horazmiy International Scientific Conference held in Tehran on behalf of the organizing committee. In the invitation the date of the conference was written as 1995, February. I also decided to send my scientific achievements to the competition and at the end of

July I had all of the documents and scientific projects translated into English and forwarded to the contest.

In 1994 I received a letter from the Head of the organizing Committee Mr Intizoriy. The following was written in the letter: "We've received all of your documents and projects. The members of the Committee have with the utmost discretion examined them all and they decided to accept your suggestion to take part in the contest". On this occasion I wrote an answer back thanking them for their approval.

In January 1995 they rang me up from the Iranian embassy and after that I met the secretary of the embassy Mr Muzaffariy. As soon as I met him, he greeted and said that they received a fax announcing about the fact that the members of the Committee found my scientific achievements worthy of the victory. He said that the date for awarding those who won was fixed on February 5, 1995. Even the secretary of the Iranian embassy in Uzbekistan, Erkin Hujayev rang me up to congratulate me with this award of high esteem. On January 28, Mr Hoshimiy Gulpayagoniy, embassador of the Iranian embassy talked to me and congratulated me on the award, reminding me to come to the conference on the appointed date . He said that we would be awarded personally by the President Hoshimiy Rafsanjoniy. I pointed out that it would be a great idea to warn the peculiar organizations in our country about my visit to Iran. He told me not to worry about it, adding that they would   send an announcement letter to the Ministry of Foreign Affairs on February 1.

Doctor: "Mr, Sarvar, the Iranian embassy staff obviously did their best for you. I think you weren't late for the conference. How was it? How did you find it?"

Sarvar: Unfortunately, for some reasonable reasons, I couldn't be present at the conference. We were late and the last departure of the plane was on February 7 from Ashhobod to Tehran. There wasn't a plane leaving from Tashkent to Ashgaba that day, and immediately the Ministry of Foreign Affairs wrote the following letter to the secretary of the Iranian Embassy, and I wrote to Mr Intizoriy.

«Dear Mr Intizoriy! I want to thank you from the bottom of my heart for assessing and valuing the scientific research and work I have done. I wish great success in all the further activities of the conference."

I am informing you that I am not able to take part in the conference of the award presentation due to the fact that I have my lecture scheduled on February 10 in the Special Council of experts of the High Attestation Commission for my doctoral dissertation. I need to take part in this occasion as an official opponent.

I have further asked Erkin Hujayev, the secretary of the Iranian Islamic Republic embassy in Uzbekistan to help me to solve all the problems relating to the award and the conference.

I also hope that our cooperation in terms of scientific development will develop even more in the future.

Sincerely professor S.Kodirov

Doctor: Oh, now I understand, and I think that it was the ambassador of the Iranian embassy in Uzbekistan, Erkin Hujayev who accepted the award for you".

Sarvar: "Yes, you're right"

On February 8, our ambassador Erkin Hujayev rang me up from Tehran to inform me that the award issued for me was handed to him personally by the President. He also added that the award would soon be delivered to the Foreign Affairs Ministry of Uzbekistan.

Doctor: Can you tell me in detail how you were handed the award and diploma?

Sarvar: Ok, well, on February 24, I received an invitational letter on behalf of Iranian embassy : "Dear Mr Sarvar Kodirov, we want to invite you to the party held by the Emergency and Plenipotentiary Ambassador of the Iranian Islamic Republic, Said Mukammal Muso Hoshimiy. We'll be really pleased to see you at the party. We'll be welcoming you and congratulating you on the occasion of the award you have been gifted with!"

Venue : Restaurant "Navruz", Small Hall. Time: 1995, February 26, 630 pm.

Twenty respected guests were sitting in a small hall of the restaurant "Navruz" on February 26, at 630 pm.

All of us were invited to take our seats in order one by one. It was the first time I was invited to such an exclusive party, and therefore I expected to take a seat at one of the ordinary seats on the edge. Instead, the hosts forced me to sit next to the Minister of Foreign Affairs Ministry, Mr Abdulaziz Komilov. I was sitting on the left, right next to him, and then there was the President of the Sciences Academy Mr J.Abdullayev. In front of us we could see ambassador of Iran, Mr Hoshimiy Gulpayagoniy and other execs of the embassy. Mr Ambassador announced the party to be opened and he mentioned the second international conference Al- Khorazmiy to be held in Tehran, which would include scientists from all the world who were privileged to be awarded. In this regard he said that the award would be handed to their owners by the President of the Iran Republic Mr Hoshimiy Rafsanjoniy, and among those scientists there was one scientist from Uzbekistan. He pronounced my name with vehement excitement. At the same time he congratulated all the citizens of the Republic of Uzbekistan with this great achievement and afterwards he submitted the award with the money to me with tumultuous applauses from the guests. He also added that any time I could visit and stay in Iran for a week completely free of charge. After that I was allowed to say a few words. I said to them:

"Good evening, dear ambassadors, dear teachers and guests!

I am really glad to be privileged to meet you face to face before such a great holiday the Eid Ramadan Khayit.

I want to sincerely thank the Council of experts of the 2 – Al-Khorazmiy technological festival, and personally to Mr Intizoriy for assessing my marginal efforts for scientific development to such a high extent.

Unfortunately I want to ask you all to forgive me that I was not able to take part in the festival personally for some excusable reasons. Besides I am also grateful to the Emergency and Plenipotentiary Ambassador of the Iranian embassy in Uzbekistan for helping to solve all the problems relating to a visit to Iran and participating in the festival. The fact that this award is handed personally by the President of the Republic leads to infer that in the East science and knowledge is highly valued. I think this award is not only my success, but it's the assessment of the intellectual ability of all the scientists in Uzbekistan.

Taking advantage of this privilege, I want to thank to all of my teachers who have been helping and supporting me in everything, and every challenge which I've faced. They are

O.Salimov, A.Mutalibov, the university administration, J.Abdullayev, P.Habibullayev, O.Lebedev and many others.

Once more I want to thank to the Minister of the Foreign Affairs Ministry Mr A.Komilov and dear ambassador Mr Hoshimiy Gulpayagoniy for organizing such a fabulous party and for making me the happiest man in the world by inviting me here.

One more very important thing I want to mention is may our President Islam Abduganiyevich Karimov live a long and healthy life because there are lots of talented scientists in Uzbekistan and they always keep working hard. Our President has never tired of helping and encouraging all of us, never.

I hope it will be decent of Iran to work with us in cooperation for scientific development as well as many other developed countries."

In order to take part in the scientific conference, I wrote a resume for my project dedicated to the problems of predicting decaying and effectively using diesel engines in the soil and climate conditions of Central Asia. That resume I also included a sample for the new air-cleaner and the results of the experiments on it.

While awarding me in the contest, I think that my work book on "Automobile and tractor engines" in the Russian language was also taken into account, because in this contest I was asked about all the monographs and books I'd published.

These days different scientific works have been carried out by the scientist of our department in our university.

In the period of transferring to market economy there are many tasks due for all the scientists in Uzbekistan. Those who are living for the sake of the motherland are undoubtedly able to accomplish them all. I strongly believe that they can considerably contribute to the development of our country.

Certainly all the ministries and other representatives of the authority have a vital role in implementing all of our plans in science.

Dear teachers, Ministers, ambassadors and guests, I once again thank you for everything from the bottom of my heart. Thanks for everything! I wish you all eternal strong health and endless success! I wish peace will prevail in our motherland longer than forever!

I congratulate everyone on the upcoming holy and sacred day Eid Ramadan Khayit dears! Thanks!"

I must admit that this award had put me on the map, and it meant that those who really try and work hard, will one day get everything they want. Today there are many talented scientists in our Republic, they are all winning in international contests and conferences from the results of their hard work and patience.

Pursuit of the biggest dreams

A university president is the chief ruler of the university. Not everyone is privileged with the happiness to become a rector who is charge of uniting the staff of teachers, and taking care of their future. To pursue this, a man needs to love justice, work in accordance with the law, and be loved by all the students and teachers as well as having high intelligence.

On November 14, 1994, the rector of the Tashkent Automobile roads institute Salim Pulatov suddenly died of a stroke while conducting a meeting. Why do people, especially scientists die of a stroke? It's because there are many people who keep hurting them all the time. There are this sort of people in our university as well, they pushed him to a stroke with their artificial complaints and with their malice aforethought knowing that perhaps after his death they would have a chance to work in his position. So, the contest started, with disputes over who can become a rector. All the deans and proctors were frankly fighting for this position. There were different rumors at the university: "Today the proctor is going to be the rector", tomorrow this rumor will change: "today the dean is going to be announced as the president".

However, there was no contest between the heads of the departments, as their position is not high to deserve it, figuratively saying. We saw the new year 1995 in, and, at that time, I was working as the head of the department "Producing and repairing automobiles", I didn't intend to take part in this dispute of being a university president because I knew what my position was, and what I had to do.

I think God decided to gift me one more time, perhaps yes. Taking into account all the disputes and rumors at the university, the State Counsellor paid a visit to our university in March gathering all the representatives of the Scientific Council. For some reasons, I don't remember I was missing from that meeting. At that time the State Counsellor asked each of the representatives to show their own candidates deserving to become a rector in a written form. Each representative could vote in favor of anyone, but only one candidate who worked as the department head, as a dean and a prorector.

Many people voted in favor of the proctor Samatov (28 votes), the dean Butayev (14 votes), the department head Askarhujayev (4 votes). Look, how surprising it was! I didn't even know some people voted in my favor as well, I got 8 votes . I got to know about this long after the meeting. So in this way they could only identify the list of the candidates possibly deserving of becoming a university president. After some time the State Counsellor came to the university to have an interview with the candidates. I think the scientific achievements, work history, and everything relating to the candidates had already been examined up to that day.

When I was invited for an interview, professor Askarhujayev was waiting for his turn. The first candidate Sh.Butayev came out from the interview. This meant G.Samatov, the second candidate before him had passed the interview exam. After that the candidate T.Askarhujayev was invited inside, he came back within about five minutes. The man who was interviewing everyone was the State Counsellor, and this was for the first time I was going to see him face to face, (of course I had seen him before many times on TV). He turned to be a very strict man, and kept asking questions one after the other. First he asked what problems there were in the university. After I counted all the problems in short, he asked me what I would do to solve them . The questions sounded exact. I gave my own opinions , and he asked me why I didn't say all this during the meetings of the scientific Council. I told him exactly what I thought and that it was impossible to prepare high qualified professionals without completely reforming the education system, I put forward the issue of preparing good specialists and professionals. Seemingly he was satisfied with the way I answered and he let me leave the room.

At that time my brother Anvar was seriously ill. In March he was admitted to the Science and research center of surgery named after Vahidov, and after all the analysis was made clear, we were asked to take him to the Oncological hospital of the city; it was useless. We took him back home on April 3.

The days were passing one after another, the ministry was busy with examining documents of several scientists, as well as mine perhaps. I think they were only examining 5 or ten documents. In this regard I talked about this with prominent people, the first university president A.Mutalibov, professor N.Rizayev and docent V.A.Urmonov. All of them gave me their golden advice promising to help me anytime. I didn't know that these promises were just promises. As I was a man who kept all of his promises, I believed that all the people were like me. I could hope for help from God, no one else.

If you remember, I was given an award by the President of Iran Republic,in February 1995 at the 2 – Al Khorazmiy International festival. In February all of my documents were brought into the disposal of our President. As I heard he became very glad to hear what he said about me: "I am glad to know that there are so intelligent and hard working scientists in our Republic whom I now know!". He signed in the license. It's with the utmost happiness that our President paid attention to me! This person always values the scientists who serve for the sake of the motherland, national fame and raising our reputation in the world.

Besides that, in order to pursue this happiness it's required to work honestly for our entire lives. After several examinations, documents of three candidates were brought into the President's office. All the recommendation letters were made ready, and I was recommended by the faculty dean and the docent of our department. To sum up, I was also invited to the interview with the State Counsellor. I don't know how the others passed the interview exam, but I was glad. At the interview he asked me: "There are several situations in the university, bribing, corporate crimes and mafia, how would you combat this all?" I said: "If you keep supporting me, I can fight against them". There was one more conversation with another State Counsellor in April in the President's office. This conversation was also very frank and open, what has astonished me to this day was that these two Counselors both knew all the illegal acts in the university. During the conversation the following statement has stayed in my memory: "The dean of the correspondence faculty requires ten dollars for each exam assessment from the students, and this sort of illegal acts all need to be excluded from the university". Then there were some opinions about the slow process of scientific research at the university.

At this time my elder brother Anvar died of a serious disease. I was in distress, it was all challenging, nearly impossible to live without my brother, and to overcome this loss. The Ministry administration , and all the teachers at the university, were a shoulder for me to cry on, and they didn't cease supporting me at this difficult time. Ok, I couldn't do anything else to ease this pain of torture without my brother, but I was forced to stand it...

Thinking about the contests and exams to become a rector seemed to be a betrayal and disrespect for the memory of my brother, I had enough to contend with and time was passing by. There was no news and the more time passed, the more rumors could be heard around. At long last on June 10, 1995, the Minister O.U.Salimov appointed the proctor G.Samatov as the person in charge of fulfilling al the tasks of the university president. (I was absent in this meeting for some unknown reasons) In my absence I was appointed as the Proctor in charge of academic affairs. No one knows the reason for making this decision. G.Samatov sat on the chair of the rector with glory over me, and I was forced to occupy the chair on which he sat up to that day, as the proctor. We started working.

On June 15, Samatov left for Surkandarya as his father had died. He left me as the man responsible for all the things at the university. The most interesting thing was that in those days, and within a week, none of my domestic phones, neither those at work, nor that at home were working. I didn't understand why. In June 17 in the early morning, the proctor J.Ruziyev congratulated me on the telephones of the local network. I took it as a congratulation of just another colleague on the occasion of my being appointed me as the proctor. A bit later the former proctor came to congratulate me, but he said : "You've been appointed as the university president!" I scolded him for that. But anyway he insisted and brushed me off saying:

"Yesterday you were wanted by the Minister all day. He phoned me, I phoned you, but no one could find you, friend! (Of course they couldn't find me, because none of the telephones

were working) Last night the President signed in the decree. Haven't you heard about it? At around 1000 pm the Minister Okil Bagdasarovich called my office number to ask about you. They informed me that the council is to be held at 3 pm, and they also asked all the staff to be here, as well as you, the former proctor."

I just nodded, and as of yet, I knew nothing about it . I asked the proctor N.Manonov to invite all the representatives of the Scientific Council into the small Hall. A bit later the dean Tillashev came to tell me that I was called up to visit the State Counselor at 12 the same day. I got to the Office of the President on time. The State Counsellor told me:

"Yesterday we decided who is to become the university president. The President signed in the decree. Now and further on you'll be trying to deserve our trust and belief in you and your loyalty. You will be restoring the reputation of the university, and you will root out bribery and other illegal acts" He said this and gave a lot of other golden advice. When I was still sitting there the State Counselor called the Prime Minister and asked: "Who is going to go to the university to introduce the new university president? It would be decent if you're going to do this." The Prime Minister informed me that S.Saidkosimov would responsible for it. The State Counselor wished me good luck and permitted me to leave.

I returned to the university, and at 1 pm the Minister O.U.Salimov arrived. After we went into the small hall, he asked me:

"How would you react if there are some negative opinions and views expressed when you're introduced as the new university president ?"

I firmly said: "While working at this university for over 33 years, I've never blocked anyone's way, and did my best to help all the people who might need my help. It's impossible that someone could say something against me here in the audience".

The Minister felt calm and we went out of the hall. The Minister then asked the two proctors about the situation, and they said that everything was ok. The Minister left after that. At 3 pm all the active representatives gathered in the small hall. Three representatives arrived from the Republic Authority, S.Saidkosimov – Assistant of the Prime-Minister, Sh.Ayupov – Special representative at the Office of the President, O.Salimov the Minister of higher education Ministry. S.Saidkosimov started his speech by saying that there hadn't been a rector at the university for seven months as the contest was quite long lasting. He also mentioned that the environment at the university wasn't good, and the corporate crimes and robberies were increasing. He said that the President made the following decision by examining all the situations prevailing at university.

"I order professor Sarvar Kodirov to be appointed as the president of the Tashkent Automobile and Roads university". The Minister ordered a halt to bribery and corporate illegal acts at university. He said:

"We know very well who is mainly involved in all these illegal acts, so no matter how much you protest, from now on all of you will be working in cooperation with the university president." I was then allowed to say a few words. I thanked our President for the trust and confidence and I promised to deserve it all the time, from now , until the future ,   to lead the university fairly, and increase the quality of education. The Council was over and a bit later I went to the tomb of my mother that day. I cried there a lot, and prayed there for her. I thought about the challenges we had come across, and about the days of hunger we had spent together. I hoped she was feeling happy in the sky, there somewhere in the sky ...

I was appointed as the university president. Thanks to God my dreams came true. I remembered how we lived in the dormitory of Ph students with Omon, Surat, Marat and Hayot, and when we all sat together. I also thought about when they told us about the opening of the Tashkent Automobiles and Roads university, and I suddenly told them that I would one day be the university president of that university. This wasn't easy for me at all. To have this dream come true, I had to pursue the candidate degree, the doctoral degree, the position of a professor, correspondent representative at the Academy, become an Honoured Scientist, win international contests and fight against the harsh rules and realities of life. The representatives of several countries acknowledged the results of my scientific work and efforts. Most importantly our citizens and our President had paid special attention to me, and they cared for me. Many scientists had also appraisingly assessed all of my inventions and scientific researches, and whatever I had pursued in life, was all due to my own hard work, honesty, patience and honest head as a representative.

Doctor: Mr Sarvar, I think that after that, you changed all the proctors and deans of the university, didn't you? Did you recruit members to your own team?

Sarvar: No, I didn't. I didn't change anything in the rectorate as a rector after that."

Even the rector who worked for a week and left after his father's death was ordered to work in his previous position. Even the position of N.Mannonov was removed within three days on the basis of the Minister's decision, but I left him to rule over the faculty of correspondence. The proctor Karimov Z.Kh. was appointed to the special administration there. Even my opponents J.Ruziyev and Kh.Dimetov continued working in their own positions. We started working , but I didn't quickly go into the rector's room. I talked to my teachers and we decided to hold a meeting dedicated to cherishing the memory of the previous university president who had died of a heart-attack. We bought a sheep and we had a pilaf cooked with its meat according to the traditions. We invited all the relatives and friends of the late rector and all prayed for him in that meeting. After that relatives of the late university president saw me off to the rector's room and wished me success in the continuation of his work. Only after that did I sit in the rector's chair .

Doctor: "If you could tell me in detail how you worked as a university president, it would help me a lot."

"Ok, I will"

After that we made a plan for three months and I urged all the chief representatives to implement it . At this time the Reception Commission had started its own activity, and we started receiving applicants to the university. All the assistants were changed at that time, except a responsible secretary, because there were different rumors about the unfair exam system. I talked to the responsible secretary face to face, and we agreed to hold all the exams fairly. He promised to do everything recommended. (But later it became clear that he was providing the wrong information to the Republican Testing and Examining Center about the working activity of the rector) On July 30, I visited the Testing Center with that responsible secretary to submit a report about all the work done, and the measures taken. The head of the Testing Center understood me well, and he said that all the information the secretary had given by that time turned out to be wrong. He decided that the secretary was no longer able to further work in this position. Therefore the secretary quit the job according to his own application (sick-leave) and docent A.Abdurahmanov was appointed instead of him to this position. All the testing occasions on August 1 – 10 passed as well as we planned. But one habit that almost all of the applicants had of "cribbing the answers", we couldn't prevent .

My working day lasted from 7 am to 8 or 9 pm. Everyday I look through these two ten-storey buildings. All the mottos and other exhibits are as good as recommended. But in October suddenly one representative came and went upstairs to the seventh floor without even going up to see me. He was from the Ministry. On seeing the poster there where he could see the motto "Lenin" and many other things, he was stunned. He called me to the seventh floor, and I was stunned to see what had happened. The night before

I had checked all the corridors and inside all the buildings. I saw nothing strange or weird. However, the next day, and this was especially arranged against me the motto "Lenin" had been written. On seeing this the representative from the Ministry , "a famous head" (who arranged this trick against me) of the department didn't even get to his feet. The representative immediately asked me to arrange a meeting in which he dismissed both proctors J. Ruziyev and G.Samatov, and after w=that he decided to appoint the two candidates I recommended and deemed to be worthy. According to my recommendation Z.Kh.Saidov was appointed as the proctor of academic affairs and R.Holikulova of education and training. The whole staff was satisfied. I didn't even show my anger to the people who resigned, and who wanted to attack me with that scary motto on the poster. I allowed them to work   at the university as the head of other departments. It is because our great ancestor Alisher Navoiy said:

Evil people don't expect good people to harm them…

But good people never forget to do many good things to them.

But problems followed problems at the university. As soon as I started working as the rector, I observed life at university and noticed that there was a negative change in student attendance. Especially correspondent students who weren't even attending summer sessions. I couldn't stand this and it, was just beyond my mind. Students not attending lessons, but being assessed without any problems. This meant teachers were still being bribed. I immediately ordered all the teachers bring in the all the students' record books into the dean's office. There's one rule, a teacher is allowed to examine and assess only the students who regularly attend all their classes. Those who don't attend aren't allowed to pass their exams without the permission of the university president.

Soon all the students heard what happened, and they all started coming up to me, but none of them had the records books. To the question : "Where's your records book?" one of them said they had given it to the dean, and another said they had left it in the proctor's office so that they could be assessed. These deans and proctors promised them to help them with the marks. This would of course cause students not to study . They would like the ease of studying by having their records book signed by the teacher without any effort. I was in a difficult position, but it became clear what kinds of employees I had around me.

A bit later we had another problem. A huge number of students in the correspondence faculties restored their studies for the second course by preparing artificial documents as if they had been expelled from other universities and had come to study at our university. These documents had basically been issued by the Polytechnical and Irrigation institutes. I came across a very difficult problem and it was big trouble for me.

I had a special committee formed on the basis of the decree, then examined the documents of the students who came from other universities to ours, trying to check if the certificates were genuine. Those which turned out to be real were forwarded to the faculty, and they could continue studying. It became clear that 75 students were enrolled in the university with artificial documents, and there weren't any document confirming that those students could really successfully pass the entrance exams. Therefore they had had artificial documents prepared about entrance into the Polytechnical or Irrigation universities, and afterwards they'd decided to come to the Tashkent Automobiles and Roads university. The Rectors of those universities sent a written report about that.

What could be done to solve this problem? The only way was to expel them from university, which I did. They were all blamed for the artificial documents they had, and none of them could deny this.

There was no dispute over the issue of expelling them. The proctor told me: "You will soon be shot to death for what you did!" I wasn't scared a bit because I was right in doing this. Whatever I was doing, I was doing taking into account my own conscience.

I reported what had happened to the Minister asking what to do with all those documents.

He said : "You can submit them all to a certain legislative organization, but you also need to think that it was the late previous rector who had signed in all those papers."

All of the students were aware of what was happening. I had plenty of advisors. Some of them advised me to submit those documents to the Court, and some of them suggested I give them to a prosecutor and many other places. Those students who entered the university with artificial papers were all scared to death, not knowing what to do, and waiting for the rector to make a decision.

I listened to what my conscience said to me: "Don't do any harm to those who are guilty, and let them feel what wrong they have done. God will punish them soon anyway". I hid all these documents where I could remember them. I didn't have any malice afterwards, but who could guarantee that someone who did this harm to me, wouldn't do this any more? No one could! The Proctor of the university, A.M.Bagdasarov, in academic affairs, apologized to me for what happened and said :

"You've done many good things for me, my children, and my family and by making this decision not to expose these … you know what I mean … actually if somebody had been in your shoes, he would've … he would've never done what good you are doing for me. Thanks that you haven't submitted them to the Court. Thanks".

He said this because I saw his signature on most of the documents as well. Nobody scared me. Neither in my office nor at my own home because I did the right thing by expelling those students from the university.

I started paying special attention to the lesson process and the quality of the lessons. The time-tables of all the teachers and professors were always on my desk, and all of them were under constant control. I started observing the lesson process of famous professors. Unfortunately, most of the Ph students or other young teachers were delivering lectures and running classes instead of those professors, I didn't like it at all. Someone was working and another man was getting the salary. It was completely unfair. I think that I was strict with this didn't seem right to some teachers, and therefore they started writing complaint letters to the State Counselor. After I was called in to have a conversation with the State Counselor, I explained my own reasons for what I was doing. He was obviously satisfied with my answers and the decisions I made, and he confirmed everything I had said. Famous teachers started looking for extra paying jobs in other universities, they changed their work time to part time, and got employed in other universities as full-time professors. Some of them quit their jobs on their own because when I was rector they were not allowed to be bribed by students, or to earn extra illegal income. The people who had malice afore thoughts against me had been writing complaint letters non stop to all the authority members ranging from the President to the prosecutors. Even though there was a law which prohibited discussion of anonymous letters, some heads formed a special commission to control how I was regulating the university. I was only believing in God and the President. There are still this type of people at the university; those who keep anonymously writing complaint letters . I can even count their names. I kept defeating all of them with only my rigid patience, and I didn't slow down my strict regulation over unfair decisions. I kept working on the basis of fair and strict decisions. Those having malicious thoughts against, all know how fairly I worked and served.

In 1995 Tashkent Automobiles and Roads university was admitted to the International Accosiation of Automobile and Roads teaching and that year I was admitted as the Honoured Professor of the MARU (Moscow Automobiles and Roads university) taking into account that partnership and my book published in Russian "Engines of automobiles and tractors". In October 1996, an International Scientific Conference was organized in which scientists from countries such as France, Germany, the Ukraine, Iran and Turkey, and countries of the Commonwealth of Independent States attended. In this conference the first convention of the International Association of Automobile Road Education (IAARE) was also held at the same time. A decree to apply new technologies were adopted, and in the same year, for the first time in the Republic, the Council of Sponsors was formed on my initiative. As a member for this organization many other organizations were admitted, they were "UzAutotrans", "UzAutoIndustry", "UzAutoRoads", "Tashkent City Passenger and Roads Transport", "Uzbekistan Airways" and Uzbekistan Higher and Secondary Education Ministry. We organized a new funding so-called "Student". I was elected as the head of it. As for the council of sponsors, professor L.A.Ahmetov was appointed as the head. This corporation issued 5 million soums to the funding, and the rest of the members remained as members just on their documents, practically, or not. All of this money was spent on financially supporting students and teachers. On the basis of the funding, we organized a company "Talaba-Tayanch" (student – support). This company has conducted the activities of selling and buying cars to the ultimate consumers by means of credit. The other half proportion of the incomes was spent on university funding. It worked in cooperation with UzDAEWOOAuto.

In 1997 September, we were going to celebrate the twenty fifth anniversary of the university, therefore we'd been seriously preparing for that. In 1996 we made up a special plan, and we appointed special professionals to implement these plans. We put forward a task of opening the university's museum. Professor O.A.Ganihujayev and L.K.Hakimov contributed a lot to all these campaigns. We also published a special book about the activity of the university in Uzbek. All the faculties and departments created special exhibitions about what they had done throughout the years after the foundation. Currently they still decorate the foyer of the university. We made a party in which we treated the guests to pilaf, and in this party representatives from all the car manufacturing and universities from all the provinces of the Republic of Uzbekistan were in attendance. Many famous scientists took part in it. My teacher professor Rostislav Pavlovich Dobrogayev and I were privileged to open the university's museum. This man contributed a lot to educating Uzbek students.

There was a change in the educational system in 1996, a and according to it all the prospective students of universities started being chosen through a testing system. The talented young people were taught 18 hours a day for this system, and it was the famous and experienced professors who taught them during this time. They learned English and Information technology in detail. Students assessed the teachers knowledge, and their salaries were appointed according to their assessments. During this time it became possible to distinguish the teachers having less teaching experience and meant each teacher needed to work at excelling their knowledge and experience. Our President opened the fund "Umid" for students, and the fund "Ustoz" for teachers at that time. Later, both these funds were combined and it was given the name "Istedod". After that this fund started working as a unique organization. Due to this fund, 300 of students got a chance to get both BC and MA degrees in highly developed countries of the world like the USA, Japan, Germany, England, Italy and Southern Korea. Teachers also gained experience in those countries.

The next three years, 1997, 1998 and 1999 around 10 bachelor and Ph.d students from our university studied in the USA on the basis of the "Umid" fund. Only four of the teachers successfully passed the contest exams to take part in that program. Unfortunately, many teachers didn't have much interest in learning foreign languages as most of them are at the age to retire. Taking this all into account we paid a lot of attention to our Master students. In 1999 a total of 38 master students were enrolled at the university on the basis of the state grant. This meant they could study for free. They were viewed as substitutes for our teachers who were day by day getting lazy, and not working to improve their own skills. If there isn't competence, there can not be development as well. Nowadays, the number of talented students at the university has reached 200, in contrast to 2004 this rate was 84, and in 2005 it was 86. These sorts of professionals are always needed for any organizations of our Republic. Most of them are working in the departments and laboratories of the university after their lessons. We won't have to invite translators if we have some foreign guests at our university. Our students can help us with translations all the time, and they can also translate all the necessary texts from foreign languages into Russian and Uzbek.

We have thousands of hard working and eager to learn students. Most of them are working in computer programs, electronic books, lecture texts, albums and creating new pedagogical technologies used for training.

I mean we can easily achieve our goals if experienced teachers educate our young students leading them to proper careers.

When I was a rector I used to show my course mates to our students gathering them all in the hall. The hall held 800 people and the meetings were always crowded . The young people there could see the people who had already found their own carriers through hard work and patience. After the meeting, I used to go to picnic in the mountains where we had a good rest with my close friends.   We never tired of talking until 2 or 3 am. The more we talked, the more things we had to say to each other. Not everyone was as happy as I was. In 1998 Lerik Ahmetov was appointed as the Assistant Prime-Minister, Temur Kamalov as the head of the Korakalpakstan Republic Joqori Kenges (Supreme Congress). They were both my close friends who did their best to contribute to the development of our university. There's a proverb : "You'd better have one hundred friends rather than having one hundred dollars". That's proved to be true for me. If you have a true friend, you won't have problems for a long time.

Dear readers, it's up to you to now interpret everything I have said for your own future! I wish you could also have friends like mine!

We need hard working professionals who are strong enough to show the world Uzbekistan's strength, and who can contribute to growth in our Republic. Who can provide us with these specialists? Of course, there are 62 university presidents and institutes in the Republic, but the teachers and the heads of the department still aren't ready for that: there's a feeling of indifference. But it's urgent to overcome difficulties, and it's necessity to organize the faculties working in cooperation with foreign countries. It's also required to conduct lessons in Russian or in English.

All the Master students and other talented people need to know these foreign languages and they all need to learn computer technology quite well. If a professional doesn't know his own special discipline, it's impossible to work effectively in that field. Even though at a slow pace, today many young people are growing to understand this harsh reality. One day only those who have enough knowledge will be teaching at the universities, and only they will have the right to lead the universities and other secondary education organizations. In this case the entire society will develop to a high extent. May God enable us to live long enough to witness this!

In this regard I have found it a good idea to tell you a bit about what I have witnessed in the educational systems in foreign countries. The students in foreign countries pay tuition fees to study at colleges or universities. The annual tuition fees range from five thousand dollars to twenty thousand dollars. Students earn all of this money when they get free lessons. They aren't shy to earn money by even having manual jobs like washing dishes, floors, selling newspapers, or working as maids in some companies. Even professors work in laboratories or in factories after they finish working at universities. So how is everything going in our country? Only a countable number of university teachers lead a better life. Unfortunately, there are some teachers who are doing nothing but waiting for the President to raise their salary. Moreover, there will not be any progress, if they keep living and working at this pace. We need to think about working hard to invent something new, and to use our opportunities as much as possible. Scientists of the world are leading prosperous lives due to their knowledge and ability to have innovational ideas. Some teachers in our university started doing the same. They are now writing work books, working out new projects, and inventing new appliances. They are leading satisfactory lives . They all drive cars like Nexia, Tico, Damas and Matiz. The teachers who are lazy are envious of them, and they do nothing for the university but write anonymous complaint letters. These sorts of people can not stand to see other's prosperity and achievements because they can't achieve what we can, and they can't work as hard as we do for that.

Tens of courses to gain experience have been opened at the university. I took the initiative for their openings all the time. Not only teachers, but students also have been working there. They have been working at important campaigns all over the Republic. Recently, it has been calculated by the Special Commission, that the additional monthly wage sums paid for teachers equal 54 million soums. How much is this rate in other universities? I don't know to be honest. Most people want to look like university presidents, and a few are envious. Everyone must admit a simple truth; what a man is destined to be or to do in the future, will certainly happen. God has created every human being and the world, and he has also created a destiny peculiar to each human Being. We will work, or live, according to what's been destined for us. Let's just try to answer one question: is there anyone who has succeeded without hard work? It's a must for every human being to work hard as soon as he is born. Being a university president means being trusted, and being viewed as the most responsible person. In this case a university president has to unite thousands of different people for the same purpose. It's a complex issue to make them work for the same aim and for the same purpose, but somehow it's possible. If a university president can't cope with it, the reputation of the university will go down. When I was a rector, the number of admissions was only 240 students . However, within 4 years, this rate reached 900. It wasn't a piece of cake for me at all. We had to make a contract for five years with the Ministry and other corporations oriented to preparing professionals. Due to the assistance of the sponsors, we bought 5 automobiles and one bus for the university. The central heating system was completely repaired, and within the last twenty years all the doors, frames and other equipment at university grew quite old, old enough to be replaced. It's required several hundreds of million soums to renew them all. Where is it possible to get the funding for that? The sponsors have been rendering assistance and providing different equipment. We've been working hard trying to pursue all that has been planned.

Each step forward is taken due to a lot of effort. There's one obstacle to any kind of development, this is bribery, and is something like a virus which eradicates human pride, reputation and the willingness to learn and excel.

I finally discovered a new way of solving this problem . Every year I used to personally hand all the diplomas to the graduates face to face, and shake hands with them. After that I would force the deans and the proctors to leave the hall where there would be just me and my former graduates. I knew quite well what they were hiding inside their heart, and therefore I used to have anonymous questionnaires filled in by them. There it was written: "I ask you to only write the truth being loyal to God and your conscience. If you got your assessment through your monitor's or big shot's help, don't write anything, if you personally paid to the teacher for assessment, then you must write."

The bachelor graduates used to write quickly and put the questionnaires back onto my desk. It became clear that out of 400 to 430 professors and teachers, 15 to 17 percent of them were bribed by students for assessment.

There used to be special conversations with those teachers, and they used to be shown all the anonymous questionnaires in which their surnames were written. On seeing the questionnaire, they would all feel scared to death. Those teachers didn't even try to deny that, because they were obviously guilty . When I talked to them face to face they would promise not to do that any more. If next year once more their surnames were written on the questionnaires, I was forced to give them the sack. In this way I could tackle the problem of bribery in our university. One day I heard one rumour. The heads of the departments such as "Physics" and "Theory of new democratic society" were all bribing the students using the group's monitors . The monitors would get the money from their group mates and give it to the head for assessment. I asked the dean to invite all the group's monitors . He did. I asked them what was wrong for clarification. They promised to confirm, or not confirm this bribery, even if they met face to face with those heads in front of me, the university president.

I called each of the department heads into my office and first asked the monitor if it was true that he was being bribed. After he nodded, the department head's head lowered, probably feeling sorry for what he had done. I asked the head to give all the money back and to quit the job immediately. After that everyone heard about what happened, and in this way all the other bribers started feeling afraid of bribing. So two "famous professors" were dismissed. The students made sure that there's justice in the educational system after that. Many colleagues suggested I allow them stay at work, but I didn't let them stay.

Consequently, all of my "favourite friends" started getting accustomed to a fair teaching and learning system. On August 1, 2000, we started testing exams to enroll the most talented applicants to the university. All the university presidents started passing assessment exams starting from September. My "Favourite friends" were starting to launch attack against me as soon as they got the opportunity. They started writing anonymous letters of complaint to all the representatives ranging from the President to the prosecutors.

They dared to confuse some of the heads a little bit, but it was useless after lots of disputes an in October, I passed the interview exam once more, and I was elected to be a rector for five more years. I don't feel upset with those "favourite friends" at all. Instead, I always thank them for urging me to yearn for tomorrow, for hoping that tomorrow is going to be a much brighter day. For ten years I didn't feel distressed about anything, I tried to fight more and more, being alert to everything, and il tried not to make mistakes. Therefore, after October of 2000, and as soon as I was elected as the university president once more, those anonymous letters of complaint didn't disturb me at all.

Oh, my unique God, praying to you all nights and days If I am on the wrong way, know you as the only guide

In your love and your care I look for the right ways Whatever happens believe in your help every day and night But envious enemies keep hurting my soul,

I beg you to defend me from their evil and attack They aren't letting me achieve my goal Please don't let them chase and hurt me back.

Enemies are all around trying to hurt me all the time Don't want to let me take a breath at least

But I don't care whatever they do to hurt

God, turn them for me into bad memories from the past You have punished them all, thanks

Thanks for creating me as a human genuine I've been living following all the ways you show

I am still as innocent as I have always and ever been. You have gifted me with dignity and patience endless

My mother had always prayed for my health and happiness Going deeper into science is my unique aim

You've enabled me to be the happiest with endless fame!

At this period I was admitted as a prominent scientist in Russia, the USA, Germany, England, South Korea, France and Israel. Due to much effort and hard work, I had auto tractor terminology dictionaries published(Russian-Uzbek, English- Russian-Uzbek). The Russian – English Dictionary of auto tractor science dictionaries have been distributed all over the Russian universities. This can certainly be counted as a historical event . I am proud to say that when I was a university president, the quality of education and teaching, and scientific research rose to the highest level at the university.

Anniversary of the university

At last, we saw in the new year 2002 . This year was much more different from the past years, as this year we were going to celebrate the thirtieth anniversary of the university. This time was a period of reporting to the university administration, and we had to make a report about our achievements and success, what we could manage, what plans we had successfully implemented, and which of them we didn't. This year was a year of making conclusions and getting energy for the next achievements. This was how I understood the anniversary. We had to prepare for the long term, and we decided to publish a book on the life at university. We had already published one in Uzbek for the twenty fifth anniversary, but unfortunately we couldn't send it to any of the foreign universities. This time we made up our minds to publish a color book in both Russian and English. We could manage this, and we could distribute this book all over the world.

On the occasion of the anniversary we got a huge sum of funding from our special university account. We spent it on publishing the book and dedicated it to the anniversary and organizing celebration parties. The administration of the "Uz auto industry" gave the university the automobile TICO as an anniversary present. I gave the key to the proctor of the University of Orifjonov. All the rest of the funding money left from the anniversary expenditures were spent to encourage teachers, students and other specialists at the university. I must say that within ten years of history at the university there had always been enough money in the fund. All the ceremonies like the sixtieth, and seventieth anniversaries of teachers were celebrated due to this fund all the time. All the books, and dictionaries were published from this fund. All of this money we received was due to the efforts of the rector, I used to order the staff to spend them fairly on only the things necessary for university life.

For ten years, neither the dean nor any proctor rendered any kind of sponsorship to someone. But I did my best to help people, those people who also helped me when I needed their help. I didn't spend a cent of the funding in my favor, I had the funding money all spent in favour of the university community. I hope that honest people, and the members of the staff who worked with me will never forget this.

The main founder of the university, academician O.U.Salimov was going to push 75. We planned to celebrate it as an anniversary, making a program for it. I took charge of writing a special book on the biography and life routine of this teacher.

I prepared a book called "The Philosophy of life is Helping people in need". The authority representatives, Chingiz Aytmatov, rectors and many other writers wrote their commentaries and articles for this book. It is never enough No matter how much we value this kind of people, we can never do enough for them.

Doctor: "By the way, I heard that people describe you as a man of business and entrepreneurship. How could you meet a man like N.I.Kucherskiy who was the hero of Labour? The field of metallurgy in Navoiy province isn't related to the sphere in which you're preparing professionals."

Sarvar: "You're right! Indeed the Navoiy Mountain Metallurgy Enterprise serves to increase gold in Uzbekistan. But geologists, miners, and economists have to work in cooperation with machine engineers, and road specialists, to sum up with us.

Unfortunately most of the specialists in this plant are graduates of the colleges in the metallurgical field."

A Special course for Navoiy Mountain Metallurgical Enterprise

Taking into account the fact that most of the employees of the plant contained only graduates of the colleges, in 1997 Kucherskiy N.I. sent a letter to me with a special request. This is what was basically written in that letter:

"We have 500 specialists working in our enterprise, and these specialists graduated from the specialty from which you graduated . Most of them today are working in high positions, and even though they don't have a diploma of higher education in this field, they have diplomas from the vocationally based colleges. Nowadays we are helping our specialists to study in Russian universities on the basis of contract correspondence learning. This is at the same time requiring a lot of money and causing an inconvenience for us."

Suggestion: "We wish you would help us to educate our specialists by organizing a three year-based intensive study program with a higher educational qualification. We are ready to render any kind of financial assistance for that on behalf of the enterprise."

I was glad to receive this request letter because due to that we could get an even stronger financial base for the university. However, we needed permission from the Higher and Secondary Education Ministry, as well as agreement with the Cabinet of Ministers so as to organize intensive teaching courses.

I sent the following letter to N.I.Kucherskiy:

"I like the idea of organizing this intensive learning and teaching course, but I think you'd better write a letter to the Minister O.U.Salimov, while at the same time, I'll also write my positive opinion about this idea.". He soon wrote a letter to the Minister, but I had talked with him by that time. The minister made an agreement with the Cabinet of Ministers to open the 3,5 year course Center at the university. O.U.Salimov once more proved that he was a man with a very good strategy.

In August we started admitting the future specialists on the basis of their correspondence learning. About 50 people successfully passed the exams , so that they could become third-year students at the university in the correspondence learning. Each applicant submitted his documents with a certificate about their prospective professional work experience, with no less than three years, a recommendation from the enterprise, and a letter of guarantee to pay all the tuition fees on time. They were prepared so that the Committee of investigation examining us every year wouldn't disturb us with their bickering.

This means these specialists got a chance to receive a higher education within three years and six months on the basis of this intensive course. Higher education based on six years was replaced with 3 and a half years. The teachers for this course were made to pass special exams, and we attracted the most talented professionals to teach them. We and those students agreed to both attend lessons, and go to work on time. Work didn't have to deter them from their studies. The teachers were ready to go to Navoiy, Zarafshon or Uchkuduk where the metallurgy enterprise was operating. All the expenditures were spent from the enterprise funding. This project had lots of benefits, and huge sums of money could be saved.

In order to implement the plans, I set the requirements for the teachers. I talked face to face with each of them. The main aim was to educate and teach honestly in accordance with the law, require knowledge from the students, and assess them fairly.

None of the teachers betrayed my trust and confidence.

Reputation is really hard to earn, it takes many years, but it can be lost within a minute. Therefore I used to have special conversations against that. In 1998 we admitted 50 students to the intensive teaching course faculty, they studied until the summer of 2002, until that time our university provided 100 professionals to the enterprise. Within this time I had been to the Navoiy Metallurgical enterprise several times where I could well get acquainted with the process of refining gold. I visited not only the gold refining plant, but also the mechanics plant in Navoiy city, the plant for producing nitrogen minerals, the technologies of refining gold and silver, and the technology of producing marble plates. We also observed all the mines in which different rare metals are derived (the plant is 500 meters in depth and several kilometers in length). In this plant the machine carried several tons of ore up and specialists will derive just several grams of gold from those tons of ore. Now just try to think, the Navoiy Metallurgical plant submits ten tons of gold to the government at least every year. Oh, so hard it is to think how many tons of ore they refined!

Within four years and six months we prepared one hundred professionals with a high education for this plant. All the specialists carried out their graduation research on the basis of the order from certain factories and plants. According to my suggestion the head of the exam committee was appointed N.I.Kucherskiy, professor of the TARU. I wanted this man to assess his own prospective professionals by himself. The main members of the Exam Committee were senior specialists working in the Navoiy Metallurgical Enterprise. Most of the graduates who defended their graduation research were assessed with excellent marks. Me and N.I.Kucherskiy were really proud of it, and we implemented our plan successfully.

I still remember, in 2000 our President gave the award "Dustlik" (Friendship) to the Navoiy Metallurgical Enterprise, because they submitted several tons of gold which was much more than it was planned to be. I was also invited to this meeting, This was also a symbol of respect and value for me. Me and Kucherskiy became quite close friends at this time. In 1997 we celebrated the twenty fifth anniversary.

In this anniversary Kucherskiy personally took an active part, and he even gave two TICO automobiles to our university as an anniversary present. He also provided our university with marble plates, iron and other materials for reconstruction. As a symbol of thanks to Kucherskiy our university awarded him with the award "professor of TARU". This award was issued to honour the scientists in Russia. They were K.Parpiyev the head of the "UzAutoIndustry", the head of the "UzAutoTrans" L.Ahmetov, the head of the "Tashkent city passenger trans" R.Fayzullayev, the head of the UzAutoRoad" R.Yunusov, T.Kamolov the head of the Joqori kenges (Supreme Congress), the rector of the MARU Lukanin, prorector Silyanov, Dobrogayev V.P., and one of the heads of the company Mercedes Bens, Volfgang.

The process of training in the intensive course center was under the control of the head organizations. One of these heads was Kostrica. Once I invited him to my home as a guest. He was stunned seeing that I was living in a flat measuring 32 meters square wide and 2 meters high. We had a good time talking and discussing. I boasted saying that I had read the holy book Koran in Russian when I was a Ph Student in 1965. Seeing the way he was interested in it, I gave that book to him as a gift. the

I have read the Koran several times in Uzbek and Russian . We investigated all the technologies closely used in the Navoiy Metallurgical enterprise. We made sure that all the equipment utilized there were up to date and modern. Members of different nationalities, from different countries, were working there in consolidation as a unique family. They are Uzbek, Russian, Tatars, Kazakhs, and many others. Therefore this enterprise was awarded with "Dustlik" (friendship) award, because people relating to different nationalities were working in cooperation to get tons of gold which was the national wealth of Uzbekistan.

I am a happy person. One day I was allowed to go into the store where gold and silver reserves were preserved, and we saw it with Kucherskiy together. For that we were strictly examined by security men in the transport. I was stunned on seeing 12 or 16 kilos of golden casts , which were deposed upon each other in the store. There were five or six of them next to the scales. I wanted to lift one of them, but I couldn't. I only could turn it over, then I could lift up because they were in conical shape. Then I liftep up the silver cast. I remember my grandfather Alimjonboy, and at that time I understood that the wealth of the motherland makes a man proud . I can never forget these moments.

A trustworthy colleague and a friend

Time passes so fast. I still remember how one young man came to the department of "Automobiles" of the Tashkent State Technical university. The head of that department Nikolai Abramov introduced him to us: "Ikromov Utkir Ahmedovich, graduated from the Ph studies in MARU, talented specialist, we'll be working together from now on."

We were admitted to Ph studies on the same day with Utkir, we have worked together for many years, and spent many years of our life being quite close friends.

If you want to know about a man much better, you'd better to travel with him, and spend some time together far from your home.

In 1963 we went to the field where we had to help grow corn with our students. There Utkir showed how hardworking, sincere and outgoing he was.

In 1963 in October I went to MARU to gain more experience and afterwards I stayed there to target my Ph.D. studies. Utkir usually sent his articles through me to his teachers professor V.V.Efremov and docent Assriyans.

His dissertation was on "Preserving the parallel state of the driving gear points while the automobile bowes are constructed". His defense was on January of 1964 in the MARU, he was awarded with the scientific degree "Candidate of technical sciences" with the common votes of experts. I understood why his parents called him Utkir (sharp), and I made up my mind to model him throughout my life.

In 1964 during the summer Utkir came to Moscow with his wife, and at that time we were students in Ph studies. No matter what happened, he kept working hard and following the advice of the professors like Okil Salimov, Abdusalom Mutalibov and Pulat Bobokhanov. He was a famous specialist.

For four years we hadn't talked to each other, because I was doing my Ph studies in MARU. Utkir was working as the vice-dean in the mechanics faculty, then he became the dean there. But if he went to Moscow on business, or if I went to Tashkent, we always had a good time together. Look, how honest man he is. In 1966 there was an earthquake in Tashkent city. At that time I was still in Moscow. He sent his friends to my home to see if my home wasn't too damaged, if my relatives were safe and sound, and then he sent me a letter, even phoned me saying that everything was alright. In 1969 after I distributed the abstract of my dissertation, I came back to Tashkent. I found out that he was working as a proctor of the Tashkent State pedagogical Institute. He was working part-time in the department "Automobiles repair" and we quite often had friendly conversations.

In 1972 Tashkent State Automobiles and Roads institute was founded. The department "Machines and equipments of building roads" was also founded at the same time. Utkir Ikromov was appointed as the head of this department. Our rector Mutalibov called me and said :

"If you work in this department assisting Utkir, it would be very decent of you to agree …" I agreed. We headed the department for four years together. We chose new teachers, and fulfilled tasks always in cooperation. We opened new laboratories. We went to see the minister of "Uzbekistan highways and automobile roads" A.Kayumov and defined the strategies there, which were really effective for further development of the department. The department became famous all over the Republic. At last in 1977 this department was divided into two parts: "Machines of building roads" and "Exploitation and repairing road building machines".

T.Askarhujayev and Utkir Ikromov were appointed as the heads in these departments. In 1978 the rector invited me and said:

"If you want, you're going to be the head in this department, Utkir Ikromov because has too many things to do". But I denied, saying that I was a scientist of engines.

Until the department was divided, Utkir Ahmedov and me were involved in some scientific research. They admitted my brother Marvar to Ph studies. He started his scientific research on the basis of a house holding contract with the Oltoi engine plant. Utkir, my brother, and I were co-authors in the publication of many articles, and all the scientific research served as the basis for my, and Utkir's doctorate, and Marvar's candidate dissertations.

Utkir Ahmedovich was the first doctor of scientific sciences who supported my doctoral dissertation results.

Utkir Ikromov worked as the proctor until 1995, gave a hand to hundreds of people, and significantly contributed to nurturing talented professionals. Many great and prominent specialists value him as a teacher.

My wife Alokhon also respects Utkir and his wife Sevara. Both of their sons studied at our institute and are contributing to the development of our motherland.

Unfortunately life is very complicated, and every person comes across with thousands of difficulties in life. However, both Utkir and his wife have overcome them with integrity. Utkir Ahmedovich celebrated his seventieth anniversary with his favorite students, friends, children and grandchildren around. He is a wonderful scientist and a great teacher who wrote many books and monographs for students in higher technical education.

*****

The university started gaining a reputation all over the Republic and being acknowledged in the world countries. I remember when we had a big meeting in the National University in 2003. Fifteen days later the same kind of meeting was held in our university as well. It was organized by the Higher Education Ministry. The State Counselor, assistant of the prime-Minister and other authority representatives participated in this meeting. I was really glad when after the meeting, the State Counselor went into my room and thanked me for the positive developmental changes we'd achieved. I am not exaggerating at all. An artificial compliment destroys behavior norms, while a fair assessment encourages a man to make further attempts, and prompts him to be even more confident.

Our teachers started feeling much more responsible for their duties, they had many books and manuals published, and I always helped them, never rejecting them whenever they asked me for help. We found out that there were some poets among our teachers, and we had their poem books published as well. All of them were published in the university publishing house. We even published some books ordered by the Ministry. On my initiative we received permission to publish books 1000 copies of each book. We also published bigger books and dictionaries. All these books were published with the money that was available in the the university's special fund. All the money the students gave to university was spent on their needs according to the rule.

At that time I was acknowledged as a scientist all over the world, I became an honored professor of several universities, an academician of several academies, twice I became "the man of the year", and I was included in the encyclopedia of the internationally famous people.

Even in my family life there have never been troubles like other families usually suffer from. In 1997 November my daughter Oydin got married to very honest man. A year later she gave birth to a daughter. This day was one of the happiest moments of my life. In 2000 she gave birth to a son, also born in February, and he is 60 years younger than me. We celebrated his birth with my anniversary together by having a party and I invited all my friends at the university and at school.

Within ten years I learned the education system of many developed countries of the world. I wrote about this in a special part of this book. But at the time when I was a rector, I had never had a vacation. All my business travels were like a vacation for me. I had a rest for treatment in Kibrai district twice or three times.

There are resting places of the university in the Parkent mountains, near the Tashkent sea, I didn't even have enough time to have a rest there.

While I was a rector I did something good for my colleagues. In 2004 I submitted houses for privatization to 25 of the teachers working at our university.

Usually twice a year we would go to the Parkent mountains to have a rest with the colleagues in the rectorate where we swam in the pool a lot. In summer our students practiced their theoretical knowledge in these places for a month. 8 cottages were reconstructed where the teachers could rest, and all the necessary equipment had been provided. I got a certificate from the governors to use these places as private property for the teachers. But this is just a part of what I did as a rector for the university.

Life is a non-stop travel to reach perfection, and those who count themselves as being perfect have already been lost to their self-esteem.

I have thousands of reasons for being proud of the life I have led because I have thousands of students who can understand me well, who are ready to help me at any time, and they are actually my future... the continuation of my life. I didn't get any rest for these ten years nor did I even go to a sauna, play tennis or go to a restaurant. I visited my old house once a year to cherish memory of my mother, and we had many guests there to have a traditional religious ceremony. It was hardly possible to invite someone to my flat, having only two rooms for these sorts of ceremonies. Just my students, my Ph students came to visit me in my flat, and no one else. I didn't disturb my colleagues for my own tasks when I failed to fulfill them, and as soon as I got some free time, I started reading books or tried to write some useful plans or opinions in the copied books. These opinions would be collected, and would be published as a book after some editing, checking, and afterwards students would use them to obtain some more knowledge.

I felt in my bones that what I was doing seemed immoral for some people, but anyway I didn't change my mind, or my way of gathering knowledge.

From 1995 to March 2005, I lived with the problems of university, and never took a moment to breathe far from that.

On February 11, 2000, I turned 60. On this occasion, and taking into account my contribution to providing the Karakalpakstan Republic with well-qualified professionals of automobiles and roads, the Joqori Kenges of the Republic awarded me with "The honored auto transport specialist of the Karakalpak Republic", I was in seventh heaven.

In 2004 the book "Automobile technology" was created in Latin script and it was awarded with the first and prime success in the contest of the technical literature which was held by the Asian Development Bank.

In 2003 and 2004 I was announced as the academician in the Academy of the engineers in the International information Academy.

In May of 2003, I was invited as a guest to the 300th anniversary of Saint Petersbourg, and I was appointed as a member of the International club of professors.

When I pushed 60 in 2000, all the proctors pushed the same age as I was. I replaced them with younger professionals, appointing these elderly professors as the heads of the departments. Their future confirmed that I had made the right choice. Three of them were privileged to work as presidents at Jizzakh Polytechnical Institute and Tashkent State Aviation Institute and TARU.

In 2005 I turned 65, but this time I didn't celebrate my anniversary again. All of the colleagues and students congratulated me in my room.

In 2004 I had monuments erected in honor of the late people who had worked in the university, and created "a book of memorizing" which I gave to all the family members of the late specialists.

In 2005 I published a book "Loyal People of the TARU" and handed it to all the loyal people working at the university. This was also no less than a monument. All of them felt happy to see this. Then after some time, on the initiative of Ganiyev Omonillo, some teachers of the institute gathered their opinions about me and published a book about me and my life. This book was handed to me when they were seeing me off while I was resigning from my position. This was a great gift for me. The book was called : "He Breathes to Help People". This was somehow a positive assessment to my activity as the university president.

Within ten years, I had several books published like "Responsibility for the Independence", "Science and culture", and "Yearning for the science". They were distributed all over the university. The aim was to educate the young students with love for the motherland, pride, and national identity.

Unfortunately there are some people who like to look for faults in whatever you do no matter how effectively you work. But so many years have passed since we obtained our independence and democracy. Sometimes I hesitate to think that these kind of people still pretend to be living in the Former Soviet period. They think it isn't incorrect to keep interfering in whatever we do as the heads of departments, even though what we do is right.

Every human being needs to try and help other people so that those people will remember him as a good person after he dies. Don't overestimate fame and reputation. Your own conscience is the main jury for whatever wrong or right you do all the time. You can hide what you did wrong from other people around, but you can't hide it from your own conscience. Try to forgive those who do harm to you, and try to be generous because God is kind and generous, he loves those who are generous, and those who help others. (Holy Hadith).

Doctor: I see that you're a man who devoted all of his life to scientific development and the development of the country. For many years you have been a rector, and I think you live in a huge and luxurious house with brilliant conditions, don't you, Sir?

Dreams about a house

Sarvar: What you say about my life is right. And of course every person dreams about living well.

From 1972 to 1977 I lived in the Korakamish district, apartment 19, flat 23 with my mother, wife and children. From 1977 to 2004 we started living in C-13, House 1, flat 59 (32 m2 flat with bedrooms). There were four people in our family at that time, 2 candidates of sciences, me and my wife and two of my daughters. My mother-in-law was living just round the corner, and she used to look after our children, therefore it was convenient for us to live there. We didn't have any desks there, and after we finished having supper or lunch, we started writing or reading on the same table in the evening. In the summer, we did our tasks on the balcony, on this old table where I had written my doctoral research in 1981.

A year later I started working as a university president, I went to see the minister of higher education, who'd been my own teacher. I wanted to buy a bit wider flat if the Ministry could help me. The policy before had been as soon as the university president started working, he would immediately be given a huge new flat or a cottage). It was impossible to get a flat for free by writing a letter of request to the governor. I was told that it was only possible if I would order a flat from the construction agency. But where on earth could I get enough money for that? I had very close friends and then I found it better to ask for assistance from the enterprises, plants and associations. In developed countries sponsorship is very well developed, because there are many opportunities for that. Taking into account the fact that our country is also developing day by day, and our President is supporting sponsorship organizations, several letters asking for help were written on behalf of the Minister to several entreprises. There it was written : "Taking into account all services and contributions, it would be decent of us if we buy a flat for TARU". The association UzIndustry was the first to give 2 million soums to the account of the Higher education Ministry, and the other ministries also decided to help, but before the money was delivered from their account, my teacher Minister was dismissed and appointed as a Counselor for the Minister. Now there was a new Minister, and four or five days later that new Minister invited me to the Ministry. He was talking about the flat, he said :

"Even though we aren't very close, your wife is a relative of mine, and if I try to help you to get a flat, there may be some rumours about that, so … I am afraid …"

Then I said: "If this problem is going to disturb you that much, you can no doubt send those 2 millions back to the sponsor UzIndustry," I immediately left the room. The chief accountant of the Ministry urged the new Minister to make this decision, because perhaps he said : "The former Minister is actually a teacher for Sarvar, and he wants to help him get this flat for free, that's something weird". I think we certainly deserved to get that flat . But we couldn't solve this problem at all.

God always supports those who he loves. I was lucky that my classmate friend became the assistant to the Prime- Minister. He was also aware of all of this as he also signed the documents as a Minister. When I went to congratulate him, he said:

"Don't feel sad, man, everything's going to be ok! Just write a letter of request on behalf of the university administration and in two or three months, you'll get what you deserve and what you're asking for! You've served our motherland a lot!" The proctor and the staff union wrote and forwarded a letter to the Ministry.

According to decision by the assistant to the Minister, the head of the Tashkent city Passenger Transport was appointed as responsible to help me with my flat. All the sponsorship money was transferred to the association account. Some time later due to their assistance I was able buy a house for 8,8 millions soums which was a very low price for a house. The house was located in an apartment which was being built in the Navoiy-Zarqaynar street. The house hadn't been built yet , so we had to wait for four more years. I got the order of ownership this house in 1999. When I first saw this half constructed house, there was nothing except the walls. There was no door or window frames, and no ceilings. But thanks to God we had honest and fair authority representatives, close friends, and I also did my best to help them as much as I could.

At last, in 2003, this flat was issued to me as a real estate and private property. For over two years, I had the walls repaired and reconstructed as well as I wanted. My student Bahrom helped me to find honest masters. As the neighbors hadn't moved in at that time, we had to wait some more, and after they moved in we had to have it reconstructed again because our neighbors were having their house reconstructed, water came down from the ceilings, and we had it repaired again, according to what the masters recommended. For over a year only three families lived in one block one block, but upstairs there was no one living there. The house was built of bricks, and twice we had problems with the water used on the fifth floor. All our ceilings got wet, but our neighbors didn't even want to think about paying for the damage, so we had it done all by ourselves.

All of our grandchildren liked this flat a lot, as it was wide and big enough to play ball inside, and the children would play on the swings around the circus as this house is quite near the circus.

I was both the architect and designer in decorating our new home. There weren't any extra decorations in my home, and it was very convenient for writing books, and reading after coming from work.

The basic purpose of my life has always been to obtain knowledge, and to honestly head an educational organization, helping those in need and forgiving everyone, even though they do much harm to you.

I've been helping, and honestly doing many good things for people just because I followed the footsteps of my own parents who led their lives in the same way. May they be blessed in that great beyond. For those who are alive, I only wish them a long and healthy life.

My family

If you remember I just mentioned my wife to you, dear readers. More in detail, she is a scientist of automobile roads, and a candidate of sciences.

On July 26,1970, my daughter, Nigora, came into existence…. the first symbol of our love. Finishing school with high grades in 1987, she entered the Moscow Pedagogical University, in the "Russian language and Literature faculty", because she really loved all the poems of the Russian poet M.Yu.Lermontov. She only studied for one year in Moscow, and after that I had to transfer her studies to the Tashkent State Pedagogical university. We had lots of problems until she changed her university, and she graduated in 1992, and helped with all of the translations of my scientific work. After she learnt many things, she started writing books with me together, and in 2001 she studied for her second specialty, economics. However, she didn't change her main profession, and she continued to edit different books in Uzbek and Russian.

On April 25, 1974, one of my daughters Oydin was born in Moscow. She finished school with a golden medal, and on her own she decided to enter the economics faculty. Having studied with excellent grades there, she brought us her certificate about her entrance into the International Relationships and Diplomacy university. We were all surprised, because she didn't speak about it to any of us. We had to change her studies in TAYI for the correspondence learning, so she could graduate at two faculties at the same time. She graduated from both universities with honors, and worked for a bit at the Ministry of Foreign Affairs then changed her workplace to the UzAuto Industry. Oydin has considerably contributed to the opening of the Sam Koch Auto Company, and she's one of the specialists who created the Technics and evidence of safety and financial efficiency of the plant. She completely learned the field of automobile industry, then she even started doing her Ph studies in correspondence courses. She finished her dissertation before the expiration date and delivered a wonderful lecture at the Scientific seminar of the TARU. She coped with some complicated questions by the experts there. I was silent, and didn't interfere. The impressions were positive, and her dissertation was recommended for a further defense.

I didn't permit her to defend it there as there could be some rumors about that, and people might think that she passed her exams because of my position and reputation, or think that I'd paid the experts to assess her dissertation positively. Those who think so are absolutely wrong.

The dissertation was forwarded to the Tashkent State Economics University Scientific Council. The head of the council was the head of the Higher Education Ministry. As the dissertation met all requirements of the SCC. I didn't even get interested in the results until after she passed her exams.

Her defense took 2 years and six months until she could successfully pass all of the Science Academy exams and scientific councils in the province universities. All the members of the council were well acquainted with the dissertation, and finally a special member of the SCC Experts Council signed a note claiming: "The dissertation meets the requirements of the SCC". After that they appointed two opponents for the defense. At last she defended her dissertation and Oydin was admitted as the candidate of sciences with 100 votes in her favor.

I purposely didn't take part in her defense exams,because I didn't want other people to think that I was there to support her in case she would have problems with assessment. I heard many good comments about her knowledge. After she defended the Minister called me to thank me for the way that I'd brought up such a clever and well-educated girl. This was my greatest victory.

My "real friends" started playing their "favourite games" with me, but this time against my daughter. Actually, after her dissertation was forwarded to the two opponents, they both wrote positive recommendations and comments. However, one of those "favourite friends" who was a member of the experts Council dared to write an anonymous letter. He was the professor who was dismissed from the TARU because of bribing. According to what he wrote in an anonymous letter, my teacher S.A.Salimov had written the dissertation for her. After that poor my daughter, Oydin was again called to Experts Council, but there she stunned all the experts with her cute answers to all the questions. Then, I later heard that she run her disputes in both Russian and English.

Several days later a professor and the head of the SCC, M.Muhitdinov invited me to his office where he apologized for what happened. As soon as I left his room, in the corridor I came across the head of the Experts Council, professor Alimov B. He also apologized for what had happened with Oydin's dissertation. They claimed that they had never seen such a clever researcher, and their opinions were sincere.

The Kodirovs have always been proud of themselves, and the life they've led. It would be unfair to not mention the mother who brought up a daughter like Oydin.

Alokhon Kodirova worked as a docent from 1972 to 1996. She headed the department of "Projecting automobile roads" from 1976 to 1986. After the university administration appointed me as the head of a department, she resigned from her position even though she was asked to stay. She didn't want to be elected for the third time.

Today my wife is a professor of the TARU, and she has an award "the teacher of all the road-builders". She translated books like "Projecting automobile roads" by V.F.Babkov and O.V.Andreev from Russian into Uzbek. Taking her all hard work into account, the administration of the technical university awarded her with "Honoured professor of the MARU" on the occasion of her seventieth anniversary. She is the only woman professor in the automobile roads field, and all the engineers of automobile roads accept her as their teacher…. Not everyone is privileged to be so happy, I think …

We can invent surely

After our country gained independence, I had a good idea to create an Uzbek automobile. Independence strengthened my feelings of responsibility even more, and I think it's a holy duty for each scientist to invent something useful for his society.

In our university, the faculty of Automobile industry was founded in 1992, I had been heading the department of producing and repairing automobiles in this faculty. I have always had the idea to invent a national Uzbek automobile. We needed enough conditions and suitable opportunity for that. One day two Russian fifth-year students came up to me. At that time I had some negative opinions about their behavior, but after we talked for some hours, they turned to be real fans of automobile science, and perhaps, therefore, they weren't interested in other subjects, or seeming to do badly at the faculty. They were drawing images and designs of automobiles day and night, they showed some of them to me, and there were some proper ideas in those images. However, they were anyway still immature. I suggested I become their scientific advisor and to write graduation work in that field, I promised to help them with the rest of the subjects with which they had no interested . The theme chosen was "Creating body construction of an Uzbek automobile" and I told them how to find the materials.

When I informed the Scientific Council of the faculty about my ideas, some skeptic teachers brushed me off:

"Uzbek scientists can not cope with this at all. 400 and 500 scientists are working hard for that in Italy, and England, but you're going to create automobile body construction with two lazy students who don't even study properly."

I insisted on staying with my decision as I was quite stubborn. We worked with those two Russian students days and evenings, drawing schemes and designs of automobile body constructions. This wasn't at a level advanced enough for construction, but close enough. Both of my graduates defended their research with excellent marks, and all the skeptic teachers were stunned.

After that I didn't meet them at all, and I got more and more work. I was chosen as a university president in 1995,and even though all the days were hectic, I still had that burning idea in my mind; automobile body construction.

In 1994, they started building an automobile producing plant in Asaka, Uzbekistan on the initiative of our President Islam Abduganiyevich Karimov. This was a joint company which was aimed to operate in cooperation with South Korean colleagues.

The first automobile Nexia was produced in the plant in 1996, and this was a great victory. Our country had become a state of car industry. But some strange mass media representatives were spreading the rumors : "Korean automobiles are being produced in Uzbekistan." All these rumors were insulting to me as an automobile scientist.

Creating or inventing something new isn't that easy , and it requires dedication from one's own life to implement a plan. Therefore, for me, a life led without any useful service for the motherland has no meaning.

I looked for professional constructors all over the Tashkent city, but couldn't find any good ones. At that time my nephew introduced his Kazakh friend to me, who wanted to live and work in Tashkent. He turned out to be a master and the constructor I was looking for. I decided to employ him, and he expressed his own opinions after he saw all the designs and schemes of the automobile body constructions.

While creating the automobile construction, we had to take our climate into account because the dust level which falls into the fuel is very high in the Republic. This causes automobile components to destroy easily. That's why it required to install special dust cleaner filters in the "SANO". Secondly the temperature of the engine in our country contains 50-60 degrees. This at the same time decreases the power of the engine and increases fuel waste. We planned to use a special liquid invented in the institute so that the engine wouldn't over heat. Thirdly we needed to focus on choosing the color of the automobile. We chose alloy steel color, because it prevents the car from heating. Fourthly our car SANO can be driven by a man of any weight and height. It's convenient for anyone. Fifthly, the automobile body construction can not be compared with to any other car; it is unique. The air opposition coefficient is 0.24 when the car is moving, that of Jiguli is 0.34. This specifically saves the engine.

Just try to imagine how much you relax if you notice a]the smell of a 5 or 6 months old baby. When my dream to create an Uzbek automobile was coming true, I also felt relaxed in the same way, as if I was hugging a baby, an innocent baby. This was the first invention and scientific exploration of Uzbek scientists. Yes, Uzbek scientists certainly can invent useful things, and they can implement brilliant ideas because they are eager to learn and excel.

We calculated all the money needed for the automobile body construction and then decided to open a small enterprise for that purpose, giving it the name SANO . The businessman Abduhalil invited his friend to work as the director of this enterprise. Me and Abduhalil were working hard at the prospective construction, and brought it to the state to meet its needs and requirements. According to our schemes we constructed a handmade body framework, doors, bonnet, wings and bumpers technology. Now this construction could be submitted to the patent agency. The authors were three people: me, the constructor and the entrepreneur. It's impossible to create a car in any other way, and someone needs to design, someone needs to construct, and one more person is needed to provide the funding for everything.

After some time I received a certificate as an author on which my name was written. It meant I could start working more seriously. We started it at first in our laboratory, we got the money for that from the funding of my house holding contract.

We bought all the necessary metals and welding tools, but unfortunately the Ministry adopted a new decree on building a modern building of an academic lyceum and academic laboratory in the same place where we were working, and therefore we were forced to find a new place to working. It was in the plant "Compressor". It was challenging for us to find a proper place to work, and after we found it, we had to move all the tools and instruments there.

We started working with creating the framework, then we started designing doors, wings, bonnet, front, and rear bumpers. This process turned out to be really complicated, but gradually we converted each complex of metals into the shape of the body. The elements were steel 0,8mm, width is 5 sentimeters, length started being collected according to the length and construction with welding. A man who hasn't tried to do the same thing we did might think that it isn't hard at all. But it took us a year to complete this task. Within this time I had to bring the car Nexia exploited in the taxopark 2 of the Tashkent city passenger transport. I always thank the head Fayzullayev R.F. for that. The engine, all the aggregations and seats of the car were deposed and installed in the car which was being constructed. We attracted the Electronic institute of the Sciences Academy and they formed the necessary electronic systems for our Uzbek automobile. This construction was to meet all the standards available. This car was also to be decided with the Automotic System of Ruling the car which was not of less quality than that of Mers. It is possible to start off the engine and heat it. The master showed me the bill 24 million soums for giving a modern view to the prospective car. This was a very huge sum and we could buy two Nexia cars for that amount. Even though the entrepreneur was the co-author for the patent, it only existed just on documents, and he didn't want to help us financially for that.

I was in the dark about where to get the money from. After a long time of brooding over it, I decided to address a rich man with a request. I wrote him a letter asking him for help, and as a result, he could also become a co-author and eventually become famous eventually. But it was in vain.

After the constructor moved to Tashkent city with his wife and children, I did my best to help him. Time was flashing by, and I still had not a penny to my name. Suddenly in 2004, I heard somehow that Abduhalil, our entrepreneur and the director of our small company wanted to close down the enterprise and steal the car SANO design from me to take it to Kazakhstan. I was really upset. Did I have to expel both of his sons from the university? But I didn't.

If he could find enough money to construct it according to my design and my plans, and if he could get some benefits due to my hard work, ok, I wouldn't try to object. This was written in many newspapers and magazines, and its photos were published in the book dedicated to the thirtieth anniversary of our university. There's an image of an automobile SANO even on the emblem of our university. The photos of the SANO designed by me and UAZ farmer-automobiles, are everywhere in our university. Even though they stole the designs and ideas, everybody in the Republic is aware that it is actually my project . It means all my contributions to these designs are deemed as historical events. My dream was to completely finish the design of that car, allow it to pass all the testing experiments, and show it to the President. But unfortunately my dreams didn't come true. This is all what God has destined us to do.

I am an optimistic man,never afraid of challenges and I can always overcome them. In 2004 I won a state grant and I started a scientific research on the second option of the Uzbekistan automobile with the docent Hoshimov Davron Ibragimovich. The model on a 1:10 scale is still kept in the museum of the university. We needed a lot of much money for reconstructing its body from metal, and according to what I read in German articles, 340 mln marks were spent to construct the automobile Mercedes. 440 million marks more were spent in order to show it in the production line. Unfortunately some specialists in the UzAutoIndustry were afraid to do this.

I made sure of all my researchers, and that all of the scientists in Uzbekistan were very talented, and if there are enough conditions, they can succeed in any field .

One of the principles that makes the state richer is its economical indications. The main part of economical growth depends on the development of a car industry. As you know the countries where the car industry is well developed are the USA, Japan, Germany, Italy, South Korea, and France which are all the strongest states of the world. Therefore the technical politics which our President is supporting is no doubt the best way to stimulation. Today we have several joint car manufacturing companies like "DAEWOO" (South Korea an Uzbekistan), "Avia" (Zcheque), «Otoyol» (Turkey), which are active in delivering cars DAEWOO company Nexia, Tico, Damas. Soon after that "Matiz" started being sold in the market, a simple car which operates using less fuel than other cars do. All the busses and trucks of the company Otoyol are making our life much more convenient for the people living in Uzbekistan.

It would be a good idea to produce a car, not expensive, which can operate with a limited amount of fuel, requiring ordinary technical care, transporting a huge number of loads, and a huge number of people. Taking all this into account, we chose UAZ-3151 as a model for farming automobiles of Uzbekistan, because they were effective for all the experiments in hard conditions. Their level of operating for a long time and transporting heavier loads are really high. To prove that we have succeeded in constructing the farming automobile needed, we are citing one article published in the magazine "On the gear":

UAZ automobile took part in car racing aimed at a distance of 4000 kilometers for the first time in 1956, which was held in Indonesia. At that time it showed its reliability and simplicity in technical service. This all put the automobile on the map. In the recent years the cars produced in the plant Ulyanovsk are easily competing with those manufactured in England, the USA, Germany and Japan. The competition Transafrica encouraged popularity of UAZ through competitions in Italy. They are used for rescuing people in mountains, geological explorations, providing countryside and mountain regions with foods and water. Fire-fighting cars are being constructed on the basis of this design. In Switzerland UAZ's jeeps are used for transporting miners to where it's hard to get to. In England it's being used for repairing a large amount of UAZ conductors.

UAZ's automobiles are widely used in the countries where the climate and road conditions are harsh: Nepal, Afghanistan, Guinea, Laos, Syria, Mozambique and Latin American countries. It is also quite often used for roads destroyed because of downpours, heavy rains, and roads on the shores where the sea water flooded. Though there are many advantages, it doesn't lack disadvantages either.

As for convenience, as we know all the seats in that UAZ are inconvenient to sit in, which makes the driver and passengers feel comfortable, especially when they have to drive for a long time. Therefore Volga seats are in this case used for the UAZ to be made. The surface of the car body is covered with tarpaulin, which makes it hot in summer and wet in winter. Taking this into account the external part of car needs to be covered with metal. Inside the automobile body needs to be covered with a rough and thick cloth so that there wouldn't be any noise. The upper roof part and the doors are covered with leather. There's a necessity to lay a thick linoleum on the floor of the car. The wall separating the saloon from the engine, needs to be wrapped with rough and thick cloth on both sides, as this blocks the noise emerging from the engine.

As the upper arch of the UAZ is not very strong and rigid, those who are sitting in the car can be seriously injured in case of accidents, if this car skids. Taking this into account, the tarpaulin roof will be replaced with the metal roof. This will increase the safety of the car body.

According to effectiveness calculations, the new ZMZ- 451M engine requires 2/14 litres of fuel per 100 kilometers distance. This is too much for one car, therefore it undoubtedly harms the budget of a farmer. Taking this into account AVIA A-712 /Zcheque/ diesel is planned to be installed instead of the carborator engines.

The automobile that we created the UAZ-FARMER has passed all the testing experiments successfully, even though they were based on difficult heavy conditions of Uzbekistan Kamchik mountain zones.

After using the new engine, the use of fuel will edge down rapidly, it decreases by 8 litres, and the force moment and working capacity is really high. This at the same time increases the cost- effectiveness and tractive force. The main gear of the rear brigade is going to be altered, and it will be moving faster than the UAZ. For that we need to replace the reductors of the GAZ-24 or GAZ-31.

The weight of the diesel engine exceeds 100 kilos, and therefore it's required to strengthen the front suspension. As a result of locating that diesel engine, the ability of the car to lift heavy details will increase. A plate will be located on each spring, which will help the UAZ-FARMER to lift a load weighing 1,5 tons or in that car it will be possible for 8 passengers to sit at the same time.

One more disadvantage of this car is its lack of light in the saloon. Since the windows are very small, the rear windows will be made bigger in size, as big as four times the size of the other windows and will also increase. This improves the design of the body and makes it easier for a driver to see and look around.

The agriculture has been reformed as a result of small farming house holdings which were organized instead of less effective collective farms. But there were again problems of delivering products to certain organizations in time. The quality of the product not delivered on time will worsen, as you know, and this eventually causes great financial damage to farmer. I think it's now high time to create a cheap, fuel-saving and convenient automobile for farmers and we decided to create this with a candidate of technical sciences, Ostroglazov.

All the changes I explained above enabled us to construct the UAZ automobile which was really suitable for Uzbekistan's climate conditions. As a result of developing some functions, we increased its ability to tractive effort, the movement of the car, effective use of fuel, convenience and safety. We hoped that this would be well assessed by the Uzbek farmers. It was as four times as cheap in comparison to the jeeps produced in the USA or in Japan, and at the same time being quite convenient for Uzbek farmers.

The scientists of our university chose the diesel engine A-712 of the "DAEWOO-Avia" company so as to construct an automobile UAZ-FARMER . Of course there are some other engines to choose, but the length of time until the first disorder is very short, and as for AVIA engine, it contains 200 thousand kilometers, and requires 8 litres of fuel per 100 kilometers, which is really cheap and effective.

It's the duty of scientists and constructors to construct an experimental copy of an automobile, and the further production and distribution of the car is the decision of the authority representatives. We had created the automobile at last. There were all the conditions to produce it further in plant 14 of the Defense Ministry. For that we needed to buy some spare parts like the front and rear bridges, conductors boxes, wheels, electric parts, and body components, which could be bought from Russia. In the future, these parts will also be produced in our Uzbek plants because we have all the conditions for that. The diesel engine can be acquired from the "Avtash" joint company in Uzbekistan, and we currently started producing seats, accumulators, tires and paints in our Republic.

In 1997 when there was a council in the Cabinet of Ministers, our President addressed the Minister of Auto Transport and criticized him for not constructing any automobile which are able to lift the load weighing 1 or 2 tons for farmers. I took it as a claim directed to me, as I am an automobile scientist, and it's my duty to do what the President orders us. Moreover, at that time I had the answer ready, and we had already started working on that type of an automobile, the UAZ- Farmer with other scientists in the TARU. After I met Lerik Ahmetov, we next made a firm decision about everything relating to the prospective automobile. He was glad, we started working, and everything was going as well as planned. Docent Ostroglazov O.G. helped us a lot as a constructor. Now, the automobile with this model is serving all the farmers in the Kashkadarya province. Producing this car as the main product in the plant is still unfortunately up in the air, because my friend, Lerik Ahmetov resigned from the position of an assistant of the Minister at that time. This happened at the beginning of 2000. It's a pity.

These days we have created a new automobile on the basis of the construction of the UAZ automobile, and my MA degree students have been helping me with that. We installed the diesel engine of the Mazda to that, and it has an ordinary bridge. The reductor was replaced with that of the automobile, we have also removed the distributor gearbox and after that we worked at the general construction. After a little bit of work on the design, we are going to experiment with the new automobile TEWNING. I hope this car will meet all the requirements of current drivers.

About to resign from the position of a university president
In February of 2005, I was asked to write a recommendation letter for three doctors of sciences who we found as suitable candidates. We had to write this:

"They are able to work as the head of a higher educational organization". I wrote recommendations for A.Muhitdinov, A.Shohidov and Sh.Alimuhamedov. On February 27, Sh.O.Butayev phoned from the Ministry and asked the Proctor M.Orifjonov to prepare his documents as well. Perhaps he was also going to be recommended for this position.

Ten days passed after that, and at this time three or four rectors of universities immediately changed. I also came to this conclusion, and on March 1 the Counselor of the Minister visited our university. I told him:

"If you've made the decision to appointing the new rector, I am already prepared to write to resign". They told me to be ready at any time, even though they had yet to resolve the situation. When the assistant to the minister, M.Kuronov called me to his office on March 10, I immediately went, and he expressed his all positive opinions and views about my activity, then asked me to resign.

I wrote a short resignation letter to him, then I told about all happened to my teacher. When I asked him which candidate was approved, he just hinted at someone. I understood. I immediately invited all of my four proctors into my office, and I told about them resigning that day, I said I of course hoped one of my students was going to substitute me there as a rector,and I advised them to work in consolidation whatever might happen.

On March at around 5 pm, my teacher called me and informed me that my resignation letter about resigning had been signed and that the new university president had been appointed. He also added that the new rector would be introduced on March 12. He said

:

"That's ok, A.Muhitdinov your student has become the new university president.Even though there were some candidates among those who were strangers, your student has won the interview! They will see you off with a special Thank you ceremony. This is a great fortune that not everyone gets. Everybody wants to thank you for all you've have done as a president". That day me and my daughter, went to see a concert by the group "Sonata" sponsored by the Navoiy Metallurgical Enterprise. Listening to the songs of Sherzod Davronov, we had a really good rest. After I got home, I phoned the new rector to congratulate him from the bottom of my heart. I was really glad to know about his success, and that he, my student, had succeeded .

On Saturday, March 12, we waited all day for the Republic authority representative and the Minister, and I gave a hug to our new rector and congratulated him on his success. I believed that he could cope with everything in the administration.

Unfortunately, nobody came while we waited for such a long time. Then I had to leave for home after 5 pm. My grandchildren were also at work with me from the early morning. On weekends we had a good rest with them, and visited our in-laws.

March 14, I supposed the authority representatives would come.

Unfortunately they again didn't show.

March 15, we were still waiting, but we were tired of it . I had already taken all of my belongings out of the rector's room, when at last they called us from the Ministry at around 12.00 pm, they said:

"The Prime Minister is going to go to the presentation at 1.25 pm." Both the new rector and I were waiting for the assistant to the Minister's arrival. We started the Scientific Council, in which the assistant of the Minister said:

"This scientist, Mr Sarvar, is always going to be a teacher and a guide for the president of the university, the new president, and though he's young, he should follow his advice." I thank God, and our President. In the Council I mentioned that while I was working with the Three Ministers, they had never negatively assessed the way I headed the university. I also said that, besides that, whatever success I had had within these ten years, I had achieved in cooperation with all of my colleagues. I then wished the new rector good luck, and best wishes to my own favorite student. The people who made a speech at that council were in total nine:

– M.Z.Musajonov, S.A.Salimov, L.K.Hakimov, A.L.Barhaniadjan, B.J.Salimova. – They expressed their good opinion about my work experience, and they positively assessed all of the hard work I had done. The Council then ended.

R.S.Kosimov led, me, the proctor and the Deans into the rector's room. Muhitdinov sat in the rector's chair , and I sat in the first chair in front of him. R.Kosimov sat right next to me. He ordered the department of house holding to solve the problem of the machine I was working at, and he gave a special order to the head of the Trade Union after that. However, even before that they made the documents ready for the new rector's appointment. As soon as the council ended I moved into the department with all of my books and documents. I ordered the replacement of all the arm-chairs with ordinary chairs because arm-chairs are for relaxing, and the department is a place for working.

On March 16 all of my dear students and colleagues came to see me in the department. We talked for a long time, and the next day the new rector came to see me. We planned to work in cooperation, and on March 22-23, two doctoral dissertations were defended. The first was by Sharipov Kongiratbay, student of the academician Lebedev, and the second one was my student Rustam Shukurov. Both of the dissertations were forwarded for official final defense with 100 % of the votes. Both of them were found suitable for the doctoral degree. There had never been a one by one doctoral research defense in the history of the TARU. This was the result of hard work. I hoped for more defenses in the next years of the university.

On March 24, we celebrated the holiday Navruz, and that day at 12 in the afternoon all the council members gathered in the small hall where I was awarded. The new university president briefly gave some biographical information about me. After that the head of the corporation "Tashkent city passenger trans" gave me a flower, a present, and I was made to wear a tun[9] .The

assistant of the Tashkent city governor expressed all of his good thoughts about me and at that ceremony I gave the book "Honoured professionals of the TARU" to the new rector. The rest of copies from the book we handed to all the other guests at the ceremony. Then professor O.A.Ganihujayev gave me the book "His breathes to help people", which portrayed my life, scientific achievements, hard work and contributions to the educational development of our country. He promised to distribute 500 copies that book to all the students in the TARU saying that it would also enrich the way that they think. There were three more representatives from the UzAuto Industry; A.M.Hakkulov, Tulaganov Sh.O. and someone else who I didn't recognize. That man gave me a tun as a present, and I was really glad for this respect.

---

[9] Tun – a type of national clothes for men, here it's given to the hero as a symbol of respect and appreciation

All of the guests were invited to have meal and they raised their glasses for cheers. My colleagues Mahmud, Gulbahor, Hikmatilla Abduboriy, and Dagar, all expressed their own wishes before we drank our drinks.

After we ate pilaf, we all went home. Starting from March 15, I started working as the head in the department where I spent my life when I was young. All in the departments required lots of attention and hard work, and I put them all in order. All the tools in the laboratory needed to be replaced. We needed to find a good specialist in electronics, needed to raise the quality of the lesson, and for that it was necessary to have a face to face talk with those who didn't regularly attend classes. At that time I understood how much I valued my own job and work here, teaching students, dedicating my energy to them, and taking care of their future. Then I understood that for a man who has spent his life on creativity, sitting from a chair of a rector to a chair of an ordinary specialist, one doesn't have any stress. I mean for me, as a creative person, it didn't cause stress to become the head of the department after resigning from the position of a university president. To be honest, I started feeling healthier, and my blood pressure started being at the normal level. My own student is substituting me as a new university president. This infused lots of happiness into my heart. He can do this job very well , and he has enough ability and talent for that. But on March 26 he came up to me and said lowering his head:

"Could you please write a resignation letter quitting the job once more? I don't understand why they want it again. I couldn't sleep all night thinking about what's wrong with them". When I visited my teacher for advice, he suggested that I take a vacation on business. So, I decided to request a vacation for a year with the aim to work on the new book "Internal combustion engines", which I wanted to rewrite in the Latin alphabet. I appointed a professional to substitute for me as the head of the department during that time.

It seemed to me very challenging to write a book in the Latin alphabet, especially while working with technical books. I think it took me seven months . Now I had to have it checked, edited, corrected, published and delivered to twenty universities of the Republic.

At the same time I met a woman, a journalist in the "Saodat" magazine, Kutlibeka Rahimboyeva. I asked her to edit my novel "The Days Recent and Bygone". She edited this book in order to make the style of writing more literary. Perhaps I wrote this book in formal language as a technician,and therefore I thought it was a good idea to ask her for help. In April I rested in the resort Kibray, where I wrote a book on "Commitments of a Teacher and a Student". A year before that I had prepared a book " The President of the Republic of Uzbekistan talks about Mass media". When I sent it to the office of the President and the university, one of the authority representatives working in that Devon brushed me off: "Don't put your nose into other fields, you'd better write books about your engines and automobiles".

At that time I prayed to god saying: "Oh, my God, you see that I am just aiming at goodness, I wish these books will soon be read by our young people. They will certainly enrich their knowledge. I am not the type that writes disruptive books and ... my intention is to teach young people how to love the motherland." I suppose God heard me, because the man who brushed me off was soon dismissed, and fired from his job.

One day I met one of my friends who was a journalist, N,Muhammadiyev. When we started talking about books, he asked me to give him some copies of the book I had written. Well, you won't believe it, but he liked it, and he said that even the head of his organization approved of this idea after he had read it once. I think you remember how one authority representative rejected my proposal and after that he was dismissed. I know because of that authority representative rejecting me, that again my "real and favorite friends", wanted to kick me out. As suggested by that young journalist, I translated that book into Russian.

Sarvar: "Mrs Doctor, now my story is going to come to an end. Now you've become aware of all I came across during my life, and I hope that I will have more things to do ahead: researching, preparing candidates and doctors of sciences, working as a teacher, teaching students using my own books, and writing books dedicated to society. I ask God to give me strength for that, and besides, doctor, I need you as well, because without being healthy, I can't cope with doing any of these things".

At this time I really want to remember two of my teachers, one of them is S.E.Nikitin, who I have known since 1992, and who, unfortunately, when I was on business travel in Nukus city (Karakalpakstan Republic), I heard some bad news about him. I heard that his heart stopped beating when he was skating in the Izmaylovo park. I couldn't even go to his funeral. I could though, somehow go nine days after his death, and console his family members on behalf of my family and the TARU. I felt calm somehow, but I had lost one of the closest people in my life. All his advice could still be heard, and they still pierce my ears, as if my teacher, Nikitin is standing by me and talking. It was he who taught me to be strict, fair and to help other people in need. May God bless him all the time. His name is eternal, and he is eternal with the book that we wrote together, "Automobile and tractor engines". All the students still read this book in Uzbek, it has also been translated into English, and it has been handed to scientists all over the world.

I learned all my administrative knowledge from my teacher Mutalibov, and to cherish his memory, I decided to open a scholarship named after him. All of his advice came in handy as the head of the university and during my life.

On my initiative the department of Internal Combustion engines was named in his honour, after him, Department of Mutalibov. Anyway, I still feel that I owe many things to my teachers as they had never been tired of teaching me, making me learn and excel and urging to fight against any challenge or harsh reality of this life.

Criterion - Justice – Good deeds

Our ancestor Amir Temur was indeed right when he said : "Justice is Power". Our President Islam Karimov highlighted his opinions by his statements: "Justice and Knowledge are Power". "No one should be dissatisfied in this home, and when any guest leaves this place, they of course need to be shown enough respect".

That's what the great writer Abdulla Kodiriy wrote in his book "Bygone days", when he said on behalf of a hero Yusufbek Hoji. During my working experience of 50 years, I have always tried to follow all of these statements. I made fair decisions for 4 thousand students, and nearly one thousand teachers at our university, because the main criterion of life needs to be justice, as N.G.Chernishevskiy said. No one who came asking me for help,or left my room feeling upset with me, because I did my best to help all of them.

I made sure that justice is the greatest power and I started believing that the head representatives with positive information would one day follow all the rules of justice. When I worked as a rector, I tried to feel the problems , and the pain of those who asked me for help, because any person who addresses the rector or another head, will be hoping for their support. Are all the heads honest? Unfortunately no. The expensive, luxurious arm-chair of a chairman is a negative energy which will make a man insane , and sometimes forget all about honesty. Therefore I didn't sit in an arm- chair at all. When I became a rector, I removed the arm-chair, and instead I sat on a wooden chair. I don't even remember when I had it made. I didn't want that magic leather arm-chair to make me feel arrogant, and now I feel that I did it all right. After a long time, I made sure that all of my students, and colleagues respected me from the bottom of their hearts. This is the greatest happiness for me. One more thing I made sure about is that power is being able to help other people. All of us are slaves for God, and one day nobody can avoid going where he is. The only thing we can do is be responsible for what we have done good, or bad . When Doom's day comes, we know that all what we did good and bad will be measured and counted one by one. If we have done more good things , we are going to stay in paradise, if not … we will be unlucky enough to stay in hell. This time, I decided to tell you one story that I have heard ever since in my childhood. One day a man did as many bad things as good things, both of were equal in his life. Suddenly he heard a voice from the sky: "If you can find one more good thing in your life record where all what you did is written, you'll stay in Paradise! You can even try to borrow something from someone's life record, or among the people you know". That man decided to ask his wife, his parents, his siblings and his children for that, but they denied saying that they needed it themselves as they also wanted to stay in Paradise. At that ti an old woman suddenly saw him and asked:

"Oh, dear, what's on earth? Why aren't you going into Paradise?"

He answered:

"Just one more good deed isn't enough for me to go in, so I am …" the old woman said:

"My dear son, do you remember that you helped me when   I went to you asking for help to solve my son's problem. Let me do you a favor. Get one good deed from me, that's it!"

Even though the man said he didn't remember, the woman saved him from staying in hell by giving him one of her recorded good deeds. So the man went into the Paradise and stayed there for a lifetime.

This story has a rich meaning hidden within it. Any trouble, or any problem can be forgotten in this life, but when someone does us a favor, it's impossible to be forgotten. And even though we forget, God doesn't forget . Even though you spend all of your life helping other people and doing nothing for yourself, you mustn't complain about that. This will be useful for you one day or the other. When I was a rector, I helped many people. For instance on my initiative many people were awarded: for instance, more than 20 teachers with "Honoured Autotransport specialist", 14 teachers with "Honoured specialist of Tashkent passenger transport", 4 professors "Teacher of road Masters", 1 professor with "Shuhrat" (Fame), several teachers with the medal "Ustoz" (teacher), more than 10 professors with "Honoured professor of the TAYI" for writing a book, more than 40 docents "Honoured docent", more than 10 professors with "Honoured Professor" and many others. There are financial supports for each of these awards, for instance those who were awarded with "Honoured Specialist of the Tashkent city passenger Transport" can use public transport completely free of charge for all of their lives.

Those who supported our university and some foreign scientists were awarded with the "Honoured professor of the TARU. This is even more closely linked to our university teachers and other staff representatives with friendship and sponsorship ties.

Business travelling (1979 – 2004)

The Prophet Mohammad said:

If those who follow me travel somewhere That will be counted as a good deed for the sake of Allah Hadis

"Dear professor, I am not just a doctor for you. As it were, I am also a sister, and I having been listening to your life stories for over fifteen years. Everything you have told me has been a very good clue for me to cure the neurological disease you have. I can diagnosis your disease correctly, but there's one more thing which is making me wonder. Do you remember that you told me about Yugoslavia, Hungary, Thailand, and your travels in these countries? At that time you only talked about them a little bit, but you promised to tell me more about them with more details one day. I really want to know about the days you enjoyed traveling and resting from your hard work at the university. Usually people can get enormous relaxation from traveling, and it's really pleasant to hear someone talking about their adventures of traveling ? I think we can learn more learn from them."

"Well, my dear sister, Dr Zulhumor Sharipovna, now you've become the director of a huge and crowded hospital. If I'm not going to take up your time by telling all these stories, and if you aren't bored, I am of course ready to tell you about everything."

The traveler

There's a wonderful proverb in our country which says "A man traveling a lot will see lots of things, experience a lot and know a lot". Indeed while traveling it becomes possible to widen our outlook, to discover new insights into culture, and the traditions of the other people in the world. In the past our ancestors used to travel riding on a horse, camel and elephants. They wrote down all of their impressions in their little books as a memory: "India" by Beruniy, "Boburnoma" by Bobur, "The Diary for My traveling Adventures" by Mukimiy and many others. Hadn't Imom Bukhoriy, at-Termiziy, al-Ferghaniy, Zamakhshariy traveled many countries with many challenges, hadn't they studied abroad, experienced life in other countries, and they wouldn't have written precious books famous all over the world if they hadn't traveled. These things, and the differences between the cultures gave them a chance to get wiser and wiser through comparing the realities of life in all those countries.

By the way we may even read what our Prophet said in the holy book, the Hadith " The travels of my successors are their loyalty for God", "I want you to travel so that you can be healthy all the time!", and it's not written in vain.

When cars, trains, and planes have developed fast, there have been quite a few opportunities to travel: now we can read a huge number of stories, novels and articles about traveling and adventures.

I have been fond of traveling since my early childhood, and I really love it. I have traveled in many provinces of our country by car. Besides in recent years I have been obligated to go to many cities of Russia and many other countries like Yugoslavia, Hungary, Czech, Thailand, Germany, India, Israel, France and South Korea. I went there by plane, and traveled in many foreign cities by car and by train. I walked in the streets on foot, talked to people there, got interested in their lifestyle, and tried to learn about their educational system.

Yugoslavia

The first time I went to Yugoslavia in 1979, in August with the docent Shavkat Sobirov, I came back with positive impressions. We stayed in one of the hotels by the Adriatic sea with our team. We were living in the same room with Mr Shavkat Sobirov . We could see the sea right through the window. We were swimming in the warm sea water. One day Shavkat turned out to have forgotten his watch at the beach and he remembered forgetting it after a long time, I mean when we came back to hotel. He said:

"It was a very good watch! I think someone has carried it away already, it's a pity."

I told him then: "You can go to sleep now, I hope you will find it right where you may have left it, but now you must have a good rest, never mind, ok?"

I was right indeed because we found it the next morning when we went there. We had a wonderful rest by the Adriatic sea, we got rid of all of our tiredness, and the fatigue completely escaped our body. At that time I found an answer to my question : "Why do foreigners travel a lot?"

Uzbek people save and collect their money for many years and spend it on weddings, building homes for their sons, and we are victims of our traditions. It's hardly possible to change them.

Hungary

The Republic of Hungary is located in the central part of Europe, in the mid current of the Danube river. In 1980 I was also privileged to go there at last. I gained some scientific experience in this country from September 15 to October 15. The train from Moscow-Budapest arrived in the morning of September 15, and for some reasons unknown to me, no one met me there, It was strange and I felt a bit awkward as we stayed alone on the platform. I immediately focused and decided to ask a soldier on the platform how to get to the university where I had been invited to study. He helped me to get to the hostel of the military servants and somehow the superintendent phoned the international relationships department of the Technical university. Afterwards he asked the soldier to help me get a taxi. This taxi was to drop me where I was planning to go . At last I got to the university where the representative Arno Konstantin ushered me in,

They immediately found a translator for me who could speak Russian and he helped me to find a private home to rent. They gave me a room to live in.

One of the famous professors Finikiu Liviu wasn't aware of my arrival, maybe that's why there wasn't any planned schedule for my time management there. It took us three days to make a plan and make contracts with the necessary organizations. But despite this, right on the first day of my stay there, I met the head of the "Automobiles" department, professor Laosh Iloshvai (I have known him since I was a Postgraduate student in Moscow) and the dean of the Transport faculty, professor Zoltan Levoi. We mainly talked to them about science and technical development . After we formed all the plans, I started pursuing my duties set for the travel on business. From September 18 to 19 I was involved in observing the scientific and academic laboratories of the departments "Automobiles" and "Aerothermotechnics". On September 20 I was busy with looking through the books written in the technical field, and the books which were available in the libraries of the university. According to the plans I was allowed to visit the theatres, and museums of the city, so I did.

On September 22, in the early morning I went to the State Technics Library, and I came across quite a few new books there. Each university in this country has their own libraries, reading rooms and even copy machines, so that each student or a teacher could use them as much as they wanted .It was enough to be registered and that's all, no extra documents, and no fees.

On September 23, I was invited to meet the head of the department "Aerothermotechnics", professor Endre Pastor. We talked about partnerships and different problems both in their university and in ours. Yes, I found out that there were many things we could learn from each other in the field of higher education.

On September 24, 25 and 26 I saw how the specialists were accomplishing manual tasks for an engineer in the "Autocout" Scientific motor university. I found a lot of valuable information here, I was glad that talented professionals rule these organizations. On September 27 and 28 I was busy with copying the information I needed in the university, even though it was Sunday and Saturday, rest days.

On September 28 I was watching the monument Citadel, Parlament building and other sightseeing places of Budapesht just like real tourists.

On Monday I went to the Chepel enterprise, plant, where I watched the technological process of producing the chassis of the bus called "Ikarus". I shared my views with the main constructor there, and found an answer to most of my questions. The next day I was introduced to the mechanism producing the buse's body's and making them suitable for the Southern and northern climate in the plant "Ikarus". I realized that people from Hungary were really responsible and eager to invent something new and useful for society.

On October 1, I went to the university of "Road construction Science and Laboratory" where I got closely acquainted with their investigations, appliances, tools and technology researching poisonous gas emissions in Hungary. On October 3, I again went to the university of Transport, and had a conversation about the confidence of the Rabo engine and Ikarus bus and the duration of their effective service.

The Hungarian automobile scientists pay close attention to the (diagnosing) troubleshooting of the car engines so that the car movements would cause less pollutions and emissions in the atmosphere.

I also went to the plants producing car engines where I learned many things about producing engines with 2 ,3 or 4 cylinders and the compressors, and then I had a talk with a number of specialists about the same issue.

October 7, I visited the town Gior where there's the plant "Rabo" which produces the engines for the bus "Ikarus". I learned many things about the technology of producing engines there, but unfortunately I couldn't see this process in an experimental workshop.

I also read about the terms for the methods of writing for the graduation work. After that I was introduced to the plans, reports, courses, paper writing methods, laboratory work, methods and the teaching process in the "Automobiles" department.

There I heard that in Hungary a teacher is required to teach 40-156 hours per semester. I even went to Hitika city where I visited the machinery plant of the Chepel enterprise. I learned to test, repair car engines and other tools as well as producing the technology of the tools used for washing cars. I talked about an article to be translated into Hungarian with the docent Ioja, then I went to the "Heat engines" department and exchanged my views with doctor Fulin on the scientific studies of the diesel engines. I also learned how to use the scientific base of the laboratory and the measuring tools they were using. There I found out that there wasn't any research carried out on the operation of Rabo engines in hot climate conditions.

In such a small country like Hungary, I witnessed their considerable development in the automobile industry and machinery science. All the students were working non stop and studying to stimulate their own knowledge. This was in the 1980 s and I think their studies have developed even more today.

Thailand

We (the delegation of Kazakhstan, Kirgizia and Uzbekistan) got off the plane in the Bangkok airport on March 3, 1996. We were welcomed at the airport, and as soon as we finished all the things with the customs, we got in a Toyota microbus and went to the AIT (Asian Institute of Technology) where we were sincerely welcomed by the President of the institute, professor Alastair M.

The institute was founded in 1959 and has 8 fields of study: ecology, biological process, agricultural disciplines, management, constructing buildings, energetic science, regional problems, and MA courses in natural resources science. After we talked to the president of university, we were allowed to observe all the faculties and the laboratories there. Being a privately owned organization this institute is financially sponsored by enterprises in countries like Germany, Australia, Holland and Japan. This institute is located 42 kilometers from Bangkok city. The university prepares masters and doctors for different countries, especially Asian countries. There were 1000 Masters students. The total square is 220 hectares, and there are all the conditions to study there. All the tools in the laboratory met the necessary requirements of the modern period. We have some laboratories which aren't equal to those. Some buildings of the AIT laboratories and classrooms were built in cooperation with sponsoring organizations In foreign countries. They have this written this on the threshold of each entrance door . The locations are clean and tidy everywhere, and no one is allowed to smoke inside. There are enough computers, fax and copying machines in each office, and in the town there are also enough opportunities for the teachers and the students to work and to live well. Moreover, teachers from different countries also work there. For example, the president is from Switzerland, the vice-president from Japan, and the deans are from India.

We visited all the faculties within four days, delivered lectures to staff of teachers and master students, and shared our opinions on the discipline.

The lessons are conducted in English, and on March 7, we went to the Ministry of Education in Bangkok city. It became clear that there were state owned and private education systems in the state, and they always try to pursue the same degrees as that of European countries. The Delegation administration made a decision to make suggestions to the Uzbekistan Higher Education Ministry about preparing professionals using the experiences of Thailand's education professionals. That same day we visited the institute of humanitarian sciences which usually prepares bachelors. There the duration of studying is four years and all the lessons are conducted in the Thai language. The cost of education is 5000 US dollars per year, and only 20 % of the applicants can enter this university. An assistant-professor's salary is 1000 dollars, and that of docent-professors is 2000. The professors who   the biggest salary, 4000 dollars,   student scholarships are 180 dollars. Most of the teachers are local people, I mean they are mostly from Thailand.

The   AIT library left a deep impression on us, and in the AIT   all the lessons are conducted out in the Thai and English , there are many computers and copy machines. While entering the library one could see the note "vandalism" in one corner. It's a method which can effectively be used in our country as well. As the distance between one faculty and the other one is very far, students have to utilize bicycles to get across campus.

In March we were invited to meeting with the head of the agriculture and reproducing oil products corporation. That day we visited the holiday held in the corporation, with students from different countries like Nepal, India, Laos, Bangladesh and many others. They showed their talent for cuisine, craftsmanship, and they played different concerts and shows for us.

On March 11, our delegation was invited to a meeting at the Royal university. We decided to carry out research for a year and we also decided to exchange our teachers and scientists who know English and who work in the field of machinery, energetics , and building construction.

I need to specifically mention the automobile routes in Thailand, which are built from concrete, and the speed of the movement is 110-120 kilometers per hour. We didn't witness any accidents at all. All the overpasses have been built from monolith concrete in five stages. The catalysis is installed into the muffler of the automobile, that's why the ecological level of the city is satisfactory, and in a city that has 10 million people, there's no trail of emissions there.

Overall, I think that we could send our teacher with a knowledge of English to Thailand in order to get some experience. Moreover, it would help our TARU bachelor graduates to study for a MA in Thailand. However, they must know English to apply.

South Korea

I have been to South Korea for four times, and because it was necessary, I once went there with a delegation, once for experience, and the next time because I'd been invited.

In April of 1997, the KOICA study centre of the Ministry of Foreign Affairs in South Korea invited several chief representatives from Uzbekistan to have a Korean experience for two weeks. This delegation was fronted by M.Tashpulatov, the head of the State Committee administration of the Uzbekistan science and techniques. We stayed in a hotel in Seoul, and the next morning we started attending courses. We got a lot of information about Korea. At that time all the Korean school children were required to pass testing exams, the results of which would be published in newspapers. An applicant had the right to apply to any university according to their scores. Every university has their own requirements for scores. The students who received scores less than those required can not be enrolled in that university. They organized tours for us on Sundays and Saturdays, to museums, theatres, the Olympic stadium and etc. We were privileged to learn about lifestyle of Korean people, their ancient and modern culture as well as traditions. We also went to the plant where their television's were produced and we watched the process of assembling the televisions. One thing that surprised me a lot was that none of the workers in the plant were interrupted from working on seeing us. They continued working even though we were closely observing the process of how they were working.

In 1998 the head of the UzAuto Industry, Q.R.Parpiyev led a special delegation consisting of 8 people, and we visited the DAEWOO company in the South Korea. The delegation's representatives were professionals. For example, me, my postgraduate student, 4 of the main engineers from our local plant and the chief constructor, the director of the plant, Mr Yusupov were in attendance. The aim was to get introduced to the working process in the DAEWOO company, and to discuss the issue of building a plant which would be used to produce car engines in Tashkent city. On this occasion, we learned the process in the plants where the engines, driving shaft, gear, head, camshaft and etc., were assembled and we also investigated automobile engine's technology, and the body. It's been 20 years since the plant was built, but the technological process was being conducted at a certain speed. For example: the uncertainty of the cylinder liner.

Even the surfaces of the crankshaft pins are being prepared at certainty levels. The aim of the Korean representatives is to sell the car tools and details which are old, having been used for twenty years. They also wanted to equip the plant with the tools and mechanisms for producing the car MATIZ. Unfortunately, I couldn't stand this unfairness because it meant they would give all of their old details and equipment to us, the advantage from that would be we'd be producing 2 thousand Tico and Dama engines every year. However, UzDAEWOO produces 20-25 thousand cars with this design every year. The rest of the engines would not be needed at all, and in that case the plant could go bankrupt. Who needs this sort of plan? As the scientific chief of the delegation I set the following terms: "The license of the engine will be issued to Uzbekistan: all the export reservations will also be included. Korea would not be producing this sort of the engine in the future. This meant, Uzbekistan was going to be the only one to sell this sort of engine all over the world. The Korean representatives couldn't do anything with that. We had several meetings there, but we insisted on our position and we informed the prime-Minister of this. What we offered was confirmed. In our opinion, it was necessary for Uzbekistan to have only new and competitive technologies. This was the only, way we could develop our Republic in the field of machinery.

There was one thing which was obvious; the Republic of Korea paid special attention to education. For many years the chief representatives of the state had to pass exams before being promoted or being appointed to state high positions. We have preserved this tradition up to now because today a good education is a prerequisite to the technical and economical development of our country and in preparing good professionals.

Nowadays, South Korea has taken a leading position in the world when one takes into account the literacy of its population.

At the same time (in 1996) there were 45 state-owned and 170 private universities, with 2.167.000 students.

The Seoul in my imagination and impression. 1997.

The plane we were sitting in, BOING of the national Uzbekistan airways landed in the Kimpo airport in the Seoul capital city of South Korea. Dusk had already fallen, but the sun seemed to be shining as if were the dawn of the day. As soon as we left the airport, we got in the bus and arrived at a luxurious hotel. After meeting a group of hosts, without any formalities, and registering, we were handed the keys to our hotel rooms.

The first day we started the training listed in the schedule for the delegation from Uzbekistan. Seven of the representatives were from the Higher Education Ministry, 6 of them were from the Science and technology Committee, and three from the Academy of the agricultural sciences. The next day we traveled to the Seoul city, the legendary centre of Korea.

Seoul seemed like a city of which we have never heard about. Now I am willing to tell you this: it's divided into two parts by the Hangan river. 12 million Korean people live in this fantastic city. The state language is Korean. 65 % of the people living in the South Korea come from the mountain regions, 35 % of them from irrigated lands. Life conditions and earning money is at a high level. The income for a year per each person is 10 000 dollars. Statistics show that if Korea pursues development like other highly developed countries, the national income per citizen will be 15 000 dollars . Evidence of this is three factors which they demonstrated: pride of nationality, strict rules, and loyalty to job commitments. These are the basic foundations of Korean economics.

At that time each of us said to ourselves: If we are also going to follow the same developmental path, our country is possibly going to soon join the highly developed countries.

In Seoul we witnessed 21st century development of the electronic products of the 21 century. Thousands of scientists and professionals are working hard to stimulate technology in the world. The Korean youth are hoping that the 21 century will be really successful for them.

The model of emerging from the economical crisis. It was not that easy for Koreans to reach these developments. Let's take a look back to the history of this economical growth. It used to be a very poor country located by the Pacific ocean until the 1960s. After their military revolution in 1961, a group fronted by president Pak Chong Hi took charge of ruling the government. The government first focused its main attention to light industry and export development . While developing their manufacturing, they took the needs and interest of the population into account and made it their most important factor. In the 1970s, the Korean people started living in prosperity, and they had plenty of food to feed their children. The field of machinery, and oil refinement has developed to a high extent.

In the 1970s, the Korean government illustrated how to emerge from an economic crisis, stabilize prices, reform the market, with liberalization as the main factor of their economy.

Starting from the 1980s, the economy started growing at a higher speed, there were enough conditions for private companies, and liberal economical competence was formed. The Korean economy is now dependent on 10 huge companies like DAEWOO, Samsung, Hyundai, KIA, and Posco. For example in order to examine the metallurgical enterprise Posco, you will have to walk 173 kilometers, because the zone is so huge, and the tankers in this company are able to lift up loads weighing from 550 000 to 1 million tons.

 The automobile industry is the engine of their economy. The plant "DAEWOO Public motors" is the unique symbol of the Korean machinery plant and it is equipped with high profile technologies of companies like "Toshiba", "Comacu", "Nagi" in Japan, "Miricron" in the USA, "Nagel" in Germany, and "Marpos" in Italy. The same plant where Korea engines and transmissions are assembled, the automobiles Tico and Damas are also assembled. By the way, I can't stand not providing some information about the Korean automobile roads and machinery as a professional. The state highways are financially supported by the government. 50 % of the provincial roads belong to private owners, and the other 50 % to the government .

In the 1970s they founded the Korean automobile industry in partnership with the "General motors" of the USA. Today DAEWOO is one of the most popular enterprises and was not long ago sold to "General Motors" of the USA. In many cities of the state, for example in Tegu and in Chon there are enterprises producing aluminum and they cast moulds. They include "DAEWOO Dong Internet", and the "DAEWOO Heavy industries". They produce different necessary details for the engine like the engine block, cylinder, shaft, bearings and etc. People from Uzbekistan know a lot about the achievements of Korea within the last two decades and five years. Besides, it's possible to prove this by referring to "UzDAEWOO Auto" which is a joint Uzbek and Korean enterprise as an example.

At that time, in June of 199, the President of Uzbekistan Islom Karimov paid a visit to South Korea and to the "Public Motors" plant of DAWOO. In November he adopted the decree to build an automobile industry plant in Asaka city. Within five years we finished building the Asaka subsidiary instead of the Tashkent tractor plant, and we, the citizens and the President completed the building of the "UzDAEWOO Auto" Uzbek and Korean joint enterprise. In short we found our genuine partner for machinery with the Korean government and company. Yes, the state, and Korea, has recently learned to produce cars from the USA and is today teaching us how to do it. Perhaps in future the enterprise of machinery "UzDAEWOO Auto" will help some of the countries in Central Asia to produce cars, as this company is unique in Central Asia.

Actually DAEWOO is famous all over the world. The automobile that we've produced in this company has put our country on the map. We did our best, worked hard at ourselves, and achieved our goal at last.

All that we have achieved is due to our intellect and scientific researches.

We can achieve success through education, learning the theory and getting knowledge. Koreans have also achieved it through their own knowledge. Even though 50 % of the secondary schools and 70 % of universities are based on profits and are paid for teaching, 90 % of the citizens have graduated from vocationally based colleges and universities.

When we were in the Seoul universities, we seldom s students walking in the corridors. When we asked the reason for this, we were told that they usually trained in the libraries independently. At that moment, I remembered our young students most of who were walking in the shops and about libraries where there is almost no student reading in our country. I always calm down by assuring myself that all these problems are going to pass us soon because at the time when our great ancestors lived and worked, they didn't have good living conditions.

The countries like Korea and Japan have found their way of development on the basis of culture and science. However, our young people aren't bereaved of interest in knowledge, they have plenty of interest in studying. I am sure that the young people who could be patient with so many challenges of life, will one day turn to reality of life, which is only knowledge.

In such a developed country like Korea, the cultural and national wealth of the state are combined with modern civilization. When we witnessed this, we grew to understand that there's lots of truth in what our President I.A.Karimov said: "we must live for the sake of our people and for the sake of our motherland".

Private universities. In 2001 in the HOSEO university of Korea we gathered enough information for our future. In this respect I want to express my own views about the considerable peculiarities of private universities which proved that we can also open a private university in Uzbekistan.

The university we have chosen to discuss is a private university founded by doctor of sciences, Kan Suk Kew, and was opened with money he had earned on his own.

New faculty buildings were erected with the money paid by the sponsors. A tuition fee (5000$ per year) is paid by every student and has been spent for the development of the university. At the present time the university is being ruled by a scientist, the former education Minister Ching Kun Ma, son of the honoured rector, Kang Il Ju who is a proctor. Every specialist and professional in this university has the same aim: to contribute to the reputation of university so that it can be included in the list of the best universities in the world.

Let's move on to the most important issue. What can we learn from this university? Can we apply what we have learned in our own universities? 10800 Bachelor, Master students and doctors are taught by just 239 teachers in this Korean university. Taking into account the number of teachers, this rate is considerably higher than in our universities. Based on the national program, if the same methods could be applied in our country as well, we could perhaps be even more successful in education because in their system of education, teachers only demonstrate how to learn, and the rest of the tasks are independently carried out by the students. The weekly hours of teaching for each professor is 9 hours. The main focus is on scientific research because in this case teacher will not only get a good income, he will also build his own reputation.

Is it easy to be a professor? The scientist who has achieved a doctoral degree can reach the degree of a "professor" in only 11 years. By that time, a prospective doctor will have to have stages like 2 years of working as an assistant and four years of working as an assistant-professor.

There will be serious requirements for the prospective professors all the time: for example, having the newest topic- based scientific articles published in the most popular science conference materials of the world. They will then show enough respect and value for the professor who has had these challenging tests in his career pursuit. 90 % of the income acquired because of his scientific research results will be forwarded to his own account.

The government in Korea pays special attention to rendering financial support to young people in their individual educational system. Every year they spend 3 million dollars on the education of each of their 80 students. These talented students are divided into twenty groups by 5 postgraduate students and 40 professors, and they all carry out practical research on the latest technologies. Most of the scientific research is carried out on the basis of special orders and requests from private enterprises, and they considerably influence the industry. As a result, both the university and the economical state of the state profit. According to the contracts with the plant, a certain percentage of its stocks will be at the disposal of the university.

Korean students must get 160 credit scores during 8 semesters (four years). There are compulsory subjects in the academic programs. However, the lectures delivered in the classrooms do not exceed 18 hours a week. Attendance of the lessons contain 95 %, all the computers are connected to Internet network, even in the student dormitory there's a special room for networking. In this room there's a computer for each student, and the student behavior, and even personal hygiene is all in order. There's no a line drawn or no dust on the desks or chairs.

As for the administration of the university, there's just one proctor , the faculty deans have wide powers, and different departments rule different sectors of the university. The way they educate students is worth gold. The main attention is paid to computer and learning foreign languages. The thing which astonished us was that all the businessmen study there in special groups. The most talented students have rights to study at several faculties. Making use of vacations, it's also possible to complete four years of study in just three years.

If we also use these skills and methods in our country as well, it will be beneficial to all of us. The assessment rating system is based on 100 scores = 20 for attendance, 20 more for homework, and 60 for the exam results. They have two test exams per term. The number of those who do well is 10-30 %. Those whose scores are good contain 20-40, those having satisfactory assessment are 20-40. This statistics have been calculated out of 100 students. Students assess professors. There's a position of the professor in the industry at the university, and the man in charge of this position teaches 6 hours a week, but gets a higher salary, for full-time job.

All the professors are assessed by special organizations,and if he doesn't carry out any research or doesn't write a book, he will be dismissed from his job or from his current position. There's only one requirement for them: professors need to bring as twice as much profit for the government than the income they get from university. Their salaries are appointed according to their contribution to the society. The motto of the professors and teachers at the university is to serve the society and the development of science. Students will also assess the professors according to their knowledge. For example, if a MA student opens an enterprise with a scientific advisor, or if he opens a company with fifteen other students, 5 % of the stock will belong to the university. A Professor, as a scientific advisor can be really proud of these achievements.

On November 8, in the town Chanon, we went to the faculty of humanities where 2000 students are getting a high education. There's a projector in each classroom, all the computers are working, and I wish we would also soon reach these opportunities .

In that university only the students with excellent grades can get scholarships. The same method should be applied in our country as well. I think if a scholarship is not paid out of the sum of the tuition fee, the students will try to work even harder. I hope it would also be a great idea to allow just talented and eager students to learn to study on the basis of a state grant.

In Korea even the state university requires tuition fees from the students, but it's a bit cheaper than that of private universities. 42,5 % of the university budget is filled in by tuition fees. This rule is more complicated and different in private universities.

There tuition fees contain 61,8%. In the state universities it's 3,5%. Expenses on Students expenses are 10,5%. and assistance from the sponsors is 7,7%дир.

10,5% of the university's funding is spent on conducting seminars for students and allowing them to study abroad.

Competence is really high in private universities, and each of the students need to attract sponsors because if they have potential, the sponsors will help covering their tuition fees. The administration will cut requirements for professors and teachers as they think they may leave their jobs here for other places.

Scientific research is oriented toward certain problems of industry and manufacturing. Great conditions are created for all the professors to open a private enterprise for their further activity in the industry. The previous president of the university founded a fund having 8 million dollars to develop small business and entrepreneurship. The professors keep offering their own new ideas making business plans all the time. Here, my dear readers, you may have a question to wonder about: "How are they going to pay back the money they get from the university fund? As I have told above, 5 % of the stock of the new enterprise will be submitted to the university. This is the strategy of the market economy; the more it develops, the more money there will be.

As regards the lessons, they are shortened and several disciplines are combined and taught in the same course. They deliver lectures in bigger classrooms, but they devote all of their energy to research development.

A Master's degree is only for hardworking students. In this university, only the hardworking students are allowed to get a Master's degree, and 70 % of the expenses are covered by the government. Even so, and again, they will pay more attention to scientific research. For that they have even built a special building. Each group is fronted by one professor. The professor teaches his students to earn money through scientific research and investigations. The fund will give 5000 dollars for all the scientific research, and in the second stage, this sum will reach 100 thousand as a result of production. After the new product is prepared, it is shown first to the juries, and if it is found worthy of being produced, the representatives will be paid 300 thousand dollars more. Twenty groups are working in this field, and the 20 students who graduated from the university are taking part in this. They will pay only 5 % of their salary as an income tax.

Previous grades are important. A Professor is usually employed by the university. For example, on the basis of a special contract, he will only have to work in this university, not in the others.

A student has 18 hours of lessons each week, and there's no missing or being late for the lessons. They will have to pay tuition fees for four years, and sign contracts annually.

In order to enter a university, the followings will be taken into account: secondary school assessment 30 %, exam results 40 %, and music, language and computer skills will also be considered by 30 %. Tens of candidates will be competing for one position as a prospective student.

The university's budget was 60 million dollars in 2000.

The president's salary at the private university is two and a half times more than that of a President of a state university.

60 % of the professors work at private universities.

The level of knowledge is assessed according to research. The best university always tries to be involved in research, and therefore scientists at a university write up 2 or 3 dissertations a year. In this way, the administration can assess their results and value of their hard work. It's really effective to educate students through research, innovations, controlling behavior and the time management of students. It's also useful to run the research and experiments on the basis of the requests from different organizations. Shortening lesson's hours have been proved to be even more effective, and this would be a good idea for our country as well to apply the same methods in our education system.

Student chooses the teacher. Three months before the next semester all the teachers start preparing for their lessons, with the topic of the lecture being made clear a week before. The student will then choose his teacher on his own . If the books requested aren't available in the library, the students may book it in advance in other libraries. Even the plans of the lectures are going to be announced on the internet. A month before that, the administration will form a list of the students who will listen to that lecture and they will request the necessary equipments and tools for that. If everything's ready, the lesson will be conducted in the classroom, and, in the first lesson, there are ten rules to follow. Before starting a lecture, a teacher must remind them that this lesson will decide their future, help them to pursue a successful career. The second rule is not to be late for the lesson. The students who failed to do homework are going to be punished.

However, first the students must learn and then practice what they have learnt in laboratories, because knowledge can be gained through revising and refreshing what we have learnt. We must always keep reminding young people to work hard for the sake of bright a future. The next important thing is to write in short all the necessary facts on the topic. In the classroom both the teacher and the students have equal rights to learn and to express their views.

A lesson should be interesting as this is a part of our life, and we must get rid of boring lectures.

The main purpose of the lessons is to attract students and to prompt them to love the subject and to learn.

At the end of the semester , every teacher should submit a report on the basis of the following factors:

1)   The criteria being assessed;

2)   Students must assess the teaching skills of a professor;

3)   All the assessment data will be saved on a computer disk and submitted to the rector, with a letter about the assessment will be forwarded to the student's parents. If a student is dissatisfied with the mark, he can apply for reassessment;

4)   Reading a lecture is like art;

In order to provide a lesson of higher quality, the university president should render assistance, the administration needs to check if there are enough conditions, equipment, and if the teacher is on time for the lesson. It's like a performance on the stage, we can imagine teachers and students as actors on the stage, ND those behind the stage are administration staff certainly.

What is the business incubator ? There are 300 technical business incubators TBI in Korea. In this field, certain countries are taking leading positions, for instance Germany the third, China the fourth, Russia the fifth, the USA the first, because the USA has 800 TBI in its own territory.

The rector of the School of technologies invited the assistant-director of NASA and appointed him as the director for TBI incubators after what these TBIs have developed at a high rate. 100 business enterprises have been founded within 20 years, and 10 of them later turned into huge companies. Even one Master organized a company and he created a bigger company after uniting fifteen enterprises on his own.

In this country each university rector visits about six universities a year to request new technology, and he applies it on his own. I looked through these measures taken for educational development and always made a wish. I really wanted the same to happen in our motherland.

Administration through information technology. Now we are moving from the period of industry to the information technological period step by step. We are living in a world of globalization . Therefore, any information can be easily distributed by means of a satellite and even a brand new invention may face a crisis in case it competes with the mass information source, because the information technology may even oppose the invention. Information technology is a decisive factor. Therefore the DAEWOO company went bankrupt, but the Ford company focused on the internet and mass media, and with ads this company overcame all the challenges of a business. The administration using information technology will soon be immanent all over the world within the next thirty years.

I've earlier mentioned that in the HOSEO university, the administration pays lots of attention to learning foreign languages and using the newest technologies as well as assisting the local technology to develop.

When requesting help to invent a new technology, higher education recommends the universities with the highest reputation to all the organizations. Their aim is to get the Nobel prize. Now it's Pilgeich who is responsible for all of this. He is said to be even stronger than Nobel, and specifically for this purpose 2 million dollars are usually spent annually. They want to increase the number of scientists like Pilgeich. 40 professors have been working for this in this system. They will be choosing the best business plans recommended.

You may read this on the internet. Nowadays there are morning and evening classes at universities which students may attend and get credit. Students are allowed freedom, all the subjects can be assessed even if a student passes the same exam at another university, and he may even be assessed after passing the exam on the internet.

A student may also simultaneously study for a BA and MA courses, and at the end of the courses all of them will be taken into account.

It's compulsory to pay if you drive on private roads. It is 4968 kilometers from Tashkent to Seoul and it takes 6 hours to get to Seoul from Tashkent, with the time difference in two capitals bing 4 hours.

Automobile roads are privately-owned, but the quality is high:

a) there are SOS telephones in each 1500-2000 meters;

b) to drive 100 kilometers of private roads, the drivers are charged 20 dollars.

Israel

It's located by the Mediterranean sea in the western part of Asia, in the near east.

We, a group of rectors and proctors went on a business trip in 2000 and studied the education system there from January 10 to January 24. The plane we were in, a Boeing, landed in the Ben Gurion after three hours. After we reached the Ben Gurion by bus, we started for Kuddus city, Jerusalem. The thing that surprised me most was the strict passport control in this country. We quickly got back our luggage, but the grapes, and watermelons we had brought for our guests were all taken away and they didn't allow us to get them back. We learned that bringing in fruit or vegetables was banned, though we weren't aware of it at all.

The roads are smooth, there are enough traffic signs there, and on the edge of the roads there is a useful information guide there for drivers and passengers. We stayed in a hotel called "Kibuts Ramal Rakel", and there we weren't required to show any identity documents. We didn't even fill in the forms for booking a room in a hotel. I started staying in the same hotel room with the prorector of the Tashkent State Finance University, Zokir Yuldashev. Since this hotel was located in the highest part of the city, the whole city around could easily be seen when we looked through the window. Here almost all the buildings were built from mountain stones, and they could easily catch the eye because of their white colour and dazzling beauty. From that day forth, we learned the moderator of the course introduced us to the plan of the program, i.e. meetings and conferences. It became clear that young people finished secondary school at the age of 18, this period lasts for

12 years (6+12=18). Only 52% of the schoolchildren successfully finish secondary school, with an honors certificate. The exams are all fair for acquiring a secondary school certificate . The need to study is really high, because the scores of the secondary school education decides the future of the applicant. Moreover, students are also charged with passing a psychometric test. The scores of both tests are added up and this is the score which is decisive in being enrolled at a university. If the scores are enough, the students will be privileged to enter a university. The scores have no expiration date. A student may use them as long as he wants. After young people push 18 (both boys and girls), they must serve in the military in defense of their motherland. Military service is compulsory, and men should serve for 36 months and girls for 20 months. Only after that can they be accepted in a university. There's no alternative to military service.

There are 600 thousand people living in Kuddus. 450 thousand of them are Jewish, 150 thousand of them are Moslems. It's a great city where three religions are united. On January 11, we visited the Asko mosque. The mosque was built on a hill where the prophet had walked . After that we visited the places where the prophet Mohammad, Abraham, and Zikariyo had prayed. We came face to face with the

history of 4 thousand years. Before it was compulsory for each Muslim to visit Kuddus city prior to going on their Hadj[10]. Unfortunately, after the 1967 war, this tradition was banned .

---

[10] Hadj is a visit to sacred cities in Saudi Arabia, this is a holy duty of all the people with Islamic religion.

On January 13, we went to the Karmiel city through Tel- Aviv. Karmiel city has a population of 45 million. Mostly Russian speaking Jews live in this city. We even saw the Gulon hills there, and after that we watched the lake in which the prophet Jesus went fishing. It is known that he fed 5000 men with two fish, and he and his disciples felt like they were walking on land, not on water. We saw many schools and academic lyceums in the city. Russian teachers were working as teachers and even trainers. Here we visited the Tekhnion university in the of Haifa where I met Leonid Tartakovskiy (DVS laboratory chief engineer). He had studied in Moscow MAMI. At that time he sent me all the documents, and a copy of the contract via fax machine.

When we were going to Karmiel we visited the Brilliant stock exchange in Tel-Aviv. 60 % of the diamonds are refined in this factory and it causes the government to get ten billions of dollars.

We came back to Jerusalim on January, and we continued to study for three more days more. We learned many things about their higher education system and Internet. On January 17 the docent of the TARU for many years invited me to his home. I enjoyed seeing the way the Jewish people lived. He told me how he and his wife had learned the Hebrew language and that they were living in happiness. Just two of them lived in a flat with five rooms. His wife, Nanel was a professor at Jerusalim university, and Leonid was teaching people to drive in his private driving courses. His son and daughter are experienced doctors. It was possible to watch 50 channel programs on their TV. On January 21, 12 rectors met in his house and cooked Uzbek pilaf to eat. My colleague Leonid showed his hospitality and respect to Uzbek people.

On January 20 we visited the place where the prophet Jesus had been born. Before that we had visited the Ben Gurion university which was located right in the centre of the desert, in Beer-Sheva city, and we met the university administration there. Can you imagine that 18 thousand students study here? Their annual budget is 205 mln dollars, and 65 % of this income is acquired because of the scientific results productivity. In this university, teachers are assessed taking into account their research and their teaching activity. It's compulsory to get a review on the research written up from at least five professors from countries in order to get a doctoral or other degrees. Their scientific degrees are confirmed by the Council of university presidents and the university president personally congratulates the candidate to be awarded. They don't have a higher education ministry. Just the university president and the President of the State are responsible for everything. The main requirement for the university is quality teaching and education. All the professors have their own school for their research. If a Master's student wants to be employed, he will certainly be asked which professor he wants as his supervisor.

Beer-sheva – means seven pools in English, and we learned that in front of one of these pools the prophet Abraham met our mother Sarah. We were very lucky to visit, that same pool, you know! Sarah is known to have given birth to the prophet Isaac. At that time the prophet Abraham had married mother Hojar, and their son Ishmael had already been born. The prophet Mohammad is also related to their geneaology. The geneaology of the prophet Isaac are Moses and Jesus. It means three religions have the same history, the same root, and they all date back to the prophet Abraham.

On January 21, we went to swim in the Dead sea, which has 28-30 % salt, you can freely rest in this sea and you won't even sink.

All the cities and places we were very beautiful. The street roads are smooth, and the Buildings are of a high quality. We didn't meet any road policemen in the street, and there were seldom drivers or passengers who broke the traffic rules. As the roads are narrow, there were some car accidents. The insurance company covers the fee of repairing the cars, and if someone feels sick there, they are certainly in big trouble because even in Israel, health is insured, and if patients have their organism X-ray examined, that costs them 175 dollars.

If you break a traffic rule or don't stop when the red light is on, you will be charged 275 dollars as a fine. There are automatic operating cameras everywhere, and they keep observing people who follow or even those who do not follow the traffic rules. No one can escape from that, and everybody has equal rights and responsibilities.

We heard that each Jewish man should plant one seedling on January 18, and all the forests came into being thanks to this tradition actually. Peasants are able to gather harvest three times using the dripping method of irrigation on the land with less soil.

We returned to Tashkent on January 24 with absolutely good impressions.

To sum, up thirty university presidents and proctors learned a lot about the higher education system in Israel on a trip funded by the fund "Ustoz".

The conclusions and debates as a result of the trip to Israel. Our President Islam Karimov: "The main purpose of our country is to fulfill the program of preparing national professionals. This should be the main duty of each chief and administrator. This should be the main factor in assessing their activity and working process. It's important to run seminars dedicated to the essential problems of our country and those devoted to development and growth. These seminars should be held as much as possible and especially younger people need to be attracted to them."

In order to fulfill these tasks I dared to offer the following measures to be looked through in the special seminars.

1.   It's effective to identify the knowledge of the students graduating from academic lyceums by submitting them tests prepared by the state testing Centre. Besides there's need to exchange experience for psychological tests. The testing results should be made equal to those used to enter the university.

2.   Nowadays the bachelor students are awarded with the degree of "Bachelor of sciences", but unfortunately some of those bachelors can not find a good job in a technical field, because just 10 or 15 % of those graduates are being enrolled in MA courses. The same rate is even worse in the far away provinces of the Republic. Students need to be adopted to universities taking into account the needs of the organizations for professionals.

3.   When it's time to prepare Master students, they need to be taught the basis of their personal calendar plans. Just the MA graduates who have written their dissertation on the scientific topic need to be recommended to be adopted to Postgraduate studies. This means the experimenting and dissertation methods of the future doctor should be chosen only in advance. This accelerates the writing process of the research of the candidate. The Master students training on the basis of the organization needs, do not need to write a dissertation on a scientific topic. They have to find ways to solve problems.

4.   Nowadays in all the faculties and departments of most universities, there are enough computers. If bachelor students are attracted to work there as operators, hundreds of students will be employed and eventually will have a job.

5.   In the developed countries all the students doing well at university should be exempted from the responsibility of paying tuition fees. This will certainly be effective for further development of education in the Republic. If this measure is taken, students will be much more eager to learn and to excel.

6.   There needs to be a new method of awarding those with scientific degrees like doctor, docent, professor and many others. In this respect the main attention should be paid to the articles and research reviews published abroad, with the value of the manuals, and textbooks on sale in foreign countries.

7.   The problem of providing all the educational organizations with the internet, computer equipment and other pedagogical technologies should urgently be solved in all the faraway provinces of the Republic. This will enable us to contact the universities and libraries all over the world. Special funding with foreign currency should also be allocated to universities for the same purpose.

8.   Carrying out research, publishing textbooks or other integrated resources needs to be confirmed as the legal duty of each teacher. It's a well known fact that the teacher who doesn't write textbooks can not excel in knowledge, so they mustn't be recommended to be awarded with the degree of a professor anyhow.

9.   All the talented students and masters should be attracted to working in well-paid jobs related to their own field of study.

10.   It's really effective to hold questionnaires "What do students think about teachers?" possibly at the end of each term.

Czech

Travelling without visa. On June 10-17, 2000 I traveled to Prague city in the Czech, Republic on the occasion of the invitation from the DAEWOO company there where I could personally see the company "Avia" . It's been more than 100 years since this plant was built. At first aviation engines started being produced here, and then diesel locomotives also started being produced. After that automobile engines have been produced since the 70s. This plant is mainly the place where the details of the engine are assembled. Most of the details of the automobiles are actually prepared in other plants. I was so happy to see Paris-like Prague. It is indeed a very ancient and beautiful city which has a thousand year history .

I remember one interesting event which happened when I was leaving the Prague airport. I was stopped by agents while I was going to the town because I didn't have a visa. I had my passport registered in a way so that I could go abroad, until the end of 2000 without a visa. Unfortunately that stamp of registration turned out to be invalid without a special visa. Immediately a representative of the Avia plant came to inspect my passport and he explained everything to me. We obtained a visa obtained the same day and filled in all the necessary documents. Luckily this problem was solved in a few minutes.

On weekends I went to the the museum of Polytechnics and Citadel in Prague. It was like a miracle . The castles kissed the sky, and all the high buildings and magnificent monuments dazzle and hypnotize anyone who comes to see them. On Monday I visited Carl university, which is the most ancient one in Europe. I also saw laboratories there.

I visited Prague again for the second time in order to get acquainted with the system of constructing traffic roads there.

This, the second visit was full of fantastic impressions. I got fully acquainted with the quality and technology in building roads. I also learned about the exhibition dedicated to the traffic movement in Prague, as well as the "Credo" program's opportunities in the framework of projecting road construction. You know what, we can easily not think of drawing with pencils and erasers because there's a computer program in Czech which can do the same task instead of us. It can draw schemes and designs of everything we want to create.Moreover, it's enough to use this program professionally The specialist of the "Prague Road projects" university went on a trip with me to guide me through the sights of the city. Within one day we travelled to the Karlovy Vary city.

Prague is so wonderful that the more you visit it , the more often you would like to go again. You can feel the energy you get from seeing the sights and ancient monuments. Karlovy Vary is a quite a different place where we could relax and rest. There are all the opportunities, and chances only for interests and benefits of the citizens, and for them to rest and enjoy. I bought a kitchen dish,and it became a gift for me to remind me about my travels in the Czech Republic.

France

The Boeing -310 plane flew from Tashkent to Paris at 14.50 on April 24 and six hours and thirty minutes later it landed in Amsterdam. I got a special invitation to go there from the initiative of the educational centre «CESMECA». From that city we went to Paris and at last arrived at the Charles de Gaulle airport. After I got off the plane, and had my passport examined , I was met by the ambassador Alisher Kunduzov.

On April 25, I went to the ENSAM Higher Technical university with the representatives of the CESMECA Rishar and Shavkat. There I was greeted by the chief director Giu Gatnerin with whom I had a talk lasting for an hour, and to whom I also handed the projects I'd prepared for our partnership. He promised to send his special representative and afterwards the contract was to be signed .

We had an interesting conversation with him. This university has 11 faculties, and the faculty director in Paris Alex Remie showed us all the university's laboratories. There are tools and instruments used for running smaller research and the students learn how to use the technology of producing details. There's an amphitheatre in this faculty which has over 1200 seats for students to watch performances. According to their statistical information, one thousand students graduated and received an engineering diploma this year.

After that conversation we went to the SUBITEO plant where professor Dube had worked before. He was the one who had organized the courses for developing skills in the TARU. He informed us that he was working on a new internet system and he also explained the advantages of that net space system. The director of this company told us about his biography for a bit while we were having negotiations. The enterprise was working on the basis of the subsidiary of the USA. He also added: "We have important aims for the future, and we also have more problems to be solved".

Dube invited me to his home, but I didn't accept because I was quite tired. The reason I was morally tired was because I didn't like the subway crowded with people, the awful smell and

… you know, in France. Suddenly it caught my eye how Afro- American people were working to lay asphalt on the roads in one part of Paris, and they were laying it just with the machine. The asphalt was 250oC. This technology was absolutely new to us. I think it could be a good idea if we could also buy this machine for road construction. Then I saw the passengers walking on the roads which had just been covered with asphalt. You must also see this miracle! How surprising, isn't it?

On April 26, I met the ambassador of Uzbekistan in France, Tohir Mamajanov. We talked a lot about our travelling impressions with him. I handed him all the books, leaflets and projects I had prepared as well as the article I had written for the French press and on the achievements of Uzbekistan in the program of Preparing professionals. Then we said goodbye to the ambassador and my partner Alisher started showing me what Paris was like.

Paris is the capital of France, it's the economical, political, and cultural centre of the state, and one of the most beautiful and biggest cities in the world.

What surprised me most was that all the buildings and establishments hadn't lost their glory over hundreds of centuries . For two hours I observed the halls of the Loeuvre, but the more I saw, the more I wanted, and desired, to look at them again. In the afternoon we went to see the Notre Dame de Paris and walked there. I was also fascinated by the Eiffel Tour. The River Sena was flowing and dazzling to the eyes. The golden cupole built on the tomb of Napoleon was even more enhancing to the beauty of the city. The hill Montmartre is deemed to be the highest peak of Paris, and if someone goes up there, he will see that it is impossible not to be fascinated by the establishments built by so clever a people.

On April 27 I went to the school that prepares and trains engineers in partnership with Rishar. The assistant of the director welcomed us there. After a conversation with him we got introduced to laboratories of bio-technology, vibro- technology, acoustics, electronic microscopy. Here scientists run researches in the field of automobile industry, aviation and cosmonautics, the experiments are conducted on the basis of householding contracts. All the tools and equipment in the laboratories are modern and suitable for experiments. We've been trying to find solutions the problems of depreciation in various conditions on the basis of the real items,when the oil is heated at 200o degrees in friction vehicle. As a result of research some new technologies are offered and they don't produce poison, reducing the amount of friction in automobiles. All the innovational items are being offered in this university for example, reducing the noise of the traffic, preventing overflow of the oil from the stuffing box, using tools from metal or non-metal polymers instead of the knee-cap, during the surgery operations. Seeing all what's happening I also wanted our university to do the same, and to give our students permission to come here to study.

In the afternoon at 1530 we had a meeting with the university president and we agreed to exchange our researchers without any necessity for foreign currency. We also had an agreement to exchange students on the basis of the TEMPUS.

On April 29 we went to Basilique de St-Denis with Shavkat together on foot, and we visited the places where the kings had been crowned and where they had been buried. The tombs of all the kings who had reigned in the 12-13 centuries are here in this place. I enjoyed looking at the king's crowns and thrones . While having a stroll in these places I made a conclusion that life is beautiful, but it is cruel as well. So many kings were crowned here with celebrations, but when they were about to die, they were accompanied to their tombs. Here I want to remember one story told by Alisher Navai. In that story we are asked to visit tombs and cemeteries, even when we are happy with our life.This infers that we will also die just like the people in this cemetery, and it means no one is eternal to rule over somebody. Therefore we need to value each instant in our life and be generous with each other.

God treats both the poor and the rich in the same way, he gives his own gifts to everyone, and he will punish us for everything wrong we do. After we die, people will remember us recalling the good things we have done for them.

I couldn't fall asleep all night as I had some keen pain somewhere in my body, and none of the drugs or pain-killers were useful. At 6.00 am I fell asleep, and I dreamt about my mother. In my dream she didn't let me go to her, and she kept chasing me away. When I had it interpreted, I was told that it would be quite early for me to die like my mother, and that my life was going to be much longer than I expected. I was glad.

On April 30 at 2oo pm Rishar took me to the Versal palace in his automobile. The weather was cloudy, and it was raining at that time. Even though I was thoroughly soaked, I watched a scene that was fascinating to me. Unfortunately we couldn't get inside the Versal palace as it was Sunday, a day to rest.

May 1 is a holiday in France. That's why all the museums are closed. It had been raining since dawn broke. That's the reason why we decided to spend the holiday at home. I fulfilled all the plans of work and I was so busy that I didn't even notice that the duration of my travel was over. That night at around 7.00 pm me, Shavkat and Alisher went to the De Gaule airport, arriving in the airport at 7.45 pm. After the passport registration I went inside, but we stayed on the chairs until 10.30 pm., talking together. I thanked the men around me, said good-bye, and afterwards boarded the plane (Boeing-310). The quality of service was absolutely high, and we started flying right at 11.00 pm. The plane landed in our motherland at 8 am in the morning. After filling in all the documents I rushed outside towards my daughter Nigora, my youngest daughter's husband Shoerkin, and my advisor Omon. As soon as I sat in the car, I heard a song by Yulduz Usmonova:

I travelled in the world far away from you, The further I got, the more I started loving you

The more I travelled, the more I yearned for you

There afar I was somehow patient longing for you I couldn't find your dark eyes nowhere in the world.

You're the unique for me wherever I go!

"Dear doctor, now I have just told you about all of my travelling adventures like a fairy tale. I think this will be kept in memories of all my students.

"Oh, dear teacher, I've known you since 1989, and we've been like a real brother and a sister. During this time I've talked to you times and shared secrets with you. We flicked through the book of your life together. This helped me to cure you correctly. Thanks to God, you're safe and sound. Now I have one suggestion for you. I think it would be a very good idea to have a book published about the life you've led, and all the experiences you gained throughout your life. This can be a very good lesson for other young people so that they can cope with the challenges you've encountered . I think you can do what I am offering you .

"Yes, I will think over, but I am not sure how other people will assess this! Won't they think that I am boasting or ..."

"Come on. Oh no. People know about you, and even those who are against you know what you deserve in life. You have travelled all over the world, and you've headed a university. Do you have any dreams that haven't come true?"

"I am completely satisfied with the life I have led. Thanks to God! All the dreams I have had came true . I have done my best to serve the government and the people I have lived with in the motherland. I have only one dream that didn't come true; my mother died early in 1977 and she didn't see all of my achievements. If she could, she would've held her chin up. I wish she could have been blessed to see what I accomplished. It is not in vain thsta it is said that even the dead can see what's happening in this world. They do not abandon us entirely. Their spirits are all alive!"

"Dear teacher! I am really glad to talk to you and listen to everything you have come across throughout your life. I have gained a huge wealth of knowledge and experience through sharing ideas with you. There are many things that I can learn from you. I know very well how hard it was for you to head the university for ten years. Every time we met when you were a university president, I have never seen you in a black mood. You are a patient person with intergrity, you keep all of your promises, and do whatever the doctors recommend you to do. We seldom have patients with the same character as yours. We needed your help to cure you, and to get to know your psychology. I have been curing you as a doctor for many years, and now that you' re safe and sound, I wish you strong health and rest for the remainder of your life."

After resigning from the university administration...

I must tell you that this woman, my doctor took care of my health whatever might happen. She always gave me the correct advice and recommendations. Thanks to God within ten years when I was a university president, I had never been sick enough to stay in the hospital, and sometimes I had back trouble. I especially had this trouble when the weather changed, or when it suddenly became hot or cold. In 2005 I decided to stay in a hospital located in the Kibray district. It was in April and my doctor recommended this to me. Telling the truth I prefer to let my nerves relax rather than going to hospital when I get sick.

My dear reader! In this book I have tried to explain how it is possible to become a loyal citizen for your motherland. At first I told you about all the secrets and other things about my parents, teachers, my life, the challenges I had, which I overcame, and those I couldn't. I hope what I have written here will be a good lesson for the young people who are about to be faced with the challenges I faced ."

"There's one more thing I am going to tell you, I know what you said about your work as a university president, as a writer, and as a scientist in the technical field. Isn't it all too difficult to cope with for just one person? How can you find time for it?

"Shall I respond to you frankly? "Of course!"

"In that case I would like you to listen to me a bit longer. I was gifted with this ability from God, and I always worked intensely night and day, of course taking into account normal hours of sleep. If I start doing something, no one can deter me from that. I work very fast, and the things that take several days other people to finish, take me just an hour. Ideas flow through my brain and through my heart. Usually, if I want to write an article, lecture, text-book or a literary work, I only write it once, and I make some corrections as soon as I finish writing; that's all.

When I was appointed as a university president, I thought that there were many things to do, but fortunately it wasn't like that at all. I used to stay at university from 7 am to 7.00 pm. But some time later, I started feeling that I didn't have any reason to be tired of doing all these things for the university, because I started employing only loyal professionals at the university. They all were working honestly and didn't let me have to bother with extra problems. That's why I had the chance to write textbooks and to create new inventions etc. I had a motto: "Each administrator is just an insignificant servant, he mustn't feel arrogant at all" if he knows that for himself, he isn't going to ignore the others who are in lower positions than he is. All the problems need to be solved taking into account the requirements of the time, politics and the government. Only in that case could it be within the remits of the rector to run the international politics and to solve strategic problems of the university. He needs to think about the social state of the university's staff and team. The university should provide all the necessary books and textbooks for the teachers and students. I always had two desks in my room when I was a university president. Sitting on one of those tables I used to do the tasks submitted to me as a university president, and on the next one I wrote my research and did many other tasks as a writer or as a scientist. I have never had dinner or lunch in cafes or restaurants. I also haven't trained for a sport. Perhaps, this is the main fault I have in my personality.

I don't even go for a walk before going to bed, not at least for two or three hours. I am very lazy with this. Maybe all the hard work I did in my childhood helps me to keep fit and healthy.

I have wrtten many textbooks as a scientist since the 1970s and I had them all published. I started my work as a writer in 1991 when I wrote the book "The Paths of

Science. This has served as a guidebook for all the young people who are trying to pursue success in science. There have been considerable changes to our intelligence since the days of independence. All the people living in our country started taking pride in this state, and they started feeling responsible for independence. I also had the same feelings, and therefore I wrote my first book so-called "Responsibility for independence". As years passed, I had my second, third and forth books published as well. I mostly included my articles, radio and TV materials as well as the lectures I had delivered. Today those four books have been published in a unique collection. I hope all the readers draw the right conclusions from them.

I worked as a university president for ten years, I didn't use the chance to rest. A vacation usually lasts for forty eight days, but I didn't take a days rest. I did all of my travelling on business, as a vacation, and to be honest, I am satisfied. I used to have lots of impressions from each of them, so these impressions at long last urged me to write the book so-called "Travelling With Special Purpose". I tried to explain all the things I learned from the educational systems in foreign developed countries. After that I wrote the other books like "Knowledge and Science" and "Lessons from Life".

I sorted out all the information about my life throughout 1991-2005 and wrote a new book so-called "The Dreams Came True", this book was distributed to all the libraries of the universities in Tashkent city. I hope students are reading them, and they are learning how to cope with challenges. This book also teaches people how to not dread the obstacles in life.

I also wrote books like "Detriment from Outer Forces", "Knowledge, Science and Behavior" and had them published as well.

As I said above, if I weren't an automobile scientist, I would prefer to be a writer. To confirm it, I even wrote a novel and I called it as "The Days Recently Gone By". This novel is a love story of two Postgraduate students, and it's really interesting. In 2007 the book I had written "The Dreams Came True" was translated into Russian and it was published in Armenia as "Science Deserves Living For" and it was delivered to readers in Russia as well as in Germany. All those books are now being published in the publishing companies of the Moscow Automobiles and Road university.

I did my best to write one more book so-called "Knowledge is the Soul of Human" and it was published in Latin and Cyrill in 2008. The books such as "The Responsibility for

Independence", "Dreams Came True", "The Days Recently Gone by" were published in 2009 and I am sure the readers will find them useful. I have always tried to praise my colleagues, to raise their reputation, show them as leaders to our students, and for that I took the initiative to celebrate the 60th, the 65th, the 70th and other anniversaries of the teachers for the money I earned by myself. I prepared books about the famous teachers and had them published, I hope this tradition will be preserved for many years.

I paid lots of attention to rendering financial assistance to students and teachers as well. The teachers working loyally and the students studying well at the university used to be supported with extra payments, monthly transport free tickets and different scholarships. They contained almost 500 in total, and of course it's the university president who must find the funding for that. There's only one way to do it, and that is to help anyone who visits you asking for help. When doing this, you won't even notice how the help you rendered was rendered back to you by God. It isn't hard for me to write these kinds of books, textbooks and novels. Instead, they are something I really enjoy doing. I feel the smell of a new born baby from the books I have published, I think that's why I am so happy, and I enjoy writing books, no matter if it's a dictionary, textbook or a novel.

I must admit that I haven't taken advantage of the time passing by so fast. I use my time effectively just like Avicenna who wrote 35 or 40 pages everyday and who included all the things he knew in his book. Of course I work less than him, but I know that everything I write will be kept in memories and will serv the younger generations for many years to come.

"Yes, I see, I hope that not only technical scientists, but also scientists of medicine are going to be interested in them".

"Can you tell me how young people in the 21 century differ from those in the 50-60s of the 20 century?"

"This question seems really complicated to me. It's impossible to respond in two words. Currently, young people differ quite considerably from those of the last one, because they are much richer. Most of these young people, except for the countable ones, eat and wear whatever they want . They have a wide range of information, including technical and internet resources. They learn whatever they want using books, the internet and other modern resources. It's not enough to only want to learn, and we haven't read the textbooks as well as lecture notes. We needed to listen to teachers, therefore we didn't miss any lessons. What about now? There are great opportunities for long distance education in developed countries (the USA, Germany, Japan, Korea, Russia and etc.). This is the right way. It's impossible to teach somebody by force, because learning basically depends on the person, not on the teacher. It's required to use the internet, and to search necessary information on the internet. If it's also possible to pass tests, and exams and get a diploma.

"How is this process going in our universities these days?

Can you talk about that for a bit, please?"

"To tell you the truth,it's almost the same. The same methods. For example, students are told not to miss classes, they must take notes and write texts into their copy books. There's only one book for each six students. The same attitude is shown towards the students who both do well and do badly at the university. Students will be expelled from university if case they have thirty hours of lessons missed. As a result of this traditional approach to higher education, the number of students doing well is always the same, just one or two, even some are rich, but stupid students laugh at those who try to study well. Most of the students who want to learn have nothing to boast about, which is unlike the rich students who have plenty of money.

I hope that one day our talented students will also be paid special attention to and they will contribute to developing our independent country.

The opportunities available for the current young people have never been created for the people who lived in the last century. There's every chance, and it's enough just to study hard and to learn. But what percent of the students are working hard? Why don't we hold different competitions like the Russia to award all the talented young people? I wish in every university at least 15-20 % of students could be included in the list of the talented students. And I wish their talent would be supported and they were encouraged to work even harder. There are a huge number of them, and we only need to find them through testing and guide them through the right way to learn and excel. This first of all depends on teachers, and the university president should value these sort of teachers. We did the same in the TARU for five years.

I think today young people have too many chances to excel, but their willingness to work isn't strong enough. I have a lot evidences of this. When saying "isn't strong enough" I mean their spiritual intelligence. To be convinced of this, we may have to talk to the clever young people of the current time. I did the same, and I asked some questions about writers and poets of the eastern and western classic literature. Most of the young people couldn't discuss them very well and couldn't answer my questions. Isn't this a lack of intelligence?

"Now, Mrs doctor, the young people who I am talking about may even say to me: "Hey, you, old man, you'd better sit at home and not think about us!"

I have an answer ready for them:

"Thanks to God, working for so many years in pedagogics, and dedicating my life to educating young people, I think I have the right to give advice to our young and immature children.

If at least one or ten of the 100 students follow what I say, I will be the happiest person in the world.

Dreams of an automobile scientist

Now we'll go back forty years… In October 1969 October two young people, a young man and a young girl are supposed get married. They are both candidates of science, and they teach at the same faculty. There was an old bus PAZ produced in the 1950s, and on the wedding day I hired this sort of an old bus to take the bride to the House of Soulmates to be. There the two young people were to be registered as a wife and husband. The young man was really shy to do it, because he could not afford to hire a newer car. However, on their first night of marriage, he said to his wife: "My darling, one day I will have lots of money and buy a Mercedes and I'll be taking you anywhere you want in that car!"

I needed thirty five years to make this dream come true, and to make that dream come true, I became a doctor of sciences, was elected as an academician, and was promoted from the position of the department head to the position of the rector.

I helped one of the administrators of the automobile shop in Sergeli a lot. After several years he came up to me with one suggestion. He said: "I know that you don't have your own car! So,I want to help you to buy a car, There's a Mercedes for a very low price, it's second hand of course, and it's been used for twelve years, but it doesn't seem like that at all." I was amazed at this suggestion, and I didn't pay any money, I just signed the document and that's all. Later on my driver Sergei took the technical passport and the certificates and acquired the number plate for the car. My student,the director of the traffic movement regulations helped me a lot with that car. The reason I liked it was the automatic gearbox , the car was very comfortable, it moved very smoothly, but my youngest daughter Oydin didn't like it all:

"It's too old to drive for a university president".

However, I didn't have enough money to buy a new one., and that car was much cheaper than the cars produced in our country like Nexia, I mean this car I bought only cost 10 thousand dollars.

Then later on, I heard about my own old car which had been stolen several years ago, so the false number of engine had been artificially stuck to the engine with a sheet made from plastic. When I was going to give the car to my nephew formally as a present, I got to know that the engine number had been changed. Could you believe that only a thief could insult and fraud a man who was heading the university, and was the administrator of five thousand people. I was just in the dark about everything, and I was stunned, as were my friends. They could not do anything to help me. I was also hesitating about what to do, and I wrote an application to the prosecutor about this case investigated. It had been a year since that car was stolen. The real number on the engine was examined by the Interpol. The car wasn't included in the list of those stolen, and this meant that my car had been stolen . I then had to formalize the car as private property and sell it as soon as possible.

After I resigned from the position of the university president, I was driving this Mercedes until august of 2005. Until and after the USSR was declared as "disintegrated" . Many people from different nationalities (Israel, the USA, Germany).

besides many friends we spent our childhood were among these

people, they are Boris Gorohovskiy, Garric Mihlin, Mihail Shapoval, Boris Krasnov, Lerik Ahmetov, Eldar Yavayev, Vyacheslav Avanesov, Estin Mark. Boris and Mark moved to Germany.

As I said, I invited all of my coursemates to the meeting in 2002 and in 2007. I even wrote a little book about all of my friends and gave it to them as a gift at this party. In our fiftieth anniversary I had a special medal prepared and organized a meeting with some honoured professors and some students. This meeting had an educational value for all the students, and honoured professionals of the motor transport field and people were happy to meet the Prime-Minister's assistant, a minister, and administrators of the plant.

My friend Boris and Mark have been living in Hannover Germany since 1994. His children earn adequate money there, and they have been inviting me to Germany since 2002. As I had too much to do at the university until 2007, I started thinking about this invitation at the end of 2007. At that time his son Alexander came to Tashkent and he made an appointment with his father's closest friends and he had a party with them. Seeing my old car there, he said in Russian: "Mr Sarvar, your car is old . I will help you get a new Mercedes, but you will have to go to Germany".

I agreed of course, and he flew to his own motherland. Then after I phoned Boris, and arranged a meeting with him.We decided to meet in March of 2008. This month was very convenient for me. I didn't have any lectures, and I was basically working with the students involved in writing graduation papers under my supervision. We had to celebrate the seventieth anniversary of A.Karunin, who was an academician, and the rector of the MARU. My wife was not able to go to Germany with me because she had lots of lectures and it would be too hard for her to go somewhere so far. Therefore I decided to go to Germany with my eldest daughter, Nigora, and we chose the route Tashkent – Saint-Peterbourg – Hannover – Moscow – Tashkent because in that case we would be able to see our friends in Saint-Petersbourg and we'd be congratulating Karunin on the occasion of the anniversary. This was both a traveling and business trip for us. My daughter had dreamed about seeing the museums in Saint-Petersbourg since she was a child. That dream was a to come true soon.

Tickets: for the flight on May 13, we'd have to come back on June 1. We bought all the gifts and presents, and we called all of our friends and solved the problems of a hotel, and seeing us in at the airport.

The professor and the dean of the SZTU, Armen Saacian saw us in the airport of Saint-Petersbourgand and he helped us to stay in rooms at the hotel of the Russian Sciences

Academy. There are two steps to the Hermitage Museum, and the One thing   that surprised me most was that all the fees of the hotel were paid in advance for us. It meant fifty dollars a day for each of us. I thanked to Armen and later we went inside the hotel rooms. My relative,my nephew Ravshan who studied there at that time came to see us. I then learned that a student had mistakenly been waiting for us in another airport, but fortunately he called Armen's number and they found each other.

I made Nigora and my nephew go to Hermitage Museum and walk along the Nevskiy prospect, and I went to the university with Armen. That same evening Armen invited us to an Italian restaurant and the four of us went there. Somewhere opposite me, a young man ran up to me wanting to hug me. He even called me with my name, perhaps he knew me, yes. I had a look at him, and yes, I did recognize him. He was my son- in-law, Shoerkin's cousin, Sherzod. After we greeted, he welcomed us there, and made us all sit around the table. We were treated as if we were sitting in the house of an Uzbek family, in Uzbekistan, because they followed all the traditions of hospitality. He was actually from Samarkand. We enjoyed eating different meals, but somehow we made him pay for what we had eaten. After leaving the restaurant we observed Leningrad, the Neva river, the monument of Peter I, and all the squares near Hermitage. At last, after traveling, we went to stay in a hotel. It was our first day in that city.

On May 14, Armen, his friend Oleg, my daughter Nigora and I went to see the Petro Palace,and the summer garden. We had breakfast when we were driving. Armen left me in Peterhoff and he went to the university after that. The three of us watched and enjoyed taking some photos, especially Nigora who was deeply impressed from spending our time there because it was the first time she was seeing those places.Especially the fountains, with the monument of the lion in this square with Solomon and lion fighting. Solomon is the symbol of Peter I, and the lion is the symbol of Sweden. Walking along the gardens, we observed inside the gardens, and after that we went to the "Sosnoviy bor" district. We walked and talked on the way and along the paths of the city. Oleg was working as a priest in the church there. All of us were enjoying the sightseeing in the wonderful garden. Then we went into the church and we saw the library and also listened to the songs the Christian people sang song in the choir. The way that they called their prophet as God was interesting, but everyone knows that God is unique for everyone. It's absolutely wrong to call a human as God. When we were walking back, I told my own opinion to Oleg, but he kept insisting that the prophet is God. The Prophet came into existence in the body of his mother, Maria, God doesn't have a husband and this is even impossible. Therefore it's impossible to have children for God.

At 10 pm in the evenings We arrived at the Italian restaurant at 10 pm in the evening, Armen, Sherzod and his brothers were looking forward to our arrival there. In a corner of the restaurant there was a table with luxurious meals, and the waiters were serving there. We enjoyed talking until 12 at night and we had a very good rest. We said goodbye to them after that and left.

On May Nigora and Davron went to see all the supermarkets to buy all the things we needed. I went to see my friend, the former rector of the Northern Western Technical University V.A.Gurecki. At the present time he works as the head of the department "Material Science". As soon as we met him, he welcomed us and we went to a restaurant together. There we enjoyed talking, and decided what to do next. In the afternoon Gurecki's wife and my daughter arrived at the restaurant we were sitting in. After we said goodbye to each other, we observed the Isaakiy sobor. This was the third day of our stay there.

On May 16 we rested until the afternoon. Armen reminded us that he had some lectures. Nigora and I walked along the Neva river on foot, and watched the Avrora ship and Petropavlovsk fortress. We went to the supermarket in the Nevski prospect and at night we met Armen and his wife near the drama theatre which we visited. We had a snack at the time of Antract, and we enjoyed the performance and went back to our hotel. The next morning they accompanied us to the Pulkovo airport and we flew to Hannover at 10 am.

We met Boris and his son in the airport in Germany and they welcomed us. We passed through customs without any problems, went outside and got in a car to go to Ratusha. It was raining. Ratusha was the palace where the Governor lived. We saw the Hannover market before and after the war. It was terrible! I wish God would save us from war all the time. My father also died because of this terrible war. After leaving Ratusha we walked around this place on foot, and watched the ducks on the lake. We then took some photos there and his wife Sveta and his daughter Rose sat us around the table where we ate some delicious foods they had prepared for us. At that time I saw Sveta worried, and I tried to calm her down. I then learned that she was worried about her husband drinking too much alcohol. I almost don't drink at all and Boris never gets drunk when he is with me. Sveta was glad about what I said. We later went to visit Sasha, Boris's eldest son, who opened the door and welcomed us inside his three room flat which was at our disposal.

Nigora started talking to Rose, I was talking to Boris, and Sasha was on the internet looking for a Mercedes with four cylinders produced in 2001. At last, he found 2 Mercedes produced in 2003 around Hannover. Their owners were both German. We immediately tackled the problem of the car, and decided to have a look at the car the next day. Both of them were silver colored and had been in accidents , but were good enough to drive and cost 11 000 Euros. The cars produced in 2004 and 2005 were very expensive. The car sellers from our country bring cars from other countries cheaply, have them repaired, then sell them saying they were produced in our own Republic. These cars are usually brought from Dubai. The real products are really expensive.

On May 18, we went to see the two cars we found on the internet. The first automobile didn't seem very good to me,with the part of the car which had been damaged as a result of the accident being downward, closer to the engine. As soon as we started the engine, we could see smoke belching through the bonnet. However, we decided to see the other cars as well so that we could compare the rest of the cars offered to us. We went to the second man who wanted to sell his car, but he was away, then came back in about fifteen minutes, and opened the car park where there were many cars. A very good-looking Mercedes immediately caught my eyes , and I felt that I liked it a lot. I have one problem with my personality; If I like something at first sight, I will try to buy it. But Nigor didn't like it very much because the front window of the car was cracked. The owner handed us the key, and Sasha got into the gear and started the engine. It worked like a clock ticking, but it didn't have a rear window nor a hatch. A tree branch had fallen on it during the thunderstorm, and that's why it had been broken. The owner of the car, Sasha, and I got in the car and drove it around the city. I also tried to drive it for a bit. The system installed to find the shortest distance to an address was also working properly. I calculated how much it could cost me to have the car body repaired. Then I learned that I was considerably wrong to calculate like that.

I told the car owner that we needed some time to think about buying that car, and we continued sightseeing in Hannover. The next day, one of my friends Mark joined us to look for a car to buy. He found a wonderful park for us to go to. It was as beautiful as paradise. Nigora walked in the shops, supermarkets and boutiques in the city for two days because in Germany all the items were very expensive. We took many photos there and we visited Mark's home later to get some rest. The next day we bought a bus ticket for a three day excursion to Paris and on May 21 we traveled to Paris. There were sixty Russian speaking tourist and all the conditions were up to date. We left Hannover at seven in the morning and had to go to Paris through Luxembourg Royalty. When we were going in the bus, we were lucky to see all the fields, German villages and places in the Luxembourg as well as Paris. My conclusion from all I saw was that a Human being has unlimited power, and If he really wants, he can turn any place into a paradise. All the roads were constructed with high quality, each meter of the field had been taken good care of, but there was no one there. We travelled for twelve hours in a bus, but we didn't see any holes in the roads, the bus didn't even skid, and moved quite smoothly. I felt sorry at that time because every year our government every year spends 300 billion soums on road construction, but where on earth is this money being spent? This also means the tens of auto road specialist being arrested every year is not in vain. When do people in our country put a halt to this illegal use of government money, and when can Uzbekistan have the quality of road as high as that in Western Europe? Automobiles used on high quality roads will last more than a hundred years. European people change their automobiles every five years, which means they have a lot of opportunities to service their cars. We buy their old and second hand cars, and we're always proud of it.

When the bus we were in got close to Luxembourg, we started to see a beautiful scene through the window. The churches were built in a glory style, with sky-scrapers. The bus stopped slowly as soon as we got the centre of Luxembourg. Everyone got off the bus and we went to a church with our own guide. For two hours we watched the main buildings and palaces of Luxembourg. The city is indeed beautiful.

 At last we arrived in Paris, the city of miracles. I was lucky to see Paris at night. Not everyone is privileged with this happiness, and I am not strong enough to describe this city when this happy. After driving for 14 hours, we decided to stay in a hotel at 9 pm at night. We crossed the city until we got to the south from the north. Then again I felt sorry for the city I live in, Tashkent, where the lights of the city can hardly be seen through the window. To enjoy these lights one has to go to the city's centre. I wish the city governors would one day feel the responsibility for their position. The hotel was brilliant, and luxurious. We were told the menu of the morning breakfast, but unfortunately we got up a bit fifteen minutes too late to eat late. Surprisingly there was nothing left on the tables to eat. We didn't say anything and got into the bus to go to the Louvre. Through the bus window we saw the wonderful buildings, alleys and prospects of the city. I had been here before, in April 2002, and I knew Paris very well. The tickets were bought, and we went inside the Louvre where we watched the main halls. Nigora was in seventh heaven. We started our travelling adventure with learning the Mona Lisa. After that we were also introduced to the the other paintings painted by other famous and well-known artists. After spending some time in Louvre, we were given a chance to do some shopping, and saw the Arch of Triumph, then visited the church of Notre Dame. The tourists in our bus were then given free chances to do whatever we wanted, and to go wherever they wished. We decided to walk through Paris on foot, and see all the opera theatres. After supper, we went back to the hotel.

On May 23 we went to the Yelisevskiy Palace where the Kings had lived, and saw the garden with hundreds of fountains, and then went into the rooms where the Kings had lived before. We went outside and bought some souveniers, returned to the bus and came back to Paris where we went into the perfume shops. The prices here were considerably low because the shop belonged to the perfume plant. We were offered fifteen types of perfumes there, but Nigora chose five of them and we bought them all. Nigora was really glad. We watched how the lights were flashing on the Eiffel tour which is something a man has to see at least once in a lifetime. We even shot some photos of ourselves there. The ship came to stop at the port, and everyone was lost because of the crowd of people. We also followed this crowd, not knowing what to do, we couldn't find our own bus, our Russian-speaking partners, and we were lost …

Focusing on where we were going, we started walking back, and at long last, we fortunately found those we were looking for. This happened on May 23.

On May 24, we went to see the Eiffel Tour, and went up to the third floor on an elevator. We could see the entire city from there. It was easy to find and recognize the place we visited. The city was incredibly beautiful. At that moment I remembered Tashkent and Seoul city, and some different thoughts entered my mind. All of us went back to the bus and again the bus driver started driving the bus to Hannover city. We again saw the same villages, and the same hills through the window. In the bus we drank whatever we wished, coffee, tea or juice. As the afternoon closed, the bus stopped near a café. We had a snack for a bit.

The thing which attracted our attention was that the price of the main course meal was about 15 Euros for two pancakes with curds costing 9 Euros. This meal cost more in our country so we thanked God that things weren't very expensive here.

The bus stopped at the bus stop in Hannover at around 7 00 pm and Boris met us in there, then drove us to a flat which Boris, and my student Sasha had rented for us to stay in. On May 25 we met the owner of that flat. That man turned out to actually be from Khorezm and had worked before as an administrator of the Uzbekbirlashuv". At that time he was living in Germany with his wife and children. That same day we cooked Uzbek pilaf together, he prepared the sauce, I mean he fried all the onions and carrots for the meal, then I added rice and made the pilaf ready. It was absolutely delicious to eat, and we gave Boris's wife and daughter some to eat.

 Early morning the next day, me and Sasha left to buy the car we had chosen, we haggled a lot about the price, and then we bought it for 10 600 Euros. After the owner signed all the necessary documents, we drove the car to the technical service where the administrator was a young man from Poland. He listed all the necessary details to be repaired or changed, and he told us the total cost was, 1400E. This was because we needed to have the front and rear windows changed, the hatch on the top, emblem, and 2 kilograms of paint. We had to pay an extra charge for cleaning both the saloon and the engine. On the same day Sasha found a trailer and we met the car owner Volodya. He said that he couldn't take the car to Tashkent, and that he could drive it just to Alma ata or Bishkek, and this service was said to cost 1300E. We solved the problem, and he agreed to give me the copy of the contract documents. At that time Nigora was busy with seeing and looking through clothes in the supermarkets and shops, and she bought some things she liked. I bought the car which I'd dreamt about.

On May 27 in the early morning we started flying to Moscow. At the airport of Hannover Boris, Sasha and Mark saw us off at the gate. We thanked them a lot for all the gifts, hospitality and the delicious meals. I have thousands of friends, and I wish them all to be healthy and happy.

At the Moscow airport a friend of my student Madamin met us with a sincere smile and then invited us to the Maru hotel. At that time we were surprised because as soon as they called us by our surnames, they handed us a key. This key was to the university president's special room and we were reminded that all the room's fees had already been paid for. Yes, it's true that something done good to people will not go in vain.

 No Uzbek visits their friends or relatives without any gifts. Unfortunately at that time the university president, professor V.M.Prihodko was away. He turned out to be occupied with the votes and elections for the Russian Academy of Sciences.

On May 28 and 29 we visited museums in Moscow and shops, and we made sure that everything was expensive, and cost us an arm and a leg. Closer to May 29, Tiymonin Volodya who worked at the MARU (MAMI) came into our room, and I gave him the zarchopon[11] and a postcard which we had brought for the university president Karunin. Because the president was at the hospital, we decided that the proctor Maximov should give him the gift because we were going to leave.

On May 30 my student Andrei came to see us when we were still at the hotel, Andrei is my friend Slavik's son. After we met Lerik Ahmetov at the airport, we went to the home of the Avanesovs. They live in a wonderful house in the countryside. When we were driving, Nigora stopped in one of the shops around there. I wish you could see how Slavik and his wife Nina welcomed us. They were so happy to see us. We hadn't seen each other for ages, and their daughter Karina and their son Andrei had already turned into Russian's as if they'd been living in Moscow all of their life. Nina moved here 5 or 6 years ago. Slavik a year ago. My friends from Tashkent continued to live in Moscow for the rest of their lives.

 May 31 was Lerik's birthday. That's why Nina prepared pilaf, and we, five friends, together, had an interesting talk for five hours. It had been a long time since I'd had such a good time. Lerik drove us to the hotel at night, there was a traffic jam in Moscow streets, and it took us two hours to get to the hotel. Nigora had left with her friend from Tashkent to go for a walk in Moscow streets.

As for Lerik, nowadays he is a professor at MARU. On May 31 we bought all the necessary things and Andrei drove us to the airport where we flew to Tashkent. The plane we were in landed safely at the Tashkent airport and my son- in-law met us there.

---

[11] Zarchopon is a type of national clothes for men, it's decorated with embroidery in golden colour

It was good to visit as a guest, but it's even better to be at home. This is a truth which no one can deny.

Now I was waiting for the car to be brought from Germany. We were forced to sign many documents to bring the car through Alma Ata, the capital city of Kazakhstan. It took a month and fifteen days for the car to be brought to Tashkent. Me and my student Bahodir made a good plan for that, because he was a specialist in Bishkek UzDAEWOO, and he could solve the problem which was worrying me. He agreed to help me to solve the problem of bringing the car into Tashkent. He agreed to help me hire someone as a driver for the car, and to do that we had to write report stating that we're hiring a driver to drive the car. Another man was working with Bahodir, but he had no rights to go to Tashkent. He was of Tadjik nationality. At that time of the Soviet Union, Tadjik people had some restrictions in certain circumstances. I paid a lot of money and [ut out a lot of energy lot for the car to be brought from Mayskiy in Kazakstan. My student Zokir and I went into the customs house, but my son-in-law Shoerkin stayed outside to wait for us. We learned that it was prohibited for the car to be exported through a driver hire from Germany, But we were forced to hire one because we didn't know how to get from Kazakhstan to Tashkent by car, that's why we needed someone who knew the route well . Unfortunately there was a decree adopted in Kazakhstan prohibiting a driver hired in a local territory. Some minutes later, we saw the car at the post and we told our friends waiting for us in the car. I then sat in my car and went to the post in Syrdarya province, Yallama post. I told my son-in-law to sit in Zokir's. Driving 150 kilometers, we got to the Yallama city. The representative of the customs house in Alma Ata didn't have any importance there, but he asked us to pay the Chimkent Traffic wardens some money. This was illegal and violated the recently adopted rule in the Kazakhstan territory. We got to the town Yallama town, and we solved the problem by paying them in Euros. Each signature on the documents costs 50 Euros. We paid 600E in total to the representative of the Kazakhstan customs house. I also gave the truck-driver 100 Euros and after saying goodbye I accessed the customs house in Uzbekistan. All the representatives here knew my reputation, positions, and therefore I solved my problems by only paying 50 Euros. We started driving the car to the customs house 11, under the control of the Tashkent customs house. I went into the post administrator's room to show him all the documents I had relevant to the car I was bringing in from Germany. He welcomed me and immediately phoned the director of the store, asking him to allow the car to be kept there inside. I was talking to the administrator of the

Tashkent Customs house at that time, because the people who have different awards can pay less customs tax for the car they are buying. But this was all in vain. I wrote an application: "I bought a car in Germany which once had an accident. I ask you to reduce the sum of customs tax taking into account the state this car is in." He asked me to address the application to the city court-experts in the Auto Technology Affairs Department. The specialist turned out to be my student, so with him I went to the post, and he took photos of the car several times from time different sides. He looked through all of the photos and details of the car, stamped the photos confirming their validity and then sent them to the enterprise where the price would be set for the car. Fortunately, there also turned out to be another of my students working there so they set the price for car repair as 6.4 million soums. I didn't wait for the price to be solved at all, and therefore this was solved in just a minute. The taxes were reduced a bit, taking into account the five year period it had been driven by the time it was sold to me. As I know they used to set the price 17600E for the cars produced in 2003, but I surprisingly bought the car for 10600E. I spent a long time registering this car as my own property, and finally I got the document requiring me to pay 24 million soums as a tax. I spent 2 million soums more for the rest of the documents to be filled in. I paid 26 million soums tax for the car I had brought from Germany. I wish the businessmen selling cars could be charged with so a huge tax... It would somehow be fair in that case, I mean. I had to gather all the money in the current account in order to get rid of that tax, until I paid it all. I had earned this money by publishing my own dictionaries, textbooks and many other books. Oh, my god, even a scientist knowing lots of things about science, may not know anything about life and they are naïve and easily convinced all the time. If I would have known that this car would cost me an arm and a leg before I had bought it, I probably wouldn't have purchased it. That is the will of God. I further wish God could help me go corectly.

On July 28 I drove my car out of the customs house post, to the university where I'd left it with Alik Shaveshian (my own student) to have it repaired. On hearing the news that I had bought a new car, most of the people rushed to see it, but they felt sorry seeing that it was in an emergency state. My real friends congratulated me anyway.

It took me 4 months to have it repaired, because even the trunk hatch had been broken. When we wanted to buy a new car or a second hand one, some people promised to bring an older one from Dubai for 1200 dollars. I didn't have a penny to my name, after having brought that car from Hannover to Alma Ata, from Alma Ata to Bishkek, wishing that it could be cheaper for us, but it was all in vain. I was also forced to address my student Bahodir at that time. We were both scientists of technical science, first learning the structure of (mashinaning tuzilishi) the trunk, then making sure that a really good mechanic could certainly repair the car without any changing of the details or other components. Bahodir took a trunk from a new car to the plant in Andijan, and two weeks later he handed me the same trunk, but in a state strong enough to operate.

Alik completely assembled the car and had it dyed. We gave some small components to my nephew Farhod so that he would repair them as well. Because they need to be repaired on the basis of the new technology. Unfortunately the masters could just repair the rear wing. We had to take the car back to Alik to have the rest of the details repaired. Within three days, he mended all the broken parts in the front bonnet, in the left wing, and he had them dyed after that. The car looked like it were brand new after that. By that time the car saloon had been cleaned several times, it was still possible to the see cracks in the windows. Then we had it cleaned chemically as well. I paid Alik for everything he had done. After I got the car out of the repair shop in July, I had already paid 1,4 million soums along with the 6 % tax. In October the Traffic regulation committee helped me to registrate the car and get the state number for it. However, I had no rights to sell the car as it had been written on a technical passport. Thanks to God, I was really happy to drive it, and I was proud of having my own students working in many organizations. They all did their best to help. All of my family members liked the car, especially my grandchildren. Even though it was not new, anyway,, as it were, it was a Mercedes, a famous brand. In 1971 I had been driving all brands of cars, they were a Moscwich, Jiguli, Volga, Espero, Nexia, and a Super-salon. They all had a mechanical box. A Mercedes has a automatic box. Only elderly people know this. On the first day of my life with my wife, I promised her I'd buy a Mercedes. As you see, I kept my promise .

When I was seventeen years old, I dreamt that in the future I would have my own driver and I'd have enough money to buy a car for myself. All of those dreams finally came true. I thank to God for this all the time. The story about this dream, which came true, has just come to end. Do you feel that there's a remedy for every torture, and a solution to every problem? Life alternates between happiness, and sadness, all thetime.

Being proud of motherland

Pride, honesty, and other features are the real value of personality. Everyone takes pride from their own point of view. Some take it as lack of modesty, some take it as the power urging the person to walk upright and to feel arrogant. If someone is insulted, he says that his pride is insulted. It's the inner feeling prompting a man to yearn for the higher peaks of life. Pride is not a feeling of ignorance, it's first strong dignity and integrity . It means to teach somebody not to forget their own national traditions and history. As time passes, elderly people give young people a chance, and development of the state depends on these young professionals. Being a good professional doesn't mean only to study well, it also represents beautiful behavior as well. If a man has beautiful behavior, he will have more reputation in his pursuit of career. For that, a man needs to have more intelligence, and pursuit of success. The road to knowledge starts with being able to differentiate something good from something bad, and to think more independently. Reading and learning non-stop, and researching is not only the source of experience, it's also the source of developing the person's overview.

Our President also mentions that young people are those who will substitute us in the future. The President of our motherland wants to see signs of intelligence in the eyes of our young people. A harmonious generation is first of all the man who can value the motherland, and who can be useful to society. A motherland seems to be appointed before each person is born. Therefore we know that we can't choose the motherland.

It's the feeling of loving the motherland. This is the pride which makes love even stronger. It makes us proud of the motherland and it's uniqueness.

If you paid attention, we often hear the expressions "harmonious generation" and "Young people of independence". This is the generation which matured during the independence period, and the feeling of love helps us to value our national and intercultural traditions.

The feeling of love serves to strengthen the independence of the state, to prepare well-educated professionals, and at first it's necessary to urge young people to be proud of their national traditions.

The citizens who work hard for the sake of their motherland are actually genuine citizens. Every citizen proud of his own motherland, and national traditions should contribute to putting his motherland on the map. This feeling prompts the citizen to do his best to work, and to overcome any obstacle in this respect.

Being proud of one's own motherland prompts people to love the land where they were born and are growing up.

Every Uzbek young citizen needs to ask himself a question: Why don't I try to work hard for motherland, like the Japanese, Korean and German citizens do. They need to make sure that they are able to in fact do it. People who love their motherland are the really happy and fortunate ones. A man only lives once in this world, and therefore they need to lead a life which causes other people to say that he was a very good man after he dies. Otherwise there's no use in living. After a man dies, nobody will remember his wealth or reputation.They will remember how helpful a man he was, and how kind he was.

Knowledge is the main factor in the development of the motherland. Even our ancestor Emir Temur valued those having much knowledge a lot, and he really appreciated them all his life. Nowadays, all the young people understand that speaking the native language and working in the motherland demonstrates a genuine love for it. They think that all the people of different nationalities in our Republic must speak and study in the state language. This is a very limited opinion. It's so good to know Russian, English and other languages. It's true that if a man knows one language, he is the only one personality, if he knows two languages, then he is like two men in one human body. Even our ancestor Behbudiy claimed that a really intelligent man should know at least four languages. Even the poet from Kharezm wrote about knowing many languages. Citizens of different nationalities know how to speak and write in the Uzbek language, and they know that they have to know it so that they could contribute to social development of the state. We can't avoid the fact that there are some citizens who were born and bred in our Republic, but they may not have even tried to learn the state language. Maybe this sort of people will do their best to learn the language of the European countries if they've got a chance to go there. Uzbek people are really kind, and honest, but there aren't any Uzbek citizens who haven't learned the state language. It's high time to try to increase the need for developing higher and secondary education. Even all of our ancestors wrote their books either in Arabic or in Persian languages. Let's suppose that you had an article or a monograph published in Uzbek. I think in this case none of the scientists will be able to read or understand this article. Some Uzbek scientists just answer this opinion with ignorance saying that they will translate it by themselves. Maybe they are somehow right. However, to develop their own comprehension and skills, every scientist should read about the most popular innovations and inventions. To do that, we have to know at least the Russian or English . We think that only in this way we may give our scientists chances which are equal to those in highly developed countries.

Something interesting is invading my thoughts: after the USSR stopped existence forever, and the states became independent, the Latvian citizens wrote a letter in their own languages to the Academy of Sciences. Therefore, the scientists of the Academy were obligated to look for a man who could speak that language in so a huge city like Tashkent. He managed to translate that letter. It took them a month to do that. Then it became known that it was written "Can you please offer some of our postgraduates time to study in your Academy?" The Uzbek scientists responded: "If a Postgraduate student who wants to apply for the job knows the Uzbek language, we will agree with pleasure." It's compulsory to know several languages for a scientist in a technical field.

I know that all the poetry, novels and the research about cotton and silk and Karakul agriculture can only be written in Uzbek. Master students should at least study subjects like medicine, physics, mathematics, biology, agriculture, machinery, chemistry and technics in English or Russian.

One more example I want to cite for you: a group of Uzbek children first studied at school in Uzbek, and we later studied in the same language at the university. We learned English and Russian at school, and we only took two courses in Russian at the university. It didn't suffice for us at all. What we learned during those lessons was only enough for us to be able to take notes during lectures, and to read textbooks. Moreover, these lessons weren't enough to retell what we learned in Russian. There needs to be opportunities for us to overcome these challenges: the two-month-practice in Minsk and Moscow, during which we had to reluctantly speak in Russian with the staff members because none of them could speak Uzbek, and where we learned the Ukrainian language while we were in the practice of pre- graduation work.

All the practical work is accurately conducted in our own language, and only the joint enterprises are allowed to organize excursions. In this case the future engineers will be learning nothing in practice.

I was an assistant of the Tashkent Polytechnical institute, and in October, 1963, I went to the Moscow Automobile Road university to gain more experience. There I remember my supervisor's secretary criticizing me politely one day: "Sarvar, you can write very well in Russian, but your speech isn't satisfactory. You still don't know how to speak Russian." I then tried to explain her:

"You're right. I learned to read and write when I was studying at school and then at the university. But we didn't a conversation and language environment. Therefore, our speech was not developed enough. I really have problems with properly conjugating the verbs in Russian."

I made the right conclusion from what she said, and I did my best to work on my speech after that. I practiced my practical lessons with Russian speaking students, and a year later that secretary complimented me and said: "Sarvar, I didn't know that you were so cute! Now you're speaking Russian very fluently. You seem to be thinking in this language, and you aren't translating your own thoughts into Russian any more. You're speaking directly, aren't you!"

I think many people come across this sort of situation when they are abroad. I was indeed able to think in Russian, but that didn't mean that I had forgotten my own native language.

My own native language is always the dearest to me, in the heart and in t he soul.

We really want our young children to be able to speak and write in at least two or three languages. Only that case can we contribute to the further development of our motherland..

Independence has made it possible for our scientists to communicate and run scientific seminars with the scholars of the world.

In 1985 with my teacher S.E. Nikitin, we aimed to write a book taking into account climate and soil properties in Central Asia, because this sort of book had never been published in the entire former Soviet Union. After legalizing all t he documents needed for that, we allocated all of them to the Republican Higher Education Ministry (request, program and the proof). We received the following reply from them: "In the Soviet Union (former) only Russian, Byelorussian, and Ukrainian scientists are able to write books on technology, Uzbek scientists are only able to only write books on the cotton and silk cocoon growing process." We could have complied with this rule and given up our idea, but we were catering to raise the reputation of our own nationality and to prove that Uzbek scientists weren't limited, and could make contributions in the technological science. Then I thought: I was a doctor of technical sciences, a professor, and I was able to invent something new for technology.

We again insisted on our decision and again sent a letter of request to the Ministry of Higher education. We eventually got a positive response, and – permission to publish a book. So the book "Automobile and Tractor Engines" was published in 1990 in Russian, and students got the chance to learn this subject more independently. Two years later this book was translated into Uzbek and 5000 copies were published . 300 copies of this book in Russian was sold to 15 foreign countries like Iran, India, Arabia, China and many others. Here we concluded that the books contributing to the world development should be written in the Russian or English, because this will enable them to be easily t ranslated into other languages and get popular all over the world. Even Japanese, Indian, Arabian, and Egyptian scientists published their books in English, and they teach their Master students in this language. This doesn't mean we ignore our own nationality or native language of the state.However, this will enable our teachers and scientists to contribute to the world development. I think it would be a good idea if we do the same. Our President more than once claimed that the young generations need to learn more than one foreign language. There are opportunities in order to implement these plans, but … Moreover, each university should have faculties full of talented students. There should also be strict requirements to know our native language as well, and this needs to begin at the primary and secondary levels. There further needs to be a demand to learn foreign languages art every university, which will serve to include our motherland in the list of the highly developed countries of the world. This could be one decisive step towards this certainty.

For anyone who wants to become a good specialist

My grandmother, who used to work as a jeweler, used to tell me : " One day in the future you will see that the only wealth a man has will be the books in his home. When he has to move to another house, he will have to load the car with books. A good book to read is more than wealth and relaxation, it's a cornerstone of intelligence, and it helps to overcome betrayal and life's challenges. A good book is an endless treasure, and the more you read it, the wiser you become".

It's easily seen that a man who doesn't read books is not nice and interesting to talk to. But the participants of the game "Intelligence" are absolutely pleasant to have a conversation with. This is a TV quiz in which a team of young intelligent people try to answer questions posted by the spectators and fans of the program.

I remember conducting the same game at our university between 2002-2003. The students whom I found talented couldn't even respond the questions I had prepared on the history of our motherland, nor on our great ancestors. However, our President makes non stop speeches about these ancestors and their contribution to the development of our country.

I hope that all of our young people will get enough knowledge and become intelligent enough to contribute to our country. They need to understand that a book is a speechless teacher of proficiency, and not reading books is a sign of decreasing literacy.

There are very good conversation clubs which are really nice to talk to. But most young people seem not to know about this at all.

When Emir Temur saw his grandson putting books into his sack, he said: "Don't be so childish, Mirzo. You may tear all these books if you ... you don't have to put them in this way into the sack, a book is something sacred. We must always value it whatever happens. Value the book as much as you value your parents and motherland."

If children don't value books, it's the parents who are guilty. The environment at school and at the university also considerably influence student's behavior. Unfortunately, most of the head representatives keep saying the same things to educate young people. They keep saying that when there's the internet, people do not need to buy books.However, this is wrong to say, and leads young people to spiritual and intellectual weakness.

People less able to think independently may immediately believe this and means it's possible to get any book you want on the internet free of charge. But this is all nonsense. Capitalists are very cunning people, and if they don't earn any profits, they will never attempt to do anything. If they foresee less profits from production, they will never produce something in huge amounts. Try to think about the financial profits of computers, mobile phones, and internet cafes.

In this case we need to address the elderly and experienced people who have never had these computers and printers. We need to ask them if they were unable to read any novels published when there weren't any printers in the past.

I think not. I still remember the 70s and the 80s, when the book I had written about technical science was first published with 5000 copies, then with 7000 copies. They were distributed to three or four universities in the Republic because the books need to reach all the students who study technology and technics as their special field of study.

Nowadays the automobile industry has considerably developed as the President of our Republic has paid a lot attention to the development of this field, and the number of universities preparing professionals in this field of study has reached 20 in total.

All the textbooks are only being published in 1000 copies editions, and the authors find it really hard to sell them. People fail to realize that books are the genuine treasure of wealth.

As for highly developed countries, after a book is published, there will be an announcement about the sale of the new book in all the lectures and seminars of university. These books are really expensive in these countries about 100-150 Euros. Books have became even more expensive in Russia, and the authors sell their books on the basis of the contracts with certain organizations. I think this is the only way for a scientist to earn money. This is in foreign countries, but it isn't like that in our country.

Another way for a scientist to earn money is to run scientific research. Unfortunately the income for that is also strictly limited to a certain sum. The additional salary of professors is only enough to buy 5 kilos of meat here. I think it's high time to think about this. How many young people do we have among our students who want to be a scientist? There's a huge gap between the older and younger generations of scientists in our country.

I am not writing these views in vain. I am writing this as a person who has worked more than a half century in pedagogical science. It's up to your own outlook how to assess and understand what I am writing about at the moment. Now I really want to give my own advice to all the students!

Every student should love to read books and to learn new things. They need to buy novels and books which seem interesting to them, If they cut down on buying boxes of cigarettes, they may easily buy good books for themselves.

Just imagine, the scientists of the 1920s and 1930s, for example Hovach M.S., Dobrogayev R.P., Voinov A.N., Archangelskiy V.M., Mutalibov A.A., Salimov O.U., Abramov

N.S.   Who wrote books, and these books started being sold in the shops of the city. If I were there, I would immediately borrow money from someone and immediately buy those books, because my teachers actually wrote these books. I would certainly read them all, and in that case, I would find myself rich and wealthy.

The "Kamolot[12]"12, youth organization, the leaders of the groups, and the teachers, need to remind the students about reading books. All the university and faculty administrators need to encourage the students to read books.However, the money shouldn't be paid in cash to teachers, and could better be withdrawn from their current account so that some taxes could be paid to the government as well. I am a teacher who has taught many students, and who has had sincere and long conversations with them. I can say confidentially that the internet is a very good thing, but it never gives something free of charge. Those who search something on the internet spend more money, but get less information. If they need more information, they will again be obliged to pay money for that. However, once a book is bought, and is always on your desk, you can read it whenever you want.

There's one more view for those who are eager to learn and value books. I think life loses its interest without knowledge. The people with knowledge of the world are the wealthiest. Money and wealth will always be chasing the man who has knowledge.

Avicenna, known as the genius of the medicine, never wasted his time, as we know. If he was free, he would read books, and if his day was hectic, he would write 35 pages of a book instead of sleeping during the nights. Therefore this person left lots of books for

---

[12] 12 It is an organization in the Republic which supports young people.

the future generations, and it has been thousands of years, but those books are still serving society. You must also imagine yourself being a prominent person in the future, and feel free to pursue this imagination. Try to make reality out of these expectations.

Being naïve

The good deeds we did, or the things we helped people do, will be eternal in this world. I used to help people, but in the end helping people it would leave me in awkward situations .

This was because I easily believed, whatever people said to me.

Even the students who are close to me take advantage of this. One day my student who had worked as an assistant with me came to see me with a good suggestion. He had been promoted to a higher position at that time. What he suggested was we open a business company in partnership. We decided to work together from that time on. I gave the share I had to pay, and though it's been more than ten years, there's still no return of the money I gave or any news about the business we were going to start at that time.

When I was a university president, I became quite close with the representatives of the television company. They used to come to shoot all the ceremonies at the university. One of those people asked me to lend him some money since he was going to soon get married . I supported him, and did my best to help.However, he still he hasn't given that money back .

The same things have happened to me more than once. I used to treat all the students very friendly, and I never made them wait when they came to ask for help. They could easily and frankly share their problems with me and ask for help or a solution. One of my former students who also asked me for help started working as the governor of the district. He came to see me before the New year and said:

"My mother is seriously ill, and I sold my car so that she could be treated. Can you please lend me your the car you're not using at the moment for three days. I will take my mummy to the doctors if you help me." He said that he will even write a document about that. How could I reject him when his mother was sick? Besides he was an orphan. We called a witness and he signed the document confirming that he had taken my car for three days, I handed him the key after that. The way that I believed everything he said caused me to fail again, and this cost me an arm a leg at the end.

That man did illegal things using my car and as a result was arrested soon after that. At last I was forced to write an explanation letter for allowing him to use my car.

Later on I started thinking for a long time even when my own siblings came to ask me for help. I know that it's not good because if there's no trust for people around you, this means honesty is likely to be fading in the world. May god save us all from that to happen.

But we are unlikely able to neglect these facts. I had a student whom I educated by myself and who was working as a traffic warden at that time. He had a brother who entered the university on the basis of the contract tuition, and he was urgent to pay for it. I did my best to help, but he still didn't pay the money he owes me. If these people lack honesty themselves, what else can I do?

Whenever I by chance meet face to face with all those people who still owe me money, we greet each other with a hug. They as usual keep making their odd promises to me. Sometimes I scold myself saying that "Why am I so naïve?" But anyway I thank God for giving me so many opportunities, and thanks to God that I don't owe a penny to anyone. I really hate to be in debt or to be slave for someone. My philosophy is that if I promise to do something, I will keep that promise.

I had close relationships with several ministers and other administrators, and I helped their children as a rector a lot. When I was a rector, they used to visit me almost every month to ask me to buy a field because they wanted to help me to build a house there. Time has passed and after fifteen years, I was allocated a land measuring 0,8 hectares. The first secretary of the former Kalinin region, Rahmatilla Kambarov, helped me with that a lot. I still remember how much he helped me. I make sure that people never forget whenever you help them.

We started building a house in 2004. All of my genuine friends helped me to buy all the necessary materials. Brick, concrete, reinforcing steel, crushed stone, door frames and water we got free of charge. I am grateful to Rashit, Botir and Shoahror for their help. Some friends neglected me after I promoted them to higher positions, though helped them a lot. The house I started still hasn't been finished even though it's   been five years . Soon, If I earn some money by publishing my own books, I will surely spend it all on this house.

God decides what will happen to us in the future and to our choices. I hope to live in a bigger house when I grow old, not in a flat like I do today.

Now I want to tell you about one more thing that happened in my life. In the autumn of 2004, the head of the council UZautoRoad came to see me when I was working as a university president. After we greeted each other, he told me that he came to see me with a request.

At that time his organization was under strict control, and there were lots of prosecutors there to investigate all of their documents. In 2002 this organization had allocated five million soums as a sponsorship to aid the university fund. This money was withdrawn by the chief engineer, but the sponsorship wasn't recorded in the operating budget. The chief engineer was at last arrested. He came to me to ask for help, and for me to rescue them by lending them some money. They also promised to pay it back within a month.

My friend was in a tight corner. I thought that it was dishonesty not to help him. I have my own current account , but if I were dishonest, I would have said that the sponsorship's money had been spent two years ago by that time.

But this organization had done a good turn for the university when it was in need, and it was wrong to forget about that. I could see my way to lending them some money and I had some money donated to them from my own personal current account; about five million soums. We wrote in the documents that it had been the sponsorship aid money, and that the money had been mistakenly transferred .

They released the chief engineer from prison, and I was really over the moon that this money came in handy for them. Unfortunately , it has been more than five years,and they still haven't paid the money back.

How could I understand this situation? I again was the victim of my own personality.

Wise sayings

I have always written what I think on sheets of paper.

I have now decided to include them all in this book.

I learned many things reading books by the great ancestors, and I advise you to conclude reading the following aphorisms I wrote. I think this could be very helpful for you to follow them all.

Save yourself from troubles, be patient when you're in pain or in a muddle. Look on honesty and the justice as a ruler for yourself, and let them rule you all the time. Live in a way that no one could look upon you as an enemy. Try to respect and value everyone. Try to save all the money and wealth you have.

Do not hurt any of the people around you. Think for a long time, talk a little. Do not let less intelligent, cunning or dishonest people into your own secrets. Try to follow whatever all the scientists and wise men advise you to do. Try to do what generous people are doing. Do not just do what you want, listen to other close people around you. Keep your clothes clean, and keep your soul free from grief. If you owe someone money someone, give it back in time. Do not be greedy with what you can help people with. Every time you put your head onto the pillow, try to make a list of the things you did the whole day, and if you did many good deeds, feel yourself over the moon. If you did something wrong, ask god to forgive your sins. Make decisions about what you're going to do the next day, and think for some time before you make a decision.

When you're counting the faults of other people around you, their unfair attitude to you, try to perceive your own faults as well. A man who can see his own faults, will not try to perceive the faults of other people either. Do not pick holes in everything.

Do not try to make an obstacle, and don't get up to anyone, because it may cause you to eventually be faced with the same obstacle. Do not try to ruin someone's reputation, or your own reputation is going to be ruined afterwards. Do not try to fight against justice and the truth. Do not try to gain fame through telling lies, or one day you will get short of fame. Try to respect everybody around you. Do not feel shy to come clean that you don't have knowledge about something. Try to learn everything you don't know, because if you don't learn, one day you'll feel sorry about that. All the good wishes you make for yourself, you need to make for others as well.

If you do whatever you like, you may get closer to death. Because the things we usually like are mostly wrong to do. Do not poke your nose in the conversations, and talks, that aren't related to you at all. Do not travel down the path leading you astray. If you are closer to people who are generous and kind, everybody will find you kind and generous.

Do not try to aim for something that you haven't contributed to. You mustn't be lazy to work, and earn money by working hard.

If something you wish didn't come true, do not panic, just be patient. Do not chat or let out whatever comes to your mind. Do not trust what others say. Do not show yourself as an intelligent and arrogant person, and try to admit that there are even more intelligent and wise people around you.

Keep valuing bread and other things you eat, and do not feel happy if someone you hate is in a tight corner. You may also get into the same trouble, so don't forget it. If you can't afford to give those people close to you gifts and presents, try to make them happy with your pleasant attitude and friendly smile. Do not try to avenge on someone, even though you can afford to. If somebody gossips about you, do not dare to argue with him, just avoid talking to that man.

If you need a friend, just look for one who can help you in need, who only speaks the truth, who keeps all of your secrets under his hat, and who understands you in all situations, no matter if you are glad or upset. Do not be friends with those who like to compliment to you.

Do not hate the person whom your friend hates, because if they get on well with each other later on, then you may get into a very awkward situation. If you do something good for someone, do not boast about that, because there are many people around who see it, even though you do not say this at all. Your own sensibility is your best friend, and the only enemy for you is lack of wisdom. Do not be afraid of crafty and dumb people. Do not forget that your good behavior is your genuine beauty.

If there's hostility among you and your friends, take the initiative to cease it at once. Do not get interested in fame, reputation and money.

Do not ask for anything if it isn't necessary, because one day they may remind you about that. Do not be quarrelsome about some little nonsense. If you suddenly meet some of your relatives or your friends, ask about their life and health. Try to respect all the guests that visit your home.

You must look on sensibility as necessary for humankind, therefore you should only use it effectively for useful things.

You need to work hard in order to be what you want. If you want to be a farmer, then you need to learn how to grow plants, or if you want to be a miner, then you must practice extracting minerals and other resources. Keep valuing and respecting your teachers all the time.

The philosophers of the East mentioned that a human being needs to have the following peculiarities:

You need to control your wanting: if you limit what you're eating and drinking, and if you are thinking before saying something, then you can be what you really want.

Be patient: do not say the things which may eventually hurt you or the others around you.

Follow all the right rules. You need to do everything in time. Everything is good in its own season.

You need to have your own aim: Do not waste your money on things not needed, try to save it.

Always do your best for something: Do not waste a minute, always do useful things, avoid doing what is not needed at all.

Look on truth as prior to everything. Always tell the truth, keep working fairly, keep yourself away from trickery, and keep your soul fresh from bad thoughts. Be trustworthy.

Keep your body clean: try to wear clean and tidy clothes, do not let them get stained.

Try to love yourself, do not ruin your own health, allowing yourself to suffer from nonsense. Think that they don't deserve brooding over. Be accurate, do not endanger not only your peace, but that of other people as well, and do not cause disagreement between them.

Always be polite, try to treat everyone politely, and do not look down on the rest of the people around you. Modesty is the best humankind feature, therefore always be modest. That will lead you to happiness.

Be brave in the heart: It's brave when a man rescues himself from the danger to come. This will save us from doing something wrong when we are frightened. Try to control yourself even when you are nervous, and do not get aggressive even if you're in a tense mood. Keeping silent and polite while you are tense will rescue you from many bad things to happen. Everybody loves kind and polite people.

This sort of people do not prefer to shout when they are angry, they just find it proper to be patient with the present situation. Getting irritated is harmful for own health and nerves. A man whose face turns red with anger, will a bit later feel sorry about what he did, and he is going to be ashamed of how he behaved when he was angry.

Modesty is the feeling of valuing other people. It prevents one from looking down on them. The man who doesn't underestimate others is worthy of many applauds. But it isn't recommended to be too modest all the time, because otherwise this will lead you to nothing. Everything is good in its own season.

Try to be consolidarity, friendly and honesty all the time.

Patience is a necessary ability helping to stand all the challenges of life.

Being a friend means being together both in happiness and in sadness. But just being together doesn't mean a thing. You should also help your friend to get out of misery.

One wise philosopher wrote these sayings for his own friends before his death:

-        Think in a right way, just tell the truth

-        Pay attention to the obvious or distinct features of what you're doing.

-        Do what you can do now, within this moment, and do not postpone this for tomorrow.

-        Be devoted to your commitments, if you feel that   you're mistaken, try to correct this mistake as soon as possible.

-        Follow your duties always in time, keep your promises.

-        Do not be friends with ill-minded people.

-        Ignore those who offer you alcohol, for this is poison, and you must keep away from that.

- Do not trust what people say about your fate, way of life, you are the guide leading this fate as a matter of fact.

- Do not be rude, always be polite.

- Be punctual for your work.

One of the great scientists Said Ali Hamadoniy said: If you don't want to be faced with an accident, do not be arrogant. If you want to lead a luxurious way of life, try to help other people, and do not hurt anyone in this world. If you want to be valued, then try to be generous. If you don't want to feel sorry for what you did, consult the elderly and wise people around you.

If you want to be loved by the people around you. Try to change yourself positively, be accurate. If you want to be respected, work loyally, and dedicate yourself to what you're doing. If you want other people to find you modest, honest and trustworthy, do not tell any lies, and think before saying something. If you get into trouble or into an awkward situation, do not panic about that at all. Rather than panicking, try to find the way to solve it, or to ease that situation.

• Science can not be stimulated when there are scientists who pretend to be scientists by having their research written by proxy.

• A real scientist is someone who doesn't want to waste even a minute of his life.

• Money decides everything, it can be the source of solving issues.

• An envious man will keep suffering from the pains of his own malicious forethoughts in the future.

• If you are a scientist, then make people want to look like you.

• If nobody wants to be like you, it means you are lazy

• Be careful in making mistakes, for those who don't like you may exaggerate all of your errors.

• If you are glad when your colleagues defeat you in competition or in a game, it means you are a good person.

• It's a real crime if a scientist is drunk.

- Hardworking people don't know how to feel bored,as they don't have time to be bored with something.

- Laziness can kill all the great inventions and ideas.

- If great and prominent people praise you, then it means you're a good person.

- Do not sleep before you calculate all the things you did today.

- There are four things which show that a scientist is a real scientist: dignity, patience, loyalty and being hard- working.

- Intelligence rules dignity.

- You may forgive the mistakes of other people, but do not dare to forget your own mistakes.

- It doesn't suit scientists to look very sad or very glad.

- The happiness of a scientist is that he is always alert no matter if he is in trouble or in red.

- There are complicated things that can take thousand days to do, but a real scientist can do it in only a day and no longer.

- The way that your eyes glow is a sign of the pureness of your soul.

- A scientist shouldn't only give an idea, he should also try to apply it.

- If there are many people who want to talk to you, then make sure that you're talented.

- If you can find a way to someone's soul, then it means you're a wise person.

- A man who can not remember own his childhood, can not be a good teacher for children.

- It's useless to give tens of advice to children about how to live, and it's better to let them see how you are leading your life, for then children will learn by seeing how you are living as a wise man.

- Find your opponent as cleverer than yourself.

- If you want to remember your childhood, then make a get-together with your old friends from childhood.

- A real friend can reduce your inner troubles by encouraging your happy feelings.

- Honesty makes a man look beautiful.

- If a man isn't honest, then he doesn't need intelligence at all, because they compliment each other.

- There will be more interest in living where there's justice.

- Truth is always painful.

- Truth is the mother of hope and trust.

- The greatest inventions are always odd.

- It will be complicated to preserve justice where there's no freedom of speech and freedom of human honesty.

- A scientist is the wealthiest man, but not financially.

- Most of the real scientists are all naïve.

- People who are both modest and proud are always sincere.

- A real scientist is a poet of his science

- The people with poetic personalities and minds are usually good scientists.

- If you want to be a good orator, then write your thoughts on paper, and retell it in your own words so that it can be understandable.

- Lectures should be short and clear.

- If wise sayings are written with a short example, it will have even more value for society.

- An orator should speak so creatively that when he says something, listeners should imagine that at that time.

- It's artistic ability to express what's on your mind in short.

- A real orator needs to deliver a wide speech in short.

- There are two types of information in the lectures: very important and secondary. It's important to change voice tones specifically for each of them and to support them with evidences.

- Wise men can distinguish liers by looking at their eyes.

- If there are no people with opposing views in a debate, then it's impossible to solve the solution of the problem, or to plumb the mystery available.

- If people do not behave well during discussions, the discussions will eventually turn into rows .

- If you lose in a debate, then you must learn to admit that.

- Music and art inspires the person, it inspires the scientists.

- A scientist can not fall asleep without dreaming or thinking for some time.

- Most accidental inventions are created by the geniuses of the world.

- If you want to be wise, then try to reach everything through thinking critically.

- Wise people can always effectively communicate with people with different personalities and different manners of behavior.

- You must love God with all of your being, with all of your heart and with all of your senses.

- Treat people the way you want them to treat you.

- The more we think we're intelligent, the sooner we'll grow to understand that this is wrong.

- A scientist doesn't even feel hunger while thinking and inventing.

- A scientist counting himself as prominent, actually has less than enough knowledge. Everybody needs to think critically about own abilities, and in that case only he will make a turning point in science.

- You need to require students to only study in case you're teaching them well .

- We can get as much as twice the knowledge as a result of teaching university students.

- Parents and teachers are the main cause of bringing up the geniuses of the world.

- The more you're talented and famous, the more rumours there are about you.

- A scientific advisor should love his own students as much as he loves his children.

- If you don't exactly imagine the importance and the aim of your research, then you can not achieve any results in your life.

- A scientist having many students should always be proud of being a teacher.

- A scientific advisor should be a teacher, a good consultant, and he needs to be kind.

- A real scientist should choose an actual topic for a research.

- An impatient man can not be a scientist.

- If a scientist has a clean and pure soul, this is the happiness of his student.

- "Now dear doctor, this has been the basic part of my life story. Now I think it's going to be much easier for you. Excuse me if I bored you with all these stories. This story covers the events which happened between 1940-2009. This is not only the fate of one person, because during the years I lived, thousands of our citizens were also living in torture."

"Now would you please leave the treatment to us?

After I left the hospital, I started writing about my life in this book. I wrote this book as a wise saying book for my own students, and for my young colleagues.

Even though this is the life one orphan boy has led, he was yearning and longing for the bright path of knowledge despite many challenges of life. It's about a young boy not having a penny to his name, who had looked forward to the university's entrance exams results, who was promoted from just being a student, to the degree of a professor and an academician. I thank the readers who are patient, and who aren't taking pity on me during their time reading between these lines. I wish you good luck if this story and experiences can help you to build your own future life a little bit. But life is going on, and I still have lots of things to do. I have to write even more textbooks and articles . Educating young people … Oh, it never ends, and this is why I am happy that I always have to do something. I am even happier about having no time to sleep.

Days Recently Bygone

We are in one more stage of the life of the main hero, Sarvar. Sarvar could have finished his story right in the previous part. But each person was born with own soulmate, and he is destined to share his life with someone in the world. Sarvar also fell in love, got married, had children like many other people. This novel is going to be like a river without any water if he doesn't tell us about his life with his other half. Family life taught him quite lots of things. In this part of the story, the hero quite frequently travels in his own soul, in love with a person of his destiny. While in this novel we move from one part into another, we can see that here he is changing his own character from time to time. In this part he is going to be in the role of Oybek. His name here is going to sound as "Oybek", not "Sarvar. Here we can also witness also some biographical extracts from the diaries of his other half, Oydin whose name is actually A'lokhon. But here the author changes her name into "Oydin", maybe so that it would sound similar with "Oybek". Yes, this is also a way to creativity, to some literary alterations.

The author says:

I live on a street named after Abdulla Kadiriy, a great writer of our motherland. I have a favourite hobby which is to go for a walk on this street sometimes in the dawn, sometimes when the dusk falls. But I always walk alone. Quite often I stare at this name: "Abdulla Kodiriy" engraved on the walls of the buildings and gates of our houses. The heroes in the novels he wrote are different. They are sometimes brave, sometimes weak ... I always remember some of them, Otabek, Kumushbibi and many others. Then I remember what Abdulla Kodiriy said when he was arrested because of a massacre. He said :"What's my crime? Why am I going to be arrested?".

In these moments, it pains me to think that he was innocent, but imprisoned due to a massacre and shot to death. Each time I think of that, I get a keen pain in my heart from the nameless tortured feelings, and I don't even want to describe these feelings in this book.

All the events in this book are written because I felt sorry for this person, who was arrested, though he was innocent. I can't be as brave as Otabek (hero in the novel by

Kodiriy "Days Gone by" perhaps, but I have as much love as Otabek had for his motherland, and for his other half Kumushbibi[13].

I preferred to name this novel as "Days recently bygone", not because I wanted to compare myself to him, but because I bear endless admiration for this writer.

Each man living in this world represents the history of his own motherland whatever he does. I wish you would be aware of the mistakes I had made during my life, I wish you would cope with the challenges I had to face much better than I did.

Foreword

The gate was open, and one could hear the sound of music from the outside, with the voices of men and women. Oybek got prepared and began to rush. Abduboriy gave him a questioning look:

-I think you said guests would be just us, friends, nobody else…

-My father said this. I think you said that if I came up to the gate, I needed to come inside further, and if the gate is closed, I needed to knock.

Abduboriy muttered with childish arrogance:

"You are not a doctor. In fact, you're a philosopher", Oybek followed his friend. There were handlamps on the trees. Thick branches of the trees and leaves were fusing with the flashes of the lights. There were some seats outside the house. There were many people, and most of them were young.

Abduboriy said to all the friends sitting there: "Here we are, now, friends!" and he greeted everyone shaking their hands.

---

[13] 13 This novel portrays the invasion and wars in Central Asia, tortures people suffered from during the XIX century. Otabek married a woman he fell in love with and who lived far from his hometown Tashkent. Her father didn't let his daughter to leave for Tashkent, but Otabek's parents wanted him to live with them, not with Kumush far from Tashkent. So Otabek's parents forced him to marry a girl whom he had never seen and loved. After that Kumushbibi moved in their home. The two wives of Otabek had rows each day. After Kumushbibi gave birth to a son, Otabek's second wife killed her giving her poisoned meal. After that Otabek also died in the war, but Kumushbibi's parents brought up their, Otabek's and Kumushbibi's son.

"Welcome you are, everyone was here but you, now we are all together." Kanoat said, he was one of the hosts there. He was also one of Oybek's closest friends, and he entered the Andijan state Medical university with Abduboriy together the same year. A group of friends were going to see them off to another city, making a get-together here in this house.

Then Kanoat started introducing all of the young people around the table: "Look, they have today come back from the international festival of the clever youth, which took place in Moscow. This is my sister, Tursunoy, this is Zahro." Kanoat introduced everyone to his friends, but at that time Oybek wanted to take a seat in the corner away from all of them. Lately he was not feeling up to taking part in this sort of get- together parties at all. He was feeling like his chest was cracked, and heart was paining a lot. Everything touched his heart immediately, everything could make him feel sad. If he joined a number of people, it seemed to him as if all the people were feeling sorry for him. His friends seemingly noticed his situation and they said:

"Look at him! Hah, he is so pale, I don't believe that love can make us so mad and sick."

"Yes, he fell in love with the daughter of a jeweler. I think he didn't know that this sort of people do not know what love is. The only thing they care about is money, gold and …"

"Therefore they said that Oybek didn't have a penny to his name, they think it costs an arm and a leg to get married, to have a wedding."

No one said this to Oybek or about him at all actually. These dialogues fierced his ears just in his thoughts, in his mind. He thought that everyone knew about the problem he had and it seemed to him as if they were teasing him about the way that he was in love with a rich girl. He was thinking non stop about her letters. He could never forget the way his mother was glad before she knocked the door of the girl's home, and then how she came back, sad and in distress. It seemed like a barrier to all of his hopes about his love, had cast a blight on all of his dreams and ambitions. He would never give up being ambitious because of someone who insulted him, would he? It pained him a lot what the jeweler had said to his mother.

The jeweler, the girl's father said: "Who is that Oybek, how can he get married if he doesn't have a penny to his name?"

No matter how poor he was, the jeweler didn't have the right to speak like that.

Suddenly his friend interrupted him while he was thinking about this all:

"Hey, mate, where are you? Wake up, look, join us, won't you? Look how beautiful the girls are!"

Suddenly Oybek felt alert at feeling the voice and breath of his friend Abduboriy.

Oybek has many wonderful friends, and Abduboriy was certainly one of those. Without these friends Oybek would sink into the sea of his anguish and pains. Anyway he was listening to everything his friends were saying:

'… so amazing shops, we saw very splendid clothes oh, we looked just like Russian fashionable girls when we tried them on.'

'Do you remember how we went for a walk in the river, we were feeling like swimming with the full moon together. I wanted to stay there for always."

Oybek was saying to himself but addressing those girls: "oh, girls, all you can talk about is just walks, strolls

and clothes…"

Oybek was thinking about that girl so much that she seemed to be much further from him, but around the same table, the same girl seemed to have said :

"Young people feel free these days to say whatever they wish. They don't have the fear of doing what's wrong at all. They may say whatever they want, maybe it's because they are living so independently."

Oybek felt surprised and he really wanted to see that girl who said this, her voice was still piercing his ears from afar:

Oh, people of freedom, they laugh quite freely They can laugh as much as they want

They may also cry, not like many others There's no shadow of sadness in their tears They may also die, but not like many others

He was still looking for that girl who spoke about independence and who recited a poem around that table. "Her voice is really nice" he thought, and he was reluctantly shy to think about this . The voice doesn't mean a thing, when this view is so brilliant. Oybek was feeling awkward looking at that girl standing up at that time, but he really wanted to see her...the girl who seemed so close to his heart.

Spring of Childhood That Never Comes Back I Want to Wear Boots

It was snowing. Oybek opened his palms wide and said: "Look, snow, so wonderful!" Snow was falling onto his palms.

Anvar brushed him off: "Hey you, throw the snow away, your hands will get frozen". Oybek's face beamed with a smile, then he squeezed the snow and threw it into the tree, dressed in white snow, looking big on the edge of the road. He used to do what his brother Anvar told him to. But he also told him:

"I wish you would walk on the traces of the cart, the snow isn't going to fill in your galoshes. The snow is thick enough, look!"

But Anvar was walking on those traces even before he said this. The snow was falling again, and thick enough to cover those traces of the cart. No matter how carefully two brothers were walking it was useless because the snow would fill in their galoshes. The white snow's happiness soon abandoned them, and they were almost crying because of the pain the cold snow was causing their feet, knees and even their heads.

Anvar's teeth were trembling, and he tried to stop it as if the pain would cease.

Oybek pulled him by his hands and said: "Bro, you must walk, or your feet will get frozen".

 He was all frozen, and there was snow even on his eyelashes. He was hardly stopping himself from crying.

As soon as they arrived, their teacher saw them , and said: "Oh, at last you're here! Oh, your feet are frozen, take off your shoes at once." The classroom was crowded with children, some of them wearing coats, some of them jackets."

The teacher was taking Oybek's shoes off and after that he started wiping them with his napkin. Oybek was crying. He was obeying whatever his teacher was doing, and he was wiping and rubbing the little boy's frozen feet by kneeling down beside him. His teacher was bidding him to turn right and then left, right and left, right and left so that he could more easily clean his feet. The lessons would begin with this episode on winter chilly days. The classrooms were never warm.

Oybek slowly stopped shivering and started reading his book bowing his head towards it.

He was reading: "A boy …" then he stopped looking at the picture of the little boy on the book page. That boy in the picture was wearing a cap and boots. Oybek was fingering the picture of the boots and he was thinking and whispering: "I think they keep the feet quite warm in winter, don't they? Yes, they do …".

The teacher was surprised seeing the way that Oybek stopped, he just asked: "What's wrong, Oybek, why did you stop?"

Oybek asked his teacher: "Why do children in the Alphabet book pictures wear boots, but we don't? Why do we wear summer galoshes in this winter?

All the students bursted out laughing.

"You're right! I like the way you ask me questions, Oybek! If a person is satisfied with his life, thinking that this is the way he is destined to live then, there's not going to be any development. Everyone in this classroom needs to ask the same questions, ok, children?"

Oybek was proud of being supported and he looked at his friends smiling. Then the teacher said again:

"As for the boots, Oybek, they are quite expensive. They are made from leather, and therefore we need to have lots of money to buy them. You need to study well and try to get well- paid jobs if you want to wear boots in future. If you study well, not only you, but your children will also be wearing boots."

Oybek wanted to laugh because he imagined his son wearing boots in the future. It is funny how a little child imagines having a son after he grows up.

He wonders who his son is going to look like, Oybek or his brother Anvar.'

The way that their teacher Giyokori Musayev spoke used to fill the classroom with joy and attract all of the children. The children seemed to be engrossed in whatever he was saying.

"One day I will also wear leather boots" said Oybek. He said this decisively, but in a very low voice. His voice disappeared through the noise children were making. He felt energy coming from his own voice and he decided to work hard from that time forth. It was high time for the break.

Mummy, could you please tell us a tale!

The chilly days of winter passed, and it was getting warmer and warmer. All the fruit trees like almond, apricot, and cherries started blooming in Tashkent's gardens. The smell of the flowers was fusing with the thunder, sunny and rainy days. After that, at last summer came, as hot as love's emotions.

If you're in a garden, you will easily feel the summer, and Oybek knew every meter of their garden like the back of his hands. Oybek heard Abduboriy's mother telling him: "Be careful sitting in the garden for so a long time. Do not fall asleep under the nut tree, ok? It may drive you mad." But as soon as Oybek's mother, Hojiya got free of her housework, she used to make Oybek work in the garden with her.

She used to tell him: "Look, Oybek, that apricot on the tree is looking at you and telling you: "Oybek, it's only a bit longer until I am ripe, and as soon as I am ripe, I will immediately fall into your hand!" Look, did you hear?"

She always made up some dialogues on behalf of the fruits: "Look, Oybek, listen to what the apple is saying: "Hey, Oybek, what's up, why don't you pick me up?"

Oybek liked the way that his mother used to say this a lot. She was reciting poems or singing songs at that moment and sang them, especially at night, outside the house, when they were sitting on the wide bench. Oybek would lie with his head on his mother's lap and used to enjoy this especially when the moon shined brightly. Hojiabonu laid her hair down on her shoulder. Everyday she had to do the same thing , cook, boil some tea, and clean the house... Perhaps she was tired of the housework, and therefore, from time to time, she used to moan:

"Oh, my God, what a pain!" It seemed like a miracle for Oybek, the way her voice trembled with tiredness, her white dress and golden earrings glittering under the moon beams. He was enjoying seeing the leaves rustling as the wind blew. Oybek said:

"Mummy, would you please tell me a tale! Is it true what Boriy's mummy says, that some mermaids come to the garden at night?"

"His mother likes to joke, come on! She was only joking with you. The garden is sacred, so if you take care of each grass and each flower, and if you don't throw any garbage in it, no mermaid or devil will haunt untidy and dirty places, keep that in mind."

Oybek wanted to hear his mother's voice on and on, and he felt like he was flying when he was there with his mother. He moaned again:

"Muuuumyyy, I want a tale!"

"Ok, well … Once upon a time, in the Tashkent city, there was a rich man, Alimjonboy. He had huge lands for farming, people used to plant and grow cotton there. They got lots of profits there all the time. That rich man had sons Tukhtaboy, Kodirboy and Abdullaboy.

"Three sons, like, me my brother Anvar and Marvar?" "Yes, like you, but you also have sisters, Bakhtia and Gulnor." "That rich man wouldn't be greedy for money at all, he used to give handful of golden coins to his children whenever they asked for money.

"Mummy, did he buy leather boots for his sons?"

"Let alone the leather boots, my honey, he used to buy them boots sewn from golden threads."

Oybek liked all the tales his mother told him, especially the one about this rich man. But he used to imagine the moon and its reflection in the canal water flowing there.

She went on: "That rich man not only took care of his own children, but also the others. Sometimes he used to have some tea chats with the rich people, and they all gave money to enable talented students to study in developed countries like Germany. Rich people wanted to change their life for the better so that their children would learn lots of good things.

Oybek didn't understand why his mother was crying when she was telling these tales. But there was something close to his heart in these tales. His heart was beating fast, he really wanted to get deeper and deeper into these tales, and he wanted to hug those people who had helped young people to study in Germany because at that time when he was studying at school, many children were unable to go to school in winter as they didn't have summer galoshes to wear. While Oybek was reading quickly, those children were reading syllables after syllables.

Alimjonboy's sons took after their father in bravery and courage. He had some hotels and concert halls built in the city. He could have lived enjoying and having fun in life, marrying more than once,and eating and drinking whatever he wished and he liked. But Tukhtaboy wanted the people around to have beautiful hotels and concert halls. He didn't want the visitors in that city to wander in the streets, perhaps therefore he built these hotels there.

"Mummy, can you go on, please? What happened next?" "Then the dragon "Soviet union" launched an attack on

these people. It has swallowed all the wealth and money Tukhtaboy and his children owned, and it swallowed them with just one attempt."

Oybek started to see the dragon with a mouth wide open. He saw the dragon swallowing golden coins, the wheat and cotton harvest, and it didn't care about his stomach getting full.

"Oybek, listen, those wealthy men who could hardly rescue themselves and their children from the dragon "Soviet" were actually your grandparents. If this dragon hadn't swallowed their money, gold and wealth, you would also be wearing leather boots in winter ..."

At that moment Oybek looked at his feet. His heels were cracked because of walking barefeet on the rocky roads of the village. Did that dragon have any rights to take their wealth away? Now because of that dragon, Oybek was suffering a lot from wearing thin galoshes on the roads covered with snow and ice. That is painful to think about, very painful.

His mother didn't always tell this sort of tales. She mostly told stories like "Stones, crack open!", and "Tohir and Zuhra".

Oybek was too weak to understand everything his mother was talking about because quite often he used to follow his own childish thoughts while she was telling him these tales.

Sometimes he interrupted his mother and said: "Look mummy, the moon is winking its eyes at us. Can you see that?"

But his mother never scolded him for interrupting.

Oybek used to listen to these fairy tales and he'd fall asleep. He usually dreamt about his grandparents, Alimjonboy, Kodirboy, and Tashpulat sitting on golden thrones.

The dragon was attacking them all, spitting fire out of his big and horrible mouth.

The nut game

"Wait a minute, let me see your soqqa14. Oybek opened his palm and handed his soqqa to him feeling still and calm.

The boy who took the soqqa tried to look through it , turned it over, and right and left on his palms. The children around were also watching that with a feeling of amusement.

"That is your turn to play" he said and handed the soqqa to Oybek. That boy didn't take his soqqa any more after that. The last time Oybek joined this game with just one nut, all the nuts were arranged in a line. They were called "gan[14]" . Children threw the nuts to the gan standing two meters away from that, if the nuts thrown hit the gan, then the participant was the winner. Oybek didn't fear throwing the nuts at all. He used to first close one of his eyes, and aiming at the gan effectively, he would throw the nut right into the gan. He used to win fifty nuts in the same game.

I think all the other participants were upset about the way that he was winning all of their nuts, and therefore one of them said furiously:

"I needed to see the nut with which he was hitting the gan, maybe he had done something to trick us" . Maybe if there had been another boy in Oybek's shoes, he would have left without even paying attention to what they were saying. But Oybek

---

[14] A stone in the game which will serve as the main target stone for participants to hit the others. This I usually called gan.

didn't dare . He turned back and asked bravely: "How did you know that? What on earth are

you saying about me?"

All the boys turned to him at once.

One of those boys calmed the others down saying: "Don't pay him any attention. He is being rude, because he is a newcomer here." Oybek wanted to prove to them that he hadn't done anything with the nuts to trick. He went up to the boy who blamed him in tricking and showed him the nuts. Although he squeezed it to break, it didn't crack open. Then Oybek looked for a stone to break the nuts open.

Even though the boys prompted him to calm down, he didn't. He found a stone somewhere, a very big one and cracked the nut open.

When Oybek wanted to bow down, all of his nuts spread out on the ground.

"Did you see it, I told you that Oybek never tricks, the nut is the real one."

"We believed you anyway, Oybek . Why did you throw all of your nuts away?"

Then Oybek immediately said: "Let's not stop the game, guys, whose turn is it?" and he started picking up all of his nuts again. The woolen jacket he was wearing was much bigger in size. His neighbor Tolib had given it to him a long time ago as his son was wearing it out . Oybek remembered what he said when he gave that jacket to him: "This is my son's jacket. He is not wearing it any more, I hope you'll wear it when you are playing outside. I am afraid it's old so...". Oybek's heart seemed to be beating slowly out of pain, then he added as an afterthought: "Maybe if my father had been alive, I wouldn't have seemed so poor that our neighbours would have to give me the clothes they're wearing out". His own uncles of means would never take care of them, no matter how often Oybek used to visit them. They seemed like they weren't welcoming at all. Oybek wasn't playing that game of nuts in vain., He believed in his own ability, and he used to win 50 and 60 of nuts in each game. He would keep them in sacks for winter.

He didn't feel upset about the way his friends suspected his fair game, and he knew that his friend was doing that on purpose. He didn't want the others to interrupt Oybek from playing by thinking that he was tricking them. He respected the boy, who played a fair game all the time.

He said: "Well done, Oybek!"

The others also said: "Yes, you are brilliant!

"I think you're going to be a sniper, aren't you?" Oybek didn't answer any of these questions. He used to play the game forgetting about himself, and about the world.

This is eager desire to be first began during his childhood. Not everyone is privileged with that, and Oybek used to be first not only in nuts game, but also in football, wrestling and many other sports and games. Every game has own special rules. For example, let's take chillak. In this game children have to hit the little stick with a longer stick called a chillak. The player who hits the stick further than the rest of the players is going to be the winner. The boy who lost the game had to carry the winner on his back up to where their stick dropped. This made children physically healthy.

In the 1950s , the game of ball was somehow like football. 6 or 7 participants took part in that game from all sides. Children living in the mahallas "Hojaparhon" and "Uzbekistan" played it and each team competed against each other. They played on the sand field , or sometimes they played in the grass field. People living in the same street would gather there to watch their game.

Still there weren't any electric bulbs in our countryside at that time. There was a grass field in the mahalla, and it bordered the village. At nights, the young men of this mahalla usually visited this place to chat and to rest. They would gather the young and little children and they would make them play the game of wrestling with each other. The games used to be played fairly all the time, nobody was tricky. Oybek was even the best in wrestling. Of course, his mother couldn't afford to buy them healthy food to eat, but despite that he was really strong. Strong enough to defeat anyone in wrestling. This demonstrates that a man doesn't have to be wealthy to be strong. It's more than enough to have strong patience and dignity. The kids started a fight between Oybek's dog "Kashka" and his neighbor's cat "Barok". I wish you could have seen this fight.

There's an idiom about these two animals, cats and dogs which isn't in vain. The cat snatched the dog with its claws, and the dog bit the cat on its neck and legs. The cat finally escaped moaning and whining from fear. Oybek's dog was a real guard in his home, and it wouldn't let cats, dogs, nor a stranger in the house. But one day the dog got lost, and he looked for it everywhere. Ten days passed but there was still no news about it. One day when Oybek was playing in the farm yard, he heard the barking sound of his dog. A week later when he was playing in the farm's field, he heard Kashka's barking. It seemed to be barking a bit further from him. Running up to it he saw Kashka wagging its tail in front of another dog. As soon as he called, Kashka took a few steps towards him, then again stepped back towards its own female partner. Walking alongside a garden (it measured about two hectares) he knocked on the door of the house there. After the house owner and Oybek greeted each other, Oybek explained why he came, as he wanted to take his dog back. The man told him smiling:

"You can get it back, of course, if you can!"

No matter how much Oybek tried, he couldn't convince the dog to go home, and at long last, he chained it and dragged it home. You can imagine it whined, looking back at its female partner. For three days, it turned down all the things I gave it to eat. I then understood that even dogs can have feelings.

A SLAP

Chilly weather. It's so icy outside that if you're going to cry, the teardrops are going to freeze before they trickle down your face. People dressed in coats or jackets were waiting for their turn in queue. They were waiting for their turn to buy bread for a cheaper price. It was the dawn of the morning, and there was no sign of the sunrise yet. If we hadn't gone up there so early, we wouldn't have been able to buy some bread at all. It wouldn't have sufficed for everyone in the queue. The people in the queue were only women and little children. Oybek was also there with his mother. His mother didn't want to stand in the queue with her elder son, because he was often sick due to weakness. Oybek was strong enough, he never avoided doing anything when there was something wrong, and he courageously tries to solve everything.

His mother was standing there in the queue, when suddenly the women around tried to speak to his mother:

"Bonu, we heard that Risolat had died, and you could not get the money back right? Or could you?" They meant the money which the chief of the mahalla had owed her husband. He had bought many things from their shops but had never paid the for them.

Then her husband had been sued because of this deficit in the income in their current account.

"Yes, you're right, he is very dishonest. How can I make him pay that? It's impossible I suppose."

Her husband couldn't stand this unfairness. The being arrested because of a debt someone else hadn't paid back, and was something he couldn't endure. Therefore, he decided to serve in the war and die for the sake of the motherland rather than being arrested. He even wrote and posted a letter when he was in the war, providing evidence that a man had owed him a huge sum of money. Hojiyabonu asked Risolat, the secretary to go up to the mahalla chief as a witness, but unfortunately that woman died. Seemingly the mahalla chief was sure that since the witness had died, the poor widowed woman couldn't do anything about that debt. Therefore after Hojiya tried to ask about that money more than once, she at last gave up because there was no use any more.

In the queue when women were reminding them about the debt, Oybek was going to interrupt them because he didn't want his mummy to think about that money at all. He I then interrupted and said: "Mummy, today we are to look for our dog again".

"Dogs are always loyal to their owners, my son". It was his mother's favourite dog, and it chased and followed her wherever she went. If a stranger visit their home, the dog would chase them back out to the gate barking loudly and snarling to frighten them.

"You think that everything is good, mum! You used to say that our cow was also good until it attacked me." Oybek was saying whatever was coming to his mind, he just wanted her not to think about his dad.

"You did something wrong, that's why it attacked you, Oybek. When an animal is made upset, it of course tends to attack a man."

"Mummy, is a snake an animal too?"

"Why did you remember the snake by a sudden?"

"I don't know, I was just thinking about my own snake, mum. Maybe if it could come back to our house again, we would've got rid of this bloody war."

Sometimes a yellow snake would haunt their home, His mother would always remind him: "This is the snake of wealth, and it will guard you. Don't be afraid, it won't do you any harm. It used to slither around the handle of your cradle."

Oybek looked upon him as a harmless guard of the house, but he was still afraid of it. One day he saw another different snake in their kitchen, and he immediately called his friends for help. His friends were older than him, but they didn't dare to go up to it. Only the neighbour's daughter Anora hit the snake with a wooden stick and killed it. Oybek was taken aback by the courage this little girl had.

In the breadline's que, Oybek had already grown sick and tired of the usual topics of talks, about war and hunger. At that time Oybek kept interrupting them all the time asking different questions. He didn't understand why so many people didn't require people to stop the war, when indeed all of their sons and husbands were cut down in their prime because of that bloodshed. He wondered why they didn't open up that they were fed up with standing in the queues so often.

When it was time for Oybek to go to school early in the morning, his mother would keep him beside her in the queue of the breadline. He would always moan: "Mum, I am going to be late for the lesson, I don't want to be here nor be late."

"You will manage to get there on time. We've been waiting for such a long time, so wait until we get some more flour or bread, my son! I need to feed you first, it's prior to your school, you know!"

Oybek imagined all the people in the breadline having just a stomach to fill, nothing more.

"But mum, my teacher will make me wait at the door holding up a brick if I am going to be late…" As soon as he said that, she slapped him in his face. This widowed mother was in torture waiting only for a loaf of bread, long before the dawn broke.

One woman there shouted: "Why on earth did you hit him? It's cold for him, don't you see? Calm down please! It isn't easy for anyone these days

"It isn't easy for anyone nowadays."

Oybek's face seemed to be burning from pain and he burst into tears.

Hard Work of Picking Soft Cotton

It was so hot that the sun seemed to throw fire all around. Drops of sweat were trickling down the faces of those who were chopping the land. Oybek was behaving like he was an adult, rubbing the sweat drops off his forehead with his hand. His palms also sweated as he was tightly holding the garden tool... His feet were also tired, he had a keen pain in his back. He would relax for a bit if he sat on the ground and chopped sitting down on the ground, but if he did so, his trousers would certainly get stained, and they couldn't afford to buy new ones.

Oybek would work in the farm field every day after his lessons. On Sundays Oybek and his mum would get up early before the dawn broke and to start working in the field. One day the two men, who were in charge of controlling the farm, went up to them riding on horses and as soon as they saw the little children, Oybek and his brother Anvar working in the field, they shouted out in anger:

"Where the heck did you find these little children? They can't work here, don't you see it? They don't even know what they are doing."

Anvar was weak by nature, and that's why his face turned pale immediately. Oybek, however, was going to go up to them and say:

"I didn't understand you sir. Firstly we aren't little children at all. We do very well in our school, so we are schoolchildren. You must first see how we are working, and if you don't like it, you may say that what you've just said, Sir. But you mustn't say whatever comes to your mind taking into account that you're senior to us."

Bakhtia, his sister, saw how he was getting frustrated, and getting ready to brush them off. She pushed him back:

"Oybek, calm down, and take it easy. If you say something wrong, it will be bad for our mummy."

A brigadier himself responded them:

"Yes, they are little, but their mother and sister are both here to take care of them. They aren't lazy boys. Trust us, they work much better than the elders. This is the cotton field, so it's important for us to choose those who know how to work."

Oybek couldn't forget that at all, and even at the present time, as soon as he starts doing some work in the field, what still hurts him, and still haunts him, are the thoughts of that time.

In his childhood he used to talk to the cotton plants, and to leaves, while he was chopping the land. Whenever he was removing all the weeds and grass from the field, he felt happy to rescue each cotton plant. He was happy about the way he was helping nature, and he would feel sorry to be there in the field when it was so scorching. He recalled his father, whom he barely remembered. What he did remember was that his father dabbed his eyes with his handkerchief after he cried before leaving for the war. The only thing he left was his name "Mukaddir" and his photo. Until they got the letter about his death, they received one letter. He wrote that his mummy had given birth in his dream. He didn't see them, and they didn't see him after that any more. They could only see him now in the Great beyond. Now his mother was alone, and the only breadwinner to feed these children. They exchanged all the jewelry his grandfather had left with the cereals and other products to eat. Whenever Oybek was chopping the land, he took a look at the field bordered by poplars. There was a channel flowing there, he wished he could leave this field   and jump into the water, then swim as fast as fish. He wished he could sunbathe on the sand after that, but these wishes were impossible to come true for him, as they had a very strict norm of working. If he didn't work, the accountant would never give him a salary, his work all day would go in vain, and Oybek wasn't the type who spent his time in vain. Though he was sometimes engrossed in his own dreams, he quickly concentrated again.

Oybek remembers: It's both hard and fun to work in the farm. A man who is tired of a hard work may find it easy to fall asleep in bed.

So good it is! Especially it's great to sleep on the grass and or the straw store.

I still feel the smell of the clover, and at home I feel the smell of the flowers, and the raihan[15] my mother used to water and take care of.

It was spring, the cotton plants were already turning into fruit, and in the winter they were going to open up and all would get picked. When workers cannot manage to pick

---

[15] A type of a scented plant with a very strong smell, it can be used as a remedy, as an ingredient for foods.

the cotton, they would have to do it in winter, when the cotton is frozen. It scratched the fingers and hands, and it really hurts when you wash them. His mother used a simple oil or an ointment of some kind on their hands every day because they hurt a lot. But all her children, Bakhtia, Anvar and Oybek were patient with all these tortures. When it rained and all the cotton they picked was wet, they laid it on the ground to dry, and afterwards they could relax, warming their feet at home. He remembered the time when his mother read the Alpomish tales to all the people in the mahalla. She read:

When horses were running, the ground troubled of an earthquake,

The Brave Alpomish was suffering due to the wound he had...,

Oybek didn't know that these people needed this national literature so much, and that they needed so courageous man like Alpomish. Their heart seemed to be beating fast when Oybek was reading to them about the Uzbek national hero Alpomish.

"Oybek, you're absolutely drowning in your dreams, aren't you? Get up and have dinner with us" said his sister who suddenly interrupted him. As soon as he stood up, he felt that his numbed feet and back got some energy back.

Then his brother Anvar started complaining:

"It's not Sunday everyday. We only work hard on Sundays, once a week."

They will now eat a piece of raw bread and a bowl of soup without any oil or meat... Then they'll climb up to the big tree and jump into the channel. What fun it is! They will forget all the pains of hard work under the sunshine and in boiling weather.

Cotton is very soft and light, but to grow it and to gather the harvest, is very hard work.

I'll Be Acting as Gulnor

Now we'll be reading littles extracts from the diary of Oydin, the girl who Oybek adores:

It was drizzling in the early morning and later it poured down in buckets for some hours at midnight. The drops of the rain trickling through the holes of our ceiling were about to stop. Even the bowls and tins we put for the rain to leak through the ceilings stopped clanking for a bit. I like summer a lot, but he is fed up with that already. Sometimes my mother used to say: "Oh, our home seems to have no roof, because all the raindrops trickle down through the holes of the ceiling." Mummy used to dig many holes inside the home on the floor, as there were not enough pans and bowls to stop the rain from falling onto the floors. Mummy sits at home with her thin scarf on her head, and each time a hole gets full, she cleans it getting the rain water with a bucket, and I go to the canal to throw it out. The faster I run, the more often I tend to fall over, and my body pains from the cold. Mother often complains as it was wet and damp in the house all the time in spring:

"I think there seems to be no end to this rain". Because her feet were all numb, I don't dare to complain. She doesn't want to see us suffering at all.

"My dear children, if God didn't want you to suffer, I wish he hadn't let your father die. While the children at the same age as you are playing in the street, I am making you all work and earn money. You don't even have a chance to feel what childhood is." She said taking pity on her children.

Oybek couldn't stand this.

"Never mind, mummy, the rain's going to stop soon. First please rest in that corner for a bit. I will clean all the holes by myself". My uncle had made our roof from some kind of black paper, and he put some special liquid on it. Under that part of the roof we keep our clothes, and in that part of the home we usually slept and rested. The musical instrument, dutar, which my father had always played used to be also kept there. If he hadn't left for the war, he wouldn't have got injured. He was a very good musician. If he hadn't died maybe, Oybek wouldn't have been cleaning the roof from the snow. His poor mother wouldn't have been buying some things in the wholesale for a cheaper price and then selling them for more expensive cost. She wouldn't have been suffering so much.

She would call me and would say:

"My sweety daughter, come here, and rest".

"No mummy, last night my uncle brought some sugar, I'll put it into a cup of tea and you'll drink it."

"Oh, my honey, I don't have any sons, but I feel that you're giving me love that even ten sons cannot give. When I have you, my daughter, I don't need to give birth to a son"

The next day was Monday, and it was wet outside. The sky was cloudy. As soon as I got a bit bored with the lesson, the sky immediately attracted me. I like to look through the window.

"Did you think about what I said last lesson, children?" said our literature teacher Sadulla Karomatov.

"Which lesson? What did you say?"

"We are going to organize a new festival of young people in our district. We need to take part in it with a little performance. We planned to make a performance on the basis of the extract from the novel "Qutlug Kon" by the writer Oybek.

Our literature teacher gave a task to two or three girls in the group to write a scenario of the performance. I was worried about the rain, therefore I forgot about it.

Our classmate, chatterbox Guli said: "Teacher, I have written the scenario"

Zebo also said that she had also done started writing.

I was feeling awkward because I used to be the first at school all the time. I promised to bring the scenario the next morning.

On coming home, I at once opened that novel and started writing the scenario. I hesitated about which extract to choose. Shall I take the first meeting of the couple in this novel? This was the first puzzle of creativity in my childhood.

So I chose an extract of this novel in which the main female hero, Gulnor, young and beautiful is kidnapped. It is when Yulchi rescues her from the trouble. So these two people actually love each other. I wrote down the scenario and the next morning rushed to school to show that to my teacher. My teacher quickly read it and asked:

"Is it you who wrote it?" Her friends started murmuring at once:

"Yes, it's she, she perhaps wrote it herself, she always writes something, it's her hobby."

Yes, I wrote the scenario, and this was my hobby. I am used to rewriting the books or the film scenarios after I get introduced to them, I even make corrections in the episodes that may seem strange to me. My classmates know it well.

"Well-done Oydin! You can be a very good writer in the future!" I wanted to tell him that I wanted to be an actress, not a writer, but instead:

"Teacher, can I ask you about something?" "Yes, you can"

"Can I be the one who will be acting as Gulnor here?" My teacher beamed with a smile as soon as I said that.

The unforgettable day

"Where's the magazine? Who hid it?"

It was Majid Kodiriy whose voice resounded around the entire classroom. All the children were scared to death. All the math teachers like Majis Kodiriy used to speak in a very low voice. But that day he was very nervous, and it could be seen from his eyes. The point is that their register disappeared all of a sudden. This happened on Saturday.

"I know that it's one of you who stole the register. Someone is not satisfied with the mark they got. If you bring back the register next Monday, it's going to be ok, but if you don't, then you will all be punished quite seriously" said the group teacher of Oybek.

It is Monday, the math lesson, and there was no sign of the register.

The teacher said: "I know that the mark I put didn't satisfy someone among you, children. Can you please come clean about who has hidden the register?

"Teacher, it's … errr… it's. .. who stole the register…" said one of the boys.

Majid Kodiriy didn't let him speak till the end: "Is it you who did it?" He was silent.

The teacher:
"If it's someone else, do not say it. Let that student come clean by himself. It isn't good to say something on behalf of someone else."

Oybek loved his math teacher a lot. But he didn't understand why his teacher was feeling so furious at that moment.

The teacher: "Now I ask everyone here to stand up." He said this so furiously that everyone was shuddering with fear.

"You must know it, all of you will be standing in this way unless someone who is guilty doesn't admit that."

"This is unfair, why do we have to stand up because of someone else's fault?" Oybek thought. He was watching all of his classmates. One of them was Nigmat who was very good at breaking and repairing things, Anvar was the type to think only about money, Mirkobil was a genius. Akrom, Tulagan and Ibodulla were all stock still and silent. Oybek was impatient with that, and he couldn't stand it when someone treated them unfairly:

"Teacher, I will sit, because I haven't stolen the register." "What if I ask you not to sit?"

"I will sit anyway"

Oybek took his seat, and the rest of the schoolchildren followed him. They also started taking their seats one after another.

The teacher Majid was watching them with different enthusiasm. He was not trying to object to them to sitting down, as they were all sitting claiming that they hadn't stolen the register.

At last there was only one boy left who didn't dare to sit. He stood in that way alone for some moments and then burst into tears:

"It's you who is guilty teacher. Why did you put me three, when you put Akrom 4? Our home task was the same, wasn't it? That's why I have hidden that register" that boy murmured.

The teacher sat on the chair and asked: "Where's that?

Where did you hide it?"

"I put it into the sack and buried somewhere near the canal."

The teacher asked Oybek to stay after the class. It seemed strange, the register was found, it was ok, not damaged, but Oybek wasn't guilty there at all. Maybe he called him to punish him for deciding to sit down first. But Majid Kodiriy sounded calm and glad.

 The teacher and Oybek's surnames sounded almost similar, and therefore the teacher would sometimes address him in a different way:

"Come here, my relative (because their surname sounded similar), I know you've got lots of questions, so I just wanted to talk to you. Don't worry. Do you know what? When you said that you wanted to take a seat, you made me glad up to the sky because nobody should allow others to punish and treat them unfairly. Or he may be further tortured to death. You know, when I was blamed for being an enemy of the citizens, the prosecutor would question me on and on and I didn't u respond at all. I thought that they would release me, because I wasn't guilty at all. They didn't release me, and instead they arrested me. Do you know what I did to be arrested? In one of the councils of professionals, one man was making a speech and he said "Stalin is our father". I whispered to him: "You need to be shy to make him a husband for your own mother". Only the two people sitting next to me could have heard what I whispered to him, and therefore either one of them, or both of them unfortunately turned out to be spies. I was subjected to torture in prison for seven years for the one thing I whispered. Staying in prison for so many years made me less energetic and less strong. Therefore, I can't stand the people who like to expose the wrong the others are doing. No matter what wrong they do, one day anyway they are going to be punished. Aren't they?"

Oybek was listening to him with all of his attention. "A man should feel responsible for all the people he is living with in the same motherland. If someone did something wrong in your presence, it means that you're also guilty. If you were a good man, you wouldn't have allowed that man to do wrong things at all."

Oybek started to feel differently after he had this talk with his teacher. He was unable to describe what happened, but there was a big change in his feelings.

Long Days and Long Nights

The light on the window sill was dimly glittering, the gentle breeze of the night was bringing the smell of the flowers outside through the window to the room where Oybek was sitting with his head down. But he wasn't feeling that smell, he was only holding the pen and his palms were sweating. He had been trying to solve his chemistry problems for many hours. He would stretch as soon as he found a solution to any of them, and would fiddle his fingers to make them relax. But he didn't stand up, his feet were numb and he would move them up and down to release the pain.

The door banged open, and his brother came through the door. His face hardly caught the light and he clattered the sack into the corner. Oybek: "How was your day? You look tired. Mummy…"

His brother interrupted him: "The police caught mummy in the street and she was forced to leave with them. I could barely escape with these heavy sacks, I was going to run away with…"

Oybek was completely shocked from what he heard. His neck wouldn't move and he sat in the same chair for hours.

"Where? Where's mummy now?"

Oybek couldn't say that "she was in the police office". He shuddered to say that, and if he did, his mum in the prison would come into his sight as a hallucination. He said:

"She is in the office close to the shop, I was going to leave all these sacks next to the shop of the Auntie Dilbar, but …

Anvar was hopefully looking at Oybek, and his eyes were asking: "What are we supposed to do now?"

Oybek was good at thinking of something to solve problems and to get out of difficult situations, so he said:

"I'll go there myself…"

"Maybe we'll go there with someone who is older" "I want to try first and then maybe …"

They were thinking that they were adults and too shy to ask help from other people.

Anvar stood and kept looking at his brother who was going to the police office where his mum was.

Oybek went out with a steady and confident look, but when he arrived to another street, he began to cry. He was upset about the way the police was torturing his mum because his mother hadn't committed a crime. She was only buying some goods like soaps, butter, tea and selling it at a bit more expensive price. She eked out her living in this way. The police should thank her for feeding her children alone when her husband had died in the war for the sake of this motherland. She didn't abandon her children to enjoy her youth at all, and she was always busy earning money wherever she went. She didn't cry out loud when she received a letter about her husband's death. She earned money to feed her children as the only breadwinner in the family. At first she started sewing jackets for the soldiers in the war. Grandma would bring cloth and she would sew winter clothes putting some cotton inside. Her sewing machine was very old and Oybek would pull the cloth tight when she was sewing, or the machine wouldn't work properly. His feet and hands hurt a lot sitting in the same position all the time, but he didn't let his mum feel that. His mum would sing a song in a crooning voice:

I'm longing for you, for your eyes, my darling My face turned pale waiting for you so long, yearning for a look into your dark eyes Waiting for you, my heart is paining and burning.

Oybek wanted to sob whenever he heard her singing, because he knew how much his mum loved his father. His father's parents objected to their marriage, but he decided to marry her anyway. That's why most of his father's relatives didn't like their children. It wasn't easy for his mum to live without her husband. After the war ended, it became fashionable for men to wear white trousers and she started sewing this sort of trousers and sold them in a bulk. After that she learned to sew clothes for women.

But it's really a hard work to sew from the early morning till the evening. Lately her eyes started aching due to tiredness. Sometimes Oybek wanted to give up his school lessons, and he wanted to earn money himself and make it easy for his mum to live. However, he didn't want to live just for today, and he knew that it could leave him as a manual worker for the rest of his life. He decided to study hard and let her enjoy her future life which Oybek was going to fill with his achievements and success.

With all these thoughts, he didn't even notice how he arrived at the police station. He knew this place very well.

After she stopped sewing she began earning money by buying all these things in the shop. Because of that job, now she is in the police office. When he went up to the policeman, the police said:

"So, what's up, why are you, a little boy here?" This policeman was dressed in a special uniform and he had a sleek moustache. Oybek glared at him quite seriously.

"I came here for my mum"

"Who is your mother? Is she a thief, a robber or an illegal seller?"

"Watch your mouth please when you talk about my mum!" "Do not be so weird, hey bastard! If we caught your   mum,

that means she is a robber or a criminal. What's her surname?"

Oybek got frustrated, and he was stunned what to do. He knew that they didn't have any right to insult his mum:

"My mum is not guilty. You're all accustomed to arresting people who aren't guilty at all. If she had given you a bit of her goods as a tip, you would have already set her free, wouldn't you, Sir?"

That policeman's eyes bulged and he came even closer to Oybek:

"You don't know that you're playing with fire, boy! Sergent, come here!" Two or three policemen came through the door and the tallest of them stood stock still and kept gazing at Oybek.

Another man who had lots of medals on his right chest also took a glance at the boy. He looked well and pleasant, but Oybek didn't want to greet any of them thinking that all of them were the same sort of dishonest people although he felt in his bones that he was not doing the right thing.

He was going to obey them for the sake of his mum and there was something burning in his heart against these dishonest people who were torturing his mum. He was thinking about his mum who everyday wandered in the bulk to buy goods to sell at a cost five cents cheaper than usual. He wanted to beat his own head against any wall as it was absolutely hard to stand that unfairness.

One of the policeman suddenly stopped them and said: "Wait. Wait. Who is your father, my son?"

"His name is Mukaddir"

"You're from the mahalla Allon, aren't you? I was sure that you are. Yes, you're his son. You're Mukaddir's son. You   have really taken after him. Are all of your brothers and sisters ok? What on earth are you doing here? Look, guys, we were in the same train to go to the war with his father. His father was a really good man"

He didn't let the man with the moustache say a word after that.

He said: "I called him with only a little problem. There, there, my son, you can go now. I am going to solve your problem by myself". He said all this in a rush. And Oybek said:

"What about my mum?"

"Everything's going to be ok. Don't worry. You may now go" The man with sleek moustache seemed to push him to the door and he whispered: "What's your mother's name?"

"Her name is Hojiyabonu"

"Now you may go. She'll go after you leave"

Oybek added as an afterthought: "Right, you policeman seem brave just to us, ordinary boys, but you're like a rabbit in front of your boss." Oybek waited a bit further from the police office. He saw that rude man seeing his mother off and after that he quickly walked away. Ten minutes later he saw his mother coming:

"Is that you, Oybek, my son? What are you doing here? You must be tired, I could go home by myself, my honey."

Oybek hugged his mother, clinging to her face with his cheeks. She was in trouble, but anyway worried about him.

"This police officer started having a bit of conscience, thanks to God, and he set me free without asking for a penny. I gave him two or three coins".

"Mooom …."

"My child, my honey, how do you know that? They must also pay for someone senior to themselves, and therefore they keep making us pay for that."

Oybek didn't tell her all the details because he was also about to be arrested for the way he had treated that officer. He bit back.

"Oh, my God, thank you for being so kind to us, and for bringing me here, home safe and sound" She said that as soon as she entered their home. Anvar was sleeping in the corner, the   light was glittering and Oybek's books were dotted all around the table, flittering as the breeze was blowing through the window.

Is it wrong to be the first?

"Oh, is that you? I don't believe it! Here you look like a groom in the wedding, wow!"

"Yes, it's me, there isn't a bride here so that I could be a groom. That's ok, one day I will find her as well."

"In this photo, you look more like your father"

"Of course, he looks like his father. He won't be taking after his neighbor, will he?"

Oybek was listening to his friends jokes and he felt something strange in his heart. Soon they would all graduate, and they didn't feel how those ten years at school had flashed by. The desks and chairs, and this classroom now seemed dear to them before they were saying goodbye to each other. They were the ones who quarreled today, but mended the fences the next day in the morning. They knew that they wouldn't meet such good friends in their future. Friends as innocent as now, as close as today. Oybek had many questions to God, many thoughts. He used to do his   homework with his friends at home. They would gather in each other's home and learn different useful things. Oybek's youngest uncle would give them mathematical problems to solve and they all used to compete to be the first to solve them. Most of Oybek's memories were connected with his own brother, because they used to go to school together and study together.

No matter how they pinched with hunger, how often they were wearing the old clothes their neighbours gave them, they really enjoyed being a child and then a teenager. They didn't have a proper suit even after they finished school, but it didn't seem like a problem for him because they had their neighbors who could help them in need.

When they were again sitting with friends, Abduboriy started talking to Oybek:

"Have you heard the news?" "What news?"

"About our school vignette. Our photos are going to be located according in alphabetical order." At first Oybek didn't pay much attention to him, but that news interrupted him from thinking:

"What?"

"Yes, that's what I heard"

"Can you explain that again? Who and where are our names going to be placed? "

Before student's photos would be placed according to how well they did during the school time. Now it wouldn't matter. Is it clear now?"

He thought that it was unfair, but he knew that he would get a gold medal. He decided not to care about that, but those who didn't do well at school within ten years would feel shy about that.

When he was thinking about that their teacher Mr. Mahmoud came into the classroom. Oybek said in a trembling voice:

"Mr. Mahmoud…"

His teacher knit his eyebrows, because he didn't like arguments at all. And Oybek didn't call the teacher unless he   intended to object to something. The teacher said:

"What else do you want?"

"Is it true that our photos are going to be placed according to alphabetical order in the vignette?"

"Yes, that's right. It's going to be the same with everywhere else. If you have the surname of your wealthy grandfather Alimboy, then you will be at the top of the list of children. But now unfortunately your photo is going to be placed a bit lower than the one on the top."

Oybek started feeling nervous.

"What if it isn't going to be placed lower   than the one on the top?

 I won't let you do that. It's unfair"

"Hey, I say, don't be so selfish! It's life, not a tale or a film. No matter how clever you are, if you don't know how to treat people around you, then you will never succeed in life. You need to be humble about having this idea to be the first all the time".

"False modesty means arrogance. A man should be open with what he thinks and feels inside. Do you really think it is bad to try to be the first?"

"You aren't exactly going to be the first in your class. You have exams soon which will decide that. Personally, I do not guarantee you to be assessed well for my own subject." Oybek knew that once Mr. Mahmoud started arguing, no one could stop him. Other teachers felt pleased when students start discussions or objected to the information the teachers gave. But this teacher was another type. They were lucky that he was a teacher being so rude to schoolchildren. If he were a governor, then he would accept every citizen with a complaint as a scandalous person. So, after that Oybek started being even more engrossed in studying and learning school subjects before the exams. He wanted to apply for the special commission in case Mr. Mahmoud didn't want to evaluate him well on purpose. Therefore, he was working very hard.

Abduboriy put his hand onto Oybek's shoulder seeing the way his eyes turned red due to tiredness:

"Leave it Oybek, your eyes are getting exhausted, don't you feel that?"

They were near the canal, and Abuboriy was sitting with his feet in the water.

"Mr. Mahmoud told you, didn't he? He will not assess you with an excellent mark, so that's why you ..."

"No, I am working hard so that it will be impossible for him not to assess me with excellent marks. I deserve it. Do not think that I am going to seek avenge, because I am not. I don't have any hatred towards the teachers. The teacher is anyway the teacher, and the person who teaches us with his hard work. God has created us all with opportunities. With eyes, a brain, ears, feet and hands, so we need to use them and value all the chances we have. We need to try to be first, then we may contribute to some development or ease in   society, I suppose." Abduboriy was staring at his friend, and he was amazed at how cute he was. He was very proud of him:

"Don't pay attention to what I am saying, Oybek. I just feel sorry for you seeing the way you work so hard. I really want you to rest a bit. I am proud of you, you know. I wish everyone in our country would be like you because then it would be developing very fast. Trust me, with loyal citizens like you"

Oybek hugged his shoulder, wanting to say that he was exaggerating.

Adolescence

It's been a long time since I've written in my diary... I was busy with exams. Once I acted in the performance in our school, everyone was surprised and they even praised me saying that I had the talent to be an actress. For a long time I prepared to enter the university of art, but then our math teacher said to me:

"Oydin, you can be a very good mathematician, don't try to study in easy subjects like art". Then one day our physics teacher said:

"You can be a very good physicist, don't make a mistake and choose another profession!"

But my mummy wants me to be a teacher or a doctor". She thinks that family life is the first thing for me as I am a girl. She wants me to only have a job at work, and she didn't want me to bring some tasks home and go on with working. As for me, I feel like laughing whenever I imagine myself getting married to someone, I was so mischievous, a mischievous girl and a family, it is something funny for me to think about.

But as for love and marriage, there's always someone in my thoughts and soul. He doesn't look like anyone, and he is quite different. Many young boys write me letters telling that they have fallen in love. But his love and feelings are quite different, I mean the man in my thoughts.

When we got our secondary school certificates, we decided to enter the university. Me and my closest friend, Muhabbat decided to go to see the Textile university, but its name seemed strange to us. We went there, but it was strange everywhere. There were only girls with long hair, from different provinces, Ferghana, Namangan and many others. There were some girls, ordinary looking, and we were looking for them. Girls were discussing other girls. One girl showed her partner another girl and said: "Look, that girl is beautiful, isn't she?"

"Your thoughts and taste about beauty is quite different. Look, she has thin lips, but thick eyebrows, they do not match at all."

We left them and went up to another group of girls in the street: "Do you know how much the scholarship here is?"

"Why do you need that?" "My mummy wants me to buy things we need for my wedding".

Both me and Muhabbat grew to understand that if we had to study with girls like them, then our life at university was going to be deadly boring.

"If these girls and their talking points aren't suitable for us, then where shall we go?" Muhabbat asked me.

"Let's go to the Technical university! Let's take a risk once in life" I said.

"I think if we enter the Technical university, we are going to have difficulties getting married. Aren't we? We are going to look like boys, not girls after studying together with boys."

"Don't be pessimistic, will you? Let's go, come on!"

We walked along all the faculties, and we were approved by the faculty of chemical technology much more than all of the rest. We applied to that faculty and started preparing for that very hard. There was a very difficult question to answer; Could we enter the university or not?

Every New Day is a New Test

"Boys, aren't you happy? Can't you feel the smell of the rain? Though the government doesn't take pity on us, God has, boys!" said our friend Zayniddin. He was from Namangan province, and he was a boy with a very warm and funny disposition.

The boys started to take a deep breath and to feel the smell of the rain one by one. They wished it would pour down with rain right at that moment. Maybe only in that case, would those poor students sit under the shadow of the tree and rest a bit from picking cotton.

They started picking cotton the first days of September, and seemingly turned into the field farmers. Oybek was also among those students who was suffering a lot because of the hot weather and the sunshine. He was a student of the mechanic's faculty at the Central Asian Technical university. He was enrolled this university after an oral exam as he finished school with a golden medal which gave him the opportunity to enter the university without written exams. Twenty-five of these students finished school with a golden medal.

"We will soon be having lessons and enjoying that boys!" -

For many years, the teachers of math Mrs. Nazira at their university was dreaming about having so talented students like them. Oybek was watching his coursemates feeling proud of being together with them. He was taking pride in studying with this sort of clever and gifted students in the same group. When they started studying with the utmost discretion, the administration made them pick cotton in the field until the winter started. Winter started, it was snowing, but they were still picking cotton.

Oybek didn't have any difficulty picking cotton as he was accustomed to working a lot in his childhood. His quick movements while picking cotton, and fast attempts, surprised everyone else. His friends who came from the city used to joke:

"Hey, man, can we please borrow your hands, they are so quick to pick cotton! If we could, maybe we would rescue all the people from the harsh winter cold and wander in the field", This was his coursemate Ziyodulla from the Samarkand province.

Oybek didn't take it amiss if his friends joked with him or called him as "patriot". After some hot days, the cold days started, the administrator also resigned, the cotton-picking season had come to end, but they were still working.

As the dusk started descending, Oybek started feeling sorry for he had spent all day in the cotton fields. He had been robbed of his whole day for a bag or two of cotton and he could have done many useful things. He also didn't want to wander in those fields in the horrible weather, and he would be very glad if it suddenly started to rain because in that case they would be allowed to rest for a bit.

What Zayniddin had predicted came true. It first started drizzling and then it poured down with rain. The students made a noise and then went into the fruit gardens. It didn't stop raining, and the students all rushed into the big lorry, but it didn't have any roof.

The driver was willing to leave with the students with pleasure, as his job was to bring and take the students from the cotton field. But he asked:

"Isn't your teacher going to scold you if I take you to your bedrooms?"

"Can you please drive? We are soaked through, and we are almost dead here!" said the students and they all started getting on the truck. As soon as the driver started driving, one of the students started singing a song either because he was enjoying the rain or he was enjoying the ride:

"Your house is there along the river on the other side" All the guys joined him in the choir:

"You look so white and you look so bright

The lorry stopped near the barracks. A man Tolib Tursunovich got off and while the boys were getting off the lorry, the administrator Tolib shouted something, but his voice faded away in the song they were singing. His eyes red from anger made them all alert, and they slowly stopped singing the song, Tolib said:

"Why are you all singing a song as if your mother is getting married? Who has allowed you to leave the cotton field, who?" Oybek couldn't stand when somebody said something against his mother, because his mother was widowed at just 34, and the rest of her life of youth she had devoted only to her children. She had been preferring these troubles of earning money for children to her own happiness. Even when Oybek gave her a pair of galoshes which he had bought from the money he had earned picking cotton, she thanked him many times. Everytime she remembered his gift, she boasted to her neighbours about what he'd done. She would keep saying:

"Other children ask their parents to give them money, but I am happy that my children earn money and do not spend it on what they need. They always give it to me!"

Anything said against his mother could hurt his heart, and therefore he couldn't stand it when Tolibov said that about their mother, trying to insult all the student's mothers. Oybek blatantly said:

"Teacher, if you ask us to go back, we will. But please, don't dare insult our mother's"

Perhaps the teacher didn't expect him to say that, therefore he was therefore stunned:

"I didn't know that you could become so weak in the rain. You should have stayed there, even if it snowed guys. If somebody comes to check on us, it means we're all dead. Don't think that it's easy for us to make you pick cotton."

"The cotton in the field is wet now, and it's pouring rain. Don't you see it? You don't want us picking low quality cotton, do you?" This time Oybek sounded a bit more gentle.

The rest of the boys also started complaining one by one: "Besides, right now it's winter, and there isn't any cotton, even that of low quality."

"Why are we wandering here? We don't understand. There isn't any cotton to pick. Can't you see?"

"We could have been learning something at the university instead. Couldn't we?"

All the students started bravely complaining. The teacher wanted to say something, but he bit his tongue and turned away, hitting the stick he was holding against the ground. After he walked a bit further, he turned back: -

"Don't think that you'll be always allowed to finish cotton picking so early. Now come inside, but try to tip-toe so that no one will notice that you've come back."

Oybek took pity on this teacher and felt sorry for what he had rudely said to him.

Dreams Mysterious

Diary… it isn't in vain called like that. I don't have enough time to write in it every day. especially after I've become a student. I have twice as many problems to solve.

By the way … I was talking about the university… entering university … The scores Muhabbat and I got on the entrance exams were a bit less than enough to be enrolled in the chemical technology faculty. It was equally painful for both of us.

Muhabbat said to me:

"Oydin, I told you that we had to pass the exams to either be a doctor or to be a teacher. Don't you see that there are too many boys in this Technical university. The boys have actually got more chances to study here than we do. We are girls, not boys, trying to learn technology. We did the wrong thing by applying for it"

I really hated it when girls discriminate themselves and believe themselves weaker than boys.

"What if we are girls, not boys? Don't you know that my mother, as a woman, is the main breadwin in our family because my father got wounded and became disabled in the war? More importantly a woman also needs to have a certain goal, and we are both going to be very good professionals in the future" I was saying this to Muhabbat, but actually I was also saying that to myself, and urging myself to be stronger. What if we did fail the exam? It didn't mean that we will fail forever.

We wanted to consult someone and we entered the office where the admission secretary was working.

"The admission requirements and score have been really high in this faculty. Don't be upset and please don't panic! If our Uzbek girls are interested in technology, we won't let them lose hope about studying in this university. so, don't be upset. If Uzbek girls like you are interested in technology, we will welcome you to our faculty."

Our Uzbek girls have to prove that they are able to do many things. They can do their best to develop technical sciences. They discussed this problem with the other staff members   and they decided to accept us both to the new faculty department of "Roads Construction". By that time, I had never even thought about what the road meant for me, to be honest. The road is something which a man needs to walk on. This road takes him wherever he wants.

These roads guide us to where we have good parents, relatives and our newest adventures. The more I think about the road, the more glad I feel, because as a future road constructor I feel myself as a very useful person for society. With these feelings, I started devoting my time and love to learning road construction. In our group, there are much less girls than boys. Our boys are serious and they are very interested in learning.

The girls started joking without letting them notice:

"Oydin, that boy is yours, this one is mine, so let's start the dates now …"

I was beaming with a smile as a reply to their jokes, but I felt that any of these boys was suitable for me. Indeed, all the boys in our group were sincere and very friendly, especially I felt that one of the boys, Mansur was staring at me, to let me know that he was falling in love. He came from the Andijan province.

I think the girls around me felt that he was in love with me, and they were joking with me saying:

"Oydin, I think you're going to get married and stay in Andijan province. Don't you see that Mansur is seriously falling in love with you?"

The others told me to be careful. And I responded to them:

"If I don't fall in love with anyone, nobody else can make me love them."

"Oh, do not be so arrogant. It depends on your destiny, not on your thoughts"

"Destiny depends on the decision a man makes.

One day your own happiness will find you itself," she interrupted all those girls reciting this poem.

Our house is not so big. It's one of the ordinary houses in an old street in the Shayhantahur district.

As we were hardly eking out a living, we allowed some students to rent in our house. We studied in the same university with Kodirjon, who lived in our house for rent. He is really a hard-working and kind boy, he runs up to help us and if he sees me or mummy with a dust pan with some coals to burn he says:

"Errr, stop there and give that dust pan and coal to me. This isn't what women are supposed to do."

My sister answered him:

"No, you will get your hands dirty. We have already taken to burning coal, Kodirjon, do not bother yourself trying to help us Don't!"

"I don't care if my hands get dirty or … my soul isn't errr…"

Mummy used to say:

"This boy, Kodirjon is very clever and … he can get married and make any woman the happiest in the world."

Mummy meant that he was a suitable man for me to marry, but I was looking for my own man, for my life, in the bottom of my heart. I knew that he was somewhere in the world. This ideal person for me had to respect me, had to be ambitious, and not ignore own aims because of me and family life. He needs to be a reliable shoulder to rely on.

No matter how strong a man is, a woman is anyway a woman. Her power is her beauty, weakness and love. My mother has been working in the school for blind students. My mother has worked hard to feed us. She has never complained to anyone, and instead she said: "Both of my daughters are the only wealth I have. They always remind me of their father, and I will do my best to bring them up, letting them eat whatever they wish." But I am not sure that they are completely happy and not alone. Maybe they want to feel that they are women, forgetting hard work, at least for some minutes. Perhaps they want to be with their father for some moments."

I have many thoughts in my mind. Many girls at the same age as we are have already started thinking about love, drawing the shape of the heart in their notebooks, love poems and many others. I don't want to hide. Sometimes I would like to do what they are doing. I also want to fall in love, and open my heart to someone. But I feel that there's someone on my mind, who I haven't met yet. It was early for me to think about him, and the only thing I need to think about is the road construction science.

It's quite a different topic

The room was very dark, one could feel the smell of cigarette smoke and alcoholic drinks. Everyone wanted to talk, and nobody wanted to listen.

Oybek couldn't breathe, and therefore he walked towards the door. The boy who invited him, looked at him with a questioning glance. Oybek said:

"I want to go outside and breathe some fresh air, can I?" His friend nodded.

It's been a long time since it happened. But every time Oybek remembers that he vomits feeling the smell of alcoholic drinks.

"I don't believe that it is possible to change life in this way, smoking and … !"

First of all a citizen needs to be alert so that he can make some changes in the social life. Oybek joined this party all of a sudden because one of his friends promised to introduce him to some very good boys there. Oybek wanted to come clean, and to bare his soul to someone reliable for a long time. At that party, all what had been said touched his heart and provoked some of the feelings in his heart. He had many questions, and he turned into two people who were talking to each other inside him:

"Our country was very great before, and now we all have all the right to live independently"

"Nobody has the right to own the gold that we have in our country"

Oybek was having the same feelings in his heart. He was hesitant about who to talk to about that. He thought that his teachers could help him. The teachers like Tursunov who was teaching Materials opposition, Aytikin Technical Drawing in geometry, Hakimov – technical drawing, Molchanov – machinery, and Isomuhammedov – philosophy. They were all calm and relaxed and nice to talk to, but he couldn't share all the feelings in his heart with these teachers. Could he?

At last he decided to bare his soul to his own favourite teacher, Okil Salimov Umurzakovich, who was teaching him Autoexploitation materials and he looked upon Oybek as if he were his own son.

Oybek remembered one of his teachers at school. he would always say: "Any experienced teacher can recognize who is the closest student to the subject of interest. The teacher will be looking at that person while teaching the entire audience because that person understands him best in this community."

The teacher Okil Salimov at the university talked and delivered all his lectures constantly looking at Sarvar all the time as if he was the only student who understood him and who valued his hard work. Oybek was also trying to write down whatever this teacher was saying during the class and would focus on whatever he was advising. Oybek was wondering how the teacher was going to treat him if he told him about his feelings. He was still wandering in his own world of puzzles and questions for which he didn't not even know the answer. Then he went up to the office where Okil Salimov worked, grasped the handle of the door, but kept looking at the door where it's written "O.U. Salimovich". Then he found the courage inside to open the door, he said:

"May I come in, teacher?"

"Of course, you may! Do come in Oybek, come in!"

Usually teachers addressed their students calling them by their last names, but here Oybek got really inspired as soon as he heard his favourite teacher calling him by his first name. This meant that this teacher was looking upon him differently   from the other students. This also meant that now he could bare his soul to his teacher:

"I'm not bothering you, am I teacher?"

"It's really nice when some of my favourite students bother me. I am ready to listen to you!"

Oybek got prepared for some moments thinking and planning what he was going to say:

"Is it the real idea "struggle for independence" what people speak about, or is it just … "

Oybek was actually seeking an answer to this question. The teacher didn't interrupt him until he ended up with what he was going to say and he also started telling his opinions after heaving a sigh for three or four seconds:

"Oybek, I value all of the opinions and views you have. Every citizen having own views are valuable for the whole society in our country. We can take advantage of these views in quite a wide range of ways. But they need to be used in such a way that each attempt needs to be effective. It needs to be beneficial for the human himself and for the whole society. I discern great power and an intuition in your personality as well as rigid integrity. In our country, we need many experienced and talented scientists to contribute to its development. They need to invent many new things and these should be important not only for our country, but for all the world countries. Independence, in every country, depends on the intelligence of the population, and we must make use of the conditions available today at a maximum level. However, I don't mean to prompt you to ignore every truth or unfair happenings in the state. Keep being alert to everything going on here and I wish you would develop the knowledge and talent you have for scientific development because in this case, you will be a useful personality for the society. Just imagine, there are thousands of young people with enough knowledge of human rights, and there may be huge important changes in the state's development as a result. It causes the society to renew every passing hour.

Okil Umurzakovich was saying all these things not just like he was talking to Oybek, but he seemed to be talking to himself.

Oybek listened to him with obvious interest and attention: "Thank you a lot, teacher!"

"Oybek, an intelligent man who admits he is Uzbek, has the feelings that you bear in your heart. I mean it isn't only you who is suffering due to these thoughts and questions"

When the dusk was falling, Oybek was going back home. He felt that there was a smell of the coal burning somewhere. He noticed all the streets, the walls built of clay, and he could now see them quite differently.

Then Oybek added an afterthought: "We need to change these old things; everything" Owing to this thought his feelings somehow changed and his heart seemed to be beating with happiness from this time on.

Only God can be alone

Tulips in the garden. If you keep staring at them for a long time, they seem to be not only wrapping up the garden, but the sky as well. Somebody is sitting on a stone, somebody is lying on the grass, and some other people are chatting in this tulip garden. One can hear the sounds of cackles and the sound of the guitar time to time.

"Friends, hey guys, we aren't here in these mountains just to sit, we came here to have a stroll, let's go and walk around those hills, boys, let's go, hurry up!"

Oybek would agree and would with pleasure go but he is wearing quite new sport shoes, trainers. They didn't fit him and they hurt him a lot a bit above the heels. Actually after he walked wearing these shoes, they scratched his feet, therefore causing him pain in each step he made.

He took them off because of the pain, and therefore he didn't want to wear them at all. He said:

"Akrom, why don't you rest for a bit? You can see both the mountain peaks and the hills right from here, can't you?"

"No, no, you can't convince me to   rest, we will be watching the sunset on the peak of the mountain. It can look extraordinarily there high up from the ground, trust me!"

Oybek knew that he was right. They had indeed come here to have a walk. But anyway, he didn't want to wear his shoes, and therefore he didn't even try to rise onto his feet. He kept looking at him for some moments and his friend said:

"Then if I am not going to come back, I am asking you to ask God to bless me in case snakes or something else might bite me to death. Of course, it's a joke!" and he started going up to the hills.

"Do not joke like that. Hey, Angels may take it seriously high up in those hills. You may even join them, and you aren't going to be bored with them together, I know" said Tulagan, one of the boys there.

Oybek beamed with a pure smile as an answer. They had been having a party and chats in cafes or in the mountains like this since they finished school.

Oybek was lying down and he could see the white clouds chasing each other and drifting back and forth in the sky and suddenly a group of ants caught his eyes. They were creeping in two rows, one of which was going forward to somewhere; the next one was coming back. Neither of the ants was breaking the rule of the team, they were all walking accurately in the same line, and they only slightly pushed each other and nothing more.

In his childhood Oybek's mother told him:

"Ants usually say hello to each other, and every time they push one another slightly, they mean to wish each other a safe journey."

Seeing what was happening with these ants, Oybek was seemingly making sure that his mother had a fair mouth. Maybe these ants are living friendly and in teams, so that they will not die the under footsteps of men, and other bigger animals. He liked his own idea and laughed. Oybek was almost falling asleep with these thoughts when Ubaydulla suddenly woke him up with his worried scream:

"Oybek, get up, Oybek, Akram hasn't come back yet. He can't still be in the hills. Where on earth could he have gotten lost?"

"What?" he asked unconsciously.

"He walked up into those hills, and if you remember, it's now getting dark, but he hasn't come back yet. Don't you understand?"

Oybek had slept for a very long time. The mountain air makes anyone sleep as it is very fresh. He stood up.

"Never mind. He left to have chat with some girls. I think he is still up there with them, having fun."

"I didn't see him. Olimjon went up to find him and the girls have already come back."

"Oh, no! He said that he was going to watch the sun rise in the mountains, I don't believe that he will dare to. Oh … doesn't he know that it is the mountain, not a town to stay in outside when it is dark?" Oybek started worrying.

"Boys, we must find Akrom!"

"Leave it. He is not a girl to be worried about, nor not a bag of money for someone to grab and carry away. He will come back" another boy said.

Everyone gave different opinions.

They decided to go back to an old holiday home where they had left their bags of foods and clothes. When Oybek was going to put on his shoes, he felt a keen pain above his heels, so he didn't wear them, and instead he put them back into his rucksack and said to the boys:

"Let's go and find Akrom!" He wanted to say he was afraid that something was wrong with him, but he held back. Abduboriy started following him as he was walking.

Then Oybek reminded them what Akrom had said before he was leaving alone: "He said some very strange things before … errr, that's why I am worried …"

"Hang it, Oybek. Stop worrying about him, will you? I think he is lying up on the peak of the mountain thinking about some things. You know, he likes surprising us all the time."

They were going up the hills, and the higher they got, the thicker the trees became. They walked through the hedges looking for their friend, Akrom. Oybek always training sports, perhaps that's why he didn't find it hard to climb up the mountains. However, his heels were sore due to the new shoes which were making it hard for him to walk. Many times hit his bare feet against the stones or the branches of the tree which had fallen on the ground. This would pain him a lot every time they touched his heels. Every minute Abduboriy was shouting to call Akrom:

"Akrom, are you there?" His voice sounded loud and echoed in the whole surroundings. They would be silent for some moments waiting for him to reply and then they moved forward again.

Abduboriy said:

"Oybek, are we lost? It seems as though we are walking on the same paths we have already walked."

Oybek was also whispering to himself: "What if a wolf has killed him and … errr no, no!

"Watch your mouth please!" said Abduboriy feeling even more worried.

"He shouldn't have left alone anyway. There's always danger for someone who's alone. He couldn't force any of us to go with him, what if there's really something wrong with him? What are we supposed to say to his mother about it? What shall we say to our parents? Shall we say that he left us and haven't returned after that? Oh, God!"

"Oybek, it's hard for me to breathe. What if we go back? Maybe Akrom will also come back by himself. Oh, what if he won't come back? We may also get lost here if we keep going like this."

Oybek was brooding over this problem, and his partners also wanted to go back. Nobody forced Akrom to leave alone. Everyone should think about safety. However, it wasn't easy for Oybek's mother to bring him up, and his mother suffered a lot for that. After his brother and he started getting scholarships, they didn't let their mother work and earn money. Until that time his mother was begging all the wholesalers and asking them to sell goods for a cheaper price. Anyway, even after that his mother didn't sit at home, she kept trying to earn money.

If something wrong happened to Oybek because of Akrom, his mother was going to die of a heart attack. But what if Akrom doesn't come back even if they go back to the holiday home? In foreign countries if a man is wanted, all the press and the policeman start looking for him. It isn't an ordinary problem when a person is lost.

"Oybek, let's go back. I think we aren't climbing. We are getting lost in the darkness. Now we did what we needed to do, so if he is destined to be alive, he will come back." Said Abduboriy. Oybek was also thinking the same things, but his heart didn't follow what he thought was the right thing to do.

"It depends on you whether one person is found or is lost, so you shouldn't miss the chance you have", This thought was urging him to go further and further.

He said: "Stop here!" grabbing Abduboriy's hand, it seemed to him that somebody groaned weakly. They stood this way for a long time.

"No, no voice here, it seemed to you like that" said Abduboriy and urged him to go back to the holiday home again.

Oybek made two or three steps and then again stopped: "Indeed somebody's groaning here" now Abduboriy also

heard it. They walked where they heard the voice.

Akrom was lying and clinging to a tree's broken limb. He was trying to get up, but had no energy to rise. Both Abduboriy and Oybek burst out crying: "Akrom, oh, no!"

"Oh, Thanks to God, I am so lucky that you're here" Akrom said.

"Don't move! Don't! Didn't you fight with angels wanting to occupy a bed in the Paradise" Abduboriy joked with wanting to remind him about what he had said before leaving. Both Abduboriy and Oybek were glad that Akrom was alive. Abduboriy was looking at his legs and hands to see what wrong was with him.

"Oh, my god, I fell over here. Something is wrong with my leg. It's either broken or ... I was thinking that I'd die if you'd gone back to the village. In vain I told about the death. Then Oybek also added: "You're right, don't joke with the things like that. Angels and God always hear what you say." He said this even though he didn't believe in this sort of superior things.

Both Oybek and Abduboriy held Akrom on both sides, Oybek on the right, Abduboriy on the left:

Don't think about it. Put all of your weight on us"

They walked for a very long time. It was very hard to go down the mountains in this way. They had to walk very carefully lest they would fall over. Their classmates thought they had left for the village because it was very dark. They suddenly heard low voices afar: "Ooooybeeeek!" "Boooooriiiiiy" "Akrooooom!"

The boys turned out to be going up the mountain to look for them t. Oybek felt stunned about that:

"We are here!" they shouted. His voice was muffled in the noise his own friends were making from afar. Oybek and Abduboriy was calling their friends by their names, and the wind was blowing forward and backwards, forward and backwards. At that time Oybek felt so strong that he could overcome any difficulty in life. He felt strong both physically and morally, , because he had loyal friends around him. Not in vain he sees ants always in teams, never alone.

Feelings

"Mummy, I know, you helped lots of people, and they prayed for you a lot. Many people wished that you'd enjoy yourself after working hard for such a long time. These wishes have come true today. Before you used to keep all the yearly records of my excellent marks at school in your own chest at home. Most people keep gold and money in their chest as wealth, but you kept my school assessments looking on them as the biggest wealth, mummy. Especially when I finished school with a golden medal. I'll never forget how happy you were, you were so happy as if you got back all the wealth you inherited from your father Tashpula the jeweler. All the wealth you had exchanged for corn, wheat, bread and other things to eat just so as to feed us during the time of the bloody war, bloodshed and the time of hunger. When you said that you wanted to hold my face with your hands, I was ready to do everything to   cure your hands which became sore and dry. These hands were fatigued because you didn't take pity on them for the sake of your children pinching with hunger. Today I am here with you, again with another happiness for you, I graduated from the university with distinction. I am here with you mum, and again you're so happy as if it isn't me who got the diploma, but you mum! So happy, so glad! Moreover, you're boasting non- stop to all the neighbours, mum, saying:

"Oybek's teachers at the university appointed him as the chief engineer in the Gulistan city automobile factory. I wish his father could see his success, I wish … But anyway I thank God that at least I am lucky to see it even if I am alone without him."

Oybek was looking at the water flowing there and he really wanted to say everything he was feeling inside to his mother. But, in fact, he didn't know what he wanted to say. It wasn't a feeling or something exact, it was the shape of the feeling that was torturing him so much. Then he decided: "I'd better express that I am grateful to my mummy, this is the best way to do it."

Oybek used to think deeply about everything, but today when all of his hard work had given the positive results, he was thinking about the future of his career, reputation and his workplace. Moreover, one beautiful girl was interrupting him from all these thoughts no matter how much he tried to stay focused.

This was the evening when the saw Abduboriy off to Andijan. They were guests in the house of the famous singer, Mehri Abdullayeva. He was sitting around the same table with the young people who had just come back from the International festival of singers. There was one very good-looking girl there, who recited a poem about independence, Oybek really wanted to know her name. As if the girls around felt that Oybek wanted to know her name, the girl's friends called her by her first name at that time:

"Oydin!"

"She has a beautiful name, besides our names sound similar, don't they?" Oybek added as an afterthought. All the songs, and laughter interrupted Oybek from all of his thoughts, so he couldn't think there for a long time. Within these five years of being a student, he met many friends, and he had friends among very good boys and polite girls. He had even gone to the cinema more than once. He thought that the girls he invited to cinema seemed to be very good, but anyway he was still thinking about that beautiful girl who recited a poem at the party they had in the singer Mehri Abdullayeva's home. He couldn't answer the question why that girl never escaped his mind, and he had to answer himself:

"Other girls are also beautiful and good, but she is the most beautiful and the best."

But Oybek didn't look for her, because he was afraid of being distracted from his study and research. He only had the aim in his heart which could unite all his desires and wishes. He said: "I must be a successful professional!", and every time he was distracted from reading, he would repeat this, "I must be a successful professional". Today he made the first step to implementing that plan.

He had to make even more steps which would all be challenging, and he couldn't miss any of them.

Something very strange was happening to him these days, and when he was going to leave for Gulistan city automobile factory as an engineer, there was something wrong which distressed him very much.

The Days of Youth

Sometimes my diary is replete with all the mathematical formulas, schemes and other drawings. My friends used to say:

"Oydin, do you know that everyone writes poems and all about their feelings in their diaries. We see that there's nothing but mathematics and calculations in yours, what's it?", and all the girls started laughing.

Yes, that's right. Today we have a test, then tomorrow we'll have exams. Today we graduated from the university, and these golden days of being a student have passed so fast, that I didn't even notice how it all happened. We are not students. We are now engineers. Before we became students, I used to dream that I would be an actress putting a dot in the middle of my forehead like Indian girls. I always tended to laugh as soon as I remember that. Today we are all grown ups, adults.

I used to want to get a well-paid job in some kind of a factory willing to make it easy for my mother and my sister to live. I wanted to take my mummy to sightseeing places where there's plenty of fresh air to breathe and where she could rest. There are lots of matchmakers asking to marry me, and maybe soon I will get married. When I was living with these thoughts, my teacher, one of the most famous scientists of the Republic, Pulat Bobokhonov invited me for a talk:

"Oydin, soon you'll get a diploma. What other plans do you have for the future?" he asked.

"I want to take my mother somewhere to rest" I said in a rush."

He laughed beaming with joy:

"Of course, your mother deserves this. It isn't easy to be a woman, especially, to live alone. But, I think the talent you have and your friend Muhabbat has is not given to everyone else.

Learning and researching is replete with challenges, and to be honest, not everyone can stand them. But I see dignity, integrity, and distinct aims in your eyes. There have been many talented women among the Eastern women since ancient periods. But in our history women have been kept under control, at home, and therefore there isn't enough information about women in our historical books. But those who were written about in history played important roles in both our social and family life."

While I was listening to him, it seemed to me like I was listening to a croon song as I was enjoying the talk with my favourite teacher. There are many people who keep urging the value of women, but most of them just urge, and do not do anything practically. When they indeed have to defend women, you can see them avoiding that. They just ignore women saying that they are just women.

But this teacher was quite different:

"Women in history served as police officers, guards and even colonels. The more women are involved in our social life, this will result in positive influences on their children. Therefore our daughters should be well-educated." After what my teacher said, I started understanding what he actually meant. He was willing to offer me and Muhabbat a chance to go to Moscow for our Ph. d studies.

"Oydin is a scientist", oh that sounded very nice to hear. But, in Moscow ... Was I talented enough to deserve the trust of my teacher? I was somehow sure, somehow not. I was assessed due to my own hard work, I studied all the time, and worked by myself. I know Russian very well. But anyway, Moscow is one of the world centres. Many people only dream about going there to study. I couldn't really believe that I was lucky to go and study there.

Teacher Babakhanov:

"Of course, it is for you to decide whether to agree or not, because I know that you need to get married, and bring up your children. However, the most important thing in life is to evolve one's own talent and skills."

"Dear teacher, I will think about what you've said. I want to ask what my mummy what thinks about this. If I had to decide on my own, I would be ready to fly to Moscow.

A Bitter Pill to Swallow

"What's wrong Oybek? Why are you staring at me like that?" Abduboriy asked Oybek as they were sitting alongside the canal   relaxing.

"I just realized one true fact, friend. A man gradually turns into part of the land where he grows up and where he drinks and eats. Now you've been living in Andijan province for five years, and you started to look like the guys originally from Andijan city"

Abduboriy laughed:

"What do they look like? Can you tell me?"

"They sound a bit rude and talk in a way that cuts each syllable in each word."

"This characteristic was suitable not for the people of our nationality, but more for the Turkish."

"Yes, I read in one book that the Turkish were very brave."

Oybek and Abduboriy had come to the Urda canal to breathe some fresh air, and there many children swimming and making lots of noise. Some of them were sunbathing on the grass. But these two friends, Oybek and Abduboriy are engrossed in their talk, as they haven't talked for quite a long time.

"Time is like wind, friend, it blows all the happiness and sadness away to the space and faraway places. Do you remember that only yesterday we were also as little as these children swimming over there? Today we are talking about some serious topics...the topics of adults. All the friends in our childhood, Sobir, Soat, Muzrob, Ozod, Tulagan, Olim, they all are all around the Republic now, which are very difficult to find.

"Yes, you're right. All the children who grew up in our mahalla and who studied in our school have become great celebrities in our country. Our great scientists Obid Sodikov, Abdulla Abdulla Ayupov, Colonel Utkir Komilov, the administrator Sodik Tolipov, many of them… yes, especially his brother. Mr. Said is a wonderful person"

"Why did you suddenly remember him?"

"It happened two or three years ago. Our neighbor Saidmurod bought a car GAS-21 Volga. His brother Utkir studied with me at the same faculty. We studied a special course teaching us how to drive a car, and we had no problem with that. Usually me and Utkir travelled along the street driving Mr. Saidmurod's car, or sometimes on the smooth roads. I was also allowed to drive, and until that time I tried to drive a car "GAZ-51" under the control of the teacher. One day handing the gear to me Utkir said that I could drive the car until we got home. I was on the cloud number nine. Our street wasn't so narrow, and after driving for some five minutes I had to change the gear to turn into the narrow street where Utkir were living. However, only one car could barely be driven in that small space. Besides that, our friend who also lived there installed and buried tram rails so that the cars passing wouldn't destroy the wall he was building. As soon as we approached the narrow street Utkir asked me to stop there. But instead of braking, I stepped on the gas pedal, so the car suddenly skidded suddenly and crashed the rails. It was quite late by the time I had pressed on the brake pedal. When we went down to the car, we saw that the bumper was ruined. The front apron looked awful, but the rest of the parts were all ok. The brand new car had to now be repaired. There was no use feeling worried, concerned or sad, it was time to think fast and very clearly. Utkir didn't even say a thing, so in order to hide what wrong we did, we decided to take the car to the Tinchlik street where we hoped to find a good master. Fortunately, we found a master and he somehow mended the front apron. Unfortunately, it was hardly possible to mend the bumper which got an awful crack. After paying for the service, I was really worried about everything and took the car to the garage. I felt like time was going to stop passing, and everything seemed to be over. I lost interest in life and I got depressed. Three or four days later Mr. Said finally saw the car and found out about everything. He had the bumper changed. After that I kept avoiding seeing that man as much as I could. One day at long last, no matter how much I tried not to see him, I came across him and I had to greet him. I expected him to scold me for what I did, but instead he politely asked me: "Why did you stop visiting us, in our home? Is everything ok with you?"

He had forgotten about everything bad I had done to the car. I can never forget his generosity, never. I want to be like these people in my mahalla."

While these friends were remembering about their childhood, three or four people drinking beer a bit afar suddenly interrupted them:

"Again, you two are boasting about your Mahalla, street, aren't you? Oh, God, when are you two going give that up, ah, when? We are fed up with all of this, don't you know that? You keep saying that you have a great grandpa Beruni, Avicenna. Oh God, please let them rest in peace! They did all what they needed to do in their own period, but we don't have to just wait to see what will happen by keeping boasting about them", That man was wearing a vest and he came up and stood looking down at them. Then one of his partners came following him there and said: "Hey, don't pay attention to them, they had enough of their lectures at the university."

"Hang it, sir, let your friend say whatever he wants, we don't about that at all" Oybek said.

"Oh, I didn't know that you were so blatant. You're even too shy to tell your names if we are going to ask you, aren't you? You're no one, and you find it enough to say "I am a grandson of Manguberdi", Am I right?"

"He's drunk, so don't take it serious, boys" his partner said. The two partners of that rude man dragged him backwards holding his hands on both sides.

"Make the right conclusion from what I've said" He shouted and he disappeared together with his friends.

Oybek was silent. Abduboriy said: "Don't pay attention to what every passerby tells you, Oybek!" Oybek raised his head: "No matter how much he hurt us, he is telling the truth, Boriy, don't you see? We are just boasting about ancestors we have, but we aren't trying to work as hard as they did in the past."

"Oh, you're too sensitive, Oybek, we have come here to have rest, but not to …"

Oybek interrupted:

"What he said is true" Oybek said as if he was talking to himself. Lately Oybek was feeling quite strange, especially when they were invited to stay at the faculty for further research. He was with pleasure willing to agree, but he was also brooding over his own family, and his personal finances. His brother had some problems to be solved, and they needed to have a wedding for their younger sister. His mother was at last just about to stop earning money to live when Oybek graduated and when he was about to work. He was now about to embark on his post graduate studies. What that tall man had said to him about his ancestors and about them hurt him a lot in the bottom of his heart. His willing to study and to put his country on the map started causing anguish in all of his body and his heart. Then at last he decided: "Mummy will understand me, she will not deny me if I say that I want to study a bit longer. After a bit longer time of tortures, we are going to enjoy the positive results soon" Oybek was thinking.

Abduboriy felt that because Oybek had became silent:

"Oh, yes, which cloud are you sailing on, friend?" They used to joke with each other in this way as soon as they felt that one of them is less alert.

Then Oybek said:

"I am sailing on my own cloud, Boriy, on my own cloud!"

Roads

The boy walking nearby suddenly fell over. Oybek turned to glance at him, but it was impossible to stop. He was almost running fast. On getting up, he emptied the sack and again ran back. The sack was rolling on the ground, and one could see some carrots dotting the ground where the boy had fallen over. That boy was trying to rise to his feet, but he had no energy, and was getting completely pale. Oybek helped him up. They started picking up all the carrots one by one:

"Was your sack so heavy that you fell over?" asked Oybek. The boy responded in his own Ozerbaijan dialect:

"No it wasn't heavy, I got a bit tired. I am very surprised that you don't feel tired."

"When I was a child, I worked on the farm and I trained for sports too," Oybek then grabbed the boy's sack without asking and walked forward much faster than he did.

He registered the sack of carrots in the document opposite the column where it's written "Akif, son of Yildiz", it was his actually partner's name. According to the amount of carrots picked here on the list, they could be paid certain sums of money every time.

The boy said that he was sorry, but Oybek thought that his face went pale not because he was tired, but because he was hungry. The boy was going to give him some money to thank for help, but he knew it was disrespect, and that's why he was thinking about inviting him to have a cup of coffee.

Oybek was destined to go to Moscow. It was autumn in Moscow, and the days of October. He could be dazzled by the beauty of the golden leaves of trees, the sky as blue as the ocean, and the water as pure as baby's skin. But the only thing that was difficult was to live there. Oybek came to Moscow because of his teacher Okil Salimov who supported him financially. At first his mother didn't agree, and she hesitated because he would live among strangers without any homemade food. He persuaded her by promising to be as a great scientist as Okil Salimov and Abdulla Ayupov five years earlier. In Moscow at the Automobile Roads university, he met the head of the "Autotractor engines department", professor Hovach. This professor was obviously confident in his own knowledge and he talked for a very long time with Oybek. He asked him about his family, aims and plans. Perhaps he got satisfied with his personality, then changed the conversation topic to science and research. No matter how much Oybek was trying to stay calm and relaxed, he was getting more and more excited while talking to this professor. Every time he answered him, he was getting confused and less sure that he was speaking correctly. Then Hovach said:

"Oybek, look!" Oybek was taken aback by the way that he could keep his name in mind so easily. "Oybek, I hope your parents gave you the name of the Uzbek writer, I read a novel about Navai by him."

Oybek was glad to hear the way the Russian scientist knew about Uzbek literature. Some scholars of technology always teased poets and writers at that time. Oybek answered:

"I was born in a very hard time to live. My parents have always wanted good and bright days to come fast. Therefore, they gave me this name."

"Yes, Uzbek people are very polite and they always have good intentions. But sometimes they do not value themselves, do they? A very important thing that helps to distinguish a human being from other creatures is his self-esteem, it's not arrogance at all. People with self-esteem will value their own family and motherland as well. A man is born with his knowledge, intelligence and integrity together." Hovach was talking in short and in brief sentences, then he gave his advice to Oybek:

"You're eager to learn, I see it, and this is the most basic factor leading you to be a scientist. But the knowledge you have is less than enough to study in our postgraduate courses. You'd better go back to Tashkent and bring a certificate allowing you to get one year of work experience here. You'll be working with the laboratory where we have foreign tools and equipment installed."

Oybek was in distress, because he came to Moscow with the hope to be enrolled in post graduate courses.

"Oybek, I have seen lots of students from Central Asia most of which do not have any knowledge and rely on the money their rich parents have. They claim that it's enough for them to get a diploma, and they don't need any research. I don't even try to talk to this sort of people. If you want to be a scientist, learn to accept and understand correct critical assessments, because lies and false thoughts are the real obstacles for a scientist."

Now Oybek was forced to go back to Tashkent, and he had no money left. That's why he was working to earn some money, carrying heavy sacks of carrots with that boy who had fallen. That boy turned out to have failed the entrance exams to the university, so he was working to earn money for preparation courses. Oybek was trying to earn money for his fare. That boy came clean about everything to him:

"I am not brave enough to go back to my countryside, as I failed the exams, you see. I have someone I love, her name is Zaynab. Her father promised we'd get married if I graduate from the university here in Moscow, and therefore I need to study. If she marries another man, I am going to die in less than no time. I couldn't stand it."

Oybek was amazed by so much love this boy had in his heart. He even suspected that it was possible to die for love in such a modern period. But he wanted to have the same strong feelings like his. That boy started having very warm and friendly attitude to

Oybek, and he realized that he had a heart of gold when he rushed to help him as soon as he fell over.

Deja Vu

We have some sayings in our oral conversations: "We have taken to it, we got used to it" and many others. This is usually used for those who are patient with all the challenges and encumbrances of life. But saying I have taken to it doesn't mean that we are ruling our life.

Like many other student girls and boys who came from Tashkent to Moscow, we have taken to the way of life here in this city. Here all people tend to treat each other freely and they say whatever they think directly. But having taken to these traditions, we don't mean to forget about our Uzbek traditions of thinking before saying something, and respecting other people. All the things like the smell of just baked bread, the smell of the raihan flowers in our yards, the atlas dress all the brides wear, and the way that women and girls water outside the house before sweeping in the early morning, which we can only see in our own motherland. It's impossible not to long for them, and it's impossible to forget about them.

Me, my classmate Muhabbat, all live in the dormitory of the postgraduate students. My topic and scientific advisor has already been confirmed. My scientific advisor Oleg Vladimirovich Andreyev is a very strict person. I have started looking for the information relating to the topic of my dissertation on "The problems of changing tributary in the Central Asian rivers". I keep attending libraries and archives every single day. All the textbooks are in Russian or in English. I am never tired of carrying dictionaries as big as pillows.

Today is Sunday, Muhabbat has left for the holiday home where one of our friends lives.

"In winter the forests are very beautiful. Russia has the most beautiful winter in the world, and we must surely see it, honey" Muhabbat said, and she somehow was also urging me to go there. I was tired of all the trainings during the week, I wanted to rest, but something forced me to stay at home. I only slept three or four hours every day, and everyday I suddenly woke up, because mum said in my dreams: "My honey daughter, Oydin, you're my lol!" I had a very good rest today, but anyway I didn't want to get up. I was looking at the snowflakes through and on the window and remembered about our Tashkent city, Shaihantahur district, my own hometown. I remembered the garden trees which flourished and bloomed in pink, white and in orange. If we watched the garden standing up on the roof of our house, those blooming trees looked like the clouds in the sky...like white clouds in the sky. My heart started with craving for my own hometown when I remembered those scenes. I got up and took the gramophone records out of my chest of drawers. I loved to listen to songs, without which I couldn't even imagine my life. Even when I study at home, if I don't listen to music, I am never in a good mood. The radio was on, and the singer's voice sounded and filled the whole room:

"The girl who looked through the window

What do your dark eyes want me to do for you, darling? La lala la"

It is impossible to describe how these songs make us feel. You only have to listen to them to feel what we feel. One of my friends used to say: "to understand these songs, you must get engrossed in them and sleep with them.". I had the same feelings. I tried to have some breakfast, and put all the books I had to read onto the table, but I wasn't able to get engrossed in reading those books like usual. Suddenly I heard a knock on the door. Is it really Muhabbat wanting me to go to that holiday home in the forest? I had an unexpected idea in my mind. I opened the door, and no it wasn't Muhabbat, it was Solijon, from the same country as I am. There are many people from Uzbekistan here.

A wonderful scientist Habib Abdullayev was appointed as the President of the Sciences Academy and after that many young people were invited to Moscow, Leningrad and Kiyev to study in post graduate courses. To pursue this chance the candidates must have graduated from the university with excellent grades. This was also a national policy, because the main factor of the nation is knowledge, and knowledge is always the first and most basic step to development. "Oh, it's you! Do come in, please. I was just feeling in my bones that I am to have a guest"

"Oh, I don't think that I can come in, then I might keep sitting for a long time then. All the postgraduates from Tashkent want to gather and go to the Poushkin museum. It was me in charge of inviting you to that get-together" he said. There were more boys among them, Omonilla, Abdusalom, Hayot. She treated Solijon as a very close friend because of his sincere attitude. He took a questioning glance at me as if he was going to ask where my friend was, then I said:

"Muhabbat has gone to see the forest in the snow"

"Ah, yes, then she left you to let you go to the museum with us. What thoughts could I have if you would have also left with her locking the door to this room? Thanks to God you haven't, I see!"

"Oh, can you really have some thoughts about us? Aren't you sure that we aren't the type who could go to wrong places at the wrong time? Huh …?"

"No no, not really. I know that you're both very good girls. But sometimes the devil can tempt us to think in the wrong ways"

"Are you sure that you're Uzbek who cannot deal with the Devil?"

We joked in this way with Solijon and started going to the museum.

We could hear the crunching sounds of the snow under our shoes as we were walking. Sometimes snow can make you feel in two different ways. When we were children, it used to snow a lot in our country, and we used to clean our own yard by ourselves, because we had no brother to rely on. The snow would fill our shoes and our feet would freeze. We used to try to get warm by jumping on the slopes of the snow, and now Moscow looked like the crystal palace built from snow and ice. The people from Tashkent were waiting for us near the subway station, and suddenly a boy of medium height caught my eyes first of all among the others. I seemed to feel hot from my hair to my heels. He looked so warm to me, so warm. I just found a reason for myself: "Ah, hang it, it's because you're seeing him for the first time." But that was a false reason. The rest of boys I had also seen for the first time before, but I didn't have that feeling at all.

"It's Oybek, he is having work experience courses in Moscow Automobile Roads university" Omonilla said.

"This boy has something that allows him to easily make friends. Yes he's a very good boy Omonilla is" Oybek said this as he stretched his hand to greet the girl, Oydin.

"Oydin, My name, my name is" … My voice trembled when he held my hands while shaking them. All the others around burst into laughter seeing the situation I was in.

"Oh, look, we have two people with similar names, Oydin and Oybek. Both of their names mean the moon, so it never gets dark unless they leave us" said one of the girls, Guzal.

We went inside the museum, and I lost myself. Oydin was relaxed and easy going. I lost all of my concentration as if I was half asleep. I wasn't even completely paying attention to what the tour guide was saying about:

"The King knew how clever and genius Poushkin was very well. He even imagined how high he could raise the reputation of Russia. But like many other kings, he didn't also like the poets who were writing poems about the freedom of citizens in the motherland. The main contrast between the King and the poet was that the poet was actually willing to write poems about freedom. No King liked the idea of civil rights and freedom. That's is the fact."

While the guide was introducing us to different facts, I was attentively watching a very beautiful image of the woman whom Poushkin adored.

The young man Oybek came up to me suddenly and asked in a very low voice and very carefully:

"I am sure you're very interested in poetry, aren't you? Am I right?"

"How do you know that?" I asked.

"I remember you reciting a very wonderful poem in Tashkent at the house of Mehri Abdullayeva".

I tried to remember… Oh, no, it's been such a long time … "You … You are …"

"Yes, I was seeing off one of my friends, Abduboriy to Andijan. Your friends had just come back from the international festival of young people held in Russia."

I was surprised. How was it possible to keep that in mind?

So strange!

"Oh, look, what a coincidence. We meet again, but now in Moscow!" I said as I was shocked and didn't even know what to say.

"I always remember that poem you recited that night. Do you know why? Because many girls like you, I mean as young as you are, are mostly interested in things like make-up, luxurious clothes and so on … but I guessed that you … errr…"

"Yes, you're right. But a woman is a woman, and she has own interests and own duties" I just said. It seemed so pleasant for me to talk to him.

"Yes, you're right. A woman should be a woman, but she must be aware of what's happening in society and in the world. Being a woman doesn't mean being a housewife and sitting at home, does it? If she is aware and well-educated, it's beneficial for both her and the future of her little children to continue the future of the state, because children will behave according to how the mother is going to herself behave."

I was always alert in a team of boys, because mostly I felt my opinions and outlook were prior to theirs. But now I was feeling myself a bit weaker, and it was nice to feel that way. I was not feeling awkward in that situation, and it was very pleasant. I suddenly remembered a poem at that moment:

I want to wake for you as beautiful as a flower, only for you!

I want to wake up for you as delicate as flowers, only for you

But prior to being beautiful and being delicate

I want to wake up to you as weak as flowers, only for you!

"Hey, guys, are you two copying out the portrait of Natalia Victorovna? I mean you have kept staring at this painting for quite a long time."

I was shy, it was obvious, blood rushed to my face, and I felt the same feeling of excitement in my partner's behavior too. -

"We turned up to have met before in Tashkent"

"Oh, here it means you're making love dialogues to each other which sounds like, "Oh, is that you who I've been looking for? Huh, Déjà vu let's say, there you go, good luck!" Solijon said wanting to joke with us.

I am writing all what happened today in my diary under the light of the reading lamp... Muhabbat is tired and she fell asleep flopping down onto her bed and the only thing she said before sleeping was: "Oydin, I'll tell you about what happened, I'll tell you, ok? But not today, let's talk tomorrow".

But I was sleepless, and his face and voice has swept everything I heard and saw in the museum about the poet Poushkin's life, paintings and his way of life. I was very happy about something. Somebody seemed to be whispering his name to me, his name to me: "Oybek" … His voice was the dearest to me, the dearest ever …

Tortures of growing up

"Oh, this smell has filled the whole room, it seems to be delicious as usual. oh my God! Oybek you will write one more minus in your notebook of debts. Yes I owe you one more dinner again. You're always cooking and I am not" Omonilla said this as usual, while taking off his gloves and rubbing his palms against each other.

Oybek responded to this joke with a faint smile on his face. Again Omonilla said:

"Do you know what? You have a brilliant mother. She always sends you a parcel with some mash16[16]. It has the odor of meat. I think she wants you to be strong and full of energy eating useful food all the time. We also want the same, Oybek!"

Omonilla usually comes very late from work, but Oybek comes back in time and makes the dinner ready to eat. He prepares it aiming at the time of his arrival. He mostly cooks mashkichri or mashkhurrda17[17] to eat. He has always loved meals

with mash, and they have quite a different and tempting taste. In Tashkent, at home, his mother used to prepare these meals not every two days, but twice or three times a week, because she knew he loved them. He was doing the same in Moscow, and his mother sends a parcel with mash asking her friends to give it to him. If there isn't anyone going to Moscow, then she sends a parcel.

"It's very good to eat delicious meals, but it's bad that after that you want to sleep" said Omonilla. Oybek nodded in response. On seeing that he realized that Oybek wasn't in a good mood, he then thought that he was perhaps tired.

"What's wrong, Oybek?"

"No, no, nothing, everything's ok!"

---

[16] Mash is an ingredient in dark green colour, usually very tasty when cooked with rice.

[17] 17 These are types of national foods prepared with mash and rice, usually very tasty.

"Are there too many minuses in your notebook of debts for cooking dinner?" he said wanting to make him glad with his funny jokes. Every time he cooks dinner or does the shopping, Omonilla would say: "Oh, then I owe you one more shopping or dinner, write it down in your notebook of debts please".

"Oh, hang it, it isn't the reason."

"Oh, you please hang it. Can't you tell what's wrong with you, man? It's enough for us that it is snowing outside, I don't want it to snow inside the home as well with your snowy mood, Oybek" he laughed.

"Errr … Lobar is getting married…"

"Ok, let her get married, but you aren't in love with her, or are you?"

"Don't you know who she is getting married to? To a very old professor."

"That's ok, even old people are liable to love"

"It's not love what I mean. That girl is getting married taking into account his wealth and money. She has been invited here to Moscow by Uzbekistan to raise the reputation of our motherland, not to get married. Our teachers wanted her to contribute to the development of our country, but within less than a year she is getting married here to a Russian man."

"Yes, you're right, Oybek. She didn't live up to our expectations. Of course, those who are patient with ups and downs of life can pursue what they dream about. Have you heard one saying: "If you want to live one hundred years, you'll have to be patient with the challenges for a hundred years". Do you know why the citizens of several states live being slaves to one country? Because they cannot stand the challenge of living independently. A man should earn, work and think independently in order to live independently. He cannot work effectively in slavery. The citizens living in slavery are the laziest people in the world. Do you know what it has to do with Lobar? She is also being a slave to that old and rich professor. Many young people are getting married to rich widowed women and they are trying to inherit their wealth. Many girls are giving birth without any marriage, this illegal birth is causing many infants to die in the streets being neglected by their own mothers. Science development is the only thing which can prevent these problems in our society.

Isn't it hard for you at the moment? It isn't easy for you, is it?" Omonilla started sounding with frustration this time.

Yes Oybek is making lots of efforts for each step he is making to work in Moscow. He even passed his exams in Tashkent for postgraduate courses. But here in Moscow at the Automobile Roads university, the administrator of the postgraduate courses required him to pass the Russian language exams. He didn't have any problems in Russian, his writing and speaking was ok in this language. However, he took offence to be required to pass an exam he had already passed. He didn't like it when people didn't trust him, and he got somehow aggressive with the man who required that. He couldn't control his emotions of anger and decided to call his teacher in Tashkent, Okil Salimov. He said:

"Akimov is a very good man and very experienced professional. He seemingly has a purpose for requiring you to pass this exam. Do not get distracted from your main responsibilities because of different thoughts and anger, please, get   ready for the exam." Oybek calmed down after that. He wasn't the type to get frustrated for a bit worse situation. When Oybek was working in Tashkent, he overheard from his friend that Ashot Pesoian had said this about Oybek: "The professors in Moscow are not as naïve as Uzbek scientists, and you cannot trick Russian scientists with two boxes of cigarettes or money. They are going to ignore and expel people like Oybek"

Therefore, what the administrator Akimov said seemed to be an attempt to expel him, and therefore he felt frustrated. Then later he made sure about everything after a telephone talk with his teacher. Akimov was present when Oybek was taking the Russian language exam. He just asked him two questions, listened to his answer and left the room. Two days later, he saw him suddenly on the path and congratulated him with a firm handshake. Oybek later learned the reason for this requirement, Akimov came clean about it:

"I know that it's quite strange in Central Asia, many postgraduates who come to study do not have any knowledge and they always depend on their wealth. If we accept these students and after some time are required to show the results of the research, they keep dismissing you: "Teacher, is it possible to cope with that somehow, we'll be ready to solve any other problems" (relating to bribing) I just hate this sort of people to tell the truth. Therefore, I always try to test all the candidates trying to study in our university."

It hasn't been a long time since Oybek was in Moscow. But he found a way to cope with the moral and financial problems within this short period. In the neighboring rooms in the dormitory, there are some foreign students living there, and they must learn Russian urgently. Oybek has learned English very well. He started teaching them Russian, and he was explaining them all the professional and effective rules. He especially and accurately writes formulas with oil paint. Therefore, all the   postgraduates asked him to write all the formulas for their dissertations. He surely gets paid for his work, and though he only sleeps a very few hours, he is patient. He is patient because he doesn't want his family to ask someone for money. He wants them to eat and buy whatever they want. He has saved up all the money he earned and bought carpets and a fashionable coat to parcel to Tashkent. His mother will sell them for more expensive prices so that she would also save up for the weddings of her children. When Omonilla said "it isn't easy for you" he started actually thinking about that. For those who planned to live better, it is never easy.

"So, Lobar is not the only reason for me to feel sad, there's no sense just sitting and brooding over it. A bit cleverer person wants to disappear in this world, and rather than watching all the unfairness in this world, he wants to change the world. But not everyone is given this chance, and it's enough for us to not be deflected from leading the right way of life and making the rights decisions. Oybek, you must think about yourself first, forget about the others, please!"

Oybek's partner quite seldom comes early to home, and he always leaves home very early and comes back very late. They quite rarely have long conversations like today. They are always busy. Sometimes they join their friends from the same town's get-togethers when they often go to theatres, cinema and the ballet. There they both have a chance to talk. He knows that Omonilla is a very sensitive and alert type of person, and today he showed that once more showed that. He remembered what he read in books: "The country which has strong and brave male citizens will never stop existing." This seems a bit strange, but he looked at himself as a brave and strong citizen for his motherland, and he smiled. Omonilla saw his smile:

"Well, look, now you're your former self. Never feel sad about anything. I want you to smile all the time. We need to dismiss all the wrongs in the world, and we mustn't take pity on what has already happened, if we are not guilty of this."

Feelings

I wonder what's wrong with me. I am not too young, I have seen many girls. There's Gavhar who quite often visits our home as soon as I go home. I can feel her love for me in each of her glances and in whatever she says to me. I don't want to hurt her soul, but I can never fancy marrying her. Or one of these girls is Dilbar. When we celebrated my birthday party at the dormitory, she stayed in our room with her friend, and she said that the chief of her dormitory wouldn't let both those girls in their own dormitory, the reason was that it was too late. But this was just a reason for her. We made them lie on our beds, and we slept on the carpets by ourselves. I suddenly woke up in the midnight and found that someone was gently holding my hair. It was Dilbar who was sleeping on the bed. I don't want to keep anything a secret, I am a man. If I had made just one attempt, she would have been mine. But I didn't want it, I couldn't live with this sort of girl. A wife for me is not just a partner for me in bed. She needs to be close to my soul, to my sense and to my being. I should never be bored with her, I should always feel happy each time I see her, every time I am with her together. She needs to value her own being, saving herself for just her own future husband, she doesn't need to be in close contact with anyone until the day of the wedding. For me the wife to be is not Dilbar, that's why I pushed her hand off my hair immediately. I said: "Dilbar, calm down, stay focused, it's not the right thing to do". This is enough for girls who value and respect themselves. This sort of girl usually becomes a victim to many dishonest men. I feel sorry for them, they are usually neglected after just a night of relaxation.

I am in love with another girl, and she is the only one for me, it's Oydin. Yes, I didn't know what she was feeling for me, but anyway my heart is longing for her. I always think about her warm smile and her beautiful voice. I know I am in love, I am worried about the end of this love story.

When I was entering postgraduate courses professor Hovach agreed to be a scientific advisor for me. But he required me not to get married unless I graduated from postgraduate courses. At first I didn't take it serious, but then I read something in historical books. In history, a great king Chinghizkhan prohibited his own soldiers from getting married or to get close to their wives. He thought that women, and love would distract men from work, and make them lose interest in their duties. Love is another thing, but I don't want to marry at all. It hasn't been a long time since my brother got married. We built a corridor and one more semi detached house in our yard. We built this house ourselves, making all the bricks from clay. Some of our neighbors are still joking: "we don't believe that you built this house in such a short time, it seems to have fallen here from the sky!" We had many problems with paying for his wedding and house to live, but the bride, his wife, couldn't get accustomed to our family environment. She is very jealous of my brother. If jealousy turns into suspect and doubts, it may destroy any strong and friendly family. My older brother still has problems with his family, so it means it is too early for me to get married. There is one more wedding we need to have; my younger sister needs to get married.

Each of my days is hectic, so it is something like a burden for me to think about getting married. But the girl I had met in Tashkent for the first time and then in the museum keeps knocking on the door of my heart, keeps invading my thoughts which I am trying to lock, reminding myself that it is banned for me to love. She seems to have the key to open my heart after I lock it. She seems to look at me here, and everywhere, with a faint smile, and everytime I put my head onto the pillow, I try to call her: "Where are you now Oydin? Do you think of me as much as I do of you?" But I never go up to her to invite her for a date with me, never. When all the young postgraduates from Tashkent meet and go to Chio Chio San and Carmen opera theatres, we happen to sit together, maybe because we both yearn for each other. Every time we sit or walk next to each other, we always have something in common, and when we start talking, we tend to never end it. I seem to have turned into the best and the most handsome man ever in the world these days. I wish these cinema films and opera theatres would never come to end. Then I say to myself: "No, Oybek, everything is good in its season, this girl has not come to Moscow to go on a date with you, it's compulsory for both of you to study now at the moment. These moments I feel like a man chasing himself off from the city of love to the desert of drought without any thoughts about love and about Oydin. But I get further from these thoughts when I am with my schemes, inventions, drawing and other plans, especially when I am researching the engines, yes the engines.

Invention in Uzbekistan

When Oybek bowed down to look at the heap of iron details, the mechanic laughed loudly. When Oybek was working with all of his energy, even a noise can distract him and make him upset. But Vlas sounded so natural and sincere Oybek was forced to take a look at him once more:

"What's wrong?"

"Look at the mirror and see your face. You look like an engineer just out of the mining tube. I wish your wife-to-be could see that, because then you can never persuade her to marry you. No, never!"

"The girls growing up in our country, do all the hard work, so she won't take it as a tragedy if she is going to see me like this. The black spots of oil on my face are the sign of hard work. It's ok, she is going to wipe it off with her own handkerchief". He nodded as if he wanted to start working again.

"Yes, you really take pride in your motherland and your own nationality. I respect you very much. Especially for this reason"

Oybek had chosen a very complicated topic for his dissertation. It was "Constructing the fast moving diesel engine with one cylinder and increasing its indications to the degree meeting world standards". Oybek was obligated to once more learn all the subjects he had already learned at the university. He read many books for materials opposition, internal combustion engines and many others. Oybek was sometimes surprised by the extreme and unexpected power he had. If a man really does his best for something, he will certainly pursue his aim.   For example, the Germans whose houses were ruined to ashes during the World war II. They restored the state to its former glory within a very short time. Oybek had very clear purpose, and he was always wandering in the libraries, factories and university. His duty was not just to learn theory, but he was obligated to invent that engine.

Actually candidates to be scientists never write up all parts of the dissertation by themselves. They use ready-made information when faced with challenging situations. For instance, creating the engine at the factory is as complicated as creating a jeweler's object. We need to know all parts of the engine ranging from the holes as thin as a needle to the diminutive balls inside. Just a bit of indifference may blow away all that you have done during the whole day. Oybek had been working very hard for many months to create a fast engine in the experimental factory. Sergei Yevdokimovich, Hovach sometimes visited him to see how things are going. The administrator of the planning department of the factory, Vladimir Golubev was working with the mechanic Vlas Prokofyevich. Every single day there's some sort of a problem, and there's less of something or something is needed there. Oybek got to know cities like Leningrad and

Harchov like the back of his hand, because he went there everyday looking for the details and parts of the engine he is going to construct. It isn't so simple to create the engine consisting of 300 diminutive details and components. After Oybek prepared all the projects and drawings, he showed them to his friends and his friends made a beautiful joke:

"Yes, Oybek is indeed going to combine one of the poems by the poet Navai with that of the poet Lutfiy and create a unique poem of his own." They meant that he was going to combine several existing details to create one complicated engine, which was almost impossible to construct. Not everyone can have this idea actually.

"Oybek, if I had a chance, I would call this engine "falcon". Its rotation frequency is equal to 3800 a minute. There has yet to be another engine with this power throughout the world" Vlas said. He was very sensitive boy and used to often interrupt Oybek from his work with his astonishment and other characters. But he was feeling that invention of this engine was just the outset of all the hard work.

Thoughts "How are you, Oybek? Are you ok?" "Yes, not bad, thanks.

"How much is the fuel waste?"

 "140 grams"

"Ok, You may go on with experimenting". This was the senior scientist-professional Hovach who would often ask me about the news in the research. Nikitin also visited us very frequently. They were assessing all of my attempts and results fairly and sincerely, but some others around said: "Let's see what this young man can do. We know that scientists of Central Asia do not even understand technology". I must work to show them what we, scientists of Central Asia can do. If I can invent the engine I am planning, this is not going to be just my victory, it is going to be the victory of all the people in my motherland. I still remember when we were in our second year of Bachelor's degree, and Okil Umurzakov was delivering lectures from the subject Materials opposition and he gave me the book "Automobiles" as a present. I value this a lot, and this was much more than anything for me. my teacher gave a me a book as a present. This meant that the teacher was relying on me and he showed this with that book with his own signature and wishes for me. From that day forth I started being valued and respected by him, because he gave me his own golden advice all the time. If I am going to succeed now in what I am trying to do, this is going to be success of my teacher first of all. This success will belong to all the teachers who taught me at school, and to all the friends I grew up with. Without them I am not going to be counted as a human being. No, without the motherland a man is nothing and nobody in this life.

At the beginning, I was reminded about fuel waste. Yes, it's actually more than enough. Again, I needed to take measures against that. I had to check that again, experiment and calculate it once more. Then it became clear, none of the screws could meet   the requirements. Our engine was made with the same methods like in the USA, Cammins. But there's plenty of difference in the technology of the USA and the former USSR. We all again gathered for a meeting.

We made up our minds to remove and reinstall the compression piston ring, with piston pins from the CMD diesel produced in the Harchov. After that everything seemed to be going well at last. I used to stay in the laboratory until 10 at night.

While I was walking the dark streets of Moscow I would turn and walk to another dormitory, from the early morning to the evening I did whatever my brain asked me to do. But when my feet did not obey my brain, meant my heart was ruling me at that time. Yes, my heart was prompting me to go to the dormitory where Oydin was living.

My heart says: "Oybek, why don't you want to listen to me? Is it only your brain you listen to all the time? Why don't you feel sorry for me?"

In these moments me and my heart went to that dormitory where Oydin lived. She will also be spending her life of youth on different drawings, schemes, books and researches like me. But she never got angry and felt sorry for the time she spends with me:

"How is your engine there?" she asks in a very cheerful voice.

"Oh, the engine? It's feeling very good, by the way, the engine, I mean she said hello to you. That's why I am here to tell you what the engine said"

They always put a pot of tea and some sweets on the table. We sit there drinking a cup of tea and talking about different things. Remembering Tashkent city. Sometimes I ask Oydin to sing a song for us. She has a crooning and nice voice. As soon as she starts singing a song while sitting on one edge of her bed, all the tiredness seems to escape and abandon me in less than no time. That's the how she sings:

Every spring this love is the same, saying hello and bye Every spring, just this hello and bye and nothing more ... But I never stay there for very long hours. After I sit here

for half an hour Oydin says:

"I am sure, your love, your engine is going to be jealous of you. She is certainly not going to let you in if you go back later than this"

It means "now you must go home" in a very polite way. Every time I knock on her door, she opens it and her eyes glitter with joy. At this time I make believe that she is not indifferent to me. But whenever I see the portrait of the singer (he had also studied in our faculty) on the wall of her room, I tend to suspect that she is in love with him, but then immediately I change my mind because I know she can never go anywhere and find a man as good as I am.

I tell her that good and handsome men like me are quite rare.   she   lets   me   hope for   her   love   saying: "You are right. Men like you are born just once in hundred years"

The next day we'll again research, do experiments... Everyday is different.... they are all different ...

Once upon a time

We had to conduct an experiment on the engine at a very high speed   to get the necessary results. But the time for the experiment was fixed at 10 pm. It was working at a 3800 frequency rate. Vlas Prokofyevich and Nicholai Petrovich were very glad that we achieved this result. Suddenly there seemed to be a spark of fire coming from the engine, and we heard some cracking sounds. We were forced to make and use measuring instruments, and conductors and tools. It was about 10 at night, I immediately pressed the emergency button to stop the engine from working. We all went home thinking that Vlas Prokofyevich, and the engineer Nicholai Petrovich wouldn't divide the engine into components, and would want to start work again the next da. I couldn't fall asleep at all, and I felt it in my bones that the engine stopped working properly, because several minutes passed until this engine started rotating 3800 times a minute. Yes it had stopped operating.

We opened the engine head in the morning at the workplace and we saw that the flap had fallen down into the cylinder. Consequently, this created a hole in the piston, and both the cylinder and   the head were in a terrible state. Nikitin helped us to rework and reinstall all the details, and after working again for three or four months, the engine started working. After we examined the motives for failure in the first testing, we found out that internal spring of the flap operating at a high speed turned out to be wrongly operating, and some necessary components were falling out of own place. When we tested the number of rotations, it was also incorrect, and the tool used for calculating the number of rotations wasn't operating at all. We found out that the engine was actually working with 4300 rotations, it couldn't obviously stand it, and it was too much for this engine. Assembling the engine once more, with all the proper components, we decided to let it work with fewer rotations and in the next experiments we got all the results as properly as we were planning.

From that day forth, Oybek started teaching all of his students to examine measuring tools and other equipment before applying them. But after we achieved our first success with so much hard work, our mechanic quit the job because of the low salary. We hired another mechanic, a bit younger mechanic, Vasya Bantush. The two young scientists were eager to excel and started working together. At last when the senior teacher visited them for the second time to know what's going on, Oybek was ready to inform him that all the things were going as well as planned. Then this senior teacher set him the requirement to construct the engine meeting the world standards after a bit longer investigations. It would take me a year and six months longer to do what he wanted.

Oydin was also busy with all of her work these days. She had many admirers around her. She treated them all equally in the same friendly manner. Her friend, Muhabbat who had started postgraduate courses with her fell in love with a man and was forced to give up her research. This huge city Moscow has own rules and norms.

Many foreign people think that they are free in this paradise like city and they can do whatever they wish. Most of them are unfortunately led astray. But some of them who are honest and trustworthy are impossible to lead astray. Our young heroes are also this sort of honest people. They have a strong conscience, eternal love for the motherland and respect for their parents.

Time to Fall in Love

Oybek guessed something mysterious in Oydin's glance. He thought that she was going to ask him something, but was feeling shy. So he decided to be the first to begin:

"So, well, are you ok? I guess you're not tired, right?"

"Oh, no thanks, I am not. How can I be tired of having fun? Living here in Moscow I seem to have missed our own national songs like "Yalla" and "yor-yor". Thanks I have enjoyed it a lot! Now can you let me go? My mum is going to be worried if you don't"

"But it isn't very late… Besides …" Oybek couldn't continue what he was saying, instead he laughed. "What besides?"

"You must go home after everybody is off". He was watching her to see how she would react. They were talking under the two willow trees which were leaning against each other.

There was a party of girls nearby. Oybek's sister was going to get married, and it was a night party before the wedding according to the national traditions. His sister looked like the brightest star among the other girls there. Oybek was feeling a very keen anguish in his heart, and anguish of feeling sorry for his sister, because he thought that she was too young yet to get married. But he was sometimes even glad that he could afford to have a wedding instead of their father who had died in the war. Oybek spent sleepless hours in Moscow lest his sister would seekingly long for the love and support of their father. So many young people at the same age as he is were all having fun at night and they were all busy with some girls. Oybek was working at his engine during the daytime, his hands dirty from engine oil, and at night he was writing formulas for his friends to earn more money. He remembered all he was doing to succeed and started taking pride in himself. A man who has a younger sister must feel responsible for her, and he must deserve it. It isn't easy to feel this responsibility and to deserve it.

So there were just two of them, Oydin and Oybek. When Oybek said Oydin was forced to be the last to leave, Oydin pretended not to have heard it. Instead she asked:

"Is the trolleybus station far from here?" "Do you really want to leave?"

"Actually this beautiful and fantastic party deserves staying in forevermore, but my mummy will find it hard to sleep without me at home, I am sorry."

It was a hidden answer for his question about love for Oybek and he said:

"If you really can stay here forevermore, I will be the happiest man, on cloud number nine!"

"If you are on cloud number nine, then you cannot get on the trolleybus with me. You will have to fly in a helicopter. If you stay here and don't go back to Moscow, what is your "Black and metal lover" going to do without you?" (here she meant the engine)

Oybek was really happy that he could understand all of her jokes and her feelings of love, and jealousy. He was happy that they were talking in an ironic language that no one could understand but him and her.

"Ok, then you may go to say goodbye to the girls, Oydin. I'll be waiting for you near that timber. Then will see you off to the station. We have very big stones in our street, and I don't want you to fall over." He meant the other young boys who might see her and set their eyes on her.

"No, all those big stones know me as a friend, and therefore they always let me pass them standing in a line". Oybek was fascinated by the way that she understood all the puzzles that Oybek was making.

Both of them were walking next to each other... It was summer evening, and there were many stars twinkling in the sky. They could easily feel the fresh air and the scent of the flowers.

"Yes, so nice. If I could, I would save all these evenings and these stars as a golden ring and wear it all the time because soon our vacation will come to end, and again we will do the same, libraries, laboratories and archives."

"You don't need to have a golden ring for that, we can keep them all in our hearts."

All the joy and happiness of his sister's wedding was giving him the courage to tell all this to her. However, he wanted to come clean about everything he was feeling for this girl. Oybek hesitated because he had gotten used to feeling alert and taking responsibility for everything he wanted to say. He didn't set his emotions run free, even on romantic nights like this. He was thinking:

"If I ask her to marry me now, and if she says "yes", then, I will not be keeping my promises to Hovach. I promised to not get married until I finish my dissertation. Besides, today is my sister's wedding, and we can't afford to have another wedding six months later. I should only tell her about marriage when I'm ready to have our wedding."

Oybek couldn't stand people who were permissive and not determined. He was having the same feelings as she was inside. The young man who was walking nearby, whose shoulders sometimes touched hers, has already turned into the main part of her dreams, and of her soul. But he didn't rush in opening his heart full of feelings and love. For both of them their scientific research is as valuable as their love is.

"Yes, I think we will again take watermelons or grapes to Moscow" Oydin tried to change the topic.

"Yes, you're right, this is what actually makes our teachers happy. But Max Samoylovich made me shy the last time, and I was a bit embarrassed. Do you know what he said? He said that he would be upset if I bought them with my own money."

"I don't understand how people can live like this limiting their own desires to eat something they want. But there are some people who never have their fill, even if they eat everything. They keep opening their mouths for food just like the dragons in the tales".

"Yes, I really want to throw a stone into the mouth of this sort of greedy people like dragons". He said this because he also hated that sort of greedy person. He was happy to have a teacher like Hovach.

"It's very hard to give presents to Hovach, because he will never accept them. Every time I am forced to lie to him saying that it is his friend Okil Salimovich who sent him those presents. This time I want to go and cook pilaf for him with our devzira rice (type of rice grown in Central Asia). How do you think about it? Is it a good idea or ...?"

"Will you cook him the type of pilaf like the one you had cooked for your teacher Bella Semenovna?" Oydin said this and she burst into laughter.

Oybek told her before what had happened to his teacher Bella Semenovna. He liked to tell her about funny things in his life. More clearly, Bella Semenovna was actually Oybek's foreign language teacher, and she treated him quite differently due to his polite attitude and character. Whenever she comes to Moscow she will surely come round to see Oybek. One day she came to Moscow and as usual visited Oybek. When they were talking, Bella Semenovna reminded him:

"Oh, by the way, tomorrow is my friend's birthday? Do you you mind cooking some pilaf for us, or …?"

It was a shame for an Uzbek boy to say: "I can't cook pilaf". because each of them must know how to do it. So, he had to cook it one day before her birthday. They didn't want the guests to smell fried meat, oil and the other ingredients while cooking fresh pilaf.

Oybek took a risk and made pilaf for twenty people. The next day, the guests themselves poured water into this meal and boiled it down for some time, then they ate it like porridge. So, after eating the meal with the spoiled ingredients, all the guests became ill, they started going to toilet much more than usual.

"After that I learned to cook pilaf. If it's going to taste less delicious than any other meals, I am surely ready to kill myself!" He said ironically to Oydin.

At that time Oydin realized why she liked this boy so much. All the boys who fell in love with her were handsome, good- looking and very talented, but Oybek was determined and he would do whatever he decided to do. Most young men don't actually have enough courage. The men who are determined can certainly have a strong and long lasting family, and they can defend their motherland from threats.

Oydin: "Now we are here, this is the station, I see. You must go home, they might need you now"

"No, I must see you getting in the trolleybus" "Even if I get in it, I might go to another place"

"I know if you get in the trolleybus, you will go to your home, nowhere else, I know it"

Oydin gave a very beautiful smile. The trolleybus arrived, and Oybek stood on the steps and said goodbye to her. He wanted all the other passengers to know that she had someone to rely on and to marry.

Oybek waved his hand to say goodbye, and he stared until it disappeared. He thought that Oydin was also looking back to see him staying there.

"Hey, can you tell me what the station this is?" He was in a very strange situation when the stranger asked him this.

"Oh, you mean this station? Oh, this is the station of love… yes, of love …" He didn't even realize what he was saying, as he was lost in his concentration.

At the station "Winds"

"Oybek, maybe that's enough. I am so tired that I'm unable to use my own hands," The mechanic put down the iron. "Now I am going to lie down and fall asleep. To tell you the truth, I can't stand it anymore"

Oybek wanted to laugh looking at Vasya's face. His face became as black as coal, as he was constantly working with the machinery and equipment filled in with oil. Oybek could only see his white teeth in that room.

"Why are you laughing?" Vasya was really intending to go to bed at that time.

"You remind me of Otello right now. You must get up somehow, friend. You must not sleep here. You have to go home, take a shower and then go to bed."

Oybek pulled him up by his hands: "Hey, get up, hurry up!" He had had this problem for a long time.

Since his first engine experiment failed, they were forced to work even harder at this research.

None of the details of the engine were sold separately, so we have to make them each by ourselves. The military servant has retired, and Vasya Bantush gets along very well with me. The man who has recently resigned from military department relishes the way Oybek works with metalwork, measuring tool pistons, details of the engine and his friendly attitude. If the military servants speak, they always speak in a way mixed with irony and criticize. Vasya discovered a man proud of his motherland, was hardworking and personally honest in Oybek's image.

At the end of the day the work to be done seemed to be over, but this was the end of only one step towards the dissertation…

Thoughts

What I hate most in this life is being helpless when there is no chance for my dreams to come true. Within three years I have to get the results of all the experiments and be ready for my defense. But it was November of 1967, and still I haven't finished my work. God is witness that I haven't spent a minute of these years on my own pleasure. Experimenting internal combustion engines is one of the most complicated spheres of engineering. The scientist who is researching in this field must know electronics and pneumo-automatics as well. He must work as hard as mechanics do. Anyway I couldn't not manage to finish it on time, and I knew it. I always feel there are reliable people who believe in my talent, but there are also some people like Ashot Petrosyan. If they get to know that I couldn't manage in time, they will be the happiest to know about my failure, they will perhaps say: "Yes, he wants to be a scientist, but he can't".

As soon as I imagined their face expression at that time, I felt like I was in hell in lots of agony. I am not here just for my own success. I may even decide the future of our motherland, and I am here to contribute to the development of our country. Some artificially talented scientists think that they can work and live there, and their lack of knowledge will not be noticed among a huge number of scientists. However, actually each professional with less than enough knowledge is a failure to his own future, and to the future of his motherland.

We needed to fix a day for our defense. Again Max Samoylovich bothered himself to go to the USSR Higher Education Ministry on behalf of the university rector and he requested that they prolong the date of the postgraduate courses for one more year, taking into account the importance of the research results. I had to meet the Minister face to face, and when he interviewed me in his office, my responses perhaps satisfied him. Therefore, he allowed me eight more months for the ongoing experiments.

"Oybek, none of postgraduates have ever been permitted to have eight more months for research by the Ministry. The maximum they have been permitted is six months. This is a valuable chance for you" Max Samoylovich said.

During this time as my teacher after Hovach, Nikitin had left for Algeria, a man A. Hachian was appointed as a supervisor and scientific advisor for me. In 1968 I managed to finish all of my experiments and created an engine which could be the basis for my dissertation. I reported everything to my teacher A. Hachian: "We'll meet in two years, and during this time, I mean after a year you'll have written your dissertation, and in another year you'll have checked and examined the results. Now you may go to your own hometown". I thought: "We'll see! Oh, he said two years". What did he mean by that? I wasn't in vain wandering in this city. He doesn't even know I think that I have spent my time effectively, and I've already written up all the chapters of my dissertation except the last one.

Fortunately Nikitin, my own teacher came back from his vacation. He looked through the entire dissertation within three days. Only three days; not even a week. God had rescued me from the teacher who would steal time from his own postgraduates.

It took a week for Max Samoylovich to look through the dissertation, and when he informed all the department teachers that the dissertation was ready, Hachian got stunned and shouted: "It is impossible!"

It is possible…..Hmmm. He should have realized that a man from the country where the greatest healer, Avicenna had lived, Beruniy had lived, could do even more than that. Shouting that it is impossible, I'm sure he then became silent, and seeing that the thing he thought impossible had been made possible, was shocking.

In the first defense of my dissertation I hung fifty-five wallpapers with schemes and drawings on the blackboard. I actually spent all of my energy on these papers. My brother Marvar, and the technician Lida, helped me to do what I needed for my dissertation. Most importantly all the scientists supported the results and it was then further recommended for the main defense. They even told me all the mistakes in it. I didn't change or edit the dissertation for the further defense, nor did I fail my fourth year postgraduate course. I was just an ordinary postgraduate for everyone. I was then declared as a candidate of sciences.

I am an Uncle Oybek
"We don't love the trees only for their beauty. Of course, firstly it is important for the green leaves, and blooms. But in fact, each human has his/her own tree. If he keeps hugging that tree for a long time, he will get a huge amount of energy from that tree"

said Galina Il'inichna while she was laying her tartan blanket on the part of the land covered with less grass. She didn't even wait for the answer:

"Serega, Tanya, do not go far. Heeeey!"

Oybek was feeling relaxed after the first defense of his dissertation. Yes, his defense was full of some challenges and many interesting ideas, and then when some people with malice aforethought started being nosy about his research, and when his documents were looked through, those people found out that he hadn't passed the exams for the subject "Internal combustion engines". This is the special field study for him.

While members of the department were discussing this issue, they decided that he needed to be automatically assessed.

They said:

"Kodirov has proved that he deserves excellent evaluation by presenting his dissertation."

At that time Oybek expressed his happiness with only: "Thank you", and he was absolutely happy that it   was possible to win. That day he went camping with his teacher Sergei Yevdokimovich, and his family, and Sergei felt quite free to talk and to spend his time with Oybek. His wife was very easy going, very calm and their children were mischievous. They kept calling him "uncle Oybek". His teacher was like the whole world to him, and every minute, he discovered something new in what he said, in the things he taught him. He had been working in Algeria for many years, but he always treated him as if he were still his own student. Sergei hadn't invited him to their time-share in the forest in vain, and he certainly needed to have a reason for that.

"How can I help you, Galina Il'ichnina?" Oybek said after he finished cleaning and tidying all around the worktop.

"You must rest now. You have worked hard for a year. That's enough I think. It's high time to rest" she said smiling. She looked upon him as if she were his sister. Oybek didn't like when people discriminated against nationalities and countries of origin. If he could, he would have classified people not according to their nationality, but taking into account their outlooks and feelings. For example brave people, rude people, hardworking people etc.

At that time, Sergei Yevdokimovich seemed to have read Oybek's thoughts and said:

"Yes, right, good people mustn't discriminate according to nationality". Oybek thought it was telepathy. Yevdokimovich went on:

"For example, there's no difference between German and Uzbek people. The only reason for the previous contrast between them is the cruel and sadistic policy of Hitler. In the war children whose fathers had died in the bloodshed used to be afraid when hearing the word "German". Just the kings and other cruel leaders needed this chauvinistic policy, not ordinary people. They devised different methods of policy so as to lead the people with fear and under strict, constant control. Therefore everybody needs to be fearful of a ruler who has the motto: "We are the best nation in the world!". This policy is their only weapon."

Oybek was walking next to him. The forest was thick with trees, and some birds were singing. It was hardly possible to view the sky. Yevdokimovich continued:

"Oh, by the way, this thought came to my mind all of sudden. Actually I invited you for another reason. I want to tell you about … Oh, it is a bit …a bit early I think. Ok, let me first of all tell you about one event if you don't mind. When I was working as the head of the department in Algeria, the university rector invited me for a talk. He wanted to actually ask about how well one of my students was doing. I gave my own opinion about him, and since then I haven't seen that student. But one day, when I was walking in the street, a Mercedes stopped nearby and a young boy got out of it. It was he, the student in whom the rector was interested. He shook my hands to greet and said: Sorry, I wasn't interested enough in technology, so they helped me to change my faculty for the humanitarian subject's faculty. I am very glad that you helped me, thanks." Do you know what? I then heard that he was the governor's son. The governor of Oran city.

Seeing that he didn't study well, the rector decided to make him change his faculty, and the governor accepted this fair decision. Do you know why I am saying this to you? I'm saying this because I have a tremendous amount of trust in your talent and ability.

I am sure that you will not stop after becoming a scientist. If one day, in future you have to decide the future of your students, if you're promoted I mean, then I advise you to make fair decisions all the time. You must contribute to the development of your motherland. Do not think that I am being too talkative like a chatterbox, I am not actually. Everybody has situations which are hard to deal with, and when you're in this sort of difficult situation, remember what I am telling you now, today, here in this forest. Now you have a pure soul, and you have become a scientist with your own power, and your own hard work. You don't have any malicious forethoughts. I hope you will live in this way, honestly and fairly, forever."

Oybek used to be afraid of missing anything his professor said, because he used to say things he was also thinking about.

But so a great scientist saying that he must live honestly even if it's hard to survive was important.

Oybek wanted to kneel down on this grass and he wanted to thank to God for making him so lucky to meet these wonderful people of science.

Being educated in atheistic behavior and methods at school, Oybek for the first time held the holy Koran when he came to Moscow. The Koran had been given to him when his friend (nephew of the King of Afghanistan, Zokirshakh) from Afghanistan when he was in Moscow. After reading that holy book, he grew to understand why that book was banned during the period of the former Soviet Union. Those who want to rob Muslims of their religion tend to ban the reading of the holy Koran.

"Why are you silent? Am I giving you a difficult task to deal with?" Yevdokimovich said after a long time of silence.

"No, Sergei Yevdokimovich, I know that a man needs to have great aims for his future. I heard about a woman who automatically lifted up a vehicle weighing several tons so as to rescue her son from dying under this car in an accident. So that means anything is possible when a man really wants something, and when he really tries."

"Yes, you're right. I trust you, Oybek."

"Uncle Oybek, Uncle Oooybeeek, daddy …" The children were calling both of us afar. Yevdokimovich laughed:

"I think the roasted mushrooms are ready. That's why the children are looking for us." Oybek held his teacher by his elbow. It was interesting to watch these two men, one of which has dedicated his life to science, another one who has just started feeling its hardships. Nobody would think about the difference in their native language, nationality or religion. If you could see that, you would also say "Oh, what a good friendship!"

He called me Sintia

Twenty-two scientists voted in my favour in the council held for the defense of my dissertation. Being supported by 22 scientists was as hard as to win as the Waterloo battle for Russia. Besides Oybek had a very complicated issue of research. That night I didn't even have a nap. I was well aware that the pre-defense discussion was very good. But everything was possible, and therefore I was very worried about that. I was allowing myself to calm down reminding myself: "Oydin, never mind, Oybek has nothing to fear, each small part of his dissertation is excellent". But sometimes, I begged God: "Oh, my God, do not let his enemies object to him. Let him be the cleverest orator in this discussion!" After the wedding of his sister, I became accustomed to imagining him by me all the time. To be honest in Moscow I didn't have a chance to have a date with him, or to fix an exact time for that. Only once did the two of us watch the French film "Mountains of Kilimanjaro". I once used to dream about being an actress, and I used to sing songs a lot. It was natural for me to be influenced by these sorts of films. But Oybek used to seem very realistic to me. While watching that French film I felt that he also had the delicate and romantic feelings that I had. After the film ended, he started calling me by the name of the main female hero of this film about love, as Sintia. It was also his own individual declaration of love.

I heard that his relatives, his sister, her husband, uncle and younger brother were going to come for his dissertation defense, and therefore it was awkward for me to go there. I felt shy to show up like I was going to introduce myself as the girl whom Oybek loved. Therefore, when they were there I just stood afar watching him there, I waited for him to glance at me. As soon as he did, I gave him my own individual look and told him all of my wishes with this glance. He understood all, of course. Besides I was due to have my own defense a week later.

I had one more reason for not coming up to Oybek's relatives. To finish my own dissertation I had to go back to Tashkent and stay there for some time because the object of my dissertation was the rivers of Central Asia. Me and Oybek didn't write letters, nor we did not even phone each other. But we felt some feelings of responsibility for each other. In the summer months, I came to Moscow to show my dissertation to my scientific advisor. I tried to visit my friend Yulia there, but she was away again.

The only friend I trusted and relied on was Oybek. His friend had left for his own motherland and his room was free for a while. Oybek asked the dormitory administrator to allow me to get one accommodation, I mean a room there. At that time, there were very strict rules about living in the dormitories. The administrator knew Oybek very well, he relied on him, and that's why he didn't refuse to help me. Until that time we used to meet each other when we were among lots of friends all the time. Even when we were alone, we used to talk about our dissertation and other issues of science. We also used to help each other. But this time we had a conversation about the love that we were hiding for so a long time in the depths of our hearts. Yes, at that time we were sitting around a table that we had moved towards the window in the room that had been given for me to live. There were just the two of us sitting there face to face. We could feel the smell of the acasia trees through the window. Oybek started:

"Well, look, all the work we had to do here is to be over soon, quite soon. Both of us are going to be back to Tashkent soon." I was used to all the expressions in his face, to his mysterious glance. I knew that if any spark of excitement glittered in his eyes, he wouldn't be talking about science or a dissertation.

My heart started beating fast because I felt that spark of excitement in his eyes.

"Yes," I said, but my voice still trembled.

"Oydin, I know, there are many guys in love with you, in Tashkent and in Moscow. I mean … I suppose there are some of them even richer, even cleverer than me. I even know personally some of them who have sworn to marry you. But I am not going to give you to any of them, I am not going to let them take you away from me, no …"

Oybek immediately said that. Perhaps I could tell him something if he asked me questions like "Are you in love with anyone?" and many others, but he said it quite differently. As he said that he was not going to let the others marry me, I didn't have anything to say.

There were many people who were in love with me. Even some of their friends told Oybek that they had seen me kissing one man somewhere. But Oybek remained as

Oybek all the time. He didn't lose himself even when he was with academicians, or with the professors. If I were from another country for example in Europe, I would have said: "Oh, I am so happy, I also don't need anyone else but you". I was born and bred in Uzbekistan, in the eastern part of the world. I was silent. One could hear only me and him breathing.

Oybek said to me:

"Do you remember the two heroes in the novel by Abdulla Kodiriy, the young man Anvar and the young beautiful girl Rano. In this novel when Anvar asked Rano when they could have a wedding to get married ... "

Oydin: "Rano says that it was ok just to date"

"But Anvar knows it well that it is immoral to break the rule of marriage. Here I also want to ask you the question which Anvar gave to Rano, I mean about the wedding."

"What if I give you the answer which Rano did?"

"But we aren't Anvar and Rano, are we? We are Oybek and Oydin. Spring is nice, but for Uzbek people autumn is the best season to have a wedding, I mean when all the vegetables and fruit are ripe and cheap to buy, I mean for the party."

I was silent again, I had many things to say, but the urge to speak seemed to be less strong that my feelings. Oybek was waiting for me to say something, and at last I told: "You are much better than anyone, Oybek!"

This night we stayed in my room. For the first time, I felt the temperature of his hands when he held mine. I felt his face touching mine so emotionally and with so much love. I trusted him with all of my feelings.

But indeed, Oybek was the best man in the world for me. This night when anything could happen between a female and a male adult, he let us both spend this night with nothing serious occurring. We were just lovers eager to love and wanting to love.

After that night, I let him know I came and I disappeared immediately. I heard about the party that Oybek and his teachers had together where they had everything from

Uzbekistan, pilaf, somsa[18], water melon, grapes and … As for me, I filled my glass in with some lemonade and drank it with cheers: "Oybek, my darling, for your success" and I also added: "With love Sintia". This was my own   individual

congratulation to him. The next day I was told that Oybek's sister Bakhtia had come to see me. I wish you could see how excited I was. I was worried why they needed me, and if, they wanted to say that they were planning to find another girl for him or …

I had met his sister in 1965 when his younger brother Marvar came back from military service. We visited Marvar to see if he was safe and sound. My mummy was also with me there. Though Oybek's mother welcomed us very well, I felt some feelings of concern in her eyes. The next time I met Oybek I said:

"YI think your mother thought that we visited your home to ask you to marry me, I think"

He took it as a joke: "Ain't I the type that girls can ask me to marry them?"

The day we visited their home with mum, I saw his sister too for the first time. I liked at the way that her husband was as kind as a father for Oybek.

I wondered why his sister visited me that day in the dormitory. I went downstairs to see what's wrong. She turned out to have come with her husband and they wanted to have a walk in Moscow. Then I heard that Oybek felt sick after the party they had had the night before.

His sister:

"Yesterday his friends forced him to drink a glass of cognac, it seems it was too much for him. He is vomiting now.   I am worried about leaving him here alone, I am here to ask you to take care of him, please, if you can."

Oybek had enough friends among the girls from Tashkent there in Moscow. But his sister seemed to have her own reason for visiting me. That meant not only he liked me, so did his family members. Maybe that's how destiny is. I was wondering if I was really destined to marry this young man who kept chasing the secret of a science he was willing to plumb.

---

[18] 17 These are types of national foods prepared with mash and rice, usually very tasty.

Close relationships

"Oh, look. You look sick and tired. Even in the recent years you have only lived in Moscow. Besides, ok, there is everything in Moscow, but nothing is equal to the energy this piece of bread will give you, the bread baked in your own motherland, my child. You must now think about yourself at least a little. You must rest for a bit. I want you to relish the results of your hard work, Oybek."

"Maybe it seems like that to you l, mum. I feel shy to say I am tired after I witnessed how so many great teachers and scientists showed their trust and respect for me in Moscow. Now I must continue my research so as to further deserve the trust of all the people ranging from my teacher who taught me the alphabet to Okil Salimov, mummy"

"Again, you'll be drawing and writing all that stuff, my poor child? Again, you'll be going to Moscow, then to Leningrad, to Moscow, then to Leningrad. I am actually proud of you, my son. I know there are millions of people, healthy, and rich, who don't know anything except ABC, or who are completely illiterate. I know some of them are serving people like a maid and earning their living. Thanks to god. You are now one of the most famous scientists when you are so young. You have a good job. Those who value the money they earn, will be valuing God as well. But I don't want you to leave again. I am a mother, I really wish to enjoy seeing that you're happy with your wife-to-be if you have one."

"Yes, mummy, I hope my sister told you about that".

"My son, this is something natural in life. If you have chosen her, I will never dare to object, and I will always agree with you whatever decision you will make. I know many of your friends who left for Moscow to study, but came back with their wives. I mean they got married there in that city, without any marriage, our national weddings …

I noticed everything, my son, everything. Thanks to god that you could some… I know what you are feeling in your heart. Oydin is now with her mother, and she has gone to Moscow, but came back. We haven't heard anything bad about her. I mean she keeps being that innocent Oydin. Girls from Uzbekistan usually go to Moscow. I don't even mind anything in her family, her sister has been living peacefully with her husband, so I think her sister will also follow in her footsteps. Her mother is good, and even though she remained widowed, she brought up all of her children. I haven't heard anyone saying something against her reputation. But there's only one problem, it is, I mean Oydin is the same age as you are, and she has the same knowledge and education as you do. According to our traditions a wife-to-be should be younger than a husband. I don't mean that we'll be ignoring her in the future. In our country, young men have always looked for a partner younger than themselves and having less education than they had themselves. It isn't in vain. In that case a man can be a woman, obeying her husband, needing her husband to rely on all the time because of her weakness.

"Mummy, we'll be relying on each other, don't worry. She is a very good girl... very clever."

"Ok, she is beautiful and good-looking. But I want you to think it over once more. I am now suffering for your brother. If you remember he also had talent and an interest in science, but he didn't use his talent because his wife is very jealous. I wish your wife would be suitable for you, I pray to God asking a good wife for you.

"She is suitable, mummy. You can go to their home without any hesitation. Why are you hesitating, do you have any reasons for not allowing me to marry her?"

"No, I don't feel anything wrong in her, but I am not sure if she can be accustomed to the good or bad days in our family. She seems very confident and determined. I am afraid that she can easily make a decision for herself. I mean she is a bit more independent for you. I heard the way she talks very loudly; not as calm as docile girls do."

"Mummy, if a scientist talks in a relaxed voice, nobody believes in what he says, and she is a scientist. They need to speak confidently. And then she is not as a rich girl as you are thinking. She has also grown up in a poor family like ours. Besides, we have already decided to get married."

It has been ages since Oybek had such a long talk with his mother. Now they are sitting together on the plank bed, and he wants to put his head onto her knees and for her to stroke his hair just like in his childhood. He understood her concern very well, but his mother also understood his feelings.

"Ok, my dear son, it depends on you who you marry. If you want me to ask her to marry you today, today I will go to her home."

Oybek didn't say anything. He wanted her to caress him like when he was a little child, but he was shy, and he showed all of his love to his mother with his warm look at her.

Happiness of Spring Came in Autumn

Oydin seemed to be a very determined and a strong girl. Sometimes when he remembered that she wrote her dissertation on a topic that even men cannot do, he imagined Tumaris just like this. Tumaris was a woman hero who beheaded the enemy of her country and put his head into a box filled with blood. She wanted him to have enough blood, because that enemy beheaded was very keen on bloodsheds and invasions. Sometimes he thought she looked like Kurbonjon who was awarded with the award Colonel or one more woman hero Kenegasbegim who poured melted tin into the ears of the King who was notorious for his sadistic behavior. But this day is a wedding day, and he changed all of his imaginations about her. While Oydin was walking into the old house inherited from Oybek's father Mukaddir, who had died in the war, Oybek saw her like an Angel in a white dress. The matchmakers who went to see Oydin said that she was very beautiful. It seemed like a fault for the matchmakers that Oydin was very thin, but today in their wedding, her thin figure seemed to be her precious beauty. The way that she is thin makes her look even more delicate, and even more beautiful. She was sitting like an innocent angel in one corner of the bed.

All the guests, hosts and relatives were sitting on the porch making lots of noise.

In the early morning party of pilaf, the sun was shining, but now when they started the evening party it started to pour down rain. Before that, his sister's husband, Hamidulla had fitted a wide overhead to stop the rain from falling onto the party hall. They actually had a party in the street, fixing many chairs and tables here in an accurate range, as if they were expecting it to rain. Then, as soon as the actor Soib Hujayev started talking in our wedding, it started to drizzle. This actor, made every expression and minute funny and said:

"Do not feel upset, but I know that the bride has already eaten what was going to be begging in the caldron."

Oybek was stunned seeing this famous actor at his wedding, and he didn't even know who invited him. Even when Oydin asked him "Do you know Soib Hujayev personally?"

He was about to say "No", but he just nodded and that's all. Perhaps Oybek's friend Rihsivoy heard her question, he said: "Your friend Salohiddin has invited this actor". Actually, Oybek and Salohiddin were very close friends in Moscow. Salohiddin was at that time working at the Reception committee of the mechanic's faculty at the Tashkent State Technical university.

Rihsivoy was working as a secretary, and Salohiddin was one of the most famous scientists of the faculty. One day he asked his students to help him with one of the girls at university, as she had some problems there. The problems was successfully solved, she turned up to be Soib Hujayev, the actor's daughter.

Suddenly Oybek laughed on hearing what the actor said: "Now, I wish this couple to have many children, I wish their children would be the football players, I wish their daughters would be the singers of the band "Spring".

Seeing him laughing Oydin asked: "What's wrong, why are you laughing?"

"No, no, nothing. I am just …"

"No, I know that you never laugh in vain. You will anyway tell me the reason" insisted Oydin.

"Suddenly I remembered how we went to the marriage registration together".

Oydin also laughed. Then they both started laughing together, even before the wedding, during the wedding many funny things happened making them laugh. Of course, there are many good people, but there are bad people as well. After they got engaged long before the wedding, some people started spreading gossips as if Oybek was going to marry and live in the bride's house. Hojiyabonu, his mother, of calm and relaxed disposition said: "I haven't brought him up to follow his wife and neglect his own mother, nobody in our family has married to stay in wife's home." This rumour seemed very embarrassing for Oybek because studying in Moscow and being valued by the greatest scientists of the world gave Oybek the wings of self-assurance.

He said to his mother: "Mummy, do not worry, if Oydin wants me to live in her own family home, I won't marry her even if she has hair of gold, and eyes of diamond." She heard it and calmed down, but women tend to bare their souls usually to their neighbours and relatives. Surely she relayed what Oybek said about that, and this was exaggerated and at last Oydin also heard about that. Look that's weird, isn't it? Her mother got very frustrated about that:

"What? What? I am giving my daughter as a bride for the widowed wife of the rich-Mukaddir, but she is looking down on me, isn't she? My daughter is not s type to marry that sort of a man then, if he said awful things like that. My daughter has   as many fans around as her golden hair". It hurt Oydin to remember that. She thought: "Oybek could ask me and I would tell him everything. But could he believe what he had heard about our family. We didn't say anything about him and I would tell him that it was not us who spread that rumour. Nobody in our family said that he would be living in our home after the wedding". She had also insisted:

"Mummy, now let him do and say whatever he wants. I don't want to marry him, to tell the truth, especially after what he said about me. Now mummy, it will depend on you to choose a husband for me. You may choose anyone you want, but not him, mum. I don't want to marry him at all. I am not going to die without him. I am not". Her mother knew what she would feel if she wasn't going to marry Oybek.

"My honey, don't get so angry, if you are both destined to be together, you will get married anyway."

Oydin tried to be busy with work all day, so as to forget Oybek, but everyday she heard some news about him like "Oybek is going to marry a daughter of their old friend, or Oybek was going to be engaged and many others. The day he heard about his sort of news, she couldn't fall asleep at all.

She would have different frightening thoughts, and she couldn't believe that Oybek could abandon her like that. No, she couldn't stand that at all, and one day her heart urged her to walk to the workplace where Oybek was working. He was there with Rihsivoy, drawing different schemes, writing and reading. As soon as Oydin greeted the, Rihsivoy left the room immediately. Oydin asked:

"What are you doing?" as if she came there to know about that.

"I am translating textbooks for my own special field of study. I started this when I was in Moscow after I heard that there weren't enough books in the Uzbek language for our students. Why are you standing like that, don't you want to take a seat?"

Oydin sat right opposite him. They looked at each other, and they both felt that they had missed each other incredibly.

"Oybek …" she started talking and Oybek put his finger onto her lips.

"No, Oydin, we'd better stop arguing about that. Tomorrow my mother is visiting you in your home."

Now they were both in the wedding hall, and they remembered what happened had before this wedding, rumors, gossips and …

The reason they laughed about the marriage registration was as follows: they hired a car, Oybek requested the university bus, and they arrived at the marriage registration office.

Oydin put on her beautiful clothes, make up and went outside with her friends, she was very stunned seeing that Oybek arrived in an old bus. If the groom weren't Oybek, she would have said: "Take away this old wrecked bus away. I am not the type to go with you in such an old bus."

But that was Oybek who came in that old bus, the best man in the world, and therefore she didn't say a word to him and got in the bus with pleasure. In the wedding hall Oydin said: I think you came in that old bus on purpose, didn't you? You wanted to test me, right? You wanted to see If I would marry you or not, am I right?" Oydin said that with a beautiful and sweet smile.

"No, I didn't have an idea about testing you or… That bus was what came to my mind. Did you feel upset with me?"

"No, just a bit shy. The girls and neighbours saw the bus" "Oh, hang it. We'll soon be going to your home in foreign cars" said Oybek and he sat closer to her this time. This was the beginning of a life in partnership which would be so, so long-lasting.

We fought against days without each other We were patient with the feeling of yearning, But we trusted our heart for one another.

And we relied on each other in every moment, each instant This wedding is for lovers, destined to be together.

"Oh, look, my daughter-in-law, Oydin is very good at cooking. She can cook very tasty rice soup just from a little piece of meat and a cup of rice. She is thrifty too."

Oybek was fiddling strings of the table mat and was enjoying listening to his mother while she was praising his wife. He remembers that before the wedding his mother was a bit worried: "I don't know if she can cope with cooking after so a long time eating in cafes, and because she didn't have time for cooking because of her research. Or did she?"

She was always boasting about Oydin's beauty, and proper behavior, besides her big talent for cooking tasty foods.

"Mom, you are good yourself, therefore your daughter-in- law seems good to you"

"Yes, she is a good happiness for us. I felt it even when you were awarded with the degree right before the wedding. I was worried if you'd be awarded or not. Fortunately now you have been!"

Oybek liked it a lot when his who was mother very innocent discussed all the things in her own way of understanding. Indeed, he got the certificate from Moscow a week before the wedding; the certificate: Oybek Mukaddirovich – candidate of technical sciences.

He knew that he would get this certificate, but didn't expect it to be delivered so soon. It was the result of his sleepless nights, long time spent in libraries flicking through big books for just a small information, and schemes drawn more than once and twice.

Experiments, testings, mistakes, successes, failures in the laboratory led to huge successes, and he was certified with the scientific degree. While sitting around the table, Oybek remembered that at the moment.

Getting free from housework of cooking and cleaning, Oydin also took her seat there. She poured tea into cups and handed a cup of it to her mother-in-law, then another cup to her husband. It was dark, this evening they were sitting together, and Oybek was watching her without letting his mum notice that. He was looking at her and wanting her to go to the bedroom as soon as possible. His mother said:

"You're tired now, my daughter. Yes, housework makes everybody tired, you both should go rest."

"Oh, yes, my clever mother, my dear mummy" Oybek thought and only drank half of his tea in the cup. The other half he threw into the yard and left for the bedroom in a rush.

"Oh, you're so slow. I know you clean and cook very well, but very slowly. Why don't you come in here after mum allows you to?" Oybek made her sit on the bed and put his head onto her knees.

Oydin started stroking his hair: "You are relaxed when we are outside the house, but as soon as you're inside, something makes it hard for you to stay here"

"Work doesn't escape my mind, Oydin. I thought I wouldn't find it hard to teach students, but now I know after I've become a scientist."

Yes, he knew that it wouldn't be easy for to him to work in this university. Last summer all the applicant admission tasks were submitted to him and his friend Rihsivoy. Everything was ok, and the exams were successful. But after Oybek started working as a teacher, a man Belorussian, who became the candidate of sciences earlier than Oybek said:

"I don't care about his defense in Moscow or his academician scientific advisor. I wish he wouldn't rely on Okil Salimov to back him. I am Belorussian (white Russian)." He meant that by being Belorussian, a white Russian was one more priority for him. It hurt Oybek to hear that. He was not afraid of anything, he was confident of his own knowledge and opportunities, but the ironic smile and glance of this teacher really distressed him.

That day he was in a very bad mood. They stayed alone at night the same day, and Oydin kept asking him what was wrong with him. He told Oydin again not to bother herself to calm him down:

"Please leave it. Could what he says decide something for you? Ok. Okil Umurzakovich is your teacher. Is there something wrong with that?"

"The problem is not with Okil Umurzakovich, Oydin. I hate the way that people discriminate by saying somebody is from Tashkent, Andijan, Belorussia and many others. I have seen many great scientists in Moscow, for example Rostislav Pavlovich, who is a doctor of technical sciences, a colonel, and a professor. He served in the Second World war, and he graduated from the Technical university. After the war, he started teaching young officers in the armored troops. He worked as the head of the "Automobiles and tractor engines" department at the Moscow Auto mechanical university. He didn't care where I was from, from Moscow, or Tashkent, and he used to treat me equally with the others. It was enough for him that his students were clever enough to carry out research.

Ok, let's take Utkir Ikromov. He is a very good man, a candidate of technical sciences, who defended his dissertation in Moscow, is a proctor of the Tashkent State Pedagogical university, and he has also never discriminated anyone. He evaluated every person according to his knowledge and honor." Oybek was talking like politicians, not just Oydin's husband in the first days of their life together.

"Oybek, this means that those who have malice aforethought will try to torture many other people around them. You mustn't quarrel or argue with them about anything. I don't want you to get nervous because of such nonsense. You'd better enjoy working, and not think about those who are envious of you."

Oydin bowed her head towards Oybek. Oybek felt dizzy feeling the pleasant smell of his wife.

"Yes, you're right. We both need to enjoy our life   together.

Let them do whatever they want."

They closed all the windows, drew the curtains and shut the door of their bedroom.

They keep doing harm

Oybek used to enjoy it when his student gave the correct answer to his questions. He had a student with a broad forehead and dark face, who was originally from the countryside. He was just five or six years younger than Oybek and had perhaps served in the army and then became a student. His answer was very clean and he spoke briefly

"Well-done! Excellent!" He felt him very close to his heart and wanted to make him know that.

"May my father rest in peace! I know he's happy seeing this in the sky" he said in a loud voice.

"Oh, it seems that his father is also dead like mine. He's living by relying on himself all the time" Oybek thought.

"Sorry, don't be sad, everyone has a different fate in this world. My father also died when I was a little child. I can't even remember his face" Oybek said. It seemed like Oybek was not examining this student, and seemed to be talking to him just like a friend. The student got an excellent mark and became very glad. This was a common situation for Oybek. He didn't want to look down on the students as a teacher of the university.

Suddenly the head of the department visited him in his classroom. He was aware that he was the sponsor of the Belorussian man who despised him.

One day his teacher Ikramov Utkir visited him and he started a talk about arrogant people like the Belorussian man:

"Oybek, science is like the sea. There you'll see both the pearls and some disgusting insects. The pearls are like your kind and helpful teachers, and the insects are like that Belorussian man. Just be indifferent to them all because the main task you have is to teach students. The state which wants to develop and become stronger will try to develop science. The government will teach not only talented students, but those less talented too. At least it will teach them how to work in a certain profession. Now you have lots of chances, and you have many students. You should interest them in learning. Some people treat you well, and some of them not. Do not be attentive to all of them, please."

Oybek wanted to complain about that Belorussian man and his sponsor, but he held back after all what Mr. Utkir Ikramov said. From that time on he stopped thinking about those people at all... people like the disgusting insects in the sea.

"Oybek, how is your wife? Have you forced her to stay at home and not to work? Are you jealous? She is a precious and rare professional. Don't force her to stay in all the time? I hope you will come to visit us. If she visits and talks to my wife, your wife is going to get lots of experience. My wife is also precious. Do you know? Oybek is now very glad to talk to his teacher and he is going to go up to the head of the department, the sponsor of the Belorussian. He wonders what he wants him to do this time.

He greeted the head of the department who nodded in response. Oybek stood there for some time and suddenly took his seat as he hadn't been asked to sit.

"Oybek Mukaddirovich, I always see everything going on here, and hear about everything here because I am always in charge. Your attitude with students is not ok for me. I don't quite like it, to tell the truth" he said in a croaky voice.

"What wrong did I do? Did I assess anyone who hasn't attended lessons for a month after one free lunch with him in restaurant?" He wanted to say, but all of his teachers, Salimov, Hovach, Dobrogayev had reminded him not to get frustrated and answer back immediately. They suggested being silent first unless you're relaxed, and then speak after thinking for some time. At that time, he felt like all of his teachers were tapping on his shoulder asking him to calm down. Oybek stayed focused and gave the head of the department an inquiring and questioning look.

The head of the department tried to make it clear after that: "I see that you've allowed your students too much freedom".   I heard what you told your students: "If you like working independently in the library rather than listening to lectures, or if you find lectures so boring, then you may go to libraries to work"

"But, it is impossible to force …"

The head of the department interrupted him:

"Do you think you're bright enough to change the higher education system which has been active for so a long time? It has been just a short time since you started working. Getting a diploma of a candidate of sciences doesn't allow you to hold reforms in the educational system. There are some other people who have grown old dedicating their life to science and education."

Oybek wanted to tell him that growing old doesn't mean being wise and well-educated, but as usual he his tongue again and waited to hear what he was going to say next.

"Oybek Mukaddirovich, if you keep working like this, you may ruin the reputation of all the scientists. It is impossible to tell students "if you want to attend, attend my lecture, if not then work independently. It's enough to pass the exam".   Therefore, students are not respecting you from the start. I know that you assessed one of the students with an excellent mark just because he told you about his father who died, you also cried remembering about your father." Oybek was only thinking: "Oh, my God, this is too much for me now. It means the Belorussian has hired a spy who keeps him posted about everything I do. I don't understand why they want to make it hard for me to work. Oybek was trying to find an answer to these questions in the conversation he had the day before with Utkir Ikramov. He remembered him saying:

"There are special groups who are afraid of their tricks will be exposed if somebody much stronger joins them. They are afraid of stronger colleagues and therefore they keep attacking them for each step they make. You must take it easy all the time."

"Seeing the way that you are sitting silent like a child who did something wrong, I am making sure that everything I said is true, right?

"Do you know what?"

"I don't need any explanations. If you want to work at this university, then please watch your step and mind whatever you say"

"I have heard everything you said without any interruption. Not because I am afraid, but because I respect you as a person older than me. Now you must also listen to me. Everything you said to me like "the baby who did wrong, crying", I'd appreciate it if you keep all these words for those who can stand them. I am not your servant. If I am working in this university and at this department, I have been employed because I am a worthy candidate. If you don't see me as worthy, I am not the type who quits his job after bickerings urging me to leave. They first of all need to prove why they want to make me quit. Students aren't elephants in the zoo, chained and imprisoned. It isn't immoral to allow freedom for a human. Besides, you told me that I was ruining the reputation of the scientists working here. You're wrong, and if any of those scientists have gained their reputation with their wonderful lectures, then nothing can ruin their reputation." Oybek said these things standing up. He didn't change his face, and didn't feel excited when he said it all. His voice sounded relaxed and low.

On hearing everything Oybek had said, the head of the department stood stunned, and lost for words. He couldn't say anything and he was silent. Oybek said goodbye and left his room without even looking at his face.

When he was walking down the corridor in a very strange mood, he came across with his Belorussian opponent. He smiled with the glory of victory. Oybek immediately understood that it was he who'd kept the department head posted about everything. Oybek didn't understand why this man was doing so much harm to him.

"Hello, dear friend, are you ok?" he said with mysterious and glorious smile.

"You know it much better than me, whether I am ok or not. Why the heck do you keep asking about that here?" Oybek said and he passed him without waiting for an answer. He was feeling his glance on his shoulder, which meant he was still looking back at him.

Who is right?

Not in vain do they call pregnancy as sickness. I am really thick and dizzy. I like nothing here, and I feel like vomiting as soon as I see the face of the students who smoke. Ok, only the students. I feel like vomiting on seeing or being in the house of my own husband. This house where I am happy with Oybek seems very terrible for me. My own mother has a flat with two bedrooms in the centre of the city, it has both hot and cold water, and the central heating operates well enough. I complained to my husband: "Oybek, don't you see that my feet are swollen from going from the kitchen to the porch, and from the porch into the kitchen. I keep sweating in the kitchen, where it's hot, and when I go into the kitchen sweating so much, I may catch a cold. It's not only bad for me, but for our baby to be born." Oybek is too shy to say this to my mother-in-law: "We can't leave her here alone and move into a comfortable flat, Oydin. Be patient for a bit more. Stay with my mum a bit more. You know she raised five children alone?" I said ok. I'll try to be patient then. For the sake of the little heart beating in my chest, I decided to be patient with everything in this house, and I try to love it because I read about this in a book by a philosopher: "A baby feels everything when a mother pregnant. If a mother doesn't like her husband's relatives, a baby will also not like them when it comes into being." Oydin didn't want her children to be indifferent to her relatives-in-law, but anyway again, on the winter days when she is about to fall over on the icy yard, she again starts to complain: "But Oybek must understand me. I don't believe that he can let me suffer so much". Besides both my sister and my mother say: "Yes, it's unbelievable that your husband has studied in Moscow, a cosmopolitan city, but we see the way that he is indifferent to your pregnancy. Why doesn't he move into the flat with you? It is difficult in a semi-detached house like this. If you don't try to move into the flat now when you're pregnant, then you will be staying there in that old house for the rest of your life. You need to be spoiled during your pregnancy".

When I am in so much agony, Oybek starts returning home in a distressed mood. He doesn't even smile at me. Why does he glare at me like that? What wrong have I done to him? I take care of him all the time, get up at the break of dawn, serve his mother like a maid, go to work, and cook the meals. I want to forget about this all in my bedroom with him, but he looks upset with me there. He is sometimes silent for an hour. What a trouble I have. Oh god! When I spoke to him:

"Oybek, I don't care how feel about it, but I'm going to live in our flat" I said making a firm decision. I expected him to say: "Can you please wait for a bit more? Let's talk to our mother first. Maybe she'll go with us", "Maybe we are destined to buy a flat one day. We'll buy it, never mind". But he got frustrated, and even he brushed me off:

"If you want to leave, there you go! You saw the kind of house I lived in before you married to me, if you remember. I have never promised you we'd live in a luxurious house."

No matter how accurate and gentle a man is, I grew to understand that a man can never see himself in a woman's shoes. He doesn't know what a woman actually needs. I know what a good and polite attitude is. He could have said: "My honey, my Oydin, one day in the future I will have big and palace- like houses built for you and where our little kids will be born", But instead, he brushed me off and chased me away. That seemed terrible for me. I only packed two or three pieces of my clothing and left the house. In my own home my mother and my elder sister were fussing over me. Here it's very good for me. I am not getting up early any more, I am not preparing breakfast or lunch, and I can sleep as much as I want. Here, I can say whatever I want. But my soul… My soul is very lonely without my husband. I am wondering what Oybek is doing at the moment, and if he changes his shirt everyday because its collar is often stained. Sometimes he'll get up in the mid-night to work, and when he did, I used to prepare tea for him. I think he is not bothering his mother for that at midnight.

But I have already left his home, and how can I go back now? My mother is also in a rush because of her anger about his indifference: "Let's go and bring all of your bits and pieces. I promise he will come here to live with you after that. He has no way out." We did. We brought all my things into our flat. Everything in my home reminds me about happy moments with Oybek. They seemed to be looking at me sadly without my husband. I hope Oybek won't leave us alone after our little baby is born. Sometimes all my hopes tend to think about him abandoning me, then I tend to call them back again.

Thoughts

I don't believe that love can live for such a short time. I don't believe that love cannot stand a small test of life. After Oydin left, we are so alone at home. My mummy looks at me, and she is hiding her anguish from me. One day my sister Bakhtia and her husband Hamidulla came to visit me:

"Marriage is forever. Loving and missing are in the past for you. Marriage is not like love to love today, or to say goodbye tomorrow. In the east, in our tradition, marriage is not just a husband and a wife. It is all the relatives in the family, siblings, uncles, aunts and so on. I want you to go talk to your wife. Maybe she is upset about something. I hope she wants to come back, and for you to try and learn what's wrong." I said o k, but I couldn't go to her, no. I wasn't guilty of anything. Besides I saw Oydin with a young man who used to love her when she was a student. What a pain it is for me! Maybe it was a coincidence, but they were coming downstairs together, I wanted to kill that man by strangling or stabbing him... a bit later I was walking, distressed and sad outside the university, Oydin came up to me by herself. I saw her face with some dark spots, and she'd put on a bit weight. At first I saw her as a weak woman needing help from me, her own husband. However, I suddenly remembered how she was going downstairs with that man and I couldn't control my anger:

"Why on earth are you alone now? Where's your fan fussing over you all the time?"

Perhaps Oydin had something to say before that, but what I said made her angry and she brushed me off:

"He has gone for some minutes, and he will come back in a car, Volga. Not all the men are the same. Some are real gentlemen, and they know how to take care of pregnant women."

What she said really frustrated me. She is not the only woman who is pregnant. There are many Uzbek women who are heavy with a child, but are working in the cotton fields. They even give a birth to their child in the fields.

"You may now go with your rich fan, and you will not be taking the bus to go somewhere. With him maybe you'll be living in a flat, not in a house like mine. I am not the type just to wait for you if you leave this way." Perhaps my eyes were red with anger. When I started to walk away, she blocked my way and stopped me:

"What a strange man you are! If I had loved that rich man, I would have chosen him before I married you. You're like a little child. I am carrying your baby in my body. Do you think I'll be dating another man? Do not be so stubborn. Please, will you go and stay in our flat at least for a week."

"No, I want to live in our house. You married me knowing that I lived in an old house, so if you come back, I will live with you, if not I will not."

"Really? Are you sure? If yes, we will get divorced. We must end this row. I am also not the type to wait for you to come… If you are Mr. Oybek Mukaddirovich, you may do whatever you want."

I found it hard to recognize my wife, Oydin. She didn't use to say things like that. I wonder how she became so rude. I was wondering whether I made a mistake in something.

God rescued me

Oybek didn't know all about the workings of the court for marriage and divorce affairs. He had only seen this in films, or read about it in books. But he had never been to that sort of places.

He has never thought that he would have to deal with the court, and he didn't even have an idea about that. Here he is, in the court building, with the judge in the centre. She is already accustomed to being in this sort of situations. She is very serious, and it is hardly possible to see if she is glad or sad. She has a secretary next to her. There is a long bench there for the defendant and for the citizen who is being sued. This cold atmosphere, with chairs with faint paint. had something which made us feel fear. Oybek immediately wanted to go back to his home and he even forgot why he was there. Yes, he is here to get divorced from Oydin, for whom he used to see and feel the happiest in the world.

Oydin has already come. She is barely sitting on one side of the bench. Her belly is bulged, and it is easily obvious that she is pregnant. He felt like somebody was looking at him through the body of Oydin, and he felt that their baby to be born was looking at him. He imagined the baby's two dark eyes, just like those of its mother. He felt a keen pain in his heart. The judge started:

"Ok, comrade Kodirov, you wrote an application here, "My character turned out to not be suitable to that of my wife. Do you still have this opinion? Shall we start the council of the court?" the woman sounded fiendish.

Again Oybek looked at Oydin. She was looking down, with both of her hands on her belly, as if she was telling her baby: "Don't cry my baby, this is what your fate is".

Oybek remembered how his mother had felt after receiving the letter about his father's death in the war.

His mother was sitting there, his poor mother, dressed in a vest, wrapped an old faint colored scarf.

Oybek knew that his mother was pregnant when his father left for the war, but it was hard for him to remember the hardships she faced when she was robbed of the happiness of living with her husband. He saw how hard it is to live without a father. Now he saw that Oydin was just like his mother, alone, helpless, weak … He thought: "Why should I let my child live as an orphan? I am not cruel to such an extent. Oydin didn't do anything worth getting a divorce. She just wanted to live in   better conditions. The man whom I had seen her with doesn't deserve my wife at all.

Judge:

"Why did you get married? Your wife is pregnant and as we can see, soon you're going to be a father. Looking through all of your documents I didn't see any good reason for you to get divorced. You are both scientists, and I see, well-educated. Other people must learn how to live together as a unique family without any disagreements."

The last thing the judge said to him influenced him a lot. If Oydin had said something bad at that moment, Oybek would not have felt sorry for that. But now Oydin is silent, she is not looking at anyone.

Oybek said: "We, I ... we aren't going to get divorced."

It seemed to him as if someone had said it to him and he was just repeating.

Judge: "Did you make this decision, Mrs. Kodirova? What do you want to say about that?"

The judge seems to sound more polite and gentle this time. Oybek took a glance at Oydin, being afraid that she would say "no", in a rush he said:

"We have already talked about that. My wife, she doesn't mind living together again. She knows, we don't want to get divorced, no!"

Since Oybek came, Oydin for the first time has raised her head, her dark eyes were full of tears…

Golden ties

"Oybek Mukaddirovich, someone's asking for you on the phone"

Oybek went upstairs jumping two steps of the stairs in a rush and ran into the reception room.

"Hello, brother, it's me. Your wife has been taken to the hospital. she is going to give birth."

He could hardly understand what his brother Marvar said in such a noisy room:

"What? When? Which hospital?"

"In the morning. Hospital number three"

"The third. The third hospital. Where was it? Oh, yes, it's in the Takhtapul district." He stopped a car and rushed to hospital. Oybek was praying to God: "Oh, God, may they both be safe and sound. Let me see both of them together. Please, both my baby and my wife". Even after that council at the court, Oydin didn't want to go back to their house, and Oybek didn't want to move to their flat. However, the situation changed a bit for the better. They used to meet each other, without any sadness, and they didn't remember the disagreements they'd had. They both had the same wish: "May the child be born first, and the rest of the problems we will solve together".

Yes, the day had come for the baby to be born. Oybek looked around the hospital, didn't even know what to do, then suddenly he saw Oydin's sister with a bunch of flowers. Oybek unfortunately didn't buy anything for his wife. He stammered:

"Oh, flowers... I was so excited on hearing that... I was in a rush and ... Oh, by the way, is she ok?"

"Congratulations. You now have a daughter. Here is a bunch of flowers for you. I bought these for you. Now go to the door and tell the nurses that you're Kodirova's husband. They will deliver your flowers to her. She's been waiting for you for a long time and looking forward to seeing you upstairs". Her sister said many things to him.

"A daughter... why a daughter? What? What's her name?"

"You're going to ask God, not me why you've got a daughter. You will yourself give her a name" Said his sister Rano.

Oybek felt shy about what he said and losing concentration: "Ok, if my wife gave birth to a daughter, then may she be

healthy for all time. That's more than enough for us".

The doctors bickered, saying that it was banned for anyone to come into the hospital and promising to deliver the flowers. But then, after he gave some money, they easily let him in. He gave them some money of joy, according to the tradition in which a person delivering good news is given some money as a sign of joy.

Oybek's feet lost their senses, and the more he tried to walk, the more he seemed to be walking backwards. "You've become a father, a father!" This is what the doctor said when she was getting the money of joy from him. Her voice sounded so loud that Oybek still seemed to hear it. Oybek hadn't imagined how happy it would make him to be a father. There Oydin was lying. Oybek heard many frightening things about giving birth, and that's why he didn't expect to see his wife looking so beautiful after birth. On seeing Oybek, blood rushed to her face. He remembered the time when the woman hero

Kumushbibi in the novel "The days Bygone" gave a birth to a child. This novel is by Abdulla Kodiriy. Remembering that the woman died several days after her birth in the novel, Oybek said to himself: "Oh, no, May God save them both!"

"Who does the baby look like?" Oybek asked. He asked the questions which came to his mind, and he was completely lost.

"They are going to bring her here now. You can see for yourself who she looks like…" Oydin said this in a low voice.

No sooner had she said this, than the nurse brought in the baby. She was very small, Oybek thought:" Oh, she's as small as a little toy". When he stretched his hand towards the baby, the nurse shook her head:

"No, you mustn't. Her mother only can …"

Oybek wanted to touch the baby's face, it was so beautiful. Her eyes, ears, and lips, were all so delicate and so beautiful … The nurse got the money of joy, but she didn't leave them

alone. She stood there reminding them that the doctor only allowed him to visit for five minutes. Oybek wanted to hold the baby, to cuddle and kiss its faces, and this desire was very strong…

But though he couldn't hold her, he felt a very strong love for that small being. This feeling was quite different among all the rest he had ever had. The disagreements about the flat they started having three months after the wedding faded away with the love for the baby.

"Who does my baby look like?" Oydin asked after the nurse took the baby away"

"Why do they keep it in another room? What if it sleeps with you here?" Oybek said. He hadn't even heard what his wife asked him. Oydin smiled, and she was now feeling that her husband was again looking at her with lots of love like before, when they first fell in love with each other.

Happiness and Problems

"Theory, dynamics and construction of the internal combustion engines". Yes, this name was etched in the heart of Oybek, just like his wife's and his daughter's name. It was like a part of his life because Oybek teaches this subject at university. His daughter, Saodat's name (it means happiness in English) gifted him with the award of being a father, but this subject gifted him with the award "a teacher". However, life at the university was full of troubles, gossips, rumors, and though he tried to avoid them as much as possible, they kept invading in his life non-stop.

He thought: "it isn't my job", but later he realized that some of the students studying at the extramural learning faculty were bribing teachers and get assessed illegal way. It was hard for Oybek to stand that situation as he didn't even request anyone to assess a student who doesn't do well enough. To bribe teachers was almost disgusting for him. The students who bribe their teachers for assessment are going to be illiterate specialists in future. Some teachers allowing bribery at the university perhaps think that marks and grades can be offered on sale, and students can act as customers here, that's something weird, and hard to believe. Oybek informed the secretary of the party commission about that, he said:

"Oybek, try to be patient with that. This is not forever. If we are going to raise concerns for all the nonsense, then none of the people around will respect us as a result. Not all the teachers are like that. For example, you never ask the students for money. I never ask. We are, two, oh, no, three people, you see?"

While leaving his room, Oybek felt relaxed, but it again pained him to ask questions "Why is it so unfair? Isn't it a betrayal for own motherland? If graduates with no knowledge start working in different organizations, this university will have no reputation left in consequence. No, it's impossible to dismiss it. Okil Salimovich was at that time one of the

secretaries of the Uzbekistan NCP[19]. Whatever position Oybek was working, he looked upon him as his own student all the time. That's why he thought to talk about it to this person. When Oybek was about to tie up all of his papers and documents, the secretary looked in:

"The secretary of the NCP is asking you to visit him"

He came into his room, he was relaxed, but his face went pale:

---

[19] National Communist party

"I suppose you think that you are allowed to have unlimited power while working as a party member". He greeted him with shouts and with this rude attitude.

"No, I don't think I have unlimited power, I am sure I have certain duties" Oybek answered in a very relaxed voice.

"I told you that we'll solve this problem together, but how did you dare to inform the administration about that? It is you who informed them, I think you won't deny that."

"No, I don't deny it at all", At this time he remembered a brave hero from one Uzbek novel by Abdulla Kodiriy. In this novel, this hero Anvar was ordered to be murdered by the King Hudoyorkhan only because he had come to save his close friend. This was actually a trap for him. But whom did Oybek intend to rescue? From whom? The teachers

who were being bribed by students for assessment, and who were dismissing their own duties before the government were all his close colleagues at the university.

To whom could he complain about his own colleagues who were poisoning their life with bribe-taking? Actually it was not only Oybek who was fed-up with bribery at the university. The main administration center would always receive anonymous letters about bribery at universities, and about 35 students had even complained about bribe-taking to the government organizations. These 35 students also didn't want to learn from the devils with the award "a teacher". But now he is not talking about the others, if this chief secretary wanted to punish him, he wouldn't settle it by himself.

The chief party secretary:

"What are we supposed to do now, hey man? Tomorrow, the representatives of the city party are going to hold a council meeting tomorrow. Tomorrow you will realize that you are barking up the wrong tree. They are going to require you to prove that some teachers are involved in bribe-taking". He was letting some drops of spit out while shouting at Oybek.

"Do you really need proof? You'll see how well I can prove that. Do you think that both the teachers and students who are involved in bribery will not say a word about this? No, you're wrong. I will prove that to you in quite a different way. I will force the student with satisfying grades to pass the final exam once more, and if they can answer the questions, then I will sue myself in court, and I will sentence myself to imprisonment for relaying incorrect information. However, you must know that these students can't pass this exam. No, they can't. The most terrible thing is that they don't even know the subject well enough to deserve a satisfactory grade". He started talking in a very relaxed way, then he got frustrated:

"Dear teacher, you're a scientist, don't you feel pain when you witness how knowledge and education is in a terrible state?" The NCP secretary who was alert when Oybek just came in sat even deeper in his armchair and held his forehead. After some time of silence, he put his hands into his pockets:

"I wish you could cope with that… I really want you to … There have been rumors and gossips about that for a week or a bit longer, it is said: "Oh, friend. Look, all the students of the extramural learning faculty are going to pass the exams again. If they fail, all the teachers are going to be punished by the party members. The next day, and after a talk with the party secretary there was indeed a council meeting. Oybek got prepared for that all night long, but the council didn't seem to be very serious. They generally talked about everything   and no one was personally blamed for bribery. They just warned all the teachers to be careful and to follow all the rules of higher education.

After several days, there was again a council, but this time in the department. Oybek was appointed as the main teacher in charge of the discipline course "Engines". They wanted to convince him that the problem was to be tackled with just this decision. But Oybek believed in justice, and he would never give up struggling for that. Therefore, he paid special attention to the course work and graduation papers of the students under his supervision. At the end of the term in the extramural learning faculty, it became known that 11 students was assessed at the standard level. When Oybek checked all the records of assessment, he saw that only 85 students could be evaluated, and the rest not. As a rule, none of the students could submit their course paper and graduation work to their scientific advisor without having it signed by Oybek. Therefore, Oybek again felt frustrated seeing the way that they submitted their work without his signature. He thought that the department had created rules and didn't follow them at all. He knew that they were assessed by paying money as a bribe. If there wasn't anything wrong, these documents could have been delivered to him for signature. Oybek couldn't stand that unfairness. He raised this question first at the university, then at the Ministry. The students who got their assessment by bribing the teachers and teachers involved in bribery were all punished according to the norms. In this way they thought that the teachers would be afraid of bribery and breaking the rules. Oybek wanted them to be punished more strictly. But they weren't.

Most people supported them and some of them weren't even punished.

After the council, again there were some disputes, and now Oybek had many teachers who hated him and keep glaring at him. These teachers were quite confident some three or four months ago, but now … He didn't know what to do with them, and how to deal with these enemies. He wanted to go up to Okil Salimov, then changed his mind, because he didn't want to bother him again.

Oydin is still in her sister's home with her baby.

Oybek had recently helped his sister and her husband to buy a car Volga, though second hand, but very good one. Oybek's brother had enough troubles on his own. His wife is very jealous of him, and that's why he didn't defend his dissertation, and lived as an ordinary manager all of his life. Wherever he was working, his wife kept going to his workplace being jealous of him, and had ruined his reputation. Marvar had started writing up dissertation under the supervision of Oybek's teacher, Utkir Ikromov. Now Oybek needed to help him. No one needed Oybek's problems, and nobody would listen to him. He started working hard to be busy enough to forget about the problems at the university. Therefore, he got to see a heap of details and metal pieces. He looked through them and got to know that they were made in a foreign country. They were the details necessary for experimenting with his new engine. He felt glad as if he had come across some brilliant jewelry. At first, he wanted to inform either the head of the department, or the party secretary, but he then grew to understand that the head of the department couldn't decide anything about that. Again, he was forced to come clean to Okil Salimov:

"I don't know what you will think about me now, and if you will think that I am eager to be promoted to a higher position or … But I think that if everybody is afraid of combating this bribery, then the society will never develop, will it?"

Oybek was feeling quite free when he was with Okil Salimov. The more that man is promoted, the more modest he is. He has never artificially praised someone for his own benefits, and whatever he got, he reached it with his own sincerity.

"I wish there had been many more honest and hardworking specialists like you. We need professionals like you in every field, law, industry, medicine and agriculture. I wish there had been more independent people to make right decisions, then we could be living much better." He then changed the topic and said:

"What suggestion do you have n for me now?"

This time Oybek started talking about the details he had found in the store that could be useful to test and experiment the new engines.

It isn't arrogance at all

The baby's hands are swollen because of injections, Oybek felt a keen pain in his own hands:

"What's wrong with her hands? Why do these nurses penetrate the needles into all of her hands? Why aren't they careful?"

"Her vessels turned out to be thinner, and the therefore nurses are finding it hard to inject. That's why they are giving her injects in her feet" Oydin said in a croaky voice, almost about to cry. "These nurses all graduated from the university and got their marks with money. That's why they don't even know how to give an injection". Oybek bowed his head and kissed his baby sleeping on the bed with a high temperature. No matter how much Oydin tried to take care of her in a warm and comfortable flat, the baby, Saodat, a caught cold anyway. She had since been in the hospital for three days. Oybek visited them every day, even when he was going to work, or returning home. He felt like his baby was looking for the arrival of her dad. He sometimes wants to say: "My daughter is a priority to everything in the world, to my work and everything". But the problems at the university had already become a part of his life. After he equipped the laboratory, he became very happy. Now he had a chance to run many research. There were many people wanting to carry out a research and now it would be much easier for them. He didn't want any applaud, but he did expect the other teachers to thank him for that. However, his friend warned him about the upcoming danger:

"Oybek, the teachers involved in bribery have now started attacking you. I wish I could help you. They are saying that you are not working hard, and that you're getting applaud for other people's hard work." It was very hard for him to get permission for this equipment.

"Oybek, it's obvious they will never cease attacking you,"

Omonilla was very upset. Oybek tried to calm him down: "Oh, leave it. Everybody sees that I haven't stolen anything from this faculty, and all of them know how hard I have worked for this department. I haven't been recommended for the State award for what I have done here for this laboratory. They may also work in here with no problem. I am not locking the doors or hiding the keys in my own home.

"Oh, come on, I am calm, but they are …" "Ok, have you read the poem:

Leave them alone, they can never let you alone,

But they can't even be as skilled as we are, on their own."

Oybek just laughed. He didn't even pay any attention to that, as he had bigger problem at the hospital, with drugs for baby. So his opponents complained about Oybek to the university president. Okil Salimov had also heard about that. Besides the problems with the laboratory, Oybek also had something funny with the drugs. He had lessons one after another one day, and he had to go into the drug store again. In the morning, he had written down the list of the drugs for the baby, Saodat. Oybek gave some money and the prescription to one of his students he saw outside the university. He felt that somebody was watching him on the second floor. When he looked at that window he saw the head of the department pointing to Oybek and showing Oybek to the university president. He showed Oybek to him, and he was satisfied that he had proved that Oybek was doing something wrong. But Oybek tried not to pay attention to them. That student whom he gave money didn't have any classes with him, and Oybek had only asked him to help him a little bit. That isn't a crime, is it? The next day the university president called him personally for a conversation face to face:

"Oybek Mukaddirovich, we found out that the list of teachers you named as being involved in bribery aren't the only teachers here involved in this. There's one more I suppose" he said with a very bitter smile. "If you want to give your daughter as a reason, saying that you wanted your student to buy some drugs for you, then you're going to fail to convince us about that"

The university president meant that Oybek was getting money for illegal evaluations in with what he had ironically said.

Oybek:

"Sir, yesterday you and the head of the department saw me handing some money and a prescription to my student, I was not taking any penny from him, was I? Will you deny seeing that? Or do you want to blame me from what you haven't witnessed?" After that the university president became silent, and didn't have anything to say. Oybek stood and left the room.

But these rows didn't end after this talk. The head of the department called him in one day and:

"I heard that you are making it hard for my postgraduate students to earn money?"

"Which of your students, sir?" "Of course, Haybullin"8888

"Is it he who told you about the drugs? That is nonsense. I am not asking him for any money, I have enough money to live on. Even if I am hungry, I wouldn't ask spies for money. You know what I mean, and I am not going to waste my time on arguments with you about nonsense that doesn't have any true facts"

"Now you may go. It is hard for a human being to argue with you. Now you must work friendly. Personally, I don't have anything against you"

He had trouble with the laboratory again, and again there was a council. Poor Okil Salimov, he was extremely bothered because that.

Oybek was confident, and he was a very excited when his teacher Okil Salimov came to the council. Oybek knew that this opponent was not just because of the equipment in laboratory. The teachers wanted to get revenge because Oybek made it hard for them to be bribed.

Okil Salimov listened to everyone, and he didn't object to any of them. When the council ended, he said:

"Let's now go and see what's going on in the laboratory"

All the NCP members followed him there. The laboratory looked very good. All the equipment was in order and properly chosen and installed.

"What other things are there to be done here?" Okil Salimov asked the chief representative next to himself. But that chief gave Oybek a questioning look:

"Just some small problems like connecting the wires and so on."

"How can we help you?"

"Thank you a lot, we can cope with it ourselves"

"Theory is like the sea without any water. Just in case we experiment with our research in the laboratories like this, we can recommend what we invent for industry. You may now go on, and try to think of applying the same type of laboratories for other subjects as well. But I want you to support and encourage each other, and please support and encourage each other."

Oybek had a very good rest that night, and he dreamt that his daughter was swinging on the crescent moon. She was swinging and smiling, swinging and smiling.

I am happy with you

My daughter was very heavy when she was born, I was afraid to make her stand on her feet, because I didn't want her to feel her weight on her big feet. Later, I felt that she was not able to hold her feet on the ground when I was holding her hands to help her. Three, four months passed after that, but my daughter hadn't start crawling. Then it became clear that it was the consequence of the misused injections. Sometimes when I am sitting in my flat, I think that it was a punishment from God to me, because my mother- in-law was upset with me. The point is that before I gave birth, I had left her house complaining that it was cold, and there were many things to do there. Oybek had enough problems   to think about, and therefore I didn't want to distract him from his work by informing him about my daughter's feet. The more time passed, the more worried I was about my baby's health. I think Oybek one day also noticed this:

"Let's take her to Moscow, and there we'll have her examined by some excellent specialists." he said. He probably chose Moscow, because we spent our happiest moments in this city. We went to Moscow with our daughter, and according to Oybek's teacher's recommendations we went to the hospital where a famous doctor, professor Petrova was working. She persuaded us both that our daughter will get well soon:

"It is possible to cure her, but she must accept all the treatments that I will prescribe"

After returning to Tashkent, we started taking her to the hospital for massages. One day I'd take her, another day my mother-in-law or her dad took her, or sometimes our students took her to the hospital.

Before, I used to carry her in my embrace all the time, because she didn't like strange people, and she would cry for any nonsense. But during the treatments, she got used to many people like doctors and to nurses. She started walking before she turned two, so we overcame the main problems we had.

At this time, we bought a flat in the Karakamish district. It was not easy to buy, and even the president of the Tashkent State Pedagogical university, M.T. Urazbayev, helped us solve this problem. At last we had a flat with three bedrooms. In the first year of our life in partnership I thought: "I was wrong to choose such a husband. Oybek is too jealous, and he doesn't understand me". Today, I am both glad and surprised seeing the way he takes care of his daughter. A human being never has enough of what he has or what he earns in his life. Yesterday me and Oybek were dreaming about having our own flat, about living peacefully, and we wanted our daughter to walk hither and tither in that flat. Today our dreams came true. She is filling our flat in, and our souls are full with happiness when she cackles and smiles. Both of us teach at the university, we are favorites, but strict teachers of all the students. Oybek has started his doctoral dissertation, and after we have eaten our meals, he starts leafing through many books. Seeing that he is working very hard, I have again began dreaming:

"there are a few people who have dedicated their life to their work. What if the government gives us a bit wider flat? Then maybe we'll start considering having a second child as well".

If we could live consider living in my mother's flat, we could be close to my mother and we would have much more free time. Oybek would also be able to finish his work much sooner. Sometimes I also dream about having a bigger house, a car and many other things. Sometimes I'm not even able to count them all. I want to talk about them with Oybek, but he doesn't have any free time. The more he lives, the more work and the more problems he's has. He sometimes falls asleep with his head on the table. I switch off the reading lamp and stand watching him for some moments. I want to wake him up so that he can lie on his bed, but he wouldn't. If he wakes up, then he starts working again, so let him sleep for some hours   on the table. These days we often say to each other: "So good that you're with me".

Happiness

One could feel the smell of some flowers. Oybek imagined all the garden trees blooming in Tashkent, because it is spring time, and in spring usually trees like cherry, and almond all start blooming. Time is passing very slowly. Oybek sat on one of the long benches of the hospital garden, and wondered how Oydin was feeling at that moment. They both longed for each other very much, and it was not easy to look after Saodat for both of them.

Oybek takes her to the Black sea every month, and he forgets about everything; work, family, everything. He did the same last summer. Oybek also went to the Black sea, and Harkkov city with her students for practice courses. She went to the shores of the sea to see her daughter and she stayed there for some three or four days. There, Oybek said:

"People say that love is forever, but I don't believe it anymore. Love is not forever, but it can be renewed because of travelings like this. We can make this feeling live longer in this way".

This night they loved each other with sugar and honey. Two souls and two minds became one,

just like two rivers, two stars and two glows.

They became one only in their very happy days This night is the endless night without any dawns, Morning and night became one in this,

Two souls became one this night, Even the sky is in the dark about that,

This night two bright starts became one.

Today at the hospital in Moscow, Oydin is giving birth to her second child. When they consulted one of the doctors in Tashkent, she had said:

"Your wife is very weak, so when she is about to give birth, it would be better if you take her to a hospital in Moscow". This time Oybek was very worried about his wife for some unknown reasons. Therefore, they finally went to Moscow. Oybek called his wife for two days in Moscow. He sent different presents to her when his students were going on business to that city. It's been a month since his wife is being treated at hospital in Moscow to preserve her pregnancy. In the middle of April she was about to give birth, and that's why Oybek requested a holiday from his workplace and went to Moscow to be with his wife. Oydin is feeling ok, and the doctors aren't worried about anything. But anyway Oybek is concerned since the dawn breaks.

He remembered his mother saying: "It isn't so simple to give birth to a child, my son. The birth of a baby is divine, so pray to God for them to be safe and sound"

He prayed: "Oh, my god, you know me and my wife have always obeyed you, and followed all whatever you want us to do. I wish you'd give her energy and that you'll help her with everything".

He is sitting on the seat, hardly patient with time passing so slowly. The lights of the hospital were glittering on the twigs of the trees, and on the flower's leaves. The nurses in white robes were walking to the right and to the left of the corridors. Oybek was watching them sitting on the bench in the garden and he could see them staring at the windows upstairs. He stared for so a long that his neck hurt. It's been a long time since they informed him that she started having birth pangs, but they still haven't told him what happened. Oybek was not the only person waiting to hear something from the doctors. All their friends, relatives in Tashkent, Max Samoylovich, the Nikitins and, the Dobrogayevs are also waiting for the news.

It is maybe the tenth or the fifteenth time Oybek is knocking on the door, and the nurses open it, smile, and immediately close it, asking him to wait. But this time the nurse smiled quite differently:

"You've got a daughter, two kilos, three hundred grams, and very healthy."

Oybek groped in his pocket and got whatever he found there. He put this money into her pocket. The nurse who was used to getting chocolates and presents as a sign of thanking, was very astonished, but she took what he gave with pleasure and smiled again. Oybek:

"What shall I bring for her? Can she eat something?" The nurse was in a bit of an awkward situation:

"No, your wife has been operated on, so she can't eat anything today"

Oybek's heart leapt out of his mouth:

"What? Why did they operate on her? Why's that?"

"The baby was not in the proper position before birth, and she spent a lot of energy giving birth. That's why the doctors were forced to operate on her. I am very sorry, but you don't need to be worried. That's something natural nowadays. Most women from Uzbekistan have to be operated on to give birth."

Oybek felt very sad about that. He was wondering why women from Uzbekistan are mostly operated on to give birth. Is the land infertile, is water less pure? What's the problem? He once had read in some newspapers that in the state where there are more and more unhealthy women, weak babies being born is the symptom of losing independence. If the state is independent, all the children and mothers are going to be healthy, even if the state isn't very rich. In an independent state, the citizens will have independent spirits.

Oybek's thoughts were invaded by these questions and thoughts about his wife and his baby.

He worry wasn't in vain. The next day Oydin started having a nonstop high temperature, and whenever he went in to see her, she was trembling from that high temperature. The doctors said that she had a cold in her kidneys, and it's not easy to cure this organ. Oybek knew it well. Oydin was not allowed to feed her baby with breast milk, because the baby may catch a virus when the mother has such a high temperature. Oybek was wandering in the Moscow streets. He heard once that all the love for the motherland, and the people close, will move into the baby's heart through the mother's breast milk.

Oybek wanted his wife to go to Tashkent with him, but he knew she couldn't because his wife was seriously sick, and obviously she couldn't go.

Everyday Oybek talked to the head of the hospital department where Oydin was being cured:

"Oybek Mukaddiirovich, I have told you many times, I don't see any other way than staying here. If she leaves with this temperature, this will exhaust her. We need to do something to help her, and we have all the medications. It has only been tested on monkeys, so we can try to give it to your wife".

"Don't you think it's harmful?" "It may influence her hearing"

"Is she going to be deaf? She is a candidate of sciences, and she teaches at the university" He asked in a rush.

"I cannot say anything in advance. We can only take a chance. I don't see any other way, I am sorry"

Oybek also felt that there was no way. He needed to brood over three people now; his wife, daughter Saodat, and new a baby daughter Shahrizoda. Oybek decided to take a risk, and allowed him to apply the drug which had only been tested on monkeys. Oybek felt that his wife was drinking that drug at that moment, and he asked God to help them over and over again. He repeated prayed to God.

A Big Challenge

There are different people, and some have an easier way of life, while others lives are more difficult.

But as for Oybek, after he overcame one challenge, the next one was blocking his way. This time, his wife got much better after the intake of that completely new drug, she is as right as rain, and together they returned to Tashkent. Oydin's sister was living with them to support Oybek, and the baby was growing with artificial milk which had to be taken for her to grow better. After he solved all of his family problems, he again started working on his doctoral research. Prior to the dissertations, he had to write textbooks in Uzbek, or translate textbooks into Uzbek for students of the Tashkent Automobile Roads university which has recently been established.

At first, he decided to make use of the books available in their own libraries. After they had their daughter cured in Moscow, they again went to that city to visit Max Samoylovich:

"Max Samoylovich, don't you think that I always keep complaining to you?"

"Why do you think like that? Don't you know that I don't like the students who keep being silent all the time by hiding their views from the teachers, or being lazy? If a man demands something, it means he is thinking. What news is there from Tashkent?"

Hovach put his hand on Oybek's shoulder of Oybek. Oybek had never felt his father's hand on his shoulder, but he felt that Hovach, Dobrogayev, and Okil Salimov had become shoulders for him to cry on. In the east scientists think that there are intuition nerve cells on the fingers of a human, and the way that friends put their hand on your shoulder means that you have support. By the way even Abdusalom Abdug'aniyevich Mutalibov was also one of his teachers, and he used to teach them "Automobiles repair". They had been very close friends since Oybek started studying his postgraduate courses in MARU. Mutalibov trusted Oybek due to his reliability, honesty and confidence. He both taught at the university and was a director of the TashAutoMach" factory.

Now Oybek was feeling that not only Hovach, but all of his teachers were putting their hand on his shoulder to support him. He felt their power and energy entering his body through those hands.

"I have already finished my translation, but the publishing house is very slow in making their decision"

"What do they want again? Why on earth are they moving so slow again?"

"They haven't said anything important, and are making me wait for the publication by asking for some sorts of annotations, recommendations and different book reviews. I've had to wait a long time for my turn to see the directors, and when I talk to them, the problem still haven't been solved." Oybek didn't only want to translate books, he also wanted to write his own textbooks. He proved that he could do it when he was only a postgraduate student. He knew that the notes of the lectures he collected for himself were used by his own friends for training, and also by some professors and the university president Lukanin for his lectures. This meant he could undoubtedly write many books for the students.

"I see that people of Uzbekistan are the best people in the world, you welcome each person who knocks on your door, and treat him to all the things to eat. Some of you block each other's way, and don't even let each other make a step further. How is it possible to combine the feeling of envy, hospitality and sincerity in the same soul? That makes me hesitate all the time". It hurt Oybek to hear that about his own landmates.

"But, Max Samoylovich, we haven't lived in our motherland alone. Many countries invaded and captured different parts of our country in the past. That's why the genetics of the nations of invaders and our own nation are combined." Oybek didn't continue, and stopped there. He didn't want him to feel upset with him after that.

"Do not brood over publishing your translations. I'm going to call Okil Salimov and help solve this problem. You must now think about writing textbooks in Uzbek. Every country should have textbooks in their own native language and in many different areas."

Hovach didn't wait for Oybek to answer and he immediately dialed Okil Salimov's phone number. Oybek felt that it could be easily solved, but he had a question that was making him suffer: "Why isn't it impossible to solve these problems on my own?"

Feelings

Mummy, why did it happen? Why did I think that you would live forever? Why did I spend my life on things much less important that your life, mum? Why is that?

The university administration appointed me as the chief for the students going to another city to pick cotton. I would be in charge of that not only one year, but every year in autumn. The administrators would always convince me:

"You can very well get along with students, cotton is a very important political issue, and we can't trust this to anyone else but you", I thought that it was my duty, and therefore I left.

But nobody warned me that this autumn was my mother's last autumn …

They asked me to hold councils as a NCP secretary, writing up reports and preparing documents. I worked very hard on that, because I thought that it was my duty. But nobody warned me that my mother was going to breathe her last breath after this autumn, nobody did.

They asked me to visit the Oltoy engine factory, to make beneficial contracts, to create newer theories, and to make discounts on the necessary details. Ok, I contributed to enriching the budget of the university by doing whatever they asked me to do, but nobody warned me that my mother was going to close her eyes forever... My mother who brought me up alone, in so much torture and pain ...

I wanted to get a flat in the city centre, and I asked many authority members to help me with that. I even offered my own flat with three bedrooms to one of the rich representatives Ibrohimov, which I had repaired, and he promised me to exchange that with a four bedroom flat. But then it became clear that he had sold the flat allocated to me and had spent the money for his own interests. I didn't know that at those moments, my mother was suffering a lot for me. I started living in my mother-in-law's two bedroom flat after that. I spent so much energy, and so many days on these troubles, that I only wanted my children to grow up in a bigger flat in the city centre, and to go to better nursery schools. I thought about my children and my wife trying to buy a flat in the city centre, but I didn't think about you mummy, at that time...

Am I a bad son for you, mummy? I have always tried to support my brothers, my sister, and my mum. But what I have done for you can never be equal to the love you feel for me, mummy. When I heard that you started feeling bad, life seemed to have finished for me, mummy. I looked for the best doctors, for the best drugs, but there turned out to be no drugs for death. Now, I let you rest in the grave on such a hot day in summer, mum, as hot as your love for me. I was orphaned in my childhood, but I didn't feel that at all. Now this feeling of being an orphan surrounds me, and this feeling reminds me of the poem by Abdulla Oripov:

So many nights I cannot sleep at all

I am not in my self, not in my own self

My mother appears in my dreams each night,

But I wake up, I am so alone, I'm just with my soul

My mother used to tell me: "I remember that my great grandfather took one strand of my hair and went to Mecca for the Hadj. She buried my hair there in that city". That means that my mother has actually also been to Hajj. She is like alive with us together, and she'll always be watching us from the sky above. I have made sure of that many times.

From the candidate of sciences to the doctor of sciences the hall of the council only had about 200 seats. There were scientists of the nine special departments there. They were sitting far from each other, which made us infer that they were unfriendly to each other. Oybek had waited for this day for them to gather here for over nine months. He was there to put his doctoral dissertation into debate. In 1975 he was enrolled in the doctoral degree course at the Moscow Auto mechanics university, "Automobiles and tractor engines" department on the basis of extramural courses. Rostislav Pavlovich Dobrogayev took charge of being a scientific advisor for him. Most of the scientists there were in a very bad mood, as if they aren't there to discuss his dissertation. Oybek of course felt their mood, as he had started writing research on a field that not every scientist would dare to learn. It had made some of the specialists envious of him. As soon as he started his doctoral dissertation he felt the pains of this envy many times, and he had even heard how those people say:

"We don't know who he is relying on to defend his doctoral dissertation. He thinks that he can do it and, it's quite weird"

One of those envious people started talking in that council, Oybek immediately took a glance at Utkir. He thought that the teachers for him would be the first to speak, not the enemies. Utkir Ikramov nodded, as if he meant to say: "Don't pay attention!". That man who started first spoke:

"I don't know why, but our friend Kodirov has chosen a very complicated topic for his doctoral dissertation. Of course, he wanted to show us that he is strong enough for that. We know he has spent a lot of energy, time and money on this. But we don't know if the result of the research deserves the money and the time spent." It was the man who for the first days dismissed Oybek as being arrogant and he also boasted that he was a docent. Oybek obviously got frustrated about what he said. A scientist like him was only discussing the dissertations extra issues, not the object of it because he doesn't have enough knowledge to discuss the object.

At last Utkir Ikramov started:

"Dear friends, Oybek Mukaddirovich has never been required to make special convenience for his doctoral dissertation, never. He has completely conducted 760 hours of his lessons effectively at the university, and he has even ruled the party of the faculty. As for the funding, as you know, this man, Oybek Mukaddirovich is the first specialist to have signed a successful profit based contract. He hasn't spent a penny from the university fund for this dissertation. If he is to spend anything, it will be later, and will come from his own share of the profits from the contract efficiency. As for the efficiency of the dissertation, it's quite necessary for us to increase efficiency of the engines of the automobiles and agricultural car engines. The problem of the whole state has been solved in his dissertation, and as you know our country is agricultural. We don't want our wives and children to bow down forever in the fields, so let the cars do what they find it hard to do. It's our duty as a citizen and as a scientist to create efficient agricultural cars and to develop those available. Friends, let all of us be friendly, so if you can't help your friend to work, please do not try to block his way. Let us all be fair at least once. I know it wasn't easy for this scientist to have a contract signed with the Oltoi engine factory. You don't know how hard it was, but I know that. Ok, they offered to run research in this area, but it isn't easy to prove scientifically why the diesel fuel transmitting pumps break faster, and to make changes in its instructions. There has been positive change in the quality of engine production in this factory as a result of the research carried out by Kodirov. This scientist wants to defend his doctoral dissertation. I am not going to claim that this dissertation is complete enough. There are special features to be edited, changed, so now it depends on all of us here, friends. Our task is to find out about them and ask him to think about that. Oybek will never avoid working, and he will take into account any of your comments as long as they are going to be proper". All the scientists were listening to him attentively, and all the scientists for Oybek knew that this silence was temporary, and that this was the first step of a struggle for justice.

Thoughts

Oybek, be a bit more patient. You are now you are in the field of a struggle. Do not dare to give up if you don't want others to laugh saying that a scientist from Uzbekistan couldn't stand researching in the technical field. I made myself go further with these thoughts. I at last got the recommendation to defend my doctoral dissertation. Two people supported my dissertation, but the rest were neither opposing, nor supporting. They weren't strong enough to oppose, but they couldn't even block my way secretly; it was too early.

I showed the dissertation to the chief of the MARU scientific council, V.N. Lukanin. Three heads of the department debated over it together. They recommended I make some changes relating to two areas of science. I worked   seven more months. I had it discussed after that again and seeing my efforts, the people opposing me ironically said:

"Oybek, how come you can stand this research until the end. I heard about many scientists who died of a heart-attack because of their doctoral dissertation before they could even finish the research. We don't want this to happen to you. We need you as you are, Oybek!"

Sometimes seeing that my eyes were sore from exhaustion, my wife complained about my job, and the hectic times. I would tell her:

"Oydin, my darling, it doesn't only depend on me, honey! You know how others treat us, so it is nonsense that scientists of Uzbekistan do not cope with technics. This isn't just doctoral dissertation for me, this is my whole life. This is the pride of all my motherland."

The second discussion in Moscow was very serious and lively. Nikitin's positive views made me feel much more confident, and the members of the scientific seminar put two proposals forward: first, to offer the dissertation for the scientific council, and the second to look through it once more for the last further debate. I chose the last option.

I was telling myself: "You must work more, Oybek, not just for yourself, but for the ancestors who had died in the massacre. It seemed to me like all the women and girls working in the cotton fields, and carrying heavy sacks of cotton were telling me: "Work much harder, Oybek, work to rescue us all!".

Victory and happiness

Oybek was used to looking at the people who love him, his mother, his sister, his wife, daughters, his teachers and   friends

… But lately he came across many people who didn't like him at all. At that moment, one of them was staring at him: "You have lied to us, man". It hurt him to hear that he was calling him a man, because now he was a scientist in favour of all the scholars of engines. He had twice controlled the Soviet Union scientific council, he had never lied to anyone, and he hated those who lied.

"So, what did I say wrong?" Oybek said, arresting the feeling of anger in his heart.

"We heard that your dissertation was negatively assessed in Moscow, but you said that the result was positive".

"It's you who is telling a lie now!" Oybek interrupted him no matter how high his position. He couldn't stand this man anymore, so he immediately stood up and tried to walk away.

"Oh, don't get so nervous, and please try to be calm. Do you need proof of that? I know that you require proof for any nonsense. Here is the proof". He threw one piece of paper to him. Oybek looked through that paper with shortened breath. It had indeed been written that negative opinions about his dissertation were stated. Even though it was signed by the rector, it wasn't officially numbered. Oybek knew how these signs could be copied. Without an official number, it meant that it was falsified.

"I will prove to you that this letter is not the real one, I will go to Moscow for that."

The chief suddenly seemed to be sounding less confident now:

"Oybek Mukaddirovich, you know that soon the political company "cotton" is going to start, and you're responsible for that. We don't want you to bother yourself to go to Moscow to proving these things." Oybek was surprised, what nonsense it is! Why does a man tend to change so quickly?

He was only scolding him by showing the letter from Moscow, and he was trying to convince him not to go there. Is Oybek guilty to punished so much? What's the reason? Is it because of his talent, or because of Okil Salimov's supervision? It isn't his teacher who is writing his dissertation. He is asking these questions, but there is nobody to answer them.

He wanted to ask this man these questions, but he held back because this sort of person wouldn't be a bit influenced by these questions.

Thoughts

Now I could not step backwards. I decided to show my dissertation to other scientists besides those in Moscow. I wanted them to read and give their own opinions, it was my own hard work, I didn't copy a word from other books or theories. First, I went to the Kiyev agricultural science university where they recommended me to address scientists at Leningrad agricultural sciences university. Everything is proved and has evidence in my research. There turned up to be a special council suitable for my dissertation topic at that university. Yes, there is justice in this world. I wasn't forcing my students to write up my dissertation at all, and I was not copying from books to write any of the chapters in this research. Every word written in it is the result of my won hard work and patience. This is the most valuable for me.

Many famous professors, specialist, the council chief and his assistant, and except the council secretary all read my dissertation abstract. They all gave similar opinions. They were all positive, but each of them recommended I make some small changes. After I returned to Tashkent, I again started working at this. Most people think that a man can get fed-up if he is continuously involved in the same thing. However, I am never fed-up and never tired. Everytime I edited the dissertation, I got even more inspired and would be very pleased with each achievement I had in this process.

Defense

The representatives of the main scientific council were professor A.N. Nikolaenko, the assistant of the chief, professor S.A. Iofinov, professor Kreps Iosifovich (Oybek had lived in hi house when he had to stay in Leningrad, he had helped him a lot), academician Kriajkov, Professor Burkov, opponents O.V.Lebedev, professors Nikolai Nikolayevich Ivanchenko, professor Boris Alexeivich Ulitovskiy. The guests from Tashkent were Oydin, brother Marvar, scientist Mirzamurod, his Ph. student Shukhrat and his "friend" B.Normuhammedov.

Oybek only slept for two hours a night, and he was still energetic and alert. There were 101 wallpapers with schemes and drawings on the board, with 20 more extra ones. The presentation of the dissertation contained 80 pages.

Most importantly it was a decisive day for Oybek's doctoral dissertation. Before Oybek started speaking he didn't look at anyone, because he didn't want to see any facial expressions. He looked at Oydin, his own wife, whom he adored. She was even more excited than Oybek, even. However, she didn't let him notice that, and instead she gave a beautiful smile. Marvar, his brother was the only one his mother and father had left as a shoulder to cry on for Oybek, Oybek had strange feelings when he looked at him. Oybek saw his father's eyes in Marvar's, and although he didn't remember his father, he seemed to urge him to remain confident, be brave, and wished him good luck.

"Dear teachers, dear colleagues!" His own voice seemed to sound from afar to him. He looked at his brother, he felt even more confident, he got the energy from his eyes and went on...

The defense lasted for five hours and twenty-five minutes. Oybek read his review, lectured for twenty-five minutes and answered questions for five hours. Professor Mishin asked him 21 questions in total:

"Yes, Oybek Mukaddirovich is answering all of my questions, and I don't want you all to think that I am here to make it hard for this person from Central Asia. No, I am not actually. I see a bit of an error in one part of the dissertation. The doctoral dissertation needs to contain the invention due to being recommended directly for manufacturing, and therefore this can't be repeatedly discussed or examined."

He wondered if Mishin wanted his dissertation to be forwarded for one more discussion, and he didn't understand. Oybek knew that he was obligated to be ready for everything, and he answered all of his questions with respect. He clarified the formula which seemed to be unclear to him, and he could prove that he was a bit wrong. Oybek thought that Mishin would vote against his dissertation, but he was the first to make a speech:

"This dissertation has been written up with a lot of energy and very hard work. This hard work is impossible to go in vain, and it will certainly serve effectively the society in your country. My sincere congratulations!" Mishin said firmly holding and shaking his hand. This old professor whose hair had already grown grey, looked just like the wise people described in the poems by Alisher Navaiy. He slowly walked out of the defense room:

"Comrade professor, what about voting?"

Frankly, I have just voted. When shall we get rid of these formalities? There you go!"

All the people there were tumultuously applauding. Oybek stood there leaning his hands against the desk. Oydin's face was as red as red roses, and longing to come up to him among the crowd of people. The defense finished with 100 votes for the dissertation. It was successful.

After the defense, Oybek found out that there was no ticket left for the train or for the plane. He and his friends, and brother, left the hotel and were now wandering, without knowing what to do. Mirzamurod suggested giving the conductor money to solve the problem of not having a ticket for the train. Shukhrat was young, and he hesitated.

Mirzamurod: "Eh, never mind, we can go by train without a ticket. It's possible, band we have no other way except that. We aren't birds who have wings to fly, are we?"

"Don't think that I can be involved in this. If you think that I can break rules, I can't. I am like a rabbit" for this problem". Oybek said feeling frightened.

"Oh, is it you saying that? Isn't it you who coped with defending his doctoral dissertation in Leningrad? Is a doctor of technical sciences afraid of a conductor on a train? Come on!" Mirzamurod joked.

"Do not conclude so early. It's enough to say MR SCC for now"

"The SCC can't do anything. All of your documents are ready".

Oybek knew that lately getting a doctoral degree in the SCC[20] required having some money to pay them illegally. He didn't want to say this to Mirzamurod.

---

[20] Supreme Attestation Committee, this is the organization in charge of assessing the candidates applying for different scientific awards and researches

Oybek was resting in the train and lying with his face to the wall. On hearing the conductor saying: "Do you have a ticket?" Oybek's heart leapt out of his mouth. Oh, no he was asking Mirzamurod, not him. His friend was trying to explain something to him. Oybek was afraid that the conductor would require him to pay a fine or to get off the train. They would both be wrong to do that to Oybek.

Now they are going to Moscow from Leningrad, without a ticket, but fortunately the conductor had already left.

"Mirzo, your purse is running out of pennies each time the conductor is passing I suppose."

"Yes, we've had a very good party. I see that the director of the Oltoi factory is a very wonderful person. He has come from Uzbekistan to Leningrad after you invited him only once. By the way, what about one of your friends who was in quite a bad mood, just like a dog having its bone stolen?"

"He was here to see and to celebrate my failure. My "very real" friends had asked him to come here, but their dreams didn't come true, and therefore none of them wanted to stay for the party. They just assessed and left."

"Yes, don't worry, sir, the rest is also going to be ok. It depends on God of course". Mirzamurod then gave him a very serious look and said worriedly:

"Look sir. Be careful. The conductor's coming, so pretend to be sleeping, be quick!"

Oybek immediately reclined and closed his eyes in a rush. Suddenly Mirzamurod's cackles shook the windows next to them. Oybek turned to look at him:

"What's wrong, friend?"

"Oh, you may now get up. It isn't the conductor. It's a beggar dressed in a soldier's scruffy uniform."

Both of them burst out laughing non-stop after that.

The very players, but the newer games

Spring in Tashkent. The sky emptied from the winter clouds looks much wider, much higher. The Swallows are flying all around, and singing their songs. The smells of the flowers are everywhere. Oybek is worried, because he's just been told to visit the rector. Usually he has heard something wrong each time he is called. It has been three years since he defended the doctoral dissertation in Leningrad, and the SAC still hasn't confirmed it. It really deserves confirming, and if it doesn't Oybek will be trying to make corrections. He knows the value of his own hard work. The university president Mutalibov doesn't wish him any harm, and he has done many good things for the TARU since he became the university president. He has worked a lot to include this university in the list of the most famous universities of the continent. He values people eager to get knowledge.

However, lately, and in the last three years, Oybek lost trust in many people as all of them are playing different games with his destiny and with his career. Now it is the time when there is a new so called massacre: "All the things wrong with Uzbeks". Oybek's favourite teacher has also become the victim of this massacre without any fault, though he was completely innocent. Fortunately, he heard that it isn't the new rector who called him, but the former. The first rector, at the moment the head of the department is the one who asked him to visit him:

"Oybek, my son, you can now be happy! The SAC gave you the award "doctor of technical sciences!"

Oybek was looking forward to hearing that, but he didn't expect to hear it like that. The news sounded wonderful:

"Teacher, I don't believe it, is it … what…"

"Yes, they wouldn't have it any other way. You have won, my son. You have, my son!"

Oybek was pushing forty-seven at that time. He was too old to be a son to him, but he found a way to accept the congratulations and the apology.

The rector was apologizing because he couldn't help him with the many injustices Oybek had suffered earlier.

"Oybek, I have some things to tell you. Take a seat!" "Maybe, you don't need to … the past is the past…"

"No, I must say this to you. You must learn how to distinguish the bad and good people around. You don't know that some people had started looking for ways to oppose you even before you defended your doctoral dissertation. You used to leave the first and second drafts of your dissertation in the department, didn't you? Your "very real friend" took advantage of these drafts by posting them and anonymous letters as a complaint to the SAC administration. It's where your dissertation was examined again. But the real copy, examined and edited version of your dissertation is still kept in the Leningrad. When the anonymous letter was forwarded to Leningrad, certain representatives examined everything. They even organized a special council with professors.

"Yes, I know about it. I was also invited and they made me write a letter of explanation" "There are plenty of things you don't know. You were confident because of your speech which lasted for forty-five minutes and the council's positive assessment. One in a thousand researches are usually rejected by the SAC. You have always believed that it's not going to be your dissertation among those failed, but your very real friends have worked much harder to make you fail. Oybek, their friends were every visited the SAC with expensive presents and gifts everyday. Do you know why? They wanted to urge them to oppose an Uzbek scientist, and they wanted to block his way to success. They didn't want you to receive a higher degree than theirs.

"Don't worry, teacher, everything is now in the past"

"I wish it were. Can you please listen to me a bit more? Do you know professor Pokrovskiy? He is as dishonest as your "very real" friends. They asked him to help them and they even requested that the SAC allow the dissertation to be examined by the energy specialists."

Oybek remembered the expert's council in which Pokrovskiy took part. He was an hour late for that council and he said: "We have come to the conclusion that your dissertation should be negatively assessed". Mutalibov went on again:

"Pokrovskiy didn't have any rights to say that on behalf of the whole council, but what he said there in secret played an important role. Your "very real friend" has not completed a dissertation in many years, and he has always been busy with blocking your way. They forwarded your dissertation to Cheliabinsk, and required additional an conclusion because thanks to Pokrovskiy you talked to the assistant chief of the OAK, Ermakov. He asked you to talk to Shapovalov, the head of the department. He had taken part in the experts council concerning your dissertation in September. When you asked him, what was wrong, he told you about everything. There you got to know that

Pokrovskiy had come to a conclusion on behalf of the whole council. The rest of this energetics council members had recently been elected, and therefore they weren't strong enough to oppose Pokrovskiy. You again visited Ermakov, together with Shapovalov and explained what had happened. They asked you to leave, promising to solve the problem by themselves. After defending your dissertation, you went to Cheliabinsk, where you wanted to offer it for debate, but you were informed that it had been given to Vinogradov. You even went to see him at that time. You didn't say anything wrong to your "very real friend", and didn't even try to get revenge. You only proved that you were right.

Oybek was surprised that Mutalibov knew so many details. This meant that not only his enemies, but his friends were also watching him. Although they couldn't help, it was enough for Oybek that they didn't oppose him. Mutalibov wanted to come clean to him about everything. These days in Tashkent, besides Bukhara and Kharezm, everybody was being arrested everywhere. Paratroopers like Gdlian and Ivanov were walking everywhere looking for a reason to arrest people.

Yes, before that Oybek had had a very long discussion with the honored professor of the Russian Soviet of the Federation of Soviet Republic Vinogradov. The longer they debated, the more he stared loving and respecting this professor. At the end of their talk, this professor said: "I will defend you not only   to the Special expert council or the SAC, I will also defend you in the great beyond". He thought about that and he felt that all his pain over the years had begun to ease:

"Dear teacher, I have never suspected anything about you, never. I have always known you as a teacher for myself. It isn't in vain that I heard this news from you. If God wanted you to hear this first, then he wanted you to make happy even before"

Mutalibov passed round the table and hugged Oybek, hugged him by his shoulder:

"Now you may go and tell it to your wife, make them happy with this news. She has also defended her doctoral dissertation, so tell her that I want to congratulate her as well. Yes, by the way, I know that you're writing letters and collecting signatures wanting to defend Okil Salimov from the massacre. It shows that you're a real honest person that you're doing your best to defend your teacher, but you'd better not play with the fire. This is a massacre which doesn't count any of the good deeds you have done. Do not let the massacre dragon swallow you by helping others. I am not telling you to just be silent and hide, but be careful!" Oybek didn't say anything in response, and just shook his hand and said goodbye.

Thoughts

The happiest moments are the quickest to pass. Yes, I was the happiest when I was a student, a postgraduate student, and when I had short time dates with Oydin. But what about the challenging times in our life? Especially within these three years starting from the day I defended my doctoral dissertation in Leningrad until March of 1987. My heart seemed to be faced with many heart- attacks because of my envious "very real friends". The people who didn't know that I grew up being an orphan, and those who don't have the same religion, belief, or nationality as I do, did their best to help me as well as my true friends did in my own motherland. My friends, and my teachers supported me all the time. My wife was also always with me. My teachers who couldn't help me in difficult situations, and who valued my talent, didn't try to block my way. But one enemy did many things to make me suffer and forced me to wander in Moscow, Leningrad, Cheliabinsk and Tashkent. I was questioned by the expert council members for many hours, and although I have never been in awkward situations owing to these meetings. I remembered the situation of the main hero in the novel "The Days Gone by" by Abdulla Kodiriy who wandered between two cities far from each other, Tashkent and Margilan. Maybe it is ok that a human's life is full of problems and troubles. I remember the poem by a famous poet Togay Murod: "May my enemies be safe and sound!". Maybe I would not have succeeded and tried so much, if my enemies hadn't tried to oppose me. I could not have defended my dissertation more than once within the three years. Oh, my God, everything depends on you, God… If you have created me for testing, and for tortures, then I am only grateful to you. What could I do if I had been born being envious and opposing other people like my "very real friends". Those very real friends didn't even congratulate me when my doctoral dissertation was confirmed by the OAK. If they congratulated me, I would have forgiven them already, but today it hurts me a lot to know that these people did many things to cause me to suffer, and to have pains in the heart.

The Star of Science

Oybek saw a very old woman sitting on a bench in the university garden. He remembered his own mother, as she used to be very good-looking. She knew her own value. She never wore un-ironed clothes. All the mothers in the world have something in common. He was now wondering who this mother was looking for, maybe her son is a student here, maybe grandson. Yes, maybe her son hasn't visited his home for many days, months, or hasn't written a letter. As soon as Oybek went into the department and took his seat, the secretary told him that an old woman wanted to see him. It seemed very strange to know that this woman came to see him:

"Let her come in, please"

This is the department of "Automobiles production and repair", which would always be criticized for its low levels of achievements and low quality of education. It's been three years since Oybek has ruled this department, and they asked him to raise the reputation of the department because he'd had ample experience having worked as the NCP secretary, and a cotton-picking leader. He agreed. A man should not stop in the same position, and now he is a doctor of sciences, and he is working now very hard.

"Come in, mother" he said and he made her sit in the chair. She asked God to bless him for a long time and said: "Kodirov my son, I thought that you looked as strong as the

chief of our village, Ali, but you look as young as our brothers"

The secretary brought in tea, and he poured a cup and handed to her:

"Thanks, my son. I am Shukrullo's grandmother. He is our youngest grandson. He always says many good things about you."

He couldn't remember which Shukrullo it was.

After Oybek became the head of the department he made many positive changes there. He organized the department subsidiary in the Auto repair factory 1, a campaign for academic-scientific study and manufacturing affairs section called "Auto repair specialist".

All the graduation works are written up on the basis of the reservations and requests of the factory. The students learned how to repair engines in practice.

"We come from Rishton district, Shukrullo has been working with you. He rarely asked us to give him money to spend every day. This year he graduated but we heard that there isn't a job for him, and now he has nothing to do and only wastes his time. I told him to visit you, but he said that he didn't want to. You taught him, and now he doesn't want you to bother your by looking for a job for him. I actually came here for a party on a birth of a baby, it's in the Zangiata district, nearby. I came here asking people how to get there. So, as you see, I am now here. I really beg you to help him because I don't think that some woman will agree to marry him because he isn't earning any money, and isn't working anywhere."

Oybek now remembered him. Shukrullo was someone who always walked round Oybek asking him questions, trying to help him around.

"Ok, don't worry too much about your grandson. Now the secretary is going to write down your full address, and we will surely help you. The university spent money on your child for five years. We'll find a job for him soon. She again started praying for him and she gave her address to the secretary. The old woman walked back to his desk again and she put something wrapped in paper on the it:

"Kodirov, my son, here's some dried fruits, and apricots. I mean from our own garden. Do not think that I have brought you less fresh apricots dried in the sun. No, this is a mirsanjar type of an apricot. It has some gold inside. Yes, it's going to give energy to your heart."

He hesitated about that woman. She looked like a telepath who noticed that Oybek often has a keen pain in his heart. He immediately shifted his thoughts to his own life. He decided to think about jobs before his children started studying. If a man with high education is unemployed, it causes the country to have economical problems. This must be in the centre of attention all the time. His phone rang suddenly, and it was Golibjon, the dean:

"Mr. Oybek, now you must make a party for us"

"What's wrong?"

"An award has seemingly been given to us."

This day had been a very different day…. that telepathic woman with golden apricots, and the award …

Two years ago many scientists at the university had been recommended for different awards. The dean Golibjon said:

"Mr. Oybek, you've become a doctor, we'll recommend all of your documents and the books you wrote for this award."

Oybek hesitated thinking maybe his books didn't deserve being awarded, and then he stopped being modest and gave all of his required documents for that competition. His colleague professor Murashov was also recommended for the same award and more than once he said:

"Oybek Mukaddirovich, I have heard that it's impossible to get this award without some expenses, I mean. I think you understand me well. So, we must find someone who can …"

"Sorry, but I don't want to get an award that is illegally paid for. No, If I deserve it let them give it to me, if not, then I don't even want it."

"Oh, God you never want to adapt to these things, Oybek Mukaddirovich. Ok, since you don't agree, then don't be upset if any… errr, ok?"

Today the award that Murashov had paid for had been automatically given to Oybek. That is actual justice actually.

"Golibjon, please, let's not declare it to all the people.

There's not a special order yet."

"Let's declare it. It's once in a lifetime. Now I feel how nice it sounds to hear: "Oybek Kodirov, honored scientist of Uzbekistan"

Oybek remembered how the old woman prayed for him in the morning.

***

"Teacher, you must not have taken your own turn to get the Volga. It was actually your turn, and the person you helped doesn't deserve it. He's rich enough. The old car you have now is not suitable for you. We've been repairing it for a month. Don't you see it?"

Oybek smiled when his talkative student was saying these things, but Oybek knew he was right. For example, Murashovv, got the Jiguli according to his turn after he became awarded. The scientists having the award "Honored scientist of Uzbekistan" could be without any turn to get a car.

He said: "No, let my teacher be the first to get it," He wasn't going to get a car before his teacher did. The teacher drove the car, but until Oybek got it according to his turn, the car became four times as expensive. The honored scientist of Uzbekistan owed money because he bought a car. That wasn't suit at all. His scientific researches were bringing millions of profits, and if his foreign partners knew that he couldn't afford to buy a car, then it would sound funny to them. During this time, his old car, the Jiguly was stolen.

The thieves thought that a scientist was rich enough to buy a new one.

Now the students are dying to have a car which isn't even worthy exploitation. What's wrong if the car he drives has a scratched or broken window. It's not important whether there's a dirty spot on the car, and it's much better to have a dirty spot on a car rather than having that in the heart.

Struggles

Oybek stood hesitating for some time. He wanted to inform Mr. Erkin about his award, but then he was afraid that he would think that Oybek was always hungry for awards. At last he decided to tell him about it:

"Mr. Erkin, I hope you won't be offended, but I recently received the award "Honored scientist of Uzbekistan" and today I am going to apply to being an academician." Oybek had known this man Erkin since he was a postgraduate in Moscow. Erkin was now the chief doctor in hospital number one.

"Why would you think that Oybek? It isn't the first time I have seen you. every person must know his own value, and the value of his hard work. Only in that case can his work be valued by others. What did you do recently? What are you going to do in the future? Can you tell me about that?"

They were both sitting on a bench outside the hospital.

"As you know after our country became independent, a new the academy of agricultural sciences had been established in our country instead of in the The Soviet Union Academy of agricultural sciences. They had even declared a competition for staff selection. It seemed to me that I can take part in this competition because I have been carrying out many researches in the field of agricultural sciences machinery, since the 1970s. I have lots of monographs and books published in this sphere, and besides I carried out my doctoral dissertation in this area.

"Ok, well, well?"

"Even the head of the Tashkent State of Irrigation and mechanization of agriculture professor Sh. Yuldoshev, my teacher Okil Salimov, submitted his documents to this academic competition. Okil Salimov had been blamed in the massacre and arrested, and as you know, he was released and has already returned to his work as a teacher. It's awkward for me to apply for this as a competitor against my own teachers."

"Oh, Oybek, they are quite wonderful people. They will never think that they are much more experienced than you are or that they must retire as an academician, no!"

"I have already talked to them. I think that old scientists who have already retired should be appointed as academicians, and that they should be the specialists serving the government being awarded. All the awards here are given according to age. Ok, leave it, I have already applied for it."

"Well done! What's the problem?"

"The engine scientists all know me very well, and now I have been told that I must get introduced to the favored scientists of agriculture. I know that you're very close friends with the chief of the experts Sadriddin Hujayevich. I wish you and I can visit him to recommend me for the award because it seems to me strange to go there alone"

"Ok, I'll will go there with you with pleasure. If my visit is going to decide something, I will go."

Thoughts

I heard that it was impossible to become an academician without bribing someone. My "very real friend" said that it was impossible for me to do that.

That's why I answered him:

"Yes, you're right, I have never solved my problems illegally. I visited the experts and members of the academy, Sadriddin Hujayevich, and Abduvali Imomaliyev who is the President of the Central Asian department of the Agricultural science academy. I haven't given them money or expensive presents. I just showed them my own books and dissertation results. My research has been positively assessed by all the members of the expert council."

I had heard positive opinions about the results of my research, but as the day for the staff selection drew loser, I heard more and more rumors about the fact that the academicians had already been declared even before the competitions, and   were bought illegally. Again, I talked to Dr Erkin:

"I don't want my enemies to laugh about me, so I need to do something."

"What does your teacher think about that? I mean the academician Lebedev. He is an academician, and I hope he knows everything about that."

"He says we'll fight until the end"

"I saw the vice-president Saidmahmoud Kodirov at a party, and he asked you to visit him".

According to what Erkin said I visited Usmonov:

"Oybek Mukaddirovich, I'm asking you to please withdraw your application and in six months we'll announce another competition for you. Don't worry about that, and please don't make it hard for us to decide." I This meant there was no way for me to be an academician.

Ok, I am patient. But I don't know why the things that some other people pursue easily is really hard for me to pursue. I am in the dark about whether it is my destiny or ... I am in the dark.

Taken aback

A huge building of the Uzbekistan agricultural sciences Academy stands high in the sky. Oybek had recently written an application to the academician Imomaliyev. He hesitated for a long time until he edited his previous application, and this time he wrote "I ask you to recommend me for the position of the correspondent academician". Today he has been urgently invited to the academy.

"You are on the additional list, and all the academicians have already been appointed" they said to Oybek.

At last he went into the hall of the meetings, and different people were looking at him with glory, while some of them with viewed him with admiration.

"Kodirov Oybek Mukaddirovich, 23 votes in favour, 3 votes against, Kodirov, you have been elected as a correspondent academician in charge of "Agricultural sciences machinery construction technology", congratulations!" Mahmud Mirzayev said.

All the people applauded, and as people were congratulating him Oybek felt tiredness in his body. He wished he could again become a baby sleeping in the cradle listening to a lullaby from his mother. He was going to run away from the phone calls of congratulation after these applauds and rest at home or at the university. It's easier to live in childhood. To live means to struggle when you are an adult.

The man who laughed at him when he applied came up to him:

"Oybek Mukaddirovich I didn't know that you were so talented! Now I am astonished, congratulations!"

Oybek just said thanks and walked away.

At this time, he wanted to go where he was born and grew up. The place where he grew up beckoned him on and on. This lure was so strong that he really wanted to go there.

Romantic traveling

My life is not only full of struggles, but also victories and problems. I have many things to be happy about. Especially my travelling adventures all over the world.

Human life contains different travelling adventures into the soul, into history, into the future and to world countries.

Now I want to tell you about my travels with my wife, because they are forevermore kept in my heart.

Unfortunately, when I was busy in Tashkent I didn't have a chance to go to resorts or to many foreign countries for a rest with my children.

Oydin has never asked me to take her to foreign countries for a rest, and she has always taken my work into account.

It's been over forty years since we got married, and within this time me and Oydin have only been to Yugoslavia, India, Germany and South Korea.

Yugoslavia

1980 August... everybody carries two pieces of luggage. Me and my wife only have a small bag. Oydin asked me to help one of the women there carry her luggage. I lifted it up, and was about to collapse because it was so cumbersome. Then we learned that people come here for trade and they return to their homes with gifts and presents in two big suitcases. But we hadn't bought anything. We have only gotten impressions about the seaside, beautiful cities, hotels and museums. The clean roads in the mountains astonished us. My wife is a road scientist, and she kept assessing the quality of the roads there.

The speed of the busses is 110 and 120 kilometers an hour. I wish you could see the water of the Adriatic Sea, all the fish could be seen through the water with three or four meters' depth. The hotel we stayed in is very nice and luxurious, and we were taken aback to learn that there's no robbery there.

Yugoslavia has lots of beautiful cities. Belgrade city, the name itself which means white city in English, infers that all the buildings there are in white colored, and built from white brick. All the historical monuments have been combined with modern architecture. The working day is from 6 am to 2 pm. It means in the afternoon everybody can run their own business or rest at home. The earlier we got up, the more effective the day became for us. Therefore, our ancestors got up early at the break of dawn and completed all their tasks when it was cool until the afternoon.

Our travels lasted for 14 days, and during these days we were able to visit 5 provinces of the state. We even went to Macedonia which had now gained its independence. We were introduced to the traditions and culture of the Greeks there.

We even went swimming to the Adriatic Sea. Our love renewed just like we were fourteen years old. The sea seemingly washed all of our troubles away.

Nine years passed after that and we went to India after that. Our department won the competition when I was working as the head, and therefore they gave us a free of charge package holiday voucher as a prize. This state has always attracted me, maybe because our great ancestor Beruniy wrote a book about it, maybe our Emir Temur had a battle there, or maybe because Bobur lived there the rest of his life. I don't exactly know the reason. While we were planning to go to India, we were feeling even happier than at the time when we went to Yugoslavia.

Leaving for India

We went through customs on November 10, 1989 at 5 am in the morning and we flew in the plane IL-62 to Delhi. According to the contract we landed in the Karachi city (Pakistan). This type of landing could destroy health of people with heart disease. The worst thing was that engines were scheduled to operate for an hour and the smell filled the plane with a terrible odor. After an hour we flew to Delhi from Karachi city. At the Delhi airport, representatives of the customs examined a group of tourists. We loaded our luggage into comfortable trolleys and drew it to the bus. We then got in the bus and went to the hotel. We stayed in the Kanishka hotel in the centre of the Delhi city. This hotel has 16 floors and it's quite wonderful with high quality service. There are four restaurants there, tens of shops, and taxis wherever you want. There are state-of-the-art TVs, a fridge and others items in each room.

The City of Ancient Monuments

Delhi is the capital of India. The population is 14 million people. It is in the north-western part of the country, on the shores of the Jamnah river. It's 216 meters above sea level, and the average temperature in the middle of July is 310, in January it is 14,20.

Current Delhi is near the ancient Indirpap. It was the capital of the Delhi Kingdom from the 8th century, and the capital of the Boburids from 1526.

In 1803 Delhi was invaded by the English, and from 1857-59 this city was the centre of the national militant actions. In 1911 the capital of British India started being built in the same city in the south-western part. It has been the capital of India since 1950.

Delhi is the huge cultural, economical and cultural centre of India, and the transport centre of the country. There are three airports in this city, many railways and automobile roads cross this city.

In this city, all the fields like textile, shoes, ceramics, electronics, pharmaceutics, metalwork, machinery are very well-developed.

In the older part of the city there is the Delhi mosque, with palaces built from white marbles by the Boburids in the La'l Kal'a complex and the Marvarid mosque is built there.

If you go to the south from the old city, you can see the ruins of the city (1351-1398), Kulon (1380) and Kilan Kal'a Palace ensemble (1540) the, Humoyun gravestone (1565) and other historical monuments.

The newer part of Delhi consists of squares, gardens and they start with wide streets. Here there is the gate of India, the central government office, administration offices and banks. There are two universities, several colleges, the internet, art and literary academies, galleries, museums, the memorial museums of Mahatma Ghandi, Javaharlal Neru, theatres and national museums.

But we cannot say that all of our stay was full of joy.

In the afternoon, we visited the greatest temple in Delhi that had been built by the richest Maharadja of Delhi. Following all the rituals of the temples, we wished peace for all the Gods of Buddhism. All the statues of Lakshmi, Krishna and Shiva were all decorated with wonderful expensive stones.

Each God has own tasks. Lakshmi is the god of love. Shiva of goodness. We walked on foot in the streets of the modern Delhi. The gate of India and the huge palace of the President gives the city a luxurious look. People rest in the grass fields. An interesting thing happened in the temple. The visitors were asked to take off their shoes and put on special socks in the temple. While leaving, visitors must leave the socks. Our partner from Kashkadarya city in Uzbekistan had taken off his shoes at the gate, and when we went out, we saw that his shoes had been stolen. So, he put on someone's shoes which would fit him. We laughed a lot, and our partner Kosimjon said that he didn't want to walk barefoot having his shoes stolen. Yes, it was very funny.

Powerful King and Beautiful Princess

Visiting the tombs of Humoyun and his close relatives was a duty for us. It was as if they were waiting for us to pray for them, and as if they were glad seeing that we had come. Muhammad Humoyun was the eldest son of Mirzo Bobur, and his mother was Mahimbegum.

Mirzo Bobur was buried in Kobul according to his own final wishes. Humoyun's gravestone was built by his wife Hamidabonu. As Gulbadanbegin, Humoyun's sister wrote in "Humoyunnoma". Hamidabonu was Mirzo Dust's daughter. Humoyun fell in love with her at first sight, and asked her to marry him. She refused him for forty days, then he sent his match- makers. His step-mother finally went to her and asked her to marry him, but she said: "I cannot marry the person in the sky. He is a king and I am an ordinary citizen". She was fourteen years old when she married him, and she gave birth to Akbarshoh in 1542. She died forty-eight years after her husband's death (1556), in 1604. The mausoleum was built from marble and red stones. There are many tourists coming to visit that. Indians preserve and value all the monuments built by the Boburids. They are holy places for these citizens. The Indians remember Bobur not as the invader, but as the person who built a great country like India. Javaharlal Neru said: Bobur was a wonderful, brave and brilliant person of the evolutionary period. He loved art and literature. He loved enjoying life given by God".

When we were leaving the Mausoleum, we burst out laughing. Our partner who had had his shoes stolen saw the man who was wearing his shoes. He was explaining everything with his mimics and gestures. That man was English and they exchanged their shoes at that moment. We saw people who were playing with snakes, and cobras. The poisonous snake was weak in his hands, we wondered how they obeyed men, or if they were the type weak enough to obey. The day ended well. …

Being Ordinary Leads to Being Great

On November 12, we went to see the house museum of Indira Ghandi. Her house was ordinary, and all the rooms were quite simply decorated. There weren't any sofas, or arm-chairs in that house. Only a desk and a desk in a small library. There is a special path leading to the place where Ghandi was shot. That path is decorated with flowers. When we walked in the square where Mahatma and Indira Ghandi were burnt, we both felt strange because these were people who gave their life for the freedom of their motherland. This place is crowded with people, with some of them are even earning money there.

In the afternoon, we visited the old city. The Red Castle was the palace of the King and Humoyun had had it built. All the precious stones used for decorating the rooms were stolen, and one could see their traces on the walls. There is one skyscraping mosque which had been built by Humoyun. I was proud of being from a generation of the Boburids, and seeing so much respect for them in this country.

In the capital city of the Baburids

Bobur Mirzo was born in 1483 on February 14 in the family of Umarshayh Mirzo. His mother Nigorkhanim was the daughter of the Tashkent governor. He was the fifteenth generation of the mogul Chingizkhan. Bobur Mirzo and was the sixth generation of Emir Temur.

Boburshakh had four sons, Humoyun, Kamron, Hindol and Askariy.

He had daughters Mas'uma Sultanbegum, Gulbadanbegun, Gulrangbegum, Gulchehrabegum, Gulzorbegum.

Bobur was one of the most influential people in the history of India.

On November 13, in the early morning, we went to Agra, the first capital of India, by bus. We inherited "Boburnoma", "Hatti Boburiy", "Mufassal", "Mubayyin" and other books from Bobur. Agra is 205 kilometers away from Delhi. On the way we stopped in the camping grounds to drink some water. We saw a thick snake three meters long on the grass. It weighed over 20 or 25 kilos. The tourists shot photos wrapping it around their necks. It became known that its owner ekes out a living by allowing tourists to shoot photos with it. After five hours of traveling we reached the city Sikandra, and there we saw the tomb of Akbarshakh, Bobur's grandson. The mausoleum is luxurious, green and beautiful, but there are too many monkeys there. Indians value this monument a lot. Akbarshakh ruled in India for forty years, the longest period among the Boburids (1556-1605). Bobur ruled for four years but his generations ruled the country for tree centuries (1526-1858). Akbarshah had three wives, but all of them only gave birth to daughters However, his Indian wife gave birth to a son, Jahangir. For that Akbarshah had visited a saint Salim Cheshtiy, living 40 kilometers far from Agra. His prayers were thought to reach God much more quickly.

His wife also went with him on foot. A year later his son came into being. Because of his belief in this Cheshtiy, he changed the capital city to Sikandra where that old man was living and had many luxurious palaces built. There you can visit the palace where Cheshtiy had worshipped God, and the king lived in this place for ten years. But this town turned into a dead city after a drought.

We heard that Salim Muhammad Jahangir fell in love with the daughter of his own babysitter. She was very beautiful and docile. The Great Mughal emperor Akbar and his wife, Mariam-uz-Zamani, had a son named Prince Saleem (later Emperor Jahangir). He was a spoiled and rude boy and because of this, Akbar the Great sent his son away to the army for fourteen years to learn the discipline required to rule the empire. Finally, Akbar allowed this son to return to the main palace in Lahore. Since this day was one of great celebration, the harem of Akbar decided to hold a great Mujra (dance performance) by a beautiful girl named Nadeera, daughter of Noor Khan Argun. Since she was an exceptional beauty, "like a blossoming flower", Akbar called her Anarkali (blossoming pomegranate).

During her first and famous dance, Prince Saleem fell in love with her and it later became apparent that she was also in love with him. Later, they both began to see each other although they kept quiet about it to others. Later, however, Prince Saleem informed his father, Akbar, of his intention to marry Anarkali and make her the Empress. The problem was that Anarkali, despite her fame in Lahore, was a dancer and a maid and not of noble blood. So, Akbar (who was sensitive about his own mother, Hamida Banu Begum, being a commoner) forbade Saleem from seeing Anarkali again. Prince Saleem and Akbar had an argument that later became very serious after Akbar ordered Anarkali's arrest and placed her in one of the jail dungeons in Lahore.

After many attempts, Saleem and one of his friends helped Anarkali escape and hid her near the outskirts of Lahore. Then, the furious Prince Saleem organized an army (from those loyal to him during his fourteen years there) and began an attack on the city; Akbar, being the emperor, had a much larger army and quickly defeated Prince Saleem's force. Akbar gave his son two choices: either surrender Anarkali to them or to face the death penalty. Prince Saleem, out of his true love for Anarkali, chose the death penalty. Anarkali, however, unable to allow Prince Saleem to die, came out of hiding and approached the Mughal emperor, Akbar. She asked him if she could be the one to give up her life in order to save Prince Saleem, and after Akbar agreed, she asked for just one wish; to spend just one pleasant night with Prince Saleem.

After her night with Saleem, Anarkali drugged Saleem with a pomegranate blossom. After a very tearful goodbye to the unconscious Saleem, she left the royal palace with guards. She was taken to the area near present-day Anarkali Bazaar in Lahore, where a large ditch was made for her. She was strapped to a board of wood and lowered in it by soldiers belonging to Akbar. They closed the top of the large ditch with a brick wall and buried her alive.

There are some other stories confirming that the Emperor Akbar helped Anarkali escape from the ditch through a series of underground tunnels with her mother, with the promise that Anarkali leave the Mughal empire and never return. It is not known whether Anarkali survived or not.

After him the kingdom was passed down to Hurram Shahjahan, who was the second most famous King after Babur because the Taj-mahal he had built is the miracle of the world. Master Iso was the chief architect who constructed this building. The garden around was planned by the gardener Raimbol.

 The weather in Agra is quite different than that in Delhi; it's mild and pure. The Taj-mahal and the area it occupies is 14 thousand square meters in total, and its height is in excess of 50 meters. The mausoleum was built from marbles glittering under the light, it's very difficult to get into this building, and the inner part is also decorated with expensive and precious gem stones. Thousands of people stand in long ques to come into this building. We could hardly go inside, and under the cupola of the mausoleum, there are decorated tombs of Shahjahan and Mumtazbegum. The tomb of Shahjahan is bigger in comparison, but both tombs have been decorated in the same way, with the same patterns. This wonderful masterpiece takes everyone aback, and is astonishing every second. We recited some surahs from the Koran, went upstairs and visited some other tombs as well. Unfortunately, there wasn't anyone among the tourists who could speak Arabic, and if there had been, we would have asked him to translate to us what was written on the walls of the tombs and mausoleum. I wished that the next time we visited this place, we would have someone knowing English and Arabic to translate all these mysterious statements. There are tens of monuments around this mausoleum, but we didn't have a chance to see them all. We had a very short time. Per what the Indian historian L.Sharba said, the Tajmahal is not only the historical and architectural memorial of India, but it is the precious wealth of the people of the world.

On November 14, we set off to the city called the Dead city where we could see Indian peasants busy growing and planting crops. We also saw some Indians who were carrying stones in their baskets and using them to build roads.

We saw no technology there, and all the things were made and created only through manual and hand work.

A famous love story

We went sightseeing in the Dead city, then we went back to Agra. We sat on the bus for nine hours non-stop, and my feet and hands started numbing.

According to what the Indian writer Nina Epton wrote, the things that were infusing beauty to Mumtozbegim were her eyes, lips, her hair hanging down to her waist. Her body was very smooth, she had a thin chin, and she also had a very delicate dimple in her right cheek. Her hands were small, but very strong, and this represented that she was of a very generous disposition."

One of the people working in high positions in the Palace, Asafkhan had a daughter, Arjumandbonu, who was born in 1594. She was also modest and docile. In 1611 on June 26, his father made her marry Prince Hurram. This Prince was famous with one more name which is Shahjahan. This name represents that Hurram would be the king of the world. Arjumandbonu gave birth to 14 children during her life.

In 1628, after Shahjahan, Hurram was crowned, became the King, and he gave his wife the name Mumtaz Mahal which meant "Nobody compares in the Palace". She was always with her husband, even in the wars and bloodsheds. Mumtaz Mahal is the symbol of loyalty. In 1631 she gave birth to her daughter Gavharorobegum. She died, because of losing too much blood. They were again in the war when she gave birth. The body of the late Mumtaz Mahal was brought from Burhanpur to the garden in Agra city.

Before she died, she is known to have begged her husband not to marry to anyone after that. Shahjahan didn't marry anyone, and besides that, he had the palace, the Taj Mahal built to cherish her memory in Agra city. 20 thousand builders built this palace within 22 years. The king was intending to have one more building built opposite the Taj Mahal, but unfortunately his son Avrangzeb started fighting for the throne and captivated his own father. He arrested him in the chamber through the window of which Shahjahan could see the Taj Mahal. The poor father died in that chamber, alone and bereft.

We were all fatigued when we at last arrived at the airport, and then we had to fly to Bombay. Again, we started flying in the sky, among the clouds, white and blue drifting from one side to another.

Waiting for Rajjesh Khanna For Two Hours

By chance, we saw a famous artist Radjesh Khanna from Bombay and Oydin got her signature for memory by speaking a little English.

We then learned that our departure had been delayed for two hours because of this artist. The plane was comfortable and there were 300 seats in it. There was almost no noise, and it was capable of taking off and reaching the necessary level within 8-10 minutes. This plane takes a very short time to land, which makes it convenient for passengers. We arrived at Bombay city in the morning, and we didn't take a nap during the flight. After we left the airport, we arrived at the hotel Horizon by bus. They welcomed us with bunches of flowers. We were in a very good mood, and went to our rooms in ten minutes. The hotel was very comfortable. There were conveniences, and it was possible to go to the Arab sea directly from this hotel. Ongoing there, we had a swim in the pool and got rid of the tiredness from spending so much time in the bus.

Bilateral Agreement

When I had a chance to rest, I telephoned the Indian Technological university, but unfortunately the dean had left for a year-lasting contract-based travels. We met the head of the department (I didn't know him very well). He is known to have defended the candidate dissertation, I know that man, Mr. Dahrival, but that meeting about science caused us to become much closer friends. We talked to him on the phone and fixed a meeting date, Dr Dahrival came into the room where we were sitting an hour later. We hugged each other while greeting, and exchanged some short information about scientific and academic researches. We got a chance to create partnership between the Indian Technological university and the Tashkent Automobile Roads University. We also decided to write a textbook together in English. We later went to see the technological university where the head of the department professor Sharma and I talked for three hours. At the end of our talks we decided to translate the book "Automobiles and Tractor engines" into English. In this meeting, we examined the report of the partnership between the two universities. After I returned to Tashkent I submitted this report to the higher Education Ministry. This technological university has a square of 400 hectares and it is situated near the banks of a lake. It's surrounded with gardens, trees blooming and with flowers. It's one small town in this city. The teachers live in this town and the students attend the university by taking different transports. The teachers there more often use books by the Scientists of the CIS (translated into English). If the scientists from Uzbekistan worked in cooperation with those from India, there would probably be progress in education and science, because the problems in their climate and automobile roads were very similar.

Oh, These Beautiful Islands

On November 16 in the early morning, we went to the Arab sea by bus. After an hour and a half, we reached the seaport and boarded a ship to go to the Elephanta island. There is a temple of the Indians on the sea shores there. It was built in the 6 century. The God Shiva is described there in nine forms.

This is the great example of the Indian masters. Here tourists walk up the stairs made like the snake traces. Near the temples the Indian perfume sellers offer different sorts of the perfumes. Oydin liked the jewelry made from blue colored jams very much. We were looking for gifts for our children, and we were thrilled when we found suitable ones.

If It's Cheap, Never of Low Quality

We returned to Bombay, had lunch there lunch, and afterwards we did some shopping. After we finished shopping, we all decided to meet at the same time with our group next to the bus. Only one person was missing, and all the tourists were waiting for him. There were 32 of them. The guide of the group was furious about that. That tourist at last came back forty minutes late. We wanted to scold him for being so late, and he threw away his shoes with anger. It became clear that he had bought new clothes for a very cheap price and while crossing the place where there was lots of water, his shoes had been torn off. He found out that the shoes had been made from paper. We did our best to calm him down:

"These are just some shoes made from paper You should thank God that you didn't buy a car made from paper."

There were lots of traffic jams at night, so we arrived at the hotel at 10 pm at night

Cultures Convers in Madras

On November 17, we prepared for a flight to Madras city. All the pilots from Bombay city were on a strike that day, and that's why they made us fly three or four hours before the set time. Bombay is a very beautiful and luxurious city. 10 million people live there, but the weather is scorching.

When we arrived in Madras city, it was pouring down with rain. All the lands were wet, and after we loaded our luggage, we were absolutely tired. As usual we stayed in a luxurious hotel where there were all the conveniences for the guests.

Madras city used to be one of the colonies of France and Portugal. It started being called Chennai in 1996. Therefore, the streets and buildings are mostly in European style. The streets are cleaner, and there are fewer poor people.

After dawn broke, we travelled around the city and the beautiful temple. Its height is 40 meters, and the most surprising thing is that the Muslims had built this temple to keep friendly relationships with the Indians. The temple was decorated with 3000 little statues. They dazzle so much under the sunshine that the eyes can be dazzled. There is a big artificial pool near the temple, and different religious ceremonies are held there. Madras had been in the past annexed without any battles of opposition. Then we saw the temples built by the Portuguese people. We took some photos next to the Statue of Mahatma Ghandi there.

On November 19, we went to a Serpentary (where snakes, crocodiles and lizards are kept). There we saw very beautiful, but poisonous snakes, and turtles weighing 100 kilos. In the afternoon, we got a chance to see the bulks which were crowded with people. According to what our guide said, near the gate of the bulk we could buy things four times as cheap by haggling with the sellers. Yes, we indeed spent very little money, but bought a great deal of things.

The Indian Ocean

On November 20, we went to Pondicherry city by bus. – Madras city is 160 kilometers far from Pondicherry, it took us four hours and thirty minutes to go there. The roads are very narrow, but the drivers are very kind to each other. Maybe that's why there are quite a few car crashes and accidents in this city. We saw many gardens and wide fields where peasants were working hard to grow crops. We could also see high and low homes of the Indians there. All the huts are built in European style. In the bus, we watched these fields, and watched the cartoons on TV of the bus, and weren't bored at all. We stayed in a two-story hotel with in Pondicherry, and through the window of our room there was a view of the Indian ocean. The ocean which seems to have no start and no ending fills the heart with emotions and wonderful feelings of happiness. There are flowers and trees everywhere, it was obvious that the hotel was built not long ago. We enjoyed sunbathing on the sand, on the shores of the ocean, and seeing the ocean waves for four days. We got rid of all of our tiredness, and we even watched Pondicherry city there. In the kitchen of our hotel, one of partners in the group cooked pilaf for us all, and the next day we ate the pea soup again, which is also our national food.

On November 21, when Oydin and I and were having a stroll on the shores of the ocean, we met some little children at the age of seven or eight. When we asked why they were not at school, they said that they didn't have, copybooks, pens and pencils to write. We asked them to come up to our hotels in the afternoon promising to give them pens, pencils and copybooks.

Indeed, in the afternoon several boys came and screamed to us from the garden, where a policeman stood. I went to the balcony to see who it was, and immediately went downstairs with my wife to give the presents I had prepared for them. Even the policeman came up to us asking for some pens and pencils, which we gave. I suddenly remembered some of our lazy students who have everything, a home, money, but do not attend classes. I compared them to these little children who couldn't even afford to buy pens to write at school.

We were usually offered smorgasboard in restaurants of other countries, but it was quite different for the Indian meals. There are 20 or 30 types of meals in dishes on the table in India, under which there are candles burnt with methyl lest the meal gets cold. You may put any of the meals on your plate and eat it sitting in your seat. However, you must eat it all. There are different types of meals, but the ones with meat were quite hotter than the others; fish and salads.

The garden of botany in Pondicherry is quite extraordinary and exquisite. There we saw one more building in a round shape which was built for people to live. There are all the conditions there, and it is called an independent city.

Good-bye Delhi

We went to Madras city in the early morning of November 23. From this city, we took a plane, and changed in Haydorobod city from where we flew to Delhi. On November 24, we went sightseeing around Delhi and even walked around the underground bulk. We spent all the rest of the Indian currency we had and went directly to the hotel. The director of the company who sponsored this travelling tour invited us all to his own garden, and country house. This invitation made us all the happiest in the world, they welcomed   us fastening different sparkling loose necklaces. We spent our time there playing tennis or badminton games. We took some photos wearing the national cap of Indian, Singh. The photos of high quality got prepared within three hours and handed in to us. There was a firework for us in the garden, and at last we said goodbye to each other and left this fascinating garden. When we were leaving, we saw a beautiful couple, a bride and a groom, both riding on an elephant decorated with beautiful flowers. All the weddings are luxurious and joyous in India. Since there are many weddings there every single day, I wanted to call India as the state of weddings to tell the truth. We came back to the hotel and packed all of our clothes and arrived at the international airport. There I was looking at the Delhi city roads with admiration, and all the transportation workers who were very polite. As there are many cows and monkeys on the roads, drivers drive their cars very carefully. There isn't any black or stinky smoke belching out of the car engines, Indians use very high quality fuel, and the technical standards are high.

We passed through customs at the airport, and we boarded the plane IL-62. We came encountered a disorder in the plane. Everybody sat on the seats which they wanted. However, the number of the seats was written on the tickets, and we could have sat on the seats numbered on our tickets. We could hardly take our own seats. After we flew for an hour and thirty minutes to Karachi city, the saloon was again filled with that stinky smell from the fuel emission. We didn't complain about that. Unfortunately, we started flying and we arrived in our hometown, Tashkent city.

Returning to our own dear city Tashkent, we had tears in our eyes. I missed my own relatives a lot, and I greeted those who came to see us in at the airport, and gave them all hugs. Oydin had a very good rest in India for fourteen days.

This was a fifty-year old couple traveling, and these memories will be kept forevermore.

The award Al-Khorazmiy

Oybek was born for science and to gain knowledge. He has never gone to restaurants and cafes which he didn't have a reason to visit. He didn't want to do that at all. That's why he saw the "Navruz" restaurant in the square "Istiklol" square. When he was travelling in India he saw many high buildings and he wished Uzbekistan to also become independent, and strong enough to build buildings, and sky scraping establishments in the style they want. Thanks to God, his dreams have come true. Uzbekistan became independent, and the President of the Republic has been paying close attention to building establishments since the first years after independence. Now Oybek is coming into one of those establishments built after independence, the so- called "Navruz" restaurant, a luxurious palace-like building, with crystal candles, and patterns decorated with flowers as white as snow. The Republic External Affairs Ministry, and the President of the Uzbekistan Sciences Academy, with the ambassador of Iran Hoshimiy Gulyapogoniy were there.

Among these great people Oybek felt a bit uncomfortable and he decided to sit somewhere with a few people. But one of the embassy representatives held him by his elbow:

"Oybek Mukaddirovich, you must sit at the center. This party is held here especially for you. He was made to sit next to the Minister of External Affairs. Oybek felt that many people on the right and on the left were looking at him with admiration. He didn't believe his eyes. Did he really make progress from his hard work? Yes, he did, and now his research is even valued in foreign countries. A person who achieves something with his own hard work might hesitate over the successful end, and might be afraid of an unhappy end. The secretary of the Iranian embassy, Mr. Muzaffariy, looked at him with a smile. This person was the first to inform Oybek about the good news of the award.

The point is that, a year ago in the summer, Oybek received a letter announcing the opening of a competition to give an award named after Al-Khorazmiy, the Second International scientific seminar. In that letter, all the requirements to take part in the competition had been clearly shown. When he heard that the conference was named after their ancestor Al- Khorazmiy, Oybek decided to apply for that competition. After that he attached all of his documents and the results of his experiments to the competition. Sometime later he received a letter from the Iranian embassy: "We have examined all of your documents and we decided to forward them for further participation!"

"Dear ladies and gentlemen! We think that the International scientific conference named after Al-Khorazmiy year by year is gaining more and more reputation in the world. As you all here know, the presentation of the conference and awarding the winner scientists with the prize was held in Tehran city on February 8. All the awards were submitted personally by the President of Iran, Hoshimiy Rafsanjoniy. The Uzbek scientist Oybek Kodirov was also among the prize winners, but unfortunately, he couldn't be present on the day of the presentation because of some reasons. Therefore, today I ask you to let me hand this award to him personally.

Oybek got the award and the money handed to him by the ambassador. He had had a little party on his fiftieth anniversary for his friends. He only invited ordinary people. He thought that he didn't need to anyone else. On this anniversary, his friend, the minister of UzAutoTransport Lerik Ahmetov, gave him the award "Honored Automobile transport specialist". After that Oybek was elected as an academician in the Academy, and now I he has won this international award. He really wanted to go Tehran, and he kept talking to Erkin Hujayev, the ambassador of the Embassy of Iran in Uzbekistan. But the time of the conference and the schedule of the flight to Iran from Uzbekistan didn't coincide at all. While the ambassador was submitting the award to Oybek in the Navruz restaurant, he mentioned the scientists from Uzbekistan and the development of science in our country. Oybek was given a chance to speak and give thanks for the award:

"Actually applying for this competition I forwarded my project dedicated to the problems of predicting erosion, effective use of diesel engines in Central Asian soil and climate conditions. There I showed the air cleaner and experiment results" After thanking everyone for the award, Oybek gave a brief description of what else he had forwarded to the competition.

"I think this award is for all the scientists of Uzbekistan, because they are carrying out very useful researches getting advantages for our independence of our motherland. All the scientists want our motherland to develop, our citizens to live in better conditions, and to exist in a country where technology and scientific advances, will have even better conditions to live".

He also said that those who dismiss scientists and knowledge will certainly be punished by God, and in his speech, he remembered his teachers and their contribution to his success.

Lie Lasts for a very short time

The biggest trouble in the world is being weak enough to solve a problem. Yes, Oybek also has a problem which he is finding difficult to deal with. His brother is ill. He addressed all the best doctors, and unfortunately they said: "We really ask you to be patient, and to be ready for anything., we did all the things we did to save your brother". His brother is suffering from the disease, cancer. Besides Oybek has a lot to do at the university.

Oybek was full of burdens to deal with as the university president of the TARU. Pulatov died of a heart attack while conducting a meeting. Ten years ago, this rector was working as the Minister of Higher Education. He even invited Oybek for a cup of tea and for an interview. He recommended Oybek to be the university president in TARU, but something happened, he resigned from his own position, and appointed a university president instead of Oybek. That's why the issue of promoting Oybek as a university president was postponed for some time.

Oybek was in the dark about what caused his brother to die so early, and the fact that his wife is very jealous cannot be used as a reason for that. But he knew what caused the late university president to die of a heart-attack, that was anonymous complaint letters, oppositions and etc.

The late university president Pulatov was very good at dealing with the organizational affairs, but he didn't cope with improve academic affairs, and the assistants started managing them   all.

Owing to lack of control, bribery has become quite common for assessment among the extramural faculty students. The postgraduate students were delivering lectures instead of their professors and scientific advisors. Pulatov actually was the victim of these burdens actually. No sooner had he died, than the struggles started for the position of the rector.

Oybek's brother was seriously ill these days and combatting the urge of death. When the selection of a new university president started my students:

"Oybek Mukaddirovich, you've also been recommended as a possible candidate for this position! Now you must try!"

"Yes, Oybek Mukaddirovich, my friend is right. If somebody with less knowledge is to be promoted to this position, then we are all in hell".

Oybek didn't have any willingness to think about anything except his brother. He wished there could be a miracle that could help his brother to get well. His brother even said many times: "Oybek, at nights I am seeing my mother, and she asks me to find a way to visit her".

Yes, indeed, life is cruel. Oybek's brother breathed his last breath, and they laid him to rest in the grave. He had previously seen his mother laid to rest, his brother-in-law Hamid being buried, and this time it was his brother.

The competitions began for the candidates to be recommended to be a rector. Oybek was face to face and sitting with the State Councilor:

"Oybek Mukaddirovich, we have heard many good things about you. Especially when you won the award Al-Khorazmiy, I know Our President is saying that we also had the scientists in favour throughout the world. The position of the university president is a reputation for some people, and for some people it's the opportunity to serve people. The person who is due to work as the university president must know all about the problematic areas at his university.

The Councilor looked into his eyes with a question.

Oybek had never seen this person before, but now when he was asked about the university's problems, he wanted to bare his soul about everything, and all the problems to be solved at this university. But he was afraid that he might think that Oybek was there to gossip about somebody. Now it was high time for that, but he hesitated for a bit. Then he swallowed all of his fear and:

"Sir Counselor, day by day the quality of education is becoming a secondary issue at our university. Besides all the students tend to only study for getting a degree, and there's no analysis of the educational process or analysis of errors in this process. There are very good decrees relating to higher education, but they aren't enforced at this university.

Oybek started his speech with a bit of hesitation, but then he felt engrossed in what he was saying, and the Counselor was listening to him without interruption:

"If you were a university president there, how would you solve these problems?"

"In our university, our salary is paid according to the position of the teachers. For example, if they are senior teachers or candidates of sciences they get average sums of salary. If they are professors or doctors, then it's usually going to be much higher. But I think a salary should be paid taking into account the quality of teaching. For example, if twenty students of a senior teacher are assessed with excellent marks they can be given a higher sum of salary for this high quality. If 5 of the doctor's students are assessed with satisfactory grades, then their salary should be less than that of the senior teacher. If the students are studying very well, normally those satisfactory are given scholarships taking into account their hard work and their results. Therefore, there can great progress in their education. The people who like to gossip and write anonymous letters should be given lots of tasks lest they would have time for nonsense. I object to the firing of a doctor of sciences involved in bribery, because he may keep being involved in this even if he starts working at another university. He must be allowed to work after at least one warning, and if he doesn't give up bribery, then he can be given the sack.

Oybek felt that his partner was listening to him attentively, and therefore he was speaking from his heart.

"Ok, Oybek, why didn't you share these opinions in the scientific seminars and councils?"

"I am only the head of the department, and I can only share the things which I have enough power to say". Besides, it's very difficult for good people to work together without any obstacles from their the opponents"

The Counselor talked to him for a very long time. When he was leaving his room, he felt that he was not alone. All of the other candidates were his own colleagues at the university.

***

Oybek's postgraduate student came to visit him:

"Teacher, there was a council meeting today at university". Oybek felt that he was looking very sad today like a guilty person. Oybek was quite busy with the traditions of burying his brother. So yesterday, and this day, he was only at home.

"What a council is it?"

"The minister of higher education. The Ministry came and he appointed Samatov as the university president, and you as a proctor"

"Oh, really?"

Oybek had very strange pain in his heart; a pain of sadness. He knew very well what he could do and what the other candidates like Samatov could or couldn't do for this university. His student was still looking at him. Oybek calmed himself down with an inner urge: "Oybek, is it your only aim to be a university president in this life?"

"Ok, if they decided, then … ok, let's forget it" he said, and he threw the twig of the tree away which he had broken into two pieces fiddling it with his hands.

"I don't understand it teacher. When does this all come to an end? This is unfair. I know that you're … and Samatov. It is too hard to believe."

"Ok, leave it, forget it. I hope you are not here just to discuss this problem. I am accustomed to seeing a research paper with my postgraduates I need to check"

Oybek's student was feeling that his voice sounded quite different, and he was feeling the pain he was hiding inside from him.

Until the next day Oybek was suspicious about if this news was real or not.

…But working as a university president is not just a game, and it requires being careful while choosing the appropriate candidate. Career future, behavior norms, initiation, the leadership of millions of students would depend on how hard the rector would work. But the next day Oybek made sure that his student was right. Samatov had already moved into the room of the late rector who had recently died, and he was reclining in his arm-chair. Oybek found it hard to get out of that awkward situation, and yes a high position changes a person very quickly. Samatov seemed to have quickly taken off his own mask and was now ready to work as that of the university president. There was also a big change in his voice:

"Oybek Mukaddirov, I am trusting you to look after everything here. I will come back within a week. You know my father died, so I must go and follow all the traditions."

Yes, time was passing very slowly for him now. Oybek was taking very heavy steps as if he was carrying heavy sacks on his shoulder. He was calming down for some moments:

"Oybek, never mind, it's just the man who is destined to be a university president". He obviously had other opposing thoughts: "Oybek, you actually deserved this position.".

***

Oybek got used to silence because of the telephones which stopped working both in his home and in his workplace since he became the proctor at this university. Somebody suddenly rang him on the local line, and he reluctantly picked up the phone:

"Oybek, congratulations!" one of his colleagues Ruziyev said.

Oybek wanted to say that he was late, because it had been a week since he started working as the university president.

Two or three minutes later, the former proctor came in and he also congratulated him with hugs. Oybek's colleague who was working in the neighboring room called Oybek to his room and told him that the Minister was looking for him:

"Oybek Mukaddirovich, it's me the Minister of higher education. Could you please tell all the teachers to wait until three pm. We are going to have a council meeting". After that Oybek was told that he was asked to visit the State Counselor. He did not understand what was happening, and he came into the room where he had been interviewed by the State Counselor. He wanted to ask why they quickly changed their mind within a week. However, it was impossible to be discussed:

"Oybek Mukaddirovich, our President signed in the decree yesterday. But I must tell you it isn't going to be easy for you. There are groups of illegal arrangements, and bribery, which are very common situations in your university. We are aware of all the things. One priority you have is you have a weapon. Oybek Mukaddirovich, you're an honest person living on what you have been earning only with your hard work.

You have achieved everything with your own talent and own force, and that's why we believe that you can also deal with all those problems using your honesty and reliability. Oybek thanked him and after he left his room, he glanced at his watch. It was one pm, and there were two hours until the council would start at 3 pm. Perhaps his wife and other relatives had heard about this news. He stopped a taxi.

Now he is in the cemetery, either because it's hot, the midday of summer, and there is nobody in the cemetery. Just at the gate on the plank bed there is only an elderly man sitting there. He has a scarf wrapped on his forehead. Oybek greeted w him and walked towards his mother's grave. His mother's grave is quite near the water, and there are many flowers and trees growing there. She loved flowers and gardens a lot. Oybek now sees the place she would stay forever is surrounded with many flowers. He squatted down in front of the gate and started reading the surah Fotiha "Auzu billahi … Sirotal mustaqim, sirotal allazina

…" When he goes somewhere, he always tries to read this surah in a very low voice, lest he will feel awkward as he may mispronounce some words in it. This time he also started reading the surah in a low voice, but he started reading loud enough to make his soul calm. He usually knows how to control himself in happiness and in disappointment, but today he doesn't want to control his emotions, and tears are trickling down all of his face:

"Mummy, look. I've come to see you, mum. I remember that you made us rush to have lunch and to go to work in the field as soon as we came back from school. But I wanted to play just like the boys in neighboring homes. Just like many other children I also wanted to sleep more on Sunday mornings. I also wanted to ride on bicycles as much as my friends did, but you made us work hard. Now I know why you did, and you did the right thing mum. If you wouldn't have brought me up as a person patient with hard work, I would have never seemed so reliable for other people." Oybek felt that his mother was listening to him. Suddenly, and on such a hot day, a gentle breeze blew for about ten seconds and showered the petals of a red rose on the grave of his mother.

Oybek was wondering if it is a sign from God to show that his mother is blessed for bringing up her child as a person reliable, trustworthy, and loyally serving the motherland.

Oybek sat there for a long time. When he had come there to bury his brother, he saw some sadness on the grave of his mother, but today, her grave seemed to have a look of satisfaction. While leaving the cemetery, he asked that elderly man at the gate to read the surah and he gave some money for that.

***

In the council at 3 o'clock Oybek was appointed as a rector. Now he was in another room, not in the rector's room, and at that moment   his   colleague   was   next to   him: "What on earth are you sitting in this room for? What about your own room? Are you afraid that you will also be made to resign after a week just like Samatov was?"

It hurt his heart to hear that from his own colleague:

"I have always been patient with all the things, friend. I am easily accustomed to all conditions. I never feel arrogant as soon as I am gifted with a higher position or bigger wealth, because I believe that if I do, I will not be distressed after I am robbed of the wealth I have. This man was our rector, and before he died he did many things for the university. I cannot sit on his chair before I ask permission from his family members. I must follow our national traditions to make a hudoyi21[21] to cherish his memory by inviting all of his relatives for that." His colleague who joked with him felt quite ashamed:

"Yes, you have a very good idea"

Let's go back to what happened in the council after he left the cemetery. All the people, the assistant of the Prime Minister, the Minister of higher education, professors and teachers all gathered in the hall for the council meeting in which the new university president was expected to be introduced.

Some of Oybek's colleagues looked concerned about something. Oybek was why they were concerned. His teacher Okil Salimov beckoned him to where he was standing:

"The authority members have received anonymous phone calls informing us that the university staff might oppose promoting you to the position of the university president. They might even make a noise, that's why. Be careful, won't you?"

"Teacher I've been working at this university for 33 years. I have never tried to block the way of the people who decide to work honestly and who want to develop their career and knowledge. I have never opposed anyone wanting to get what belongs to them, I don't even know who started these rumors about the staff's opposition" Oybek sounded a bit frustrated this time.

---

[21] Religious ceremony held for praying to God, thanking for something or asking God to bless the late people

"Ok, never mind. Higher positions require bigger arguments. That's why stay relaxed, calm and focused". They both entered the hall.

Nobody objected, and everybody listened to the assistant to the Prime Minister.

He also said whatever the State Counselor had told Oybek during the interview. Yes, everybody was silent, but something was hidden under this silence. Oybek could struggle against his opposition if they were open, but silent and secretly planned opposition was something hard to deal with.

21 Religious ceremony held for praying to God, thanking for something or asking God to bless the late people.

Oybek tried to catch a glance at these who tended to oppose him, but they didn't even look at him, and were avoiding looking at his face.

Now Oybek is the university president, and it's been two or three days since he was promoted. He still hadn't gone into the room of the university president. When he had visited his mother's grave, he had an idea about cherishing the late rector's memory by cooking pilaf with the meal of a lamb, and inviting all the previous university's president's family members. Today he is organizing the tradition which he has been planning. He didn't care about the people who might laugh at what Oybek was doing.

He felt satisfaction in the eyes of the late university president's relatives, and they even went into his room with Oybek together. Before, when the late rector was alive, he and Oybek didn't visit each other if there wasn't an important reason.

Now they are in the room, and an old man asked them to open their plans for praying:

"My son, Oybek, we ask God to make you healthy and happy all the time, may you always be in God's care!" Others joined him saying "Omin".

Before when I was not married, I used to write in diaries, but then I realized that a man needs a diary when he is isolated. After we got married, I was mostly busy with bringing up our children. For a long time, we weren't able to enjoy living in the flat which Oybek had bought with lots of difficulties and troubles. After my mother's flat was free to live in, we moved into it and lived there with my husband and children. My mother unfortunately died. Yes, I lost her. After that we inherited this flat from her. My daughters Saodat and Shahrizoda both grew up in this flat.

I was not completely involved in childcare. I headed the department of "Projecting the automobile roads" for ten years. I taught the students from the city centre, and those from the far countryside. I was both a teacher and a reliable friend to them all. I realized how much my hard work was valued when I was awarded "The first woman specialist in the field of Automobile roads". Then I was awarded as a professor. I had a book published in the Uzbek language which is called "Projecting Automobile roads" and there are two volumes. This is the first book ever written in this field of study for Uzbek students. I was also awarded as "The Teacher of the automobile road specialists" with the presentation of that very book. I didn't feel any need for diaries as I was not isolated or bereft and I only have some short notes in my copybooks; nothing more.

"Our daughter Saodat started studying at the Moscow Pedagogical university, because this Moscow city was the reason both me and my husband got married and became one. She only studied there for a year and then we hardly forced her to come back and continue her education in our own country."

She takes after her father a lot, and oh my god, she is as naïve as he is, and as honest as he is. It is very hard to live with this sort of person.

My youngest daughter, Shahrizoda is quite different. We usually call her "our son daughter" as she acts like a boy in character. She has studied and achieved excellent grades at school for ten years. It was great fun when she got a golden medal while finishing school. Usually the candidates applying for golden medals pass their specific exams not at school, but at the District department of mainstream education. Shahrizoda is always confident in her knowledge, and she always sure that all her grades are going to be excellent. But three or four days after the exams she came back home and she furiously said that she had a four for math. The thing which Oybek hated most was unfairness. So, he cancelled all his plans for the next day and went to the department of mainstream education. When he had all her control work examined, there was no error, but the grade was four, good, but not excellent. He asked the juries to repeat their assessment, which they did, so she coped with getting an excellent grade with lots of challenges.

We thought that our daughter could be enrolled at university quite easily, as soon as she received an excellent grade for math. But then we heard that the excellent grade that she had got could only be confirmed after her certificate is signed by professor Bagdasarov. So anyway, she was assessed with good mark instead of excellent. When her father requested the juries to examine her knowledge twice, they assessed her with excellent grade, but they didn't write this data on the certificate. It was Gafurov who did not change the grade which was unfairly recorded.

Gafurov wanted to support our daughter, and tried to convince Bagdasarov:

"Teacher, she completed all the controlled work and achieved an excellent mark. Moreover, pay attention to her surname. All the people in this family are hard working and honest, I think it would be unfair if you don't support them fairly"

Oybek felt happy that at least his surname could help them to achieve something fairly.

Shahrizoda graduated from the university of International Economics and diplomacy. Her secondary specialty is economics. No, she didn't take after her father professionally, but we have many hopes for her.

Saodat is a translator, she always helps her father, she also studied, and her second specialty is economics.

Shahrizoda got married, her husband is also hard working, and he is a businessman. She earned a postgraduate degree, and defended the dissertation of a candidate. She was at first working at the Ministry of Foreign Affairs, then she changed her profession to production. She is a genius of her own profession. She gave birth to a healthy and very sweet daughter. When she started crawling and walking a bit, she played with drugs and accidentally swallowed one of them. She was poisoned because of her granddad's drug.

It was the most frightening time for me and for my husband, and that night I didn't even have a nap. The baby's father, and all of our students were bothered and fussing over the baby. That day I had a blood pressure of about 220. She got well in the morning thanks to god.

Sometimes when I open my notebook, I tend to read these short notes which are short, but they are something which reminds about the Kodirov's life episodes.

Germany

Everybody values their own motherland. If they are in another country for three days or for a week, they start craving for their own country despite the life full of problems there.

Travelling is great fun, and to appreciate your own motherland, people must try to travel for some time. Again, we were lucky to travel, this time in Germany, and then of course with my wife. On the initiative of the head of the organization "Automagistral" in the UzAutoYul", the representative of the WIRTGEN GROUP of Germany Oygen Schpenst invited me and my wife to Germany to be introduced to the machinery, automobile roads, concrete and paved roads.

The company paid all the expenditures on these tours. In accordance with the suggestion of the German embassy in Uzbekistan we planned to visit the machinery universities in Germany.

On May 28,2002 in the early morning at 7 am, the plane BOEING 310 flew to Frankfurt and landed at 10.30 according to the German time zone. Mr. Oygen personally met there in personally. The airport our plane landed at was very huge and luxurious. Then we heard that this is the biggest airport in Europe. Two planes take off and land here every minute. We were wearing summer clothes, but it was very cold there, and therefore we rushed into the taxi immediately after passing through the customs. Within five minutes Oygen had a rented Mercedes with a diesel engine. It is the most up-to-date car requiring 6 litres of fuel per 100 kilometers. Three of us went to Kioln city, which was 200 kilometers from the airport. Oydin soon started assessing the roads of this country as a specialist of the road construction: "Ideal roads!". There are luxurious buildings and scene all around, with six lanes on the autobahn. Before we arrived in Koln, we stopped at a small village where there was a small house inside of with every room decorated with flowers. The rooms were very clean and tidy and even outside the houses were decorated with flowers. Not long after that we arrived at the company's main administration, and fifteen minutes after that we were informed that the assistant director of the Uzbekistan Road Construction concern had already arrived at the factory.

Soon we also arrived at that place to join their group. We even saw our own former students there who welcomed us with smiles.

There we were introduced to the technology of producing the razors cutting the asphalt and producing frame details for the machinery of laying asphalt on the roads. These details measure from 3,75 meters to 15 meters. After we examined the factory, we were taken to a hotel in a bus, and they gave us the keys to our bedrooms without registering. We didn't have to write any declarations of customs at the airport. Both sides of the roads there are surrounded by forests, and we were amazed how while watching all the scenery, we didn't even feel how the car traveled 200 kilometers within an hour and a half.

At night, we went to a restaurant with Oygen where we had Koln beer and meals This was how our first day came to end in Germany.

On May 29, at 9 am we had a breakfast in smorgasboard. The fee for the meals were included in the fee for the hotel rooms which had already been paid by the company. We got in the bus and then went to Belgium. We were not asked to write an application for a visa and so on, we were only asked to get a passport for any emergencies. In the territory of The European union no visa is needed. We were going to Belgium through Holland. Oh so far!

Our aim was to see the concrete roads constructed using the cars produced in Germany. The distance between two countries exceeds 300 kilometers, so we got lost. Oygen somehow found the phone number of the director of the Belgium construction plant. He immediately arrived and guided us further. We saw the process of constructing concrete roads there, and we witnessed how the concrete 3,75 meters wide and 12 centimeters thick were covering the roads there. We learned the mechanisms and principles of the operation of the road construction cars.

On May 30, together with the road specialist's delegation t we were introduced to the production technology in other cities. In those plants road construction cars were being produced, and after looking through the plant in the afternoon, we went to see the highway which was being reconstructed. The thickness of the asphalt was 18 centimeters. It was aimed to serve drivers for one hundred years. Oydin also made a wish that in future the quality of the roads in Uzbekistan will also reach the same degree.

On May 31 Oygen made us take a fast train to Berlin and we arrived in this city within only five hours. The representative of the Uzbekistan embassy in Germany Mavlon met us there, then a bit later our ambassador Vladimir Norov came, we talked for three hours, and had a fabulous lunch.

Svikau University

Mavlon drove us to Svikau university through Drezden in his own car, since the meeting was appointed in advance, and that's why the rector, proctor and the dean personally welcomed us. The Proctor freely spoke in Russian as he had studied in Russia. We shared our ideas about the scientific and academic process. They mentioned the possibility of allowing Uzbekistan students to study in Germany for practice The. students at the Svikau university are taught in the English. They also told us that the teachers of the TARU who would write lecture books in English meeting their requirements would be paid 3500 US dollars and invited to work there for a year or six months.

After saying goodbye to the university president, we were introduced to the laboratory which experimented on automobiles and engines, and where the proctor was being our guide. They were only using modern tools and appliances. The postgraduate students were testing these appliances. We traveled to Drezden city later at 6 pm and saw the famous gallery once more. As for the safety of the transport movement, the German roads are modern, they all have road signs, but one could see no traffic warden there. Electronic machines control the movement of the cars and they record all the cases breaking the rules. Therefore, in this way, there is no way for a driver to escape. In the case of breaking the rules, the driver will receive a letter about a fine in their own homes.

We only saw one car accident in Drezden, where there were only three traffic wardens. After that we returned to Berlin at about 8 pm. Mavlon welcomed us in his own home. There were different kinds of fruit on the table, but the fruit of our own country cannot be found throughout the world. After supper, we went to a hotel to stay. The next morning Mavlon drove us to the supermarket where everything was expensive, and that's why we couldn't buy anything there. Then he saw us off to the railway station, and we went back to Koln where Oygen saw us in. It was pouring down with rain, we visited the church in this city. We rested after supper, it was Saturday, Oygen apologized and left for his country house.

We spent our weekends walking in the cities and visiting different places. The next morning the three of us went to the Frankfurt airport where we passed through customs and boarded the plane. In the evening the plane at last landed at the Tashkent city airport.

Thanks to God, we were able to relax and gather a wealth of knowledge due to this tour in Germany. I think that all the tourists coming to Uzbekistan come here to get very huge wealth of knowledge as there are unlimited places to discover in our country. When we got to our own mahalla Oydin said:

"Darling, I feel the smell of the newly baked bread." My heart seemed to be beating fast, because I was feeling smell of the raihan.

South Korea

According to an invitation from the President of the Yoshu National University, Kim Ha Jun, a delegation consisting of five people, me, my wife, O.V. Lebedev, E. Fayzullayev, and G. Tursunova travelled to South Korea on business in 2005 from February 10 to February13.

Most of the Korean scientists don't know English, and therefore the embassy and the university had to hire a translator. We boarded the Boeing 770 in 2004 on February 9 at 9.00 pm and then flew to IN Chon International airport after six hours of flight. We passed through customs within a few minutes and immediately got our luggage back. We went outside and the first secretary of the Uzbekistan embassy in Korea, Shukur Sobitov met us there with our Korean friend Kim Chung. The representative of the embassy accompanied us to Kimpo airport in Seoul city in a mini-bus. The airport is 80 kilometers away from the In Chon airport. It was 11 am, and we had to have breakfast at the airport. Resting for some two hours without any customs, we flew to Yoshu in a small plane Boing It took us an hour to get there. At the Yoshu airport the proctor and the chief representative of the international relationships Choy Meyong welcomed us and after that we went to a hotel with him.

The hotel rooms were very well furnished and decorated. There was a pool on the balcony. When we opened the windows, rain started pouring down in buckets. We could hear the rain roaring outside. There was everything we wanted in our room; a fridge, coffee-maker, TV, everything. From 4 pm to 6 pm, we watched the bridge and the seashores of that city. At 6.30 pm there was a party and we really enjoyed it.

National university. On February 11 at 9.30 am, the President of the university invited us for a conversation. They'd hung a poster there at the entrance of the university: "Welcome the delegation of the TARU!" It was   considerable attention and respect for all of us. After we talked for thirty minutes, they started a formal reception at 10 am. The conversation and exchange of opinions lasted for more than two hours. We watched different videos about universities. Then, we, the guests exchanged our own gifts and books with them. We went to have lunch on the initiative of the university president. This time we also sat in a Korean cuisine (restaurant). There we ate around a low table. We took off our shoes, and all of the meals were national Korean cuisine, ranging from seaweed to the crabmeat. We even visited several laboratories until lunchtime. We saw a laboratory equipped with measuring tools for inspecting the quality of water which had cost the university 3 million dollars. In the afternoon O.V. Lebedev, Erkin Fayzullayev and G. Tursunova made certain plans to work with the Korean deans and the heads of the departments. The university president ordered his driver to take me and my wife on a tour of Yoshu city. We saw many wonderful monuments, ocean banks, the town of fishermen, and museums within two hours. At 6 pm the university president threw a party for our delegation.

I always think that I am a man loved by God, because this day was my birthday and as I turned 64, I was destined to celebrate this birthday in one of the countries of the sunrise. On this occasion, we treated Korean hosts with the fruit we had brought from Tashkent. They were very glad, and they all applauded and congratulated me. It was a wonderful experience for me. After the party, they accompanied us to the hotel in a car though it was only 150 meters away from that place. We said a friendly goodbye to the president, because we had to be at the KATECH university the next morning at 9.30 am. The party came to end with tea, coffee, Uzbek national kazi, apples and pears.

The Scientific research university. In the morning after having breakfast we went to the machinery researching scientific laboratory. We were welcomed there very well.

After watching a video about the university for two hours, we observed the working process in the laboratory. We exchanged presents, said goodbye and left the laboratory. At 6.30 pm we came back to the Seoul hotel where we were welcomed by the translator Shukur Sobitov. After supper, we went outside for a stroll in Seoul. Shukur's wife Sanobarkhan also was also a partner for us there. She also   speaks Korean very well. There were many electric screen posters in the streets, I was wondering where they get so much electric energy from. The women partners did the window shopping and they even bought some several things. The meals were quite expensive, as were the clothes and wearings. They don't have cars and goods from foreign countries on sale, but they have all the things on sale. The smallest sum of salary is 1200 dollars. In the streets, we could see the most modern cars like Hyundai, Kia, and those by DAEWOO companies. There you could see some cars produced in Russia, Germany, Japan or the USA, but quite seldom. The Korean citizens love and adore their own motherland, and therefore they always keep buying goods only produced in their country.

Sharing experience with the Seoul National university. I went to meet the president of the Seoul National university together with O.V. Lebedev, Sh. Sobitov, and E. Fayzullayev went to a museum with the women. The university is located in a very huge territory, and the faculties are in buildings far from each other. They all have laboratories equipped with modern tools and instruments. We watched a video about that. We submitted mutual contracts for a project, exchanged our own gifts, then we left this university with very good impressions.

I hope in the future we will be able to allow our master students to study here. We were then introduced to the laboratory of the internal combustion engines which is equipped with the latest technology, it is working for producing engines for the Hyundai company.

Seoul National university is in the second position in Asia for educating and researching.

After that we went up to a tower located on the highest cliff of a mountain. We had lunch in a wonderful restaurant inside this tower and were lucky to watch the whole Seoul city standing 150 meters high up in the tower. An exciting landscape! Skyscraping buildings, 28 bridges built over the Sangan river and the Central Government building of 63 stories looked fantastic. Then we went to the In Chon airport. Saying goodbye to our new friends, we passed through customers and entered a plane of the Asian company. The plane landed in Tashkent city within eight hours, our students welcomed us inside the airport, we passed through customs again, but we had to wait long time to get our luggage back. We stayed in Korea for four days, and thanks to God we were again back in our hometown safe and sound.

Korean culture. All the gardens and streets are and clean and shiny. There are flowers and small trees grown around the offices, shops and other buildings. Visitors must take off their shoes before entering restaurants, and they sit around low table to eat. Meals are mostly prepared from sea ingredients, and usually 6 or 9 types of meals are offered to guests as a sign of hospitality. They consume hot and spicy foods a lot.

The Koreans are all patriotic, and they rarely buy foreign cars from foreign countries because they want to buy their own national products. They are very hardworking, and work 10 or 12 hours a day. In their free time, they rest in the parks and in the gardens. The main religions in this country are Christianity and Buddhism.

The travel which lasted for three days will be kept in our memories for the rest of our lives.

What a Question Is It?

Oybek tried to open his eyes, but he felt his eyes were laden. He felt as if his feet and hands were tied, and he couldn't move them at all. He was wondering where he was, at the hospital or in the great beyond. He was feeling a pain in his left chest, and he was alive, but feeling dizzy. Oh, he understood that he had been knocked unconscious, but he didn't know when.

He was seemingly in the great beyond, because somebody started questioning him like a prosecutor. Oybek couldn't see if this person were a ghost. Every word he said echoed in this room surrounded by four walls. Oybek felt sick. The man asked:

You are Oybek, Mukaddir's son, aren't you?

"Yes, I am" Another person seemed to talk instead of him, because Oybek's mouth was closed as if with a zipper.

"Oybek, God gifted you with the talent for science. Have you ever betrayed god? Did you deserve his trust?"

"Yes, I tried to deserve it. I translated tens of books, and I wrote many books and monographs. I had a book "Automobile and tractor engines" published in three languages, Uzbek, Russian and English. It takes thirty years of challenges to write a book in a technical field because most of the terms we need are all in foreign languages. I have also published a dictionary of automobile terms in Russian and in Uzbek in cooperation with others. Most of the administrators spend their energy on their duties as a chief, and maybe this is somehow right. But my pursuit of scientific achievements has urged me to be an administrator. I shared the knowledge I have with everyone who needed it. I used the initiative for recruiting talented students and making them study in special groups on the basis of certain books. The university which I headed was adopted into the Association of the International Automobile Road education. In 1996 we held an international seminar in our university in which scientists from France, Germany, Iran and Turkey took part.

Oybek didn't even know who was saying these things instead of him so bravely and so confidently.

"Ok, why did you organize the council of sponsors in the university? Did you receive any benefits from that?"

Before organizing this council, I was introduced to the activity of the rectors in Moscow universities. I had a fund "Student" opened at the university into which the sponsor Council allocated 5 million soums. All of this money was spent supporting orphaned students and encouraging talented young people. All we have done has been very effective and as time has passed, tens of our students were awarded with the "Umid" fund grants and got a chance to study in the USA and in England. The university has enriched its own fund, and the sponsors helped us buy 5 cars and 1 bus.

We had the central heating completely repaired and several companies have been opened in our universities. They work on the basis of the research carried out by our scientists. Oybek felt that there was a garden, with a smell of flowers near. That invisible man, started questioning Oybek again. Oybek:

"Yes, I have dream about living in a house, not in a small flat. I even wrote an application to the district governing asking them to allow me to build a house on the land unused near the Aviation plant. After having my application signed by the Higher Education Minister and the governor, I visited the Assistant of the Prime Minister:

"I see that you're a university president. Why don't you buy two old houses in the center and have a big house built instead of them?"

"If I had a chance like you're thinking about, I would have never asked you about this land." Seemingly the man Oybek talked to counted all the university presidents as men of means. He said that he would help if he had a chance to, but there was no result. I thought that I deserved being given a very good house from the government because I was doing my best to work hard.

Yes, if god has loved somebody, the others can never hurt him, never. The department of our university which prepares professionals consulted all the professors and they decided to buy me a house on the basis of sponsorship.

In 2003, when I pushed 63, the last age of the prophet, I got the flat I was dreaming about. Some of my opponents wrote many letters to the authority claiming that I had already had a house with two stories, with a palace-like luxury, and they complained about this for five long years.

Again, the same voice: "Did anyone oppose you in secret when   you   were   a university   president?"   "Actually, our President was introduced to my achievements and he decided to appoint me as a university president. This was a gift to me from God.

During ten years, I did my best to deserve the trust of our President. I had to unite all the staff members with the same purpose, and for the further development of our motherland and society. This was not easy at all, and it required sleepless hours at night. A university president must do his best to help everyone who asks him for help. A university president will have some visitors who ask him for help according to the request of the people in higher positions, they start having friendly relationships with you, then at the end, when it is time for entrance exams or applicants, those people come up to you asking you to help their relatives to enter the university. A university president must then change the topic saying that the student must attend the applicant preparation courses.

"God hasn't created us for accepting things as they are. Have you tried to change something?"

"Yes, I tried to change quite a few things. The representatives of the OAK must be present during the expert councils of the dissertation defense, and after the votes are counted to be more in favour of the candidate, then his documents should not be allowed to be groped in for search. His opponents should be kept secret until the day of the expert's council.

This is what I wanted for the sake of the scientific advancement in our motherland.

I have been to universities in foreign countries where education is based on tuition fees. The scientists in these countries work in different organizations besides teaching at a university.

In America those who don't pass attestation are given some time to train for further testing. If he doesn't develop his knowledge within the given time given, then he will never be allowed to work anymore.

"Don't you owe your teachers something?"

"I think not. I have always tried to support all the tasks they had attempted. I have teachers in Moscow and in Uzbekistan. Some of them are dead, and some of them are still alive. For example, my teacher Dobrogayev will soon turn 90."

"Don't you owe your wife something?" "She had enough knowledge to continue her research, and she could have been a doctor of sciences. But she was busy with looking after me and my children Sometimes I feel guilty about that."

Oybek felt an even stronger pain in his heart, but he was wondering if he hadn't let his wife carry all of his burdens in life. He didn't abandon his wife like many other men working abroad and who didn't even send any money to their wives.

"Tell me, are there enough talented people in your country in every field of science? Has someone analyzed it?"

"It's very hard to answer this question. I have headed one of the most famous universities in the Republic for ten years. I have many plans I didn't manage to implement.

"You are one of the prominent representatives of higher education. Can you tell me frankly does the quality of higher education meet your standards? Let's be frank, they don't. So, what's the reason?"

"Why is it so hard to answer? To be honest, the quality of higher education doesn't meet the requirements our President has set for us. The main reason is the absence of free talk and the freedom to express all opinions. None of the administrators are brave enough to speak about all the problems to be solved… They are all afraid of losing their own positions.

Tell us how many bachelors graduate with the diploma of honors, and how many of them enter the master's degree on the basis of government funding?" "Unfortunately, I don't know anything about that. I on know these things about my own university:

For example, 84 students out of 650 graduated with the diploma of honors. This 13 percent. This is too much. None of the universities has this sort of high result. Other universities it only have 5-6 %.

There are usually more talented students from low income families. In our universities, we used to have 100 seats for masters students, 40 of which are based on government funding. The rest of the applicants will study on the basis of tuition fees. Young talented students don't know how to earn money to cover their tuition fees.

"Ok, what should be done to solve this problem?" "I think the graduates with three years of work experience should be enrolled in the extramural postgraduate and master studies programs.

I know how the talented students will feel about failing the Masters exams, I have helped most of those students to be honest. I wish the students who got their diploma fairly with honors should enter a Master's program without exams. If students are awarded on the basis of fair competitions, then students will be eager to study and to have more knowledge than each other. When I was a rector, a student who only had one satisfactory mark in Bachelor studies didn't have the right to apply for a Master studies program. The quality of education has been raised to a very high level.

I wish there would be a special experts group to assessing the dissertations of the Master students. If all the failures and success in the research are exposed, there will be greater progress in the future. I wish all the talented Master's students would gain higher positions in our country so that they could work fairly for the development of our country.

"Can you tell me where the students from Uzbekistan who studied in abroad are working?"

"I wish you hadn't asked me these questions. I told you that ten students from our university have studied in America, Germany and England. Only two of them are now working in Tashkent. The other eight have stayed abroad when the foreign companies offered them very well-paid jobs.

I organized the faculty of talented students in our university. I wanted to show that we could also prepare professionals who could meet the requirements of the world. However, they will have to have a love for their motherland, which is so strong that they will not to leave for other countries. I tried to prepare young people who are ready to die for the sake of the motherland.

There are some students who studied abroad and are ignoring their own motherland. They keep saying that they will work in Uzbekistan if they are paid as high salary as in foreign countries, or they will leave. They count money before everything... even before their love for their motherland.

I don't think that they are our children No they aren't. They are just dishonest people who have sold their conscience for money.

You have been working at the university since 1962. What could be done so that Uzbekistan will develop as much as many other European countries?"

As a scientist who has learned the educational system of both the west and the east, I would accomplish the following: I would declare a special decree after learning all the positive experience of foreign universities; I would divide all the children in the nursery, primary, and secondary schools into several groups according to their interests and talent. All the trainings would be specialized in accordance with their abilities. If any of the children were a bit lazy, I would make him study in a group of ordinary students. At the same time, the less talented students should also be given a chance to join the special groups in case they work hard. This system was active in our university until 2005.

I would organize something like golden and silver medals for school levels and think about their advantages for further education. To accomplish this all the teachers and the way they work do should be seriously controlled.

I would support the testing system active in foreign countries. According to my intention, all the applicants should pass only one type of exam with certain subject ranges and the scores they get should be valid enough to apply to all the universities in the entire Republic if they are good enough.

The students with the diploma of honors would be allowed to enter Master courses without any exams;

All the scholarships like the President's scholarship, Navaiy, and Beruniy should be given according to a contest for which at least ten students must apply from each university faculty. The student who succeeds until the final stage, but eventually fails, must be recommended for an honored scholarship at the university.

Dissertation of doctors should be defended in the OAK special council of experts. If the defense is successful the diploma should be handed next morning. Teachers should be awarded as professors only in case they write successful books in Uzbek.

"Who will take charge of this? Look I think this is a revolution in higher education."

"Oh, do you think so? But these dreams are just a small part of all of them. I wish at least they could come true… I sincerely wish this."

"Why do you think all the people in higher positions tend to resign quite soon?"

"I will give my own personal opinion. As we know our President founded a Special Academy. There are enough talented young people, but they should be supported so that they could work in the positions they deserve.

"Why do you think Emir Temur is famous for being great?"

"The point is that he has never did something without the permission of his teacher Said Baraka. He did everything only on his golden advices. But there are only a few people who value teachers who really deserve valuing."

For 47 years, whatever I did, I did on the advice of my teacher Okil Salimov. Our President appointed me as a university president, and after some time I awarded my teacher as "Honored university president of the TARU". This garnered brilliant results, and our university became one of the most famous in the Republic.

"Look, you're older than 63. Why don't you retire and enjoy taking a break from work?"

"Thanks to God I have lived to the same age the age as our prophet, so the rest of my life is at the disposal of God. I am a servant for all the students. I cannot imagine my life without books, without teaching and without students.

This is my life. I cannot live in any other way. No matter how long a life I am given to live, I will dedicate it all to our young children in our motherland."

Oybek didn't know how long he was unconscious, or if it was summer, winter, nor which day it was. The thing that didn't let him open his eyes, set him free at last.

Something was ticking beside him... it was an injection.

He wanted to smell a lemon.

"No, no, no! Don't try to move! You have frightened us all. Oh, God, you've opened your eyes at last."

Oybek saw a young doctor next to him.

"What happened to me? What's wrong with me?" Oybek sounded very weak.

"Your heart troubled you a bit, don't worry. It will pass soon. Oybek again closed his eyes. Was it the doctor who questioned him so long and so cruelly? Oh, no, not this young man, he can't be that intelligent. Was it his own conscience who asked him so many challenging questions? Oybek started closing his eyes again, and again he was in the clouds, flying, because he was falling asleep again.

The End

"Can you stop the car here?" Oybek said this when it was about to get to the university. The driver looked at him wanting to ask "why?"

"Don't worry, I want to walk on foot for a bit. Yes, the weather is always fresh after it rains". The driver quickly got out of the car and opened the door of the super saloon for him. Oybek would usually tell his driver: "Oh God, no, don't bother trying to open the door for me. It isn't difficult to close and open this". But this time he just thanked to him. He started walking very slowly, and he remembered the poem by the poet Oybek. He stopped for a bit under the trees with leaves wet because of the rain and he took a deep breath. Since his heart troubled him he made it a habit to walk outside to get a breath of fresh air.

The doctors had said: "You work too hard, Sir. Moreover, you never stop working. Every year you're writing new books, you supervise three or four postgraduates, institute reforms in the department, at the university, which all may eventually cause a heart attack". However, doing all this actually made him enjoy life. The things that made him sick were anonymous letters, wrong oppositions, bribery and many others injustices.

Suddenly he felt that somebody had stood behind him, and when he looked back he saw a man whose hair and beard had turned grey. He stretched his hand towards Oybek.

That man was drunk, and a beggar in the streets. He always asked people for money to buy a glass of alcoholic drinks. Oybek wanted to vomit on seeing him, and he was going to pass him, but the man wouldn't let him: "Please, I beg you, to give money for only 100 grams of …"

Oybek tried to recognize him, because his eyes were quite familiar to him… yes he was. He was the man, one of the men who for three years has tried to block his way when he was working hard on his doctoral dissertation. This old man was one of those who tried to cause troubles for Oybek. Oybek had exposed him as a teacher involved in bribery. But this man then decided to fight against Oybek for the rest of his life. Oybek heard that that teacher had become a businessman, and after that was arrested for illegal acts in business. It was he… that very man…

Oybek started trembling from concern. He groped in his pocket and gave him whatever he had in his pocket. He shook his shoes as if he'd stepped on something disgusting and went into the university building:

"Good afternoon, teacher?"

"Good afternoon, Oybek Mukaddirovich, are you ok?" Oybek greeted all the students and postgraduates in the corridors, and while he was walking into the department, the sunshine coming through the windows was playing off his forehead and eyebrows.